Step Up, Mrs Dugdale

Lynne Leonhardt grew up on an orchard in Donnybrook in the South West of Western Australia and travelled extensively as a young adult. She studied music and English literature at the University of Western Australia while bringing up four children, and later completed a PhD in Creative Writing at Edith Cowan University. Her first novel, *Finding Jasper* (Margaret River Press, 2012), was longlisted for the 2013 Dobbie Award. Lynne is the great-great-grand-niece of leading Australian suffragist, Henrietta Augusta Dugdale.

Step Up, Mrs Dugdale

A NOVEL BASED ON
A TRUE STORY

LYNNE LEONHARDT

MATILDA BAY
BOOKS

First published in 2019 by Matilda Bay Books
Claremont, Western Australia
matildabaybooks@iinet.net.au

National Library of Australia
Cataloguing-in-Publication entry:
ISBN 978-0-6483788-1-5

Cover design and internal text by Sandy Cull
Front cover image by Mark Owen/Trevillion Images
Typeset in Adobe Garamond Pro 12.5pt/16.5pt by Kerry Cooke
Printed by Lightning Source/Ingram Australia

FOR HENRIETTA

⌇

Virtue can only flourish amongst equals.
MARY WOLLSTONECRAFT

CONTENTS

PROLOGUE

She braces herself against the boot-room door, her senses on high alert.

The hypocrisy of *her* being accused of adultery. And the danger … This will follow her for the rest of her life.

Her throat is a burning rush, heart beating so hard she can barely breathe. And some instinct deep inside her bones is telling her to run.

A few deep gasps, then she collects herself. Claps twice, gathering her three young sons together in the hallway.

'Now, listen. Be good for Mama.' Her voice cracks as she tries to temper her words. 'We must leave for town immediately. Gather your clothes and any special playthings.'

They look up at her, uncertain.

'Boys, boys! Go on now, hurry.'

From room to room she runs, emptying drawer-loads of clothes into boxes, stuffing them with as many precious items as will fit.

'Right,' she pants, 'five minutes, boys. Wait for me by the front steps ready with the boxes, while I get the cart.'

Gathering her skirts, she sprints towards the harness shed. The mare pricks her ears and comes trotting.

'There, steady, my friend, steady,' she whispers. Gently slipping the collar over Gypsy's head, she harnesses the mare and hitches her to the large spring cart.

No time for doubts. She gathers the reins between fumbling fingers and jumps into the cart. Boys and belongings aboard, they are off, flying over puddles and ruts, sticks and stones, at a crisp canter. Sweeps of grassland and straggling scrub flash past against an unforgivably grey sky, but not once does Henrietta look back.

The melancholy colours of the landscape begin to blur, her eyes watering in the wind, and, as they approach the shadowy tunnel of cypress, the boys clutch her, pale and quiet.

'Hold tight, my darlings!' Bouncing about on the seat, she can barely see, her heartbeat drowned by the rattle of wheels and the agonising squeak of axle. God help her if he is waiting at the crossroads.

Part I

1863–1868

Chapter 1

✑

QUEENSCLIFF, VICTORIA

5 MARCH 1863

Henrietta stood at the edge of the Bluff, drinking the wild air. Ah! The mingling smell of lime and brine and the relentless energy of the ocean beneath. Spread out before her was the hard, rough-cut sparkle of Port Phillip Bay. Beyond, evaporating into that endless blue haze, the old world she had left behind.

The bay would look safe enough were it not for the Heads. The two pincers of land that welcomed with the promise of new life were still there, but so too was the wild greenishness known as the Rip. There was the meeting place for the coming in and going out of ships and the conflicting forces of two masses of water.

Ten years to the day, she thought wistfully. The honeymoon over before it began.

Flickers of white smudged against the blue. Gulls wheeling, orange legs outstretched to land. At the last second they stalled, hovering in the updraft. For a while she watched them hawking above the crag. Scavengers. Rats of the sea. But there was a human element to their desperate, piercing cries that struck at the core of her heart.

Sorrow had not chastened her. Pitching across the water was a steady stream of vessels, the midday light painting their sails with silver. And

5

now the wind, the first whisper of autumn, turning, its sough whistling through the grasses and low-lying scrub.

Heavens! She snatched at her bonnet as a sudden gust tore through her redingote, raising her very hackles. Only a fool would stand here, skirts billowing up like a parachute.

Her husband would give her a grilling. There was work to be done. Quickly, she turned to make the ten-minute walk back home over the ridge to the Hermitage Dairy.

∾

'Where have you been?'

Afternoon rays of sun spilled across the floorboards as she pushed open the door. It was a large, longish room with closet-style bedrooms either side, and a simple kitchen-cum-scullery attached to the back. Gracing one end was her most beloved possession and nightly companion, her piano. At the other, a pair of easy chairs and a sizeable fireplace with a small array of hooks, kettles and cast-iron pots – the family hub, the hearth from which she could look out of their Stevens Street home upon the protected back shores of town, the gentler waters of Swan Bay.

Finger to her lips, she tiptoed into the nursery. The two older boys, Einnim and Carl, were quietly playing, mercifully. She lifted up Austin, who had just woken, and came out, pressing him onto her hip.

Her voice was quiet and calm. 'I just slipped out to the draper … some fawn silk.' She lowered her eyelids for a second, allowing a faint mocking smile to play about her lips. 'Or would you rather go around with holes in your stockings?'

William drew out a spindle chair for himself and, looking down his nose, began to read, mouth in a downward 'u'. It seemed she would have to find some way of supplicating his lordship.

'There, there, patience, little one.' She drew her skirts aside and sank into the rocker, feeling at once the letdown mapping her bodice wet.

'Must you continue to suckle the child?'

6

Henrietta looked up, startled. Fourteen months was well nigh time to wean the child, she knew, but she had been hanging on in the wisdom that a babe at the breast oft holds the next at bay. With each infant, it had been the same. The thought, at thirty-six, of having to face another birth remained a constant fear. Austin's – the last – being ill timed, was long, lonely and very frightening, made worse by William's unexplained week of absence.

Austin, having had his fill, sat up, all moist and smiling. She kissed his plump, rosy cheeks.

'You're making a sissy out of him. More time on the floor's what a boy needs. If he's fed and done, then put him down.'

She sighed, and, having let the tot find his feet, went to the fireplace and placed the iron guard against it, all the time longing to ask, *Have you thought today of your loving bride of ten years gone? Time flies, does it not?* But she was too proud. And she suspected she already knew the answer.

Later, after supper, she draped a passing arm across William's shoulder and said airily, 'So, Captain Dugdale, what are they saying in the newspapers?'

'Oh, still the same old question.' He snickered and flung a leg over his knee. 'Who should have the right to vote. The so-called evils of universal suffrage. There is talk of a new Electoral Act and much debate.'

The topic of universal suffrage was nothing new. She'd grown up with it literally nigh on her doorstep. Young as she was then, part of her had understood. She remembered watching from the dining-room balcony of their Bloomsbury home as angry hordes came trooping down the street. 'Papa, quickly, the Chartists are coming. They're heading for Holborn!' People shouting, chanting, 'One man, one vote! Join the march, comrades. Remember your starving brothers!' Urgency, passion in their voices; tradesmen in fustian jackets with their white aprons folded up; men – a few women, too – from all walks of life.

What was so dangerous about it – 'horrid' democracy? And if a woman could be a miner, or a storekeeper, or a dairywoman, why could such a woman not vote, too?

She could feel her colour coming and going.

'All very well to talk about universal suffrage,' she said, checking herself. 'So far I hear no talk of women.' Reaching behind him, she replenished the candelabra with fresh tapers and placed them back on the mantelpiece.

William continued puffing on his pipe as she busied herself about the room. Every now and again, he would narrow his eyes through the drift of smoke and, because of his beard, it was hard to tell whether he was more amused or annoyed.

But, having found her voice, she could hardly stop. She pointed out that there was an economic imperative, too, as in their case here at home. On the face of it, their partnership was an equal one.

'Since I hold claim to what we own in trust and effectively pay half of the taxes, I feel I have as much right to a vote as you.'

'Of what good is a vote to a woman, let alone a married one? You promised to obey me and would vote as would I, thereby granting me two votes. Think, now, would that be fair?'

'You, sir, come up with the same old argument and yet beg to presume.'

'Count yourself lucky, Mrs Dugdale.'

Admittedly, she was in a better position than most women. A dairy provided a domain where a woman could attain a certain degree of economic control and authority. What was owed to them she personally and very proudly collected and accounted for clearly in neat two-sided ledgers.

Money aside, it was the physical freedom she valued, rounding up their bountiful herd with William. Of course, truth lay in nature. There was purity in their labours – spiritual and moral – she had liked to believe. Once back before the hearth, everything seemed to change.

Sparks shot up the chimney as William poked a log in the grate with his boot.

'Tell me, then, what do you mean by democracy?' He stood, elbow on the mantelpiece, pipe in palm. 'Do you mean Chartism or Republicanism?'

'As I see it, so long as they can read and write, it is the right – the right of nature – for every citizen, women included, to have a voice in making the laws he is called upon to obey – a single, equal vote.' Her breast swelled and her eyes flashed. 'I, for one, stand up for that. In fact, I have a good mind to write to the newspapers and add my say.'

'Politics, pff. I have only to mention the word "democracy", and look at yourself in the mirror – see how easily it excites you, sullies you, makes you manly.'

How in a few words he could suppress her by playing upon her virtue. She stood looking out the window, her hands firmly united in front. She was testing him again, could feel it coming, the clunk as he put down his pipe, the meat in his steps. She flinched. Very gently he spun her around and tilted her chin with his thumb so he could better see the glow of her deep grey eyes.

'You may think what you like, say it within the realms of our own house, if you dare, but I won't have my wife expressing her views in public.'

Her brows froze as she took the full weight of his gaze. Somehow she managed to compose herself, snuff her breathy fear into a sigh. As much as he liked to think of himself as an intelligent, freethinking and enlightened fellow, William could be as stiff as a raisin in a very stiff plum pudding.

⁂

Dairying was not quite the genteel life either had first envisaged. They had not gone in green. But the same intensity could not be achieved in the Bellarine as in the lush meadowlands around the Dugdale home in Dorset. Four times as many cows were needed to furnish the same amount of milk. Here, in this rough-and-tumble land of bounty, you often got what you paid for – ill-mannered horses with feathered fetlocks, and scrub cattle, either absconders or ones that were bred and brought up in the bush. It had taken much time, patience and hard bodily work over the last seven years to tame these errant beasts.

Running a dairy, they had quickly discovered, was a relentless, grinding life ruled by the sun. Early to bed, early to rise, every hour of the day run to the strictest schedule.

Being calving time, it was up to her, Henrietta, the woman of the household, to take careful note of springing, strutting udders, a reluctance to trot.

'The last of the heifers has dropped, William,' she mentioned the following night. 'She's lying by herself away from the herd. I've strewn some trusses around in case she calves.'

'Leave it to nature. Cows don't like fuss or interference. Neither do I.'

But now it was well past midnight and she had barely slept. Eiderdown pulled up over his whiskers, William was dead to the world. She trudged out to the holding yards, lantern in hand, to see splinters of light igniting a heaving loin, the roll of a dark liquid eye, tongue frothing silver in the pitch of night. As a mother, she knew what to expect. To witness such stoicism, hour after hour of what must have been agony, and the poor beast uttering little more than a single pathetic moo. It took her breath away, the mucousy blood and the slippery balloon-like capsule wriggling forth the marvel of new life. Gripped by the intensity of nature's beauty, she stayed put, watching the little darling being licked dry before it was allowed to suckle. All senses alert, she held the lantern aloft, to find an audience gathering. The mother's instincts had triggered a licking response among the herd. Through the darkness, she could make out their movements, the nodding of heads in approval.

Come dawn, the baby steer was up with his mother. Within days, he would be prancing around, pawing and tossing his head at her, kicking up straw and dust like all the others before. For hours, Einnim and Carl would hang off the gate, enchanted, but none the wiser when William finally whisked the calf away. Of course, separation was essential; one had to make a living. But her heart bled, knowing the calf's fate rested in the slaughter yard. For nights and days, the mother's agonising high-pitched bellow would follow her about, leaving her stricken with complicity and pain.

⁓

There was not just the rounding up of the herd and milking. Creaming and butter making had to be carried out twice a week in the coolest hours to avoid it going sour or rancid. The warmer the day, the earlier she had to rise. The middle of March being no exception.

After skimming the previous night's milk in the shallow trays, she poured the takings into the keg by light of the lamp, and sniffed to see if they were tainted. What remained in the pan she would save for the calves. Hitching her skirts over a stool, she began to churn, constantly checking the smell. She tried to remind herself of the semi-sacredness of milk – simple notions of healing and rebirth – and the aesthetic beauty of running a dairy. How silly to imagine that in performing these dreary menial daily tasks, her life might somehow get better?

Milk and honey! As if that alone were enough.

To and fro she pushed the lever, as if the heavy monotonous rhythm might push her grievances aside. Yawning over the dreamy swish of creaming froth, she found herself floating backwards across the sea to a time when she was young. It was always his touch she could feel: Junius taking her elbow, helping her down the broad white steps into the streets of London.

Now, in the cool, dark, musty room, scraps of that day emerged – the curving row of terrace houses drenched in golden slabs of sunlight; the canal a flood of shifting colours. Junius, her fiancé, for the most part lying in the narrowboat, arms pillowing his head as she manoeuvred them through webs of floating lilies. He, the consummate mariner, exercising little more than the creases in his half-closed eyes; she showing off without a care in the world. The two of them, alone, beneath shadowy strands of willows; the tingle of touch, the delightful squirm, her laughter rising like cream to his banter.

'Look! A tea-garden, a veritable Hermitage.' Just in the nick of time. They had sat side-by-side under an arbour of climbing roses and honeysuckle surrounded by fruit trees. Fallen apples lay half-concealed beneath a carpet of crisp autumn leaves. The trees bare but for a few apples, hanging round and conspicuously red against the grey craggy branches. In low-lying meadows, soft-eyed Jerseys lay chewing their cuds, oblivious to stinging nettles pressed against their bloated udders. 'If I could live here, Junius, I might live a better, truer life.'

'Life is true enough wherever you live, but truth might not suit your fancy.'

The lamp by now had died, the dawn light filtering through the thin white cotton curtains of the dairy. Henrietta paused for a moment, eyes fixed on the yellowing mass in the green-painted barrel. Hadn't she enough labour, setting her raw hands to churning for hours, without the task of working the butter, reworking it, mindful so as not to injure the grain, keeping it cool and firm enough to mould and wrap for the Melbourne market.

Jerseys? Those darlings of the world, with their placid manners and their grace, they had become something of a pipedream. By comparison, what they had here in Queenscliff were good old bush cows. 'Ragged razor-backed bags of bones, get along with you.' William yelling at them with a crack of his whip.

The sudden clump-clump of footsteps on brick courtyard outside booted her heart. He had obviously finished the milking. Quickly she set aside the trays of butter on the granite bench, covered them with damp salted cloths and slipped back to the house.

The children were already up, dressed and fed, and the morning's mail spread out on the breakfast table.

'Please, Pa,' cried Einnim, 'let me open the parcel.'

Carl peered on tiptoes. Austin pulled at her skirts, paddling his feet up and down amid cries of protest. Mama! She swept him up, gave him a cuddle and a kiss and took him through to the kitchen to their young Irish servant, Millie, who was busy peeling potatoes.

William eased himself onto a bentwood chair with a grunt.

'Father's will has arrived. About bloody time.' Pushing tea and damper aside, he began poring over the contents of a long, fat brown envelope.

It was a good twelve years since William had seen his father, the father he hardly knew. Distance and the disparateness of their worlds had shredded the long rope thin. The Reverend Dugdale's recent passing had sparked little emotion in William other than a sense of entitlement.

'Einnim and Carl, come.' Henrietta waved her hand. 'Outside and play.'

As much as he played the profligate, there was a mercenary side to William's nature. Oh, but how she begrudged the waste – money spent on his pleasures, money earned mostly through her hard toil.

Through the window she kept an eye on the boys, who were now tossing fallen pine cones into a cream pail. What a racket. Oh, Einnim! Now she would have to go out and supervise. She stopped. William, scraping back his chair, was fully venting his spleen, papers, envelopes and all sent flying across the floor.

'Hell and damnation!' His closed fist struck the table. 'May he go to the devil!'

She could see it in a flash. Unbeknown to William, the will had been changed and now he would not inherit a penny until after his mother had died. Meantime, he would be even more beholden to Henrietta and her money.

Chapter 2

⁓

O nce Austin was weaned, a good deal of Henrietta's day was spent in
the saddle. Besides helping round up the herd for milking, there
were calves to poddy, the dairy to run and deliveries to be made on
alternate days. By the time she had seen to the children at the end of the
day and put them to bed, she was worn thin and tired.

Her new routine was barely a month old. Clearly, a number of things
would have to change.

Though they did not 'dress' for dinner as one did in the Old Country,
she still insisted on freshening up. Now, in the privacy of their bedroom,
she quickly stripped down to her chemise, her bosom half-exposed as
she completed the rest of her evening-toilet, brushes and towels laid
out at the ready. She unloosened her hair. Nimbly patted her scalp with
brandy and rosewater and gave it a thorough brushing in the simplest
of daily rituals. Rather than fiddle-faddling with rolls and braids and
broken strands of hair and silk nets that slipped through her fingers, she
had reduced things to a very graceful spartan knot behind her head.

Candlelight glinted on every wave, adding to the natural gloss of her
copper-brown hair. Spread out dark and burnished upon her shoulders,
her crowning glory was more of a burden, subject as it was to daily sweat
and dust. With so little time to play to the mirror, there was only one

solution. Henrietta tossed aside the white polishing brush. She reached for her scissors and began to cut. There! Her wealth of femininity lying tumbled upon the bare boards.

She stretched out her neck, shook her head and gave herself a subtle smile. Parted in the middle, her remaining locks fell in short loose curls like Raphael's angels'. Easy to wash and dress and deliciously cool. No, she was not George Sand-ing, nor would it make her any less of a wife or a mother. As for corsets ... she gasped, feeling again the rebel blood surge in her veins.

'Oh, Mama, you are squeezing me to death!' She remembered running round and round, screaming in rage. The hiss of her mother's ceaseless whispers, 'My child, you must! A lady must ... it's a sign of noble posture.'

She had later shown her childish contempt by hacking into the hideous contraption with a pair of shears, removing every inch of baleen.

To make the charge that doing away with corsets unsexed a woman was obnoxious and unfair. As to the score of delicacy, nuns found no reason to wear corsets. Nor did Turkish or Indian women, and they embodied feminine qualities. Henrietta always felt at ease with her own willowy grace. Very few women were naturally dumbbell-shaped, she figured, and nothing, nothing, would make her so.

Eyes tight, she splashed her face over and over, allowing the cooled water to trickle down her breasts before patting herself with a cambric towel. How good it was to be free of binders, her figure back, riding again; oh, and how she revelled in it, the sensuality of movement – the smell of grass, flying clods of salt marsh, of horse and leather breathing in the sun.

Being aside her favourite mount again elevated her body, spirit and mind. Already it had helped her regain her self-respect, her authority, her refusal to work in long dresses. To have them trailing through wet scrub and mud and long grass was sheer lunacy. Travelling in the tropics, she had seen Englishwomen riding *à la mode de l'indienne*, an apron effect with bloomers underneath, and other modified clothes – even women who rode astride. Upon arriving in Australia, she had been quick to fashion her own garments, dresses of comfort and workability, riding outfits with skirts that were a little bit shorter and gave no cause to blush. Neat as a clothespin, too. No flapping skirts about the left flank. With topper and tails, they looked perfectly charming and nobody the wiser.

William, old bear, always betwixt and between. He burst in.

'What have you been up to? Good grief!' His eyes seized upon her fallen locks.

Dark lashes masked her downcast eyes. 'It is for the best, since I've been moulting of late.'

William joined her at the washstand. She could smell his body amid the scent of the cow yard. He stood behind in shirtsleeves, unbuttoning the fly of his dusty moleskins, waiting for her to finish. She felt the pressure of his barrel chest, his hand upon her belly. The walls were thin. No matter how liberated she was, in her heart of hearts, she was more than chaste, she was a prude. The thought of anybody being in any way party to the intimacy of her bedroom was off-putting.

'You must be more discreet.' Her whisper came out hoarse and urgent. 'The children are still awake.' She flushed. She would have to lecture him again. Millie had barely left the house this minute.

From behind the Chinese screen, she followed his movements, anticipating every little ritual. The soaping of hands, the cup-like splashes at face and underarms, raking his wet fingers through his hair, smoothing it till it shone like tortoiseshell. Having caught her reflection in the mirror, he came over, undressing her with his gold-green eyes as he patted his whiskers dry. Would she ever change him? Since he no longer loved her, it was beginning to feel like nightly degradation rather than a duty.

⌣

Henrietta wheeled Gypsy around as the cattle disappeared into the threshing scrub.

'For God's sake, man,' William roared at their new cow hand, 'hold him tight, or he'll be off!'

Trying to teach a novice how to round up cattle was a lost cause when it was obvious the man had never been on a horse in his life. Through the sheoaks, she could see the poor fellow, clinging convulsively to the saddle, his mount head-tossing from side to side as it broke into a canter.

'Stick in your knees, you damn fool.' William let out a bellow. 'Watch out, keep him from the trees!'

Now the cattle were at sixes and sevens for want of help. Henrietta was dreading the thought of the weekend.

'Never marry a sailor,' Papa had cautioned her, 'a sailor is always married to the sea.'

Like Junius, William could not forsake the sea. Any excuse to take 'French leave' and William was off to sail at Sandridge – the principal seaport of Melbourne – leaving some greenhorn straight off a ship as his replacement. Wages were rising like the devil, William complained. No matter who he engaged for the job, the rascal would as quickly be up and off, following the others to the diggings.

Henrietta waited by the west flank, overlooking the swan ponds. Here, she could be at peace, knowing the cattle would eventually emerge onto open ground of their own accord. So few were the opportunities to stop and reflect in the ever-revolving timetable of her daily life.

There were moments of intense tenderness, the brief delight that came from immersing herself and the children in the natural beauty around them. For, as she tried to explain to them, everything on earth is part of a cycle, or part of a pattern therein.

She never tired of the way the light moved over the mudflats and the bush, an embankment of tea-tree scrub veiled creamy-white with profusions of sweet-smelling clematis blossom or 'traveller's joy', as they called the star-shaped creeper.

There was always some miniature drama unfolding out on Swan Bay, should one chance to look. Fishing boats came and went through the course of the day. Chinamen clad in white pyjamas and coolie hats drifted through slaty meadows of seagrass with their gentle art of sculling. And, ever mingling, the ubiquitous swans; by milking time, black hooks suspended against a setting sun. Here, there were birds aplenty, birds of all kinds – black duck, snipe and teal, as well as wattlebirds, bronzewing pigeons, parrots and stately pelicans. For the past few months, it had been a theatre of wings.

The swans could often be heard homing in the gorse, an occasional honk arresting her in her tracks. Early this morning, while searching for a stray calf, she had found herself party to their rituals. The only sounds the whisper of sheoaks and the jingle of her mare champing at the bit. She had let drop the reins and sat quiet in the saddle, transfixed by the beauty of two mates face-to-face quivering their wings at each other as the wind gently pleated the water.

Now, by late day, she could just make them out, the swans, their tiny movements, wink-like, against the porcelain-blue sky. Then, louder and louder, as every flurry of fresh air accompanied the high-pitched *whooo* of them coming in to roost. It was low tide, the surface rippling quicksilver. Lying undercover were local shooters with punt guns. Gypsy shied as a volley of reports split the air. But still it hung, the sickening smell of shot, as the birds rose clumsily and swung away seawards. In her heart, she was with them, could feel every wingbeat, willing them to soar, away, free from harm. For the grace and music of these creatures never failed to mesmerise her.

As soon as the two men reappeared through the scrub, she gave the mare her head. In front of them, the cows plodded knowingly towards the open gate in ritual. Deepening shadows crisscrossed, consuming the town amid the dust and bluish wisps of woodsmoke. Glistening in broken blocks of light, the dark oiled weatherboard that was their home, its shingles weathered silver-grey.

Gorgeous multi-hued parrots hopped half-hidden in the wattles and honeysuckles. Paperbarks quivered in the breeze. And the sun, the magical way it hung so red and round and mellow, languishing across the still waters of Swan Bay, the tint of its glow distant on the sandstone dairy. Within minutes it would all vanish, dissipating into the straggly silhouette of stringybarks and sheoaks.

After closing the gate on the cows, she rubbed down the mare, gave her some oats, then hung up the saddle and bridle. The desire to capture such moments on paper quickly melted with the sun. The sending home of leaves and pressed flowers had long fallen away; there was little she felt inclined to preserve. Keeping a diary – even with lock and key – was a dangerous habit with William around, and *bons mots* best kept inside her head.

Come the following weekend, William was shirking again. Saturday he had set off after early milking for Sandridge, informing her he would not be back till late Sunday. Since there was no milk round, she was able to spare the children an hour by the waterside. She left Austin with Millie, and, boy on either side, made her way down the path to the back shore with a bag of socks and sewing silks. Here, clear of conscience, she could sit and sew – yet with no respite – her hands never idle, her mind never resting, her eyes forever watchful.

No matter how tired, though, she wouldn't stand for any nonsense. Einnim, little rascal, had a tendency to dart hither and thither like a water beetle. Either that or wading out too far and falling into swans' holes.

She hoisted her eyebrows a little higher and wearily stretched the toe of one of William's socks over the wooden darning egg. Length of grey silk held to the light, she threaded the eye of the needle and set to work, shuttling the spine back and forth. Carl, at five, was happy enough to sit by her side, examining shells and specks of silver mica. Not far away was Einnim. In shirtsleeves and bracer trousers he stood, bare feet anchored in the sand as he twisted this way and that with his newfound toy.

'If you want to sail, laddie, you'd best learn about the wind first before the water. Your finger is a tad small for a tester. But if you're ever in doubt as to which way it's blowing, you can always check up there.' William had pointed up to the weathervane, a red wooden rooster standing atop the gable.

A kite was more than a plaything. It was obvious William could see himself in Einnim. 'Run free with it, sonny, feel the pull of the wind. Get used to the principles of how a sail actually works, then we shall see about getting you a boat.'

The boy was easily taken with the idea. He hung off his father's every word.

William often spoke to his sons as if they were cabin boys, in rude or colourful parlance.

'Lots of stories to be told about boats and kites, boy.' Dead pipe in his hand, he had gone on to relate in gory detail the legend about Chinese sailors preparing to leave port. They would find a fool or a drunk and tie him into a kite and launch him from their ship. If he flew straight up, it was a good omen for the voyage. If he failed to rise, no merchant would load his wares onto that boat.

'I want a kite.' Einnim would not let up. All morning he had been sulking. 'Oh, I wish Papa was home.'

'Very well, then.' Having equipped the boy with an empty cotton reel for a spool, a thin rod for a handle, a goodly length of cord and a slice of sailcloth, she had left him the task of hunting down some nice sturdy sticks for a frame.

Anyone looking at the child now would fail to detect one ounce of devilment. He was an angel personified: the brim of his straw hat a yellow halo pivoting against the clear blue sky as he leaned back, keeping the kite in check. In his right hand, he held firmly against his heart the spool, while the other leaned out to control the running of his kite. With hat askew, he dashed this way and that, flashes of sunlight capturing the purity of his sweet young face. Yet his focus was unmistakable. It was not until he turned and called 'Mama! Mama!' that she observed his sheer wonder and delight at his own skill and mastery. She knew at that moment that she had lost a son. His dependency on her was a thing of the past.

'Look, Carlie! See the kite? Wave to your big brother!'

It seemed to float one second, then, like a dragon, ducked and dived. Yet all along the boy had control of this mythical being.

The desire to fly was innate. One had only to look back to the Ancient Greeks. Daedalus, while shut up in his tower, had set to work fabricating feathered pinions for himself and his young son Icarus. Time and again, man had sought to bind himself to a set of wings. As for woman? Just imagine, the sensation of taking off, up, up, the freedom of soaring up and away. Over the years, it had been the essence of a recurring dream. To experience the most wondrous feeling, to will it to go on, only to wake up and suffer the reality of having been cheated.

⁓

To argue in front of a servant would be to lose respect as equally as to let the matter slide, so Henrietta resolved to put William on the spot upon his return from Sandridge once Millie was out of earshot. Palm over palm, she smoothed a thin film of cold cream, paltry balm for her poor hands which were aching after being left the bulk of the milking again – so much for their new apprentice. No, she would not let William get off scot-free.

Mid-afternoon, she made her way over to the Bluff with the boys, faithful Millie pushing Austin behind in the wicker perambulator.

'Is that Papa?' Einnim ran on down the path towards the jetty, pointing. Boats of all kinds spread stock-still across Port Phillip Bay. Far out she could see a ketch or a yawl. She must have been unconsciously tracking it for some time, reckoning against the jetty. Was it real or just a mirage? Its sails billowing out, then collapsing into the haze like some phantom of the sea. Every so often it would reappear, its masts so close as to appear married to one another.

That was how William saw their marriage, always in a nautical sense, he leading in front and she automatically following behind as the natural order of things. Whereas she saw it in a grounded way – not in some tandem harness but as a team or pair working together side-by-side with mutual respect. Much fairer, and far more sociable to boot. But in William's world there was one captain, under whom all others must bow to command; endless leisure time at his fancy.

Her boots punched footprints out of the crisp, cream-coloured sand. Today the water could not match her mood – it was exasperatingly calm. From time to time, she would hear the slap of a flaccid sail taking up its slack. Eventually a wake would find its way to lap lazily against the shore.

So beguiling, so belying. One of the most treacherous stretches of water in the world, Junius had warned her with almost reverence and dread. Then to finally experience it hand-in-hand – the excitement, the trepidation unimaginable as they had entered the Heads at dawn, and from this tawny strand of beach, one of the pilot boats had come through the whitecaps to meet them, led the *Caroline Agnes* down the channel into safe waters. Ah, the glow of the early-morning sun on the face of the Bluff, to see it unfold and the shelving sands. She had wanted to cry out like a seabird – this new golden land bursting with hope and freedom.

Freedom at a cost, well she now knew. The mere tongue of the tide and the narrow channel could fool the most experienced of mariners. There were horrifying tales about the Rip. Even on a day like today, the constant turmoil below the surface was enough to crack a mast or a boom, snap a fellow's neck or knock him unconscious into the sea. Let alone the rocks.

In but a blink, the outline of the reef had deepened, the shoal waters lying still and lucent against the point. At once her nostrils took in the clinging dampness of grit and sandstone. High above in shadow, the cliff-face and the new black lighthouse, fast looming as one.

Henrietta put her hand in her pocket and drew out her watch. It was four o'clock. And still no sign of William and no hint of a breeze. Within hours it would be nightfall and the cows waiting to be milked. Millie had already gone on home with Austin. Einnim and Carl, no doubt hungry, idled about, bare feet dragging through clumps of seaweed dyed white and yellow to deep red, and the water barely a flicker.

Fine dark figures emerged like grace notes caught in a dance of late-afternoon light. She drew the boys respectfully to her side. Stalking the shallows were a couple of natives – proud, erect steps while they speared at fish. Their shy lubras, clad only in opossum skins, pointing out moving shoals from above.

The blast of a horn brought her around abruptly. Carl plucked at her skirt in search of a leg. Einnim let go of her hand and ran back along the beach, calling 'Papa! Papa!'

As soon as William stepped off the jetty, the boys were beside him, jumping up and down. She closed her parasol with a final click.

*

'But you see, William, it has to stop – this frittering away of good time and money.' She broke a switch of tea-tree leaves, swishing away sandflies as they climbed the path to the Bluff. 'I'm doing more than my fair share, more than is humanly possible, while you've been out traipsing around here, there and everywhere. We cannot afford your style of life.' She had been through the ledgers systematically, like her father had taught her, accounting for every fractional farthing, and things did not balance.

'Must you lower yourself to cheeseparing, Madam? How many times have I told you? I am not interested in money for money's sake.'

She rolled her eyes to the heavens. 'But money, William, is a necessary vulgarity, for how else are we to live?'

Once home, she pointed to the growing pile of 'accounts rendered' on her desk. It was not her habit to live in debt. The very thought of bankruptcy sent a nasty shiver down her back.

William, frozen into silence, would hear nothing more on the matter. She waited until the boys had gone to sleep that night, set the cruet back on the dresser and, having shaken the cloth, folded it crisply in four. Everything clear and tidy, she sat herself at the piano, her nightly custom.

Candles in sconces flickered either side of the music rest. Normally the dark umber graining with its veins and head-like knots conveyed a uniquely human power. But tonight no company could be brought to bear out of the burr walnut panels. Her hands were uncommonly cold and stiff; the only sound in the room, the beating of her own heart. She took a deep breath and spun herself around on the piano stool.

'You throw money away in folly and dissipation. Then have the cheek to come home and treat me as if I were nothing more than your mizzen.'

William took out his tobacco pouch. He filled his pipe in slow, deliberate movements, packed it in with his thumb, inspecting his handiwork again and again, testing her patience.

'Mizzen, you say?' He raised an eyebrow. 'Rarely are they the same size, and since they are not the same size, they cannot claim to do the same work.'

'Have you forgotten what Mr Emerson said about the rights of women?'

'Emerson?' He let out a sour laugh. 'The savant of our century! But perchance your good learned man is in two minds about women.' William puffed and popped his cheek, appearing to ponder as he clenched his pipe. 'What did he say now? *Man is will, woman sentiment ... In the ship of humanity, will is the rudder, sentiment the sail; and when woman attempts to steer, the rudder is only a masked sail.*'

Something new crept into her voice. 'Mr Emerson also said that *the slavery of women happened when the men were slaves of kings.* Women's position is changing, William. What women say and think may be the shadows of new events, but new events they will eventually bring.'

Chapter 3

～

William had never seen a census paper, let alone filled one in. When it had arrived two years ago, in 1861, she had tried to gently hold sway.

Henrietta looked over his shoulder. 'Oh, William, how can you say that? I am not a dependant. I work long and hard, every day of the year, and I contribute as equally if not more than you.'

'Forget about me, that is how the law likes to put it, the statistician. That is the way it is in society.' He had thumped the edge of his hand down on the paper. 'The population of a country is naturally divided into "breadwinners" and "dependants" whether you like it or not.' His eyes glared, face red as a cockscomb.

'But you are not the sole breadwinner. We are both legitimate breadwinners, for remember I am a working woman.'

'All this fuss about nothing. A piece of paper, that's all it is.'

She had given him a chiding look. 'This is not a pleasure dairy, William. It's no good dreaming of Minton tiles and porcelain basins filled with milk fresh from little Jerseys that come when they're called. We are not in Camelot, you know.'

'I am your God-given natural protector, damn it.'

William had put down his pen, stroked his bottom lip slowly with the pad of his thumb. He had had that slightly pinched look in his eye that he sometimes got, as if he were sizing up some man-o'-war across the waves.

Since they could not see eye to eye, she had tried again later that night within the walls of their bedroom. 'You may call yourself the bread-winner, if you so choose, but what about this house?' she said. 'What about the dairy and sheds, all of which are mine in trust? What about my time and labour? You dismiss my work.'

'I give you the right to nurse our children. I give you the right to ride a horse, to be your husband's helpmate. That is all.'

'Please do not insult me, William. You dismiss my work, my rights.'

'Damn your rights. All your fiery demands! They are not worth a brass razoo, and nor are you, if it comes to that.'

'I have a right to expect you, my husband, to be home at a decent hour, with enough sleep to be up, ready to start the day at the same time as me.'

'For pity's sake, woman. What I do in my own time is my own concern and mine alone. So you should not trouble yourself about what hour I get home so long as there is food on the table when I get home.'

The very thought of there being other women was degrading. What he was wanting, she had come to realise even then, was an illustrious mistress, not a rational wife. She had slid away from William onto the cold side of the bed, and when he turned she had watched him with growing qualm. Waking at dawn, she had lain, waiting to see who'd be first to rise. A finger of raw light poking its way tentatively through the blind, and there was a nip in the air. Outside the low, soft moos of the cows from the holding yards were becoming more intense: deep, pressing moans, begging to be milked. William had reached over and slid his hand up her nightdress, seeking out a bare breast or the warm clamminess of bush below. She had dashed to the washbasin. Could she be *enceinte* again? Surely not, but the taste of rising bile was unmistakable.

'Oh, for God's sake, don't be so damned melodramatic. Now what are you doing?'

She had let him wait, then rinsed her mouth and spat in the basin. 'Brushing my teeth. There is work to be done.'

With Austin now toddling at her feet, it seemed she could do nothing to please William.

$\backsim$

Just as William was always against her, these days he seemed to be against the government, too. He had raged against the thinly populated town of Queenscliff becoming a municipality. He resisted change, so long as it suited him.

Over time, she had come to like the popular watering place, its restful order and lie of the land. The town stood alone. It saw what came in and what went out of the bay. A veritable Janus of the Heads, yet it did not stand on ceremony. It only saw what it wanted to see, often turning a blind eye. Overall, the town had jogged along with its leisurely air – a welcome resort for the wealthy traders and miners. Now that it was a municipality, Queenscliff would be subject to change. Their grazing rights on common land – which William saw as an entitlement – would undoubtedly be affected by new regulations. He huffed and puffed at fortnightly municipal meetings, stumbling home with prodigal disregard.

'It is all very well arguing against rising rates and progress,' she said at the dinner table the day after the last meeting in May. 'You stay on for hours, drinking and playing billiards, running up bill after bill at the Royal Hotel. It is we who must change, William. Adapt to the times.'

He thrust down his napkin and stood before the fire, glowering, legs splayed, hands on hips. 'Madam, I have sailed a ship around the world without aid of a woman. 'Twas I, by Jove, who pioneered the port of Sandridge.'

Bluster and bravado. If she had heard it once, she had heard it a thousand times, the story about William bringing in the *Duke of Bedford* against pilot's orders. Little wonder he had been blackballed by the Pilot Board. William, harping back to how his ship had for days prior been stuck in the ice in the Southern Ocean, and he, without complaint or injury, had managed to get all aboard safely to landfall. William and all his charm.

'What is it you want in me? A wife who bathes herself in milk, waiting for you to come home?'

William put on his mask of sangfroid. 'As to beauty, who knows? But if it lowers your nervous system and softens your skin, well and good. It will at least have achieved something. You have grown hard, Madam. Where is the delicate young lady I met all those years ago aboard the *Duke of Bedford*?'

⁓

Bound for South Australia in the year of 1848, the *Duke of Bedford* was ready set to sail. Masts and half-slackened sails came floating through the musk-coloured haze. Beyond, suspended from the clouds, the steeples and the ghostlike dome of St Paul's.

'Just one more run.' Junius had taken her up onto the poop deck so they could talk in private.

'Promise me?' She had locked fast to his arms, searched his eyes, mapping every line and crinkle.

He had pressed her to him, run a finger over her lips, allowing it to linger. 'A year, I swear. Then I will take you away to far-off places you would only dream about.'

Inside, she was burning. Barely wed the week, they were being torn apart for yet another year.

The ship listed gently, feeling the mellow breeze. The vaulted awning a mass of floating pillows gathered at the main. Either side of the deck, braided bluejackets shifted from one foot to the other. Brass buttons winked in the sun.

'Come, my love. Come and meet my new mate. Dugdale is his name.'

She had offered her hand and turned on a smile. William tucked his hat under his arm and made a bow. The two officers were of similar height, bronzed and stamped with crown and lion.

'How very good of you to come bid us a safe journey, Mrs Davies. My first voyage to Australia! Wish me good luck!'

Turning to Junius, she adjusted his stock. 'Some say it is a talisman to touch the collar of a sailor's suit. But I prefer to think luck lies more in one's making. Either way, sir, you're sure to be in safe hands with my husband.'

⁓

The next day, William returned from the auction sales in a foul temper. 'Our names have been sullied, Mrs Dugdale.' He was pacing up and down, smacking a rolled-up newspaper against his palm. He thrust it open on the table.

'Dear God! Whatever do you mean?'

He drummed a weathered finger on the page of *The Times*, his face mottled with rage. Words began to jump about and the room shimmered before her, everything swept up in a blur.

Principally because romantic notions are sometimes formed by gentlefolk in England as to the free, unconstrained, and therefore, happy country life of ladies and gentlemen in a colony, I lately noticed a case in the bush, rather rare and, I think, very interesting.

Returning from the township of a Victorian watering place on a Sunday evening after a very long stroll in the country I heard coming up behind me at a trot about 30 head of cattle. I observed, as they approached, that they were all milch-cows, and that a sort of gentleman in his shirtsleeves and well mounted, kept them together on one side, and a woman, also on horseback, was rounding them up on the other side.

As she galloped after some errant animal, her habit graceful, flying behind her, and her seat (as she jumped logs and little creeks) safe and

29

*assured from long practice, she looked like Die Vernon turned useful,
and anyone would have pronounced her a lady, and an elegant lady
too, had she not been driving cattle, which to my prejudiced eye rather
complicated her personal appearance with a touch of Smithfield.*

*The whole group swept by, and in a minute or so were lost sight of
in the bush. Early on the next morning I was walking through the little
township before breakfast, when I saw a milk cart with the most modern
style of shining tin pails in it; standing at a door, a man serving the
milk, while a woman sat in the cart handling the reins. As they drove
off I had a dim recollection of having seen them before, but where or
in what circumstances I could not call to mind. I described to my old
Scottish landlord what I had seen as above described and at once he told
me what he and all his neighbours evidently regarded as one of the most
romantic little stories of which the neighbourhood could boast.*

*The pair of equestrians in the bush and the pair in the milk-cart were
one and the same pair. The doctor in the township had discovered all
about them. When young and poor they had married in England despite
the opposition of friends. The gentleman had been in the navy; the lady
had been delicately nurtured.*

*Soon after their marriage, they resolved to begin afresh. They arrived
in Victoria very poor. Mr D. nearly related to noble family, with
honourable strength of will worked hard and his delicate young wife was
a devoted and self-denying partner in his hardships. He put by a little
money and bought a few head of stock. And now Mr D. declares that
he is as happy as the day is long, and that he would not exchange his
position for the command of the best ship in Her Majesty's Navy. They
have three children pronounced to be wonders of pretty behaviour and
good training and the father and mother (say the gossips) after nine years
of married life speak to each other more like lovers than man and wife.*

*Together they round up the cattle of an evening and serve milk in the
morning. In the evening when the cattle are in she solaces herself and
the little circle with the piano and gives an hour or so to the education*

of her little ones. But it is said that she is not altogether as contented as her lord. Why? Said I, deeply interested in this little romance of real life. After many questions, and many answers here is the outcome of the cross examinations of various witnesses. At the bottom of all the rural lady's felicity is a little something that poisons it somewhat – human pride. She is often addressed as a common milk woman, when she knows she is not a common milk woman, and she shrinks from the vulgar but extremely natural mistake a woman who serves milk when she is a princess in disguise, is still a milk woman to the eyes of the flesh and suppressed accomplishments can hardly secure recognition. Such a life then, after all, is a mistake.

They are a misfit in the social scheme. They may say and try to behave that they are roughly happy, but not associate with those with whom they are fit to associate, and hold aloof from the vulgar and ignorant, they are in effect almost without society. The troubled pride, therefore of Mrs D. If, after all, only the involuntarily expressed consciousness of the unappreciated lady, she is playing a part in the midst of serious life and is perhaps unreasonably indignant that the life does not more applaud the little drama and admire the milk woman and the lady so gracefully rolled into one. It is difficult to write so hard against the custom bound world and yet receive no smart from the process.

'You and your "troubled pride", Mrs Dugdale. What lies have you been telling?'

Lies? Say nothing of historical inaccuracies and misconceptions made public by a London broadsheet. The late Captain Junius Augustus Davies, the husband who had left her without kith or kin, lost to local folklore, whitewashed from her life. How to confute this mythical portrait of herself without further damaging William's pride?

She dared not look up. William's face was a mask. When he acted like this, so suspicious, it made her shiver inside. This man, whom she had first thought so artistic, poetic of temperament, a man who would appreciate a woman like herself, a young widow of sensibility, of pioneering spirit, one who could buckle to as the need arose. He had fostered her drive, her penchant for hard work, seemingly proud that she could work equally by his side, but he did that to the point where it had isolated her from other women. She had unwittingly distinguished herself, endorsing his moral smugness. The way she conducted herself – lively but a little standoffish – pronounced her a lady.

As for 'dairywoman' … far from demeaning, in her mind, it made her of equal importance in the marriage. Under the new *Electoral Act*, 'all Victorian ratepayers' would be eligible to register; in effect, that included those who were women. Soon she too would be enfranchised and able to demonstrate her legally equal partnership. But she knew it was not quite as simple when the law that made man and wife 'one flesh' did not allow them equal rights to the property they had in common.

How to stave off the tittle-tattle of town talk while maintaining her self-regard, William all the time watching her from a distance? The last thing she wanted to do was make herself look guilty or vulnerable. By evening Henrietta could work no appetite. Throughout the meal of roast beef, bread and potatoes, she was conscious of William's stare accompanying his every mouthful of protracted chewing.

Even after the meal, she could think of nothing to say. She fingered the spine of her book and frowned, the flames of the candelabras dancing across the chimney breast in a blaze of ever-changing light.

Somehow she must take the heat off them both. What they needed was a grazing property of their own rather than having the cattle range free on the common. The idea of taking out a mortgage on the dairy and buying up eighty-five acres out on the Portarlington Road had already been broached. She could draw in advance on a family bequest, should she so need. Well, then, go ahead with it they would. It would add to their assets, prove the town wrong.

William could have his share with her as third party, with the added proviso: 'The deed is her act – privately and apart from her husband.' They would override the old law of coverture and be on an equal footing. Papa, long-time London land agent and accountant, who knew the law as well as any chap in Lincoln's Inn, had advised her well on the ways and means. The motto 'Mine is thine' should really be 'Thine is mine but mine is my own.' Papa had seen it all too often. Why, he said, should a married woman resign her money to an idle scapegrace who spent it as soon as it was won?

Henrietta closed her book, marking her place with a feather.

'What are you reading?'

She held out the morocco binding.

'George Eliot. I see. Where did you get it?'

'Sarah Harding lent it to me.'

William pinned her with the dots of his narrow green eyes. I am your natural lord and master, they said. How could he begrudge her anything from Sarah, the wife of his closest acquaintance in town?

'As to the article, I shall write a letter of protest – with your permission, William – and thereby put an end to it.' She moved closer and slipped her hand in his. 'Let us make a speedy offer on the Portarlington Road property.' What better show of marital solidarity than to expand the business and make it more efficient.

~

Sir, As you have given Times publicity to a portion of my private history in your Melbourne correspondence in yours of June 15th, I trust you will also allow me to rectify an error therein which otherwise might act banefully upon the worldly prospects of our little nest in the bush, subject me to unmerited annoyance, and what is worse, cause dear ones in England to blush for the littleness of mind your correspondent so mercilessly ascribes me, for the details of his account being tolerably correct and my husband's own words quoted, the portraits were at once recognised both 'at home' and in Queenscliff and Melbourne.

After discussing us – husband, self, and our birdies, most kindly, though in some respects too flatteringly, he winds up with a sort of essay on my 'troubled pride' and in vain pining for what is termed 'society' and represents me as being really a contemptibly unhappy person because I am a 'milkwoman'. Were it the truth, I should merit all his polished sarcasm and to be thus universally ridiculed, but as facts are, he has treated me less than fairly and had he honoured me with a visit of inspection, which he ought to have done before making my history so public, he would have discovered instead of 'troubled pride', only gratitude I am able to be a milkwoman, and that my husband's society is amply sufficient for my happiness.

That I have pride I confess, but only the pride of being loved by my good and truly noble husband and so long as I can assist to earn our bread by his side, no one will ever find me ashamed of any occupation that is not dishonourable.

I remain, Sir, your obedient servant,
Henrie A. Dugdale
Hermitage Dairy
Queenscliff, Victoria, Australia

Chapter 4

$\backsim$

It was early December the same year when news came of her mother's death. Henrietta was busy preparing the usual creature comforts for Christmas, the morning spent stoning plums, washing currants, chopping citron and suet, and beating basins of eggs and sugar. Today the smell of mince pies baking in the oven was of little consolation. Her brother Charles's letter had caught her off guard. It was all she could do to try and hide her distress in the guise of seasonal spirit and industry.

Wiping flour from her hands, she slipped out to the washhouse to check the copper. Clouds of steam greeted her as she threw another piece of wood on the fire and immersed the calico-covered puddings, one upon the other, into the boiling black well of water.

Later that evening after supper, as the puddings lay cooling, she read Charles's letter again. Mercifully, she had been spared the duty of having to stand by and witness the old lady's slow decline to cancer and all its hideous workings. Mouth and tongue riddled; the growth steadily strangling her inside and out, or as Charles had delicately put it, 'imagine a bunch of grapes rotting through the neck.' Now she could not even think of Mama without having to retch in another surge of grief.

'Papa is devastated,' wrote Charles.

She adored her father, could only imagine what he was going through. At this precise time in London, Papa would have finished breakfast. A copy of *The Times* lying folded by his napkin. She pictured the old Norfolkman alone in his loss, looking about, searching, the poor devil having to wait for the everyday formalities of mealtimes to ease his heartbreak. Then to endure the long tail of summer light into the veil of nightfall. Here on the other side of the world, most people were asleep. Outside in the cold inkiness, the sheoaks shimmered as the ocean settled itself into a respectful shush broken by the occasional hoot or beep of a bird.

Not far away, she could hear the cows grinding at their troughs, the soft scuff of hoof, a sigh or stamp carrying easily in the cool breeze. She unlatched the door of the dairy, taking in the rush of ripening cheese. The lantern flickered against the stone walls to the clang of milk can lids as she went about checking everything was clean and ready for milking again at first light. Breaking the crust of cream, she ladled a pint of milk into a jug for breakfast. Then, slipping out, she pushed the latch of the door down firmly behind her. In a trail of breeze, a sudden shiver ran through her body and something made her look up. A dark, silent butterfly shape was drifting low over the new church tower on the hill behind. She gasped. It was only a swan. The moon, almost full, but now ever so slightly distorted, looked rather like an enormous owl's egg that had been thrown up into the spray of stars. All those heavenly bodies looking down at her in cold regard had been there far longer than any being on earth. What lay beyond would forever remain a mystery. However many civilisations worshipped an afterworld was of little consequence, there being nothing to substantiate one.

Yet no matter how long and hard she might argue against it, she knew that an afterlife was precisely what her dear long-suffering mother would have prayed for.

She had read somewhere that every time a woman gives birth to a child, she gives away something of herself. Often that child takes what it needs and gives little back in return. Time and distance had enabled her to shelve her guilt. Now it touched upon every nerve, playing on the knowledge that she had been unable to give back in her mother's greatest time of need.

Henrietta sniffled and gulped. She had always prided herself on never being a burden to her already overburdened mother. Yet shadowing this were the awful scenes: answering back, slamming doors and storming out of rooms. 'No, Mama, I cannot be demure. I simply cannot!'

When she thought about it, their most intimate times had been those spent outside the home, together, when she did not have to compete with her six brothers for love or attention. Whether at London galleries, the British Library, the Foundling Hospital, the Polytechnic, the concerts and theatres of Covent Garden, where her grandfather, Joseph Austin, had made his fame, outings tended to unite and liberate. By herself, her mother provided a well-educated chaperone.

She remembered that first time sailing back from France to Dover, a sudden breeze that had brought with it a rancid smell and wafts of rising bilge. In desperation, she had sought out the green land and moss-grown turrets, grasping at any fresh focus that might help to quell her seasickness. The churning ocean, the awful build-up, then heaving her insides out as the ship was dumped into a trough.

Mama, without so much as a thought for her own discomfort, holding back her hair, enabling her to retch over the gunwale, wiping her mouth clean – she, Henrietta, the healthy, robust child, the one who had never been sick. Oh, to see those chalky cliffs rising out of the mist and buttresses the colour of bones.

⁓

If she were to drop dead tomorrow, William would not so much as blink, let alone shed a tear, there being such little affection in his heart. But it was May, and the lingering weight of her grief had yet to pass.

'Have you heard from your brother Joseph?'

Joseph's silence had been mystifying.

'No, why do you ask?'

William humped his eyebrows and uttered a rude sound.

She knew he found her brother an arrogant fellow, a bit of a silver tongue. Blowing his own trumpet when there was no real cause. But Joseph was more than glib and insufferable. Sometimes she preferred to forget he ever existed.

'Odd fellow.' William tossed a nod at *The Age*. 'Have a read of that.'

Sir, A lank shadow, which looks like a thin boy, is seen daily walking the Long Beach, dragging after him a miserable wretch that has some mystified shape of a horse, with a mailbag at times on the back of the beast, and not infrequently on that of the boy. Both horse and boy are the pictures of extreme misery and privation – the beast, according to the boy's version, lives on the produce of the Long Beach, which is sand, and the boy goes without food all day, sometimes for twenty-four hours; on one of which occasions he was benighted on the road, and had the benefit of the mailbag for a pillow. But the unfortunate lad toils on – cold or heat, sunshine or rain, it matters not, the shivering being, habited only in a shirt and trousers, plods his wretched course, day by day, striving hard to deliver a mailbag, which he manages to do at some unknown period during the interval of four hours and twenty later than the proper time. Pray advise your readers that there are no real ghosts on the 'Long Beach', but that the boy and beast are actual flesh and blood, employed in the mail services.

I am, Sir, your obedient servant,
Joseph E. Worrell
Mornington

Was it some florid delusion? She could never be sure with Joseph. Expressing sympathy for a woebegone stranger was one thing. It would give her much heart to think Joseph capable of having sympathy for all the lame ducks in the colony, were it not for the way he had shamefully and cruelly treated his daughters.

In a few quick snips, she cut out the letter with her scissors.

'Heard an odd rumour about him the other day.'

'What did you hear?' She kept very still and her cheeks began to burn.

'Oh, didn't believe it for one minute,' he said. 'One hears all kinds of rummy tales.'

She closed her eyes for a moment. Had William been delving in her private papers? Henrietta rose quietly in one assured and fluid motion, and slipped out to the kitchen. She reached for her mother's old tea caddy – though it was not tea she was after – and turned the key to her secret hidey-hole, infused as it was with a faint dry aroma redolent of home.

There, beneath her marriage certificates, were the cold hard facts – the now faded news reports of the London court case. The whole family beset with shock and grief and shame. Joseph, gaunt and wretched, standing alone in the docks in the dark, austere courtroom. Imagine, poor little waifs, the humiliation, having to give evidence against their own father – and to have it splashed across every broadsheet in the country.

The stain was still there, with all its memories. She wouldn't want William to find out. He would lord it over her. With one eye on the door, she quickly tucked it all away, including her clipping of Joseph's letter, and turned the tasselled key, hearing the click of safekeeping. Haunting her, the question: how could my own brother have sunk to such black despair? Three months' prison, penance at a pittance.

She slid back into her seat in the living room, quiet and grave, rearranging her skirts with a sigh. Perhaps grief for Mama had at last come to humble Joseph, she thought, reaching for the newspaper again. If not, what could be the underlying impulse for his very public letter? Its bizarreness belied a truth of its own. It was well known that young lads were employed in the mail service for a penny a mile, if they were lucky.

'It's an outright disgrace,' she said at last. 'One should be grateful if the mail arrives at all.' It was indeed right and proper of Joseph to draw this shameful matter to the attention of the powers-that-be, but in no way could this absolve him of his own abuses of power.

⁀

The task of teaching children right from wrong was paramount. This morning Henrietta began wading through a series of graduated grammar exercises, a dreadful book which she quickly abandoned. There was no point in unproductive toil. And of what use was a pedant to the world? Beginning with her children's first efforts of speech, she had set standards crystal clear. By two-and-a-half, Einnim and Carl could speak so correctly that people wondered how it was possible when neither even knew the alphabet. But it took precious time, and try as she might with Austin, her littlest still had no desire to repeat anything.

Oh, for one of her three nieces. She could forget any of their failings. From time to time, they had come to stay, to help lighten her load. The benefits were mutual. The girls had learned new skills, and their visits offered them respite from their frenetic existence. Emma – light auburn loops either side of her pale face – would have made an ideal governess, but she was already a teacher under her father, who was now living a new life in Mornington as a headmaster. *Emma, Little Bread-and-butter Miss*, as William put it unkindly, *plain as a pikestaff.* Fanny, the youngest, forgot instructions. A wisp of a child, spent of all life. One, two, three puffs were enough to send her flying away like thistledown. Fanny seemed happiest in the dairy, dewy-eyed, talking to the animals, or milking, head pressed into flank, gathering the warm white rhythm in her hands. It was the eldest, Hattie – her namesake – William had taken to: dark, flashing eyes and wineglass figure and her long, black tresses escaping from under her bonnet. Of pluck she had plenty. But now Hattie, having refused to go to Mornington, had run away with her sister, Fanny, and was living heaven knows where.

Good girls were hard to come by. Being so few women to men in the colony, they could pick and choose, or try their luck in the goldfields.

Millie had enough work, as it was. Henrietta begrudged having to leave her three young sons with others whom she considered unsuitably equipped for the position. Apart from the threat of physical dangers, it was her boys' social and moral advancement she jealously guarded. How would her children learn to behave and speak properly if left with unschooled girls for long periods?

Their education would be left to her. She did not want her children to experience the harsh classroom model of learning she'd had to endure in London. As a child of six or seven, she had been kept standing until her delicate limbs ached, to say nothing of sundry cuffings and other assaults, because her young mind refused to be saturated with knowledge of bloody deeds. Tender, innocent children, she believed, should not have to endure canings and other barbarous punishments.

Rote lessons on unnecessary subjects did immense harm to children. At least she and William seemed to agree on that score. William said he had learned more at sea during the first year of cadetship than in the entire years of his schooling. Much of which was no doubt unpalatable, she thought, especially when repeated innocently from the mouths of babes. When Einnim was just a little fellow of four, she'd had to bring him to task.

'I forbid you to use that word.'

'Men speak differently,' the scamp had replied. What impudence! William had merely popped his eyes and stuck his tongue in his cheek.

Loath as she was to wheedle, she had taken the boy out for an afternoon drive in the trap, just the two of them – a special treat – on the promise he be good. But they were barely at the end of the street when he began to behave badly. Standing up on the footboard, no hands, shouting his lungs out to the wind. She'd pulled over the pony.

'I won't say it again, Einnim! Sit down, hang on to the railing and, for goodness sake, keep quiet.'

'Why?'

'It is dangerous, that's why.'

'Men do it.'

'Little boys must obey their mothers.' She'd given him a lecture there and then about spooking horses. 'A sudden movement could cause little Bob to rear or bolt. Throw you out of the trap.'

Einnim cast her a dark look that said, *Don't care!*

But it was William who was at fault. He took great delight in undermining her authority in front of the boys. And this, she told herself, was how the world perpetuated itself, from father to son, generation after generation. It was grossly unfair, and the recall of Einnim's words still stung.

Chapter 5

In September a letter arrived from Henrietta's youngest brother Charles in London, advising her that their father too had succumbed. Poor man had not lasted a year. Without a wife, he had nothing to live for. The prostatic disease that had been plaguing him in his latter years had taken a sudden grip for the worse.

As to whether Joseph was aware of Papa's death, she dared not enquire. Although the eldest son, he could expect to inherit nothing; he was still in disgrace, and incommunicado with the rest of their family.

The double blow of her parents' passing left Henrietta bereft; her strongest sense, one of utter loneliness. Images from childhood gridlocked her mind at all hours of the day and night, in her fear she might lose them and the refuge of memory, as well.

She pictured her father at his best: a proud, magnanimous-looking man in a long grey frock coat, leaning back from the chess table, enabling his little darling to climb upon his knee. 'You're such an engaging child, aren't you, love? Now, my little champion, how about you pour me a fresh cup of tea?'

Holding steady cup and saucer, negotiating the fine blue line of steam curling upwards to the ceiling, she would make her way towards him.

'Put it there,' he'd say. 'Now come and give me a great big hug.'

Her fascination with his face, his parchment-like cheeks and his fool of a nose, which glowed like a port beacon from morning to night. Examining his ears, lacing her fingers through his fine grey hair.

Images spun before her, like pages flipping in a penny picture book. Her first visit to the seaside at fourteen years old, just her and Papa, and miles of mudflats shimmering silvery blue and bronze. Boots and stockings in one hand, steadying her bonnet against the wind. All the while, her father watching in amusement as she skipped and ran, spreading out her arms, wheeling around and around, wild with exhilaration.

'Look, Papa. I am a spinning top. I am a bird. I am whatever I want to be. Why cannot it always be like this?'

His wry chuckle returned in a rush. 'If Mama could see you she would scold me for giving you such licence.'

Poor Mama. No capacity for words in her last days, just the blush of shame for her contrary dairywoman daughter. According to Charles, the article in *The Times* had hastened Mama's death.

Henrietta mopped her eyes. What a disappointment she must have been. All those battles, whether it be over corsets, eating too quickly, laughing too loudly or acting inappropriately with her cousin.

Throughout the day, the memory of that short time on the beach with Papa returned again and again. The dizzying delight of imagining herself dancing with Junius barefoot in the sand, squealing, wheeling around, a flock of seagulls beating inside her breast. Even now, she could still feel the occasional peck at her heart. 'Now now, Henrietta, come along! Can't you see the tide is coming in?' Funny old Papa running after her on the beach, pulling her by the arms, bringing her to her senses. She, laughing and panting, her hair flying; in her mind, she kept dancing around, dancing forever.

The immediate seclusion and silence of the pinewoods in contrast upon them leaving the sands, every footfall absorbed into the dry bed of needles beneath – their cool, calming aroma – and the sounds of the ocean and the wind but a distant memory. Looking up into the canopy of branches, she had been captivated, shafts of light jiggling up and down like puppet strings. Twenty years later and thirteen and a half thousand miles distant, she could still recall the details of that image. Now, unmitigated adulthood seemed a bleak prospect amid the hard practicalities of life.

～

Henrietta guided Gypsy through the marshy shrubland to their new property on the Portarlington Road. The cattle appeared to be well settled, having spent the winter months here, fenced in their new pastureland. The new situation would make calving time a lot easier for her.

Gently, she drew on the reins, attuning herself to the sounds of wildlife. Hiding in the shadows were snipe, quails and curlews and the occasional plover. But today everything was perfectly still. Raindrops crystallised the trees as the huge, dark skies began to part. In the moist air, she could smell the onset of spring; anticipate it in every one of her senses. The land began to take on new intensity; leaves, grass and beaded glasswort glistening as the sun sharpened its beams. Peeling grey-barked tea-trees veiled themselves in white. How she rejoiced to see rusty sheoaks give rise to flower, fallen beds of needles blushing red with pollen, and the air bursting with the scent of gumleaves and wattle and mingling expectation.

She told herself she must try again, remould her relationship with William. 'Greenleaf' was not a name she would have chosen for their new property. It was William's – a way of feeding his ongoing bouts of nostalgia. The more he wallowed, the more extravagantly she had played English ballads. She had never allowed herself the luxury of mooning, having no real desire to go back. *En avant* had always been her motto.

The beginning is always today, Mama would say. Now that the bequest from her mother's family had arrived, they could pay off the Greenleaf mortgage and make their home more commodious. The rest of her entitlement she expected would remain safely in the hands of her Melbourne trustee. It was what Papa himself would have recommended.

With her father's spirit still hovering brightly, a model of generosity and goodwill, she mulled no longer. Perhaps she had been a bit standoffish over the years. Small-mindedness and insularity could easily get under one's skin. She resolved to open their house and extend some hospitality. She would give of herself with Saturday night singsongs and soirees, enjoy the company of John and Sarah Harding, plus the postmaster and registrar, the schoolmaster of the common school and the local doctor among her trusted coterie.

⌒

On the first Sunday in October, the scene was set for a picnic at Greenleaf – a gathering of townsfolk to help them celebrate their new acquisition. Buggies and drays arrived in the best of spirits. Together in good company they feasted *en famille*. White napery spread fresh with offerings: cold ducks, rabbit pies, sandwiches, Scotch eggs, tarts, baskets of oranges, bottles of ginger beer and ale. Everywhere, children on the run: rollicking in the long grass, building humpies and playing hide-and-seek, or cooking jacket potatoes around the fireside as they watched the tea billies boil.

What would he think of it all? Dearest Papa. Later, on the way home, she pictured him sitting beside her, holding the reins, appraising their land like a good auctioneer. 'Hardly a Gainsborough,' he'd probably say. She still found herself talking to him, unconsciously seeking approval. Every so often she would close her eyes and settle her head on his imaginary shoulder, allowing it to take the brunt of every jolt.

How tickled he would have been to hear that women ratepayers were now eligible to exercise their electoral rights in the forthcoming 1864 colonial election. William had pooh-poohed the new legislation. A bureaucratical blunder, he claimed, a mere oversight that wouldn't stand the test. The qualifying term 'all ratepayers' was certain to be redressed by an immediate amendment confining it to 'all *male* ratepayers'.

The crack of the whip brought her to her senses as William gave the four-in-hand a *cluck*. 'C'mon, you bloody brutes! Get a move on!' Rather putting a blot on the idyll. She coughed amid the cloud of dust. Forget about Gainsborough. She was thinking of poor Maggie Tulliver and all her suffering in *Mill on the Floss*.

She must pass it on to Sarah Harding now she had finished. They usually shared whatever books came to hand, there being few enough novels at the local Mechanics' Institute, tucked away on the top shelf where only men could reach.

⁓

Before long, volumes of books arrived in a consignment of old family keepsakes shipped out to her from the Old Country by Charles. As she unpacked, the joint distribution of deceased estates, the passing on – for her, the last demarcation between parent and child – began to unleash more memories, her senses alive to the raw fragrance of clean timber shavings amid softer muted smells of nutmeg and cloves that clung to the empty tea chests.

A glass-doored cedar bookcase now boasted a row of old but merrily bound books embossed with gold. Grandfather Austin's famed collection of comedies, farces, songs, novels and poems she had devoured as a child. Whether she would ever more than look at them again was another thing.

There was also a new focal-point to the room as the children played among the packaging. A heavily framed portrait of Mama, painted at the height of youth, hung on a previously empty wall. It was still recognisably her own dear Mama. The classical profile. Long, white neck and shell-like ears, the dark ringlets she had fingered as a child and the distinctive bow-shaped lips that had kissed her goodnight.

As for Mama's jewellery, there would be little occasion to wear such dainty trappings here. Pieces that were old-fashioned or ornate were out of place. They did not suit her colonial preference for dressing down in simple day-to-day attire without need for feminine affectation.

In London, there was a dress code for this and a dress code for that. Going outside was a major expedition, especially for children – polished boots and gloves and hats and no end of preparation. Here her youngsters could roam barefoot, with the shores at their disposal. If they fell playing 'possum up the trees', they fell softly and came to no harm.

Now, with everything in its place, she sat, under the sheoaks, sans shoes, sans stockings, workbox by her side, watching the children play by the waterside. Time permitting, she would take them there daily over the summer months. A luxury, granted, but an hour invested by the waterside was a very good way of getting the steam out of the little pets. Here, they lost all desire to bicker, any claims to rights lost in their total sense of freedom.

In the low tide, they were moulding a sandbar out of mud and seagrass so as to launch their new pond yachts.

'Here,' she said, pressing a cabbage-tree hat upon Einnim's head, 'now keep it on.'

He squinted at her, brushed away a fly that had settled on his nose, and pointed.

'Oh yes, a fine harbour you have made! We must tell Papa about it when he comes home.'

William had never been comfortable with babies. 'Give me a boy of seven and I will give you the man,' he would say. For some months he had been helping Einnim build a toy boat out of balsawood. At first it had made her nervous to see the boy whittling and splicing over spread-out pages of newspaper on the kitchen table. Any moment he would lose the top of a thumb, and then where would they be?

She knew she must let her son have his rein. That way a child could learn informally – in her mind, the healthiest, best way for a child to learn.

'Me too!' Austin toddled off to the waterside, pulling at his frock and drawers.

She had to rush and check him before he wet himself completely. It would soon be time to breech the child. Only natural, Austin wanting to be the same as his brothers in white sailor suits.

48

'Not too deep, boys. Careful.' Swans were known to be aggressive, especially when nesting – strong enough to capsize a small boat. Last summer, a boy was knocked out of his canoe by a swan, which set upon him, pecking at his face, hindering his attempts to swim ashore until he drowned. The thought terrified and sickened her.

She snipped a fresh length of brown silk and threaded the needle again, thankful there was only one more stocking left to darn. The swans had moved, she noticed. They drifted quietly in the distance now, a navy of black ships.

Chapter 6

~

The sky was as fickle as the sea, and the sea was always breathing in its sleep. Sea breezes and prevailing winds strongly influenced the tides of Port Phillip Bay and, anywhere within a hundred mile radius, one could experience four seasons in a day. Here, in pilot waters, a sailor had to constantly guard his leeway.

Junius had come and gone with the tide. Today, twelve years on, it seemed as if he had just drifted off into a night fog and never come home. In her early days of widowhood, he had been there at every turn. At the old lighthouse or on the beach or walking down the street. Once, she'd gone rushing towards him, only to be left stricken, battling to free herself from his shadow, the burn of his dark eyes, the twist of his lips mocking. *Whether for love or money, it was too rash, too unadvised, too sudden, too like the lightning ...* It was indecent to marry again so soon.

Last night she had heard it, a dolorous sound like someone groaning, that kept eating into her soul.

'William, William, wake up. Listen!' she cried. 'Someone's out in the bay.'

'What? What?' He sat up, threw off his nightcap and rumpled his hair. 'Only person out there's the new buoy,' he snorted. 'Go back to sleep, you silly woman.'

With stomach churning, and in need of proof, she had risen early before milking. The morning, grey and vaporous, with faint yellow stains in the east. Standing on the Bluff, looking out at the mist rising off the channel, she could just pick it out, that black blot of a whistling buoy being buffeting about by the waves. Ears cocked, she waited in mounting dread. *Ooooh!* Again and again, it wearily moaned its warning. Like a last dying breath it came, its repeated bellow, each time defying the dense, wraith-like conditions, which in the still night would have muffled all other sounds around.

Later, after finishing in the dairy, she returned to the Bluff with the boys. A brief shower of rain had freshened the dusty streets, the air thick with the smell of damp sandstone and passing whiffs of brine. Broken mirrors of blue sky and cloud lay caught in the puddles. Approaching the row of pilots' cottages near the clifftop, she took Austin's hand. Carl ambled a few paces in front, while Einnim ran on ahead with a stick in his hand, delighting in the clatter as he scraped it along the wrought-iron fence palings. Carl, ever on the lookout, had stopped to pick up a feather floating in a puddle. Its black and white markings looked vaguely familiar.

'An albatross, Mama?'

She was surprised to catch her image in the puddle, her own absent frown. Carl twirled the feather, studying it with concern. Once, he'd found a stunned petrel. Poor creature must have flown into the lighthouse, temporarily blinded by the weather. Being blown off course could happen just as easily to a sailor as to a bird.

'Come!' She gripped Austin's hand tighter. 'Do walk a little faster, dear.'

The moaning sound had gone now. So freely imagined, that haunting human sigh of a signal would forevermore hold harrowing associations. 'Stop it!' she reprimanded herself. Surely, after all this time, she could let him rest – Junius, a dim, distant glow, like an oyster shell lying on the ocean floor.

51

However much she tried to please William, he gave nothing back in return. The licensed libertine continued to take much latitude. He would hire a man to do his work at great cost, and off he would go for three or four days and think nothing of it. In his absence, the children would become rude and pesky, especially around mealtimes, all the while her resentment building.

As if she didn't have enough to do and delegate in a day, all the time waiting for his lordship to come home. Yet, in a sense, fearing it, too, this game he played for his benefit alone. It sapped her strength at the worst possible times, and she could feel her patience, all her powers, gradually waning. William would return home his genial self, olive branch in hand. Once accepted, it made her vulnerable. Then at every turn he would try and thwart her. Belittle her. Amusing the boys at her expense.

Early Friday morning, he had ridden off to Geelong to meet a stock and station agent, saying he would be back by Saturday afternoon at the latest. It was now Sunday evening again, the dairy still to be cleaned, and she felt at wit's end, having given poor Millie the day off.

'Mama, Mama!'

'Now, you greedy boys.' She rushed back through the scullery door with what she hoped was her sternest frown. 'What are you looking at me like that for, empty plates in your hands?'

'Please, Mama, may we have more?' Their voices started up again, each competing louder and louder, one against the other.

'Where are your manners, boys? You have eaten far too quickly and none of you has touched so much as a forkful of cabbage.'

Austin kept banging his spoon on the table. 'Don't like cabbage.' He spat at his food. 'More meat.'

The door creaked open.

'What have we here? A right little mutiny, by the sounds of it.' William took off his oilskins and flung them over a chair. He sat himself down, his hair damp and dishevelled, whiskers crusted with salt.

'Eat up,' he said, 'and since my supper is not ready and waiting for me, I shall tell you a story.'

Henrietta brushed the tablecloth briskly with the palm of her hand and threw the crumbs into the fire. As she set a place before William, she was at once assaulted by his grog-soaked breath. The boys knew no different. They were all ears and eyes, under his spell.

'What story, Papa?'

William paused to pinch the drip off his nose. 'You wouldn't read about it – the greatest unhung scoundrel who ever sailed the seas. That murderous cut-throat of a cook baled up the captain of our ship with his butcher's knife. Took him to the block in front of us all, then made the mate and steward walk the plank. Only a cabin-boy at the time but I was old enough to see how sharp and shiny that darn blade was, and oh, that wicked sneer on his face as he slashed this way and that, blood spurting, the master's noddle lying bespattered on the deck. Next day he served it up well cooked with a tasty sauce and made us eat it all. Moral of the story is, my pretty lads, never argue with the cook.'

The three boys squealed with delight.

'So, what have we here, then?' William opened his napkin with a flourish.

Henrietta's appetite was long vanished but his, she knew, would be voracious. The sooner he ate, the sooner he would sober up. Steam rose as she lifted the lid of the bain-marie and left him to serve himself.

'Broiled chicken, eh? Broiled chicken is chicken spoiled, in my opinion.' William leaned down and gave Austin's ear a tweak. 'Be thankful for what you get from this galley. You never know when it might be your last.'

'Lucky it wasn't your head, Pa,' said Einnim, rocking back and forth with a cackle.

'No, but by the looks of your mama, it might well be in store.'

'What happened to Cook, Papa?' Carl's face had turned suddenly pale and thoughtful.

'Yes, do tell us, Pa,' said Einnim. 'Did they hang him by a rope?'

Eyes on stalks, the boys watched their father pulverising mouthfuls of chicken.

'No fear.' William sucked on a drumstick before pushing it, the caper sauce and the cabbage to the side of his plate. 'They sent him across the seas to the Swan River Settlement. Locked him up.' His teacup he held poised, little finger ridiculously hooked. 'Lucky man. I understand he went on to become a perfectly respectable citizen of Fremantle, a tobacconist, I believe, which reminds me ...' William drained the dregs and went over and eased himself into his comfy chair by the fire.

'Einnim! Hoy! Where are you hiding?'

'Here, Pa.' The boy jumped to attention.

'Bring me my pipe, there's a good lad.'

'Ah, thank you,' he said, stretching out his legs. 'Yes, yes,' he nodded, 'go on, you may light it for me if you wish, so long as you give it straight back, otherwise your mama will have my head.'

~

The next morning was routine as normal. The daily milk round, droving the cattle with William, and a list of chores she'd left for Millie. Upon her return, she heard squeals and scuffling coming from the dairy. Quickly she slid down from the saddle and secured the reins to the railing. Carl dashed out, followed by Einnim brandishing a pair of butter pats.

'Mama! Mama! He's whacking me.'

'Einnim, come, come! This won't do! You must be kind to your brother, really you must.' The boy squirmed under her grasp like an eel as she tried to take off her riding gloves.

William snickered. 'Oh, let them be.'

'I will not have my children growing into monsters.'

Einnim ducked as William made out to tug a lock of hair or take hold of an ear.

'What would you have him be, a tragedienne like his mother?'

Mischievousness was not necessarily a bad thing. Often it was simply a sign of an inquisitive mind. To put her foot down only drove Einnim further into fearlessness; his stripling body was always searching for a challenge. To see the boy relish in his physicality made her swell with pride, for he was more than dexterous for his age. Already he could ride Bob, bareback, unaided, and wield a pair of oars as well as she. A born fish. Before long he would be outswimming his father.

Einnim had been hankering to go and see Buckley's Cave. She had been telling the children the story of Buckley, an escaped convict, who, having gone to live with the blacks, had not seen or spoken to a white man for thirty years. The story was useful. In one sense, it was a lesson on the social mores of the natives, the remaining few left in the Bellarine. Yet it was also about universal morals – the crossing of lines, compassion, being cast out by one society and taken in by another. The idea of living in a cave appealed to Einnim, who fancied himself as Robinson Crusoe.

The first Saturday in the Christmas holidays, they drove the four miles out to Point Lonsdale. After a picnic and a quick bathe in one of the protected little bays, they made their way up to the point to see the big hole and the middens. Einnim couldn't get out of the cave fast enough.

'Smells something awful!' he said, fist against his nose. 'Nothing but old bones.'

Then William insisted on climbing the new lighthouse. It stood solitary, a bold banded tower boasting a light that could be seen ten nautical miles out to sea on a clear night. She looked on, heart in mouth, as Einnim scrambled up the steps ahead of his father and stood on the balcony, pointing beyond the passing ships, screaming, 'I can see Antarctica!'

William turned and grinned at her. 'He'll be clawing his way up the ratlines to the crow's nest afore you know it.'

She knew what sort of life that would be. A life at sea. A wave of angst swept over her. Grasping the two younger boys, she clamped them to her sides. A sudden gust and they would be gone forever. Below, the rugged precipice with its serrated platform, the bottle-green turbulence and swirling tides. Was it a trick of the eye? For, there! Every now and then she would sight it – Junius' face – rising, falling, in the play of waters whirling on the reef, in the windswept spray against that heaving blue mass to the cliffs on the other arm of the Heads, and all the while the breakers kept pounding, relentless, from the back beach behind.

～

At home, keeping a check on the children's whereabouts remained a strain, with water at every turn. Every now and then she felt the need to let out a *cooee*! The awful nerve-racking wait. Carl could usually be spotted anywhere – that shock of red hair shining like a torch against the grey gorsey scrub, the rawness of his white skin turned pink by the sudden chill of salt water. Yet the sturdiness, the dependable plod of his legs climbing the Bluff, was her brother Charles all over again.

Einnim began to leave Carl behind, his placid good nature, his desire to please. At eight and a half, he was old enough to go out adventuring alone. It began to alarm her, his rush for life. Bird nesting or chasing a calf, he insisted, was for sissies. He would come back, rabbits on a belt, blood dripping down his legs.

William, very much against her wishes, had been teaching him how to use a pea-rifle. Foolish thing to let a young lad loose with a firearm – but, give him his due, William was strict in his licence.

'Always treat a rifle as loaded. Never, never point it at anyone. A mere tap of the bolt-head, boy, could make it fire and you might end up with a murder charge on your hands.'

Together, mid-afternoon, before bringing in the cows for milking, father and son had gone off to practise, taking potshots at a tin can nailed to a nearby gate-post. The boy imitated his father. The jauntiness with which he kicked at dried-out pieces of dung. The set of his face as he sat on the stool, learning how to milk. Already there was definition in his muscles, his young face crisp as if chiselled out of local sandstone.

Her eyes followed him now, playing ball with his brothers. The lingering rays of sunlight catching the red-gold of Carl's hair. Austin was of a different mould: dark and fast as a whippet. His three-year-old face a miniature of William's, minus the middle-age podge.

'Captain Dugdale' lived up to his name with much aplomb. He, with his fine aristocratic nose, his discerning eyes, could be high-hatted when it suited or a gentleman salt of the sea. In good company, nothing was seen to cross him; his brow unsullied, not even a flinch of the whiskers shielding his weatherworn cheeks. Beneath the weight of civility, his mouth betrayed a cruel and obstinate streak.

She struck a match, and, having lighted the candelabra, rang the tea bell. Outside, in the soft, ample shades of dusk, her three sons appeared inseparable, their tones and forms fleetingly diffused as they played around the garden.

One had no control over one's looks, one's blood, only one's manners and actions. Whatever else her sons may have inherited from their father, it would not be cruelty. That was one thing she would not tolerate. When she looked out again, it was to see her three sons charging around, waving broken sticks for swords.

'Einnim!' The boy had Austin piggyback on his shoulders, threatening Carlie. '*Aagh!* Got you!'

Little brutes! Once before, these rough and tumbles had left Austin nursing a broken collarbone for weeks.

William waved her off in exasperation, as he came in from the dairy. 'Bah! Don't fuss. The boy will live.'

Chapter 7

⁓

The long, hot, trying summer had taken its toll. Feed was low, feral goats competing on the common with their herd. By the end of February 1865, the Dugdale family had left town and relocated to Spring Hill, a property west of the narrows, just past the Point Lonsdale junction, that had once been a cattle run. With its freshwater springs perpetually bubbling nearby, it was ideal to lease: eight acres of grazing land and four under cultivation, plus a granite dairy purpose-built on site.

The homestead, built of solid limestone, was somewhat grander than the dwelling they'd left in town – more rooms than Henrietta cared to manage, and far more than they needed. Here, at Spring Hill Court, she began at once to feel cut off from the comfort of her familiar surroundings. She missed the intimacy of Swan Bay, the brisk walk to the Bluff, the blue relief wherever she looked. Once past the narrows and the market gardens, one took in only an occasional gulp of seawater. Stunted trees and scrub hugged the land and silenced the wind.

The view from the homestead was somewhat hindered: a narrow paddock in the foreground, and darker tussocks alternating with lighter grazed-down patches of grass where the cattle ranged, brindle like the gums across the rise. Either side, pasture and a mix of yellowing crops stretched into bush scrub and neighbouring lots through which a dirt track, overshadowed by an avenue of young cypress, seemed to lead to nowhere.

Their nearest neighbours, their oldest, staunchest friends, were the Hardings: Sarah, with her charm and wisdom, and her husband, John. How oft had the tale been repeated of John and William's brief visit to the diggings in 1852? The two men, having been robbed of all their belongings, had had to traipse back to Queenscliff by foot. Perhaps that was why Henrietta sometimes felt somewhat the interloper amid their laughs. Her own story held a different bond — a friendship wrought out of loss and tragedy and the sudden woes of widowhood barely months after her arrival in the colony. But for Sarah taking her under her wing, she would, at least in the short term, have been no better off than one of the thousands of deserted women in Emerald Hill, living in destitution with little more than a sheet of canvas over her head. Sarah had seen her through her lowest, most vulnerable moments — for Henrietta, a life-changing experience which made her treasure her self-reliance. Could she not shed her cloak of invincibility for one moment and share her problems with Sarah again?

For the last fortnight, Henrietta had been up nightly, tending sick calves with Bleeding Nose. She was puzzled, since they were only the orphaned ones she had reared by hand. Worried the disease would infect the herd, she rode over to Sarah's house, knowing her friend was very knowledgeable about animal husbandry.

Why the Hardings had sold their cattle and were now solely sheep farming was hard to fathom. Nervous, dopey-minded animals, William called them, whereas a milch cow showed curiosity and generally knew where it was going. Henrietta loved all animals, though some, she conceded, were easier to manage than others. A cow might not have the elegance and nobility of a horse, but one could not help love such a creature for its appearance and attitude to man.

'What am I doing wrong, Sarah?' She described the coughing, the swelling under the tongue, the heavy snoring, the blood in the manure. 'It's heartbreaking. I've lost three in the past two weeks.'

'What do you feed them?'

'They turn away from whatever I offer.'

Sarah took her hand and pressed her further. 'Tell me, what is their bedding?'

'Dried bracken, fresh from the scrub.'

'Oh, then the poor darlings will be breathing poison into their lungs. I steer clear of bracken with my lambs. It's well known to be noxious.'

Henrietta was mortified. To think she had been unconsciously killing her own stock. Observing her faraway frown, Sarah poured her another cup of tea. 'Poor dear, you look exhausted.'

'If only I could get a proper night's sleep.' The calves, Henrietta knew, were only partly to blame. In the hectic busyness of day, she was like an automaton, but when darkness came she found she could not unwind. William beside her, like a steam engine, taking in all of her air. So overpowering that it often brought on the feeling of suffocation, the continual compulsion to check, hand on breast, that that vital part of her was moving. Up and down. Up and down. Even then, she would end up placing her hand under her nose to prove she was still alive, before finally shutting her mind to the shadows.

'Break one of your patterns. It will lead you out of your troubles.' Sarah Harding's suggestion had been to sleep outside. 'Air once breathed is not fit to breathe again,' she claimed. It poisoned all the 'bodyworkers', as she called them. That's why a closed room, where the air was breathed over and over, caused sleeplessness and headaches.

'What you really need, Henrie dear, is a holiday. Why don't you and William spend the weekend in Melbourne? Once the calves are up and on their feet, go. Stay overnight. Leave the children with Alice, and John and his man will take care of the milking.'

'How kind of you, Sarah.' Henrietta turned to the Hardings' eighteen-year-old daughter. 'Are you sure, Alice? I wouldn't want to impose upon your generosity.'

'It would be a pleasure, Mrs Dugdale,' said the young woman. 'I love children, especially yours.'

'We will do what we can. But you must try and eat more, dear.' Sarah offered Henrietta a plate of shortbread. 'Don't envy you the dairy and a fair-sized herd to handle as well. Sheep, in our experience, are pretty much self-sufficient, apart from a few lambing problems. They excel in any environment, we've found, and are generally not as difficult to hold.'

On the way home, Henrietta spotted the lambs – white blobs shimmering against the blue and gold palette of the sun-drenched landscape. But soon enough they would be no different from the rest of the flock. It was true about sheep all doing the same thing, following the one in front. The way the first will jump a gate, but once the gate is pulled aside the others will still jump in the same spot over an imagined hurdle. Was it a learned habit to follow or a born trait? There was much to learn from Mr Darwin.

She too could blend in to her surroundings, when and how it suited. But she never felt bound to follow, knowing she could see horizons that others failed to see. Saluting the eerie stillness, she drew rein. Even with the raking light on the open parched stubble and the shapes of the scrub casting their long shadows, she could see signs of things to come.

～

It was almost the end of March before they could get away for the weekend. Before passing the boys over to Alice, Henrietta kissed each in turn with the assurance that, come two sleeps, Mama and Papa would return to Spring Hill Court. Together, she and William took the ten o'clock steamer to Sandridge and from there the short train ride into the city. No sooner had they arrived at Scot's Hotel in Collins Street than William excused himself.

'I need to see a man about a horse. What say we meet up at the Botanical Gardens at three,' he said breezily, leaving her vexed and alone in their rooms.

Henrietta picked at the light lunch she had ordered and, after a rest and a read, began to freshen up. All week she had been looking forward to attending the outdoor concert. Eyebrows aloft, she dabbed either temple liberally with lavender water. Did William expect her to find a chaperone at such short notice? Respectable women did not move through public spaces alone, here as in Queenscliff. If they had to, they did so as quickly as possible.

Rather than prevailing upon a chambermaid – a complete stranger – to accompany her, she would act singly. Selecting the best of her summer hats – a circular one with a stiff crown – she studied her reflection in the cheval mirror. Her paisley gown, with cuffs and collar of spotless lawn, and her quiet, genteel manner would not invite attention. Silks tied, she pulled on her gloves, and within a few minutes had stepped out into the street with her white parasol held elegantly aloft.

A hot wind swept through the city, lifting clouds of grit and dust. Henrietta narrowed her eyes at the women. Froth and trains trailing, their dear little waists squeezed beyond extinction. It was supposed to be the height of summer and here they were, niminy-piminies, unnecessarily encumbering themselves from head to toe. The sheer burden of their garments, their ridiculously large hoops swaying, bumping into each other, showing off their extravagant trappings.

Such pain and inconvenience. All this unnecessary weight greatly wasted a woman's strength, made her unable to walk far, inhibited every movement, like a bird in a cage – it was opposed to every law of nature. Surely walking was as much a matter of health as expediency. The March of Intellect, she had read, depended very much upon the bodily powers of marching. Garments that distorted the body distorted the mind.

The sun beat down. How she longed for the smell of rain, the pungency of freshly dampened soil. Parched and panting ever so slightly, she pushed on over the bridge and made her way along the embankment amid the deafening wheels of carriages and hansoms and brightly decked-out crowds. Beside her lay the River Yarra, a slimy brown slug amid the dried-up slush.

Henrietta put the corner of her lace handkerchief delicately to her nose. Oh! Foul effluvium. She had all but forgotten its stench.

Once inside the gates of the Botanical Gardens, she embraced the long green walk, the fragrance and tranquillity of the precinct. A large throng had already gathered around the open pavilion to be near the bandstand, but no sign of William. Having found a bench seat, she sipped a lemonade. To look out and see the city mushrooming against the bluish swell and the dry rolling cache of hinterland was to look back on Melbourne's history, and through the haze she found herself dwelling not only on the timeline of the colony but on her own twelve years of marriage. The sudden rush before love ran dry.

In hindsight, she had been stupid and impulsive, lacking in judgement. All in good faith, for what were her options? William had insisted. 'The least I can do is provide you with shelter.' Some accused her of exploiting the situation and making a play for him, Captain Dugdale being a handsome naval man. There were rumours about the sordidness of their relationship, with a husband lost at sea, the body yet to be found and buried. Suspicions ran rife on the nature of Junius' death. At the time, with no immediate funds, no friends or family living in Melbourne, she had fallen for William's charms. Within months they were 'spliced'.

Troubled, her eyes, roving the big metropolis, came to rest on the church where they were wed. There, barely distinguishable among the grey conglomeration, St Mark's – God's gift to redemption.

Henrietta agitated her parasol. The pretence of promenading was over. The orchestra had finished tuning up; the final gong sounded. Had William been here, he would have pressed her arm, propelled her forward to some vantage point while there was still some time. But he was one hour late, as it was. Quickly she found a spare chair near the back and sat down, folding her hands in cool repose. The bandmaster was now up on the podium, his air one of solemnity, a gracious bow of his head; everybody, even the orchestra, watched expectantly as he took up the baton. Then, as he brought it down, the music that came forth was medicine to her soul and, until the end of the program, she gave William not another thought.

Music had form of its own. Music, Beethoven claimed, was the mediator between the spiritual and the sensual life. Ah, but there was good music and bad music. Good music like this removed one from the dross of life in a way that transcended all spiritual and physical boundaries.

'Bravo! Bravo!' Henrietta leaned forward and wiped her eyes. It was all too short. People were standing amid hails of applause. Her mood buoyed, she tagged along in the crowd. To be transported into the deepest wells of human experience and washed of all her worries was a blessing. As for William, to put her in such a position. What a bumpkin she was beginning to feel.

A hand touched her arm.

'Henrietta!'

She swung around to catch the wave of a top hat and a pair of thick, dark dundreary whiskers. 'Joseph! Fancy seeing you here.' Her face froze amid a flurry of conflicting emotions.

'You look bemused. May I be of brotherly assistance?'

The last person she needed was Joseph. His sudden presence, his devilish blue eyes, had disturbed her equilibrium. She stepped back, her stomach gone sour.

'Well, the thing is, you see, I appear to have lost William.' Somehow she managed a hasty smile. 'Ah, but Joseph, you look in fine fettle, I must say. Life in Mornington must be suiting you well?'

Joseph tucked his top hat firmly under his arm and beamed. 'Yes, yes, our family growing by the year and, may I say, there is not a happier man on earth.'

Henrietta looked at him in a state of bewilderment. The news of Joseph's second marriage five years earlier had come as a shock. Margaret Downward was a good woman from a good family. Not for one minute would Henrietta begrudge her brother the opportunity of a new wife just because she herself had been deluded into the toils of matrimony yet a second time. Success often begets success. Joseph, as headmaster of the Mornington School, had risen in standing. Working by the light of the moon, he could now lay claim to a line of titles: Registrar of Births, Deaths and Marriages, registered auctioneer and land agent, Secretary to the Church Trustees, and Worshipful Master of the Mornington Lodge. With his good looks, his perfect manners, and perfect smile and demeanour, he would have set out to charm. How else could he have built himself such a fine reputation, having arrived in the town with barely a horse to his name, and bankrupt?

How extraordinary! Joseph, despite his tumultuous ups and downs, appeared to have barely aged. A full head of dark springy curls, and bushy pillars of whiskers bestraddling his cheeks. Remarkably, there was not a white hair to be seen. She eyed him askance, longing to bring up the passing of Mama and Papa, only to think better of it. The subject of death had always been difficult to broach, casting its chain of old shadows.

'And Hattie, Emma and Fanny … how are they faring?'

They were grown women now. But in London, when she had first taken them into her care in her parents' Bloomsbury home, the tots had struggled to eat properly. They had suffered terribly – half-starved, feral and used to eating with their hands. Oh, the frustration of trying to earn their trust. She remembered trying to spoon soup into the two littler girls, whom for their own safety she had tied into chairs. Fanny, still with snarls in her hair and her face red from rage, had batted the spoon away with her fist, causing the liquid to spill. Try and cuddle or cajole her, and she would squirm or push one away with a very definitive 'No!'

Joseph's eyes grew restive as he pressed her aside.

'Pray, let me introduce you … Mr Frederick Johnson, the son of our esteemed bandmaster and, I believe, filling in for the fiddles. My sister, Mrs Dugdale. Her husband, I assume, will be with us any moment.'

Henrietta's lips rose to a smile as this tall young man took her hand. A face round and fresh, elegantly framed by light brown whiskers that gave him a youthful grace.

Joseph was explaining their connection and with such gloss, having met the Johnson family in Montreal back in the early 1840s.

'Oh really, what a small world,' she murmured, and yes, to think of the Johnsons arriving here in the colony within months of herself. 'Of course, of course! I've met your father, heard him play many many times – a wonderful musician. Everybody's heard of the famous Mr Henry Johnson of the 40th Regiment, but, until now, I did not know of his son.'

'Only a lad when we arrived, Mrs Dugdale,' said Mr Johnson. 'Barely a year in the colony when the regiment was given the call to Ballarat. Terrible business.' The young man stopped short at this oblique reference to the storming of the Eureka Stockade.

She nodded thoughtfully, the sun catching her eyes beneath the brim of her hat. 'Lives lost on both sides, Mr Johnson, more's the pity. Poor diggers were sacrificial lambs.'

A shadow had crossed Joseph's face. Sweat beads shimmered on his brow. He drew his thumbs from his waistcoat and checked his watch. 'Well, I'm afraid you must excuse me.' He shook hands. 'I have a steamer to catch. Good day to you both.' He bowed and put on his top hat.

'And your father.' Her eyes returned at once to the young man with relief. 'He is engaged in teaching these days?'

'Yes, winds and woodwinds: trumpet, of course, as well as saxophone and the clarinet.'

'And what about you, Mr Johnson?' She trailed the point of her parasol in the sand for a few seconds. 'What are you doing with yourself – that is, when you're not playing the violin?'

'Living with my parents at present. I'm with the Melbourne Philharmonic Society, you see. I take what's on offer, bit of this, bit of that.'

She tucked her chin into her neck and gave him a snug little smile. 'Have you not been tempted by the diggings?'

'Oh no. I do like the fresh air, Mrs Dugdale, and I'm not afraid of hard physical work, but that sort of life is not for me. Besides, they say gold fever is dying.' His dark brown eyes strayed for a second. 'My mother, father and two sisters will be looking for me. Ah.' He gave them a nod. 'Perhaps you would care to join us until your husband returns.'

Upon introduction, the little party made its way to some bench seats under one of the tall gum trees, where they sat exchanging pleasantries in the shade. Henrietta cast her eyes periodically towards the empty pavilion. Suddenly, she spotted William, silver swallow tails flapping, as he turned this way and that. He looked a bit put out and noticeably hot and uncomfortable in his pinstripe pants, and silk cravat adrift. She raised her parasol as he made his way towards them.

'You are not the wife of Captain Dugdale, are you, by any chance?' said the elder Mr Johnson. 'Fellow I knew back in the early days, master of the *Duke of Bedford*. Look, here he comes; the man himself.'

Chapter 8

⌒

Henrietta had been reading about how Mr Dickens' son, Alfred, having left the idleness of London, was now a conspicuous figure on Collins Street. This 'lion of the hour' cum bushman was said to have his eye on a sheep station. From this scrap of gossip had come her novel idea of a jackaroo.

There was no need for a character reference. As Frederick Johnson was the son of a highly respected military man, William made him a proposal without hesitation. Their Spring Hill location was not exactly up-country, he said, but it was a pretty good place for a young fellow to cut his teeth. A wattle and daub hut going empty behind the dairy was quickly fitted out with a few home comforts, and their new dairyman installed at Spring Hill Court.

Henrietta watched Mr Johnson's progress with interest. New frontiers, she well knew, brought the challenges of new occupations, which were character-building. Going bush was meant to bring out the best in a young man. From the homestead, she could see Mr Johnson throughout the day, going about his business. Released from her day-to-day drudgery, Henrietta felt at once gay and good-tempered. Her brief visit to Melbourne, with its lasting impressions, had confirmed that the cultured town lady side of her had not entirely rubbed off in the bush.

The thought of attending upcoming concerts and galleries, and the odd ticket to the Haymarket, had her salivating. And her dear mare, she had not forgotten.

After setting the boys some lessons, she went out to the lower paddock, sugar lumps in her pocket. Even at a distance, she could hear the horses' soft nickers. Curious, they came trotting over to the fence, flicking their tails. Noses between the rails, they waited. She gave the blaze on Gypsy's forehead a good rub and reached out for her muzzle, the soft velvet fluttering against her palm. William would have raised a fist, never allowed a horse to nibble or lip.

Gypsy was a good, faithful companion. At least she could ride her now for riding's sake and still find time in the day for the company of the printed page.

Henrietta unleashed her cravat, shook free her hair, and quickly splashed about the basin. Fresh curls sprang from her dampened crown, giving her a fresh, girlish look. Was it true 'the face was the index of the mind'? Her cheeks, in the mirror, glowed with good health and humour. Her eyes. Was there a bit of a sparkle in those deep-set lights of the sea? Her nose was longish, though slightly turned up. Her most endearing feature, she'd been told, was her mouth. Wide and asymmetrical, with unusual mobility of expression. Every flash of thought, every change of colour of feeling, fancy or wit, showed in the charm of her mouth as her beauty came alive. Something had struck low in her body, stirring flutters of desire she had thought extinct. But she dared not give it away.

It was August. For three months now, Frederick Johnson had been working for them, and, my goodness, what a difference it made. Never had the dairy been run so efficiently. Vats, pails and pans brought to a gleaming shine. Mr Johnson, scrupulous in his methods, took pride in even the smallest and most mundane of tasks. It showed in the superior quality of butter and cheese making, cloths and linen soaked and boiled daily of every trace of scum. This young man was quick to learn and his daily company came as a blessing. Mr Johnson, she found, was good with the boys, too. They looked up to him. It was his youthfulness, presumably his understanding of what made young boys tick.

After milking, Mr Johnson, as a rule, joined them for dinner. Invariably, this would lead to an impromptu singsong and recital. His quiet, relaxed gentlemanly presence at mealtimes came as a tension-breaker. The singing of the kettle was a calling to table. Any earlier feelings of angst seemed to have long been stemmed by the presence of her new go-between. Over the months, Spring Hill Court came alive as friends gathered for regular Saturday night soirees. Mr Johnson, who played flute and piccolo as well as violin, was in high demand and was only too happy to perform. A talented, worldly, intelligent young man who fitted in well, who could converse on all manner of subjects, could meet her eyes, engage with ease and candour, and yet, at the same time, whose character was so pure and clean.

'Oh, and by the way, William, dear, I've asked Mr Johnson to give Einnim some lessons on the fiddle. The boy is well old enough now and he's at an age, I feel, where he needs to extend himself.'

'The boy will learn what he chooses to learn, and that, to date, he's managed more than amply.'

'Boats and water are all very well, William, but the world goes beyond the blot of Queenscliff. High time to expose him to some culture. There is a wild streak in the boy, I fear,' she said with a liberal roll of her eyes, 'God knows whence, and learning the violin I feel will help to challenge his mind.'

William, legs spread-eagled, head behind the newspaper, buried in every word.

'I can see you are not attending.' Henrietta smiled dryly to herself. She had lately learned to make little of the ambiguity of William's silences. Clearly, he had no regard for her wishes unless they tallied with his own. 'Well, then, since you have no objection, I will arrange for Einnim to start immediately, and Carl as soon as Mr Johnson sees fit.' She rubbed her hands. 'All credit to Joseph – a fortuitous introduction.'

The opportunity of bringing Mr Johnson into their dairy partnership was ripe. By early the following year, the young man had more than proven himself. As inducement, they offered him a five-acre parcel of land at Greenleaf for peppercorn.

This duly signed over for thirty pounds, they raised a toast the following evening. Doors and windows flung wide and with the bay breeze filtering room to room, the house took on an air of almost lightsome playfulness. The boys filed into the parlour in their flannel nightshirts to say their goodnights, each having been instructed to sing or recite something while standing upon the ottoman.

Enchanted, Mr Johnson bent forward, clapping enthusiastically.

Henrietta, beaming, blew each in turn her kisses. *Bravo, my darling!* It was what her mother had done when she was a child, since dressing up and acting were daily pastimes.

William drained his brandy and sat up. 'Time performing ponies were sent to their stalls.'

She would have to temper her exuberance. William did not approve of little boys being spoiled and petted and put up in the world. 'Stage fairies', he claimed, invariably developed an unhealthy thirst for admiration.

'Now, then, boys.' She whisked them away, and, having tucked them into bed and kissed them goodnight, brought in the oyster stew and placed the quince pie and cream on the cedar chiffonier.

At the end of the meal, Henrietta leaned forward to Mr Johnson, hands clasped on her knees. 'You have your fiddle with you, perchance?'

'I left it in the hall, Mrs Dugdale. Shall I fetch it?' Having returned to the room, he kneeled down and took his violin out of its box.

'Shall we do the "Spring Sonata"?' She shot him a teasing glance. 'I promise not to play over you.'

Waiting, she swivelled upon the piano stool, watching his long, strong elegant hands, the left one caressing the scroll, the right tightening a string here, plucking a single quivering note there. The tips of his fingers shiny white with rosin dust.

'Shall we?' Mr Johnson raised his bow and, in a nod, their eyes fleetingly met. From the first note, she felt at once in rapport, as if her youth had miraculously returned. The pastoral element to the music, so beautifully lyrical and relaxed, with just enough movement that the melody floated as easily as leaves lightly blown by the wind. Her body, a supple reed, swayed as she played, with her fingers, not her arms, in deference, echoing his passages, as he did hers. The two of them seemed of the one mind. Every phrase, every pause, every breath sensitively matched.

William, without so much as a clap, reached for his pipe and pouch, signalling for Mr Johnson to follow him out to the verandah. Henrietta, still flushed – for it was rare to find a musical partnership so completely balanced – took the lamp through the French windows and placed it on the wrought-iron table. Drifting back inside, she put the music sheets away in the cabinet and retired to the window seat, hands in her lap, where she could see them. Men's business, smoking was as much a test of character as anything else. It amused her, with all its silly rituals, the drawing out of interchange as to who would be the first to talk. William cupped the bowl of his pipe as he lit it, before settling back into a series of shallow puffs.

In the quiet stillness, she could hear the frogs croaking and the distant sounds of the bush, for as yet neither man had spoken. William, with a set to his face, gripped the pipe in his teeth, hooked his tongue around the stem of the pipe and drew it into the corner of his mouth.

'Still no pipe, I see?' he drawled.

'I have yet to acquire the taste, sir.' Mr Johnson stood up. 'You must excuse me, I must be getting on.'

The young man came inside and, after thanking Henrietta for her hospitality, bade them both goodnight with a little bow. Formality having fallen into the shadows, William kicked off his boots and socks and stretched out his toes. Quietly, she set to, plumping the cushions, snuffing out lamps and candles.

'How lucky we are, William. Our good man is well connected. Apparently he knows Mrs Caroline Dexter, young Mr William Lynch's new wife.'

'Who?' William swung around and his eyes bore down on her. 'Oh, yes, I remember now,' he said with a grunt. 'The famous Mrs Dexter, the bloomer lady – the one who likes to wear *troosers*?'

'Mrs Carrie Lynch, she is now – a woman of many talents, a lecturer and gifted authoress, a publisher in her own right. And excellent company, according to Mr Johnson.'

'Talents? Rubbish. I hear she dabbles in clairvoyance. All that rapping and tapping and calling down of spirits. The New Creed, so they call it. Sheer quackery.'

'Never mind spirits. Mrs Lynch is right up on medicine and art, William, and … I've been invited to her next exhibition.'

'What kind of woman would marry a man half her age?' He came over and pressed a hand on her shoulder. 'Careful what company you consort with, my love.'

She shrank, noting the twist of his thumb on her neck.

⌢

Though Henrietta's trips to Melbourne were few, her life at Spring Hill Court had become more than tolerable. The beginning of September 1867 brought the promise of a healthy harvest in the Bellarine district. Here, from the height of Spring Hill Court, one could almost see the growth in the crops since the change of weather, the distant ribboning of colours.

Henrietta lingered a few minutes longer at the French windows, sopping up the warm, buttery sunshine. She was pretending not to hear the childish tussles in the hall. Sunday afternoons had always been devoted to chess lessons. Today it was Carl's duty to set up the wooden chessboard before the fire. If only Austin would sit quietly. At six, the imp was hungry for knowledge but a wrecker of games.

'*Neigh!*' he cried, prancing around the parlour. 'I've got the white horse.'

'It's a knight, silly,' Carl called after him. 'Here, give it back or Ma will get cross.'

'Austin, really!' Having caught the boy between her knees, she prised the chessman from his fingers and gave it to Carl.

Heavens, she would never have dared do such a thing. But she knew Austin too would be quick to learn the game. Papa, an old master, and chairman of the London Chess Club, had taught her before she could read. Having mastered draughts, she had easily progressed to the Game of Kings.

Apart from memory skills and fair play, chess taught the virtues of foresight, circumspection, caution and courage, the ability of each participant to exercise free will within the physical constraints of the game. Far better that than having boys running riot, trying to waddy each other every minute of the day, as William would have it, all in the love of conquest.

'We shall have to ask Mr Johnson if he plays, won't we, Carlie?' Gazing down at him, she smoothed his curly red forelock.

William, who appeared to have been catnapping, opened his eyes and slid his tongue over his bottom lip.

'Well, then, time I'll be off.' Chess bored him to death. Didn't take kindly to anyone getting the better of him. Rather than risk losing face, William chose not to play. It made her laugh, his silly fear of being beaten.

He was out in the boot room when she found him. Ignoring her, he snatched his hat and Albert cape. She followed him quietly over to the stables. He remained with his back to her, Kitty lowering her head to receive the bridle. She watched him as he straightened the saddle rug before setting the saddle and giving it a good smack.

'William, where are you going?'

He had earlier mumbled something about selling off some of the non-milkers. A quick way to raise some money, but dealing in stock was always a gamble. Why could he not come outright and say?

William bent down, reached for the girth, tightened it, waited a few seconds, then cinched it again as Kitty let out her breath. Gathering the reins, he swung a leg over the saddle. Not once did he meet her eyes, his face sunken into his beard, whip tucked tightly under his arm.

'William, you have not said.' She had to raise her voice against the wind. 'William, will you not answer me?'

Swinging the mare around, he prodded the air with the butt of his whip. 'Tell Johnson I'm leaving him on his own. See if he's not just a puppy-face.'

He clapped his spurs into Kitty's flanks and, clearing the cattle pit, disappeared over the hill in a cloud of dust.

Well, she thought, he's gone. Good riddance. Since Mr Johnson would not be joining the family this evening, Sunday being a day of rest, she would honour her promise to the children. Amid armfuls of pillows and blankets, she set up four camp beds on the verandah. Her early colonist days living out of a tent remained vivid. There was nothing quite like staring up at the blanket of darkness and seeing those four bright stars standing out in the shape of a cross to give one a sense of protection, a sense of place in the world. This land, once so deliciously foreign to her, was now more like home. Her sons were not little Englishmen, as William liked to treat them. They were little Australians, born and bred. They had learned to smell, to touch, to taste, to explore this land and find their bearings.

Together, she and the boys had been making a study of the moon, plotting its nightly face, its nightly place in the universe. Now, with the aid of William's new telescope, they could learn about the planets. She had mentioned it to him earlier in the day, while polishing the instrument.

'Nothing makes me happier than feeding fresh minds. I have promised the boys they may sleep on the verandah, William dear, under my strict eye, of course.'

'What's this? Next you'll be promising to teach them the basic principles of navigation.'

'Indeed.' It was not that difficult. Any woman could navigate as well as a man, so long as she applied her mind.

And with no William at home to worry about, and now no Millie – for Millie, having faithfully fulfilled her working engagement, was no longer with them – the evening was hers. After an early tea of boiled eggs and soldiers and sago pudding, she had them all bathed and bedded before the sun was down, ready to see who would be the one to sight the first star.

Later, lying close by, she listened to their night sighs and sighed back at them in turn. Three young bodies curled up like loaves of warm bread were all the more endearing. It seemed they were growing into little men all too quickly. Where did that leave her? She could feel the crisp night air cutting her out, defining every part of her in opposition. Not far away in the pitch of dark, vague reminders of their whereabouts – strips of low shrubbery, brush fences and the various farmyard landmarks seemed to be taking on supernatural forms.

For most of the night, she lay waiting, waiting for sleep to come. The silence deepening, disrupted by the last of nature's rhythms: the occasional *swish-swish* of a wild duck's wing, a solitary cricket or a mosquito singing in her ears; all the while, the moon waning in and out of the clouds.

She lay looking out at the sky. She had easily mastered the art of navigation under Junius' tutelage. He had bought her a sextant for her sixteenth birthday – a pretty brass affair in a mahogany box – with a sight glass and calibrations, which she first learned to use on land. It was a joy. With one of its arms on a celestial body and the other on the horizon, she practised and practised until she could plot a course – all the time secretly plotting with him paths to a more adventurous life.

On the passage from England, she had often, with Junius' permission, put this knowledge to practical use to assist a sick or overworked crewman. Junius was full of praise, for even when the sun was blocked or the horizon swamped by waves, she had developed her skill at dead reckoning with near accurate results. That mahogany box, which lay at the bottom of her Saratoga trunk, hadn't been opened for fifteen years. Next weekend, she would clean and oil the sextant and show it to the boys.

Time drifted in the cycle of her thoughts, forgotten questions returning again and again. At one stage, she thought she could hear the crunch, crunch, crunch of gravel and the crackle of twigs. The whinny of a horse, the sound of hooves and a sliprail let down.

It was far too early for Mr Johnson to be up. An easygoing young man, but perhaps there were nights when even he couldn't sleep. The wind, gathering in full force, began to howl, and the roof creaked, the canvas awning knock-knocked against the verandah railing. Were they in for a squall? She propped herself on her pillows, searching the darkness. All around, the trees groaned and the tussocks hissed and writhed, and she found herself dreaming the most unimaginable things.

At first light she woke, exhausted, her face and nightdress damp with dew. Greeting her, three empty beds – imps already up and off to help in the dairy. Bleary-eyed, she peered at the trail of evidence, their freshly wrought imprints across the wet capeweed and its crumpled golden stars.

The grunt, the rough snort, of a steam engine from behind the French windows made her start. Surely not! That snore she knew only too well. She dashed inside, flung back the bedroom curtains to the glaring white tumble of bed linen. William's body half-stirred as she cleared aside the trail of clothes on the floor with a bare foot. Mouth open, beard stretched full upon his chest. She had never noticed before that his two front teeth were notched and yellowy brown from clenching his pipe.

The room was stuffy and warm, his clothes tainted with the smell of smoke and whisky and, yes, women. So vile it made her bilious, and she knew then and there that she could never sleep in the same bed with him again.

~

Henrietta drew the screen. After washing, she dressed, and, closing the bedroom door quietly behind her, went outside to call in the boys for breakfast.

The last thing she felt like was eating but she must stick to weekday routine until she had planned her next move.

Breakfast over, she set the boys up with some arithmetic, and sat at her desk, attending to some monthly accounts.

By lunchtime a surge of unease had crept over her. William was nowhere to be found.

'Einnim, have you seen Papa?' she called from the verandah.

'He's over at the sheds with Mr Johnson. He sent us away.'

'Very well, then. Stay here with the others and I shall go and see.'

The two men were in the dairy. William in Captain mode. She could tell from the tone, the cold clip of his words as they ricocheted off stone. She laid herself flat against the outside wall. The sound of her heart a tambour trapped inside her; the thrum in her chest, in her ears, the whoosh of blood pulsating. William had Mr Johnson bailed up, she could see through a crack in the door.

'Listen here, my good man. And listen hard.' He drilled a finger hard into Mr Johnson's chest. 'Get out of my dairy. Get off my land. Never on any account set foot in this town again.'

'But what about the land that is rightfully mine?'

'I will buy back that land so you have no excuse to come near my property ever again.'

'You may say that but you cannot make me do it, sir. I will not be bullied.'

'If you value your reputation, Johnson, you will do as I say. In no uncertain terms. Otherwise I will take you through the courts and have you ruined.'

Henrietta stole back to the house and stood hugging herself. She felt instinctively in some way to blame – a vague, yet hideous fear she dared not shape into any definite form that she had perhaps become too familiar with Mr Johnson. Her inner voice reminded her to stay calm. She had seen this kind of behaviour in William before – the ferocious extent of his temper. So suspiciously jealous. Only she had seen the worst of it. His displeasure coming down like thunder in the midst of his love. The love that had long grown thin.

She could hear him banging about in the boot room.

'Where are you off to now?' Her voice came out high and uncertain.

'Going to borrow one of Harding's men,' he called. 'Johnson's taken his leave. Damn lucky I didn't take a horsewhip to the devil.' He stood in the kitchen doorway, bracing himself against the architrave. 'As for you, Madam …' He came at her, whiplash fast. 'You stinking whoring bitch!'

She stiffened, her eyebrows like wings. It was not the vilest of curses she had heard from the mouth of a mariner. But dare she question his language, he would only tighten the screw.

'But how have I displeased you, William? I don't understand.'

'You were not in your rightful bed when I came home last night. Where were you?'

'I slept on the verandah to keep an eye on the boys. I swear on my heart I told you – yesterday morning – of my movements, don't you remember?'

'It is you who needs keeping an eye on.' He pinned her against the wall, her body rigid against his hold. 'If you ever do anything like that again, God help me, I will break your bloody little neck.'

Chapter 9

⌣

The desperate night ride from Spring Hill Court, jostling through the sandy backroads to the sanctuary of Queenscliff, took the better part of an hour and a half, leaving Henrietta exhausted and the children bewildered.

Once inside the house in Stevens Street, Henrietta locked the door, consumed by shock. Nothing seemed real. Boats cast their moving shadows upon the mirroring tide. As she looked out on Swan Bay, it was as if a sail had suddenly snapped and slapped her in the face. She was blinded, cut adrift, flailing, feeling that life was abruptly coming to an end. Then it had come like a black flash of lightning, the horror and recall of William's threat.

Where to go? Their old house was currently rented to a man called Behan. The only option had been the smaller, spartanly furnished dwelling next door, which they kept vacant as their town house.

It was now a week since she had ensconced herself here with the boys, with no communication. The silence was insufferable. Every day she passed in dread, expecting William to show up, craving resolution yet wrung out at the very thought of coming face-to-face with him. Parched, she lifted the hatch to the well, drew some water, gulping freely, yet unable to quench her thirst. She dabbed at her face. Loosening her top button, she ran a timorous finger under her lace collar and recoiled at the thought of any bruising. Whether in body or mind, she could not fully escape William, and, as she paced about, his threat seemed to echo in every room.

The boys, happy to be back in their old stamping ground, remained oblivious. On the first hot day, they were out canoeing in the Swan Ponds and looking for cockles in the mud. For her, the bank of decisions was rapidly mounting. The lease on the Spring Hill Court property would be coming up for renewal at the end of the year. Inevitably, things would come to a head.

Enshawled, she wove her way down the embankment to call the boys in for tea. How she envied the waterbirds as they dipped in and out of the glassy surface. Tripping nimbly along, an elegant dotterel without a care in the world. The ominous feel of the air – warm and hazy, unusually still, with a scattering of black thunderclouds scowling from above – only added to the sturm und drang of the past week, as did the boys' growing antics. Carl let out a squeal. She tightened her muslin shawl. Austin was egging the other two on, furiously waving his paddle. Einnim and Carl stood at either end of the gunwales, rocking this way and that. Harder and harder they bounced, testing their might, their balance, to see who would be the first to tip the other into the water. Give them nothing and in minutes the little water rats would devise some new battle that only compounded her stress.

Looking around, she searched for respite. Pink-eyed oystercatchers piped the tideline. Pelicans perched on the buffer pylons, bills pressed down upon their breasts. The swans, she noticed, had grown in number. Their cygnets, cream-coloured powder puffs riding on their parents' glossy backs. Swans were known to be monogamous for life. Model parents, she had read. Equally involved with the young.

Her jaw ached. Her stomach twisted and turned and tied itself over and over in knots. There had been no tryst, nothing dishonourable. William in reddest rage threatening to sue Mr Johnson for all he was damn well worth. 'Criminal conversation.' Adultery. The very word caught at the back of her throat. Legally, as a married woman, her husband's chattel, she did not even exist.

No, no. She would not allow herself to be gulled or bullied into signing a *confessio delicti* – an ugly document that could be used against her as a confession of misconduct. It was vile, cowardly and corrupt. She could not have remained another minute under the same roof with William. If he divorced her for adultery, well and good. Let the newspapers make a meal of it, this mockery of a marriage, for either way she had no redress.

⁓

The short whinny gave him away. She shot a look out the window to see Gypsy lowering her head, nudging noses with her old friend, Kitty, chestnut and bay reunited in a caring exchange of nickers. Henrietta knew she must think clearly. The law, he would say, makes a man master of his wife and children, their natural protector. How to outwit William without having to grovel? But in a flash, it seemed, he was standing over her, using the children as pawns.

He tossed his hat on the chiffonier. 'I'm changing the deeds,' he announced coolly. 'I shall arrange for a witness and you will do as I say.'

'Have you forgotten my share of Greenleaf? You are constrained, remember?'

William was not listening. 'It is simple. In return for your share of Greenleaf, I am making over Stevens Street to you.'

Their first home, next door, he had already transferred to her eight years ago in trust, as the final part of their marriage settlement. The cottage in which they were now standing, together with the yards at the back, was safely held on her behalf in dower trust; indeed, the bulk of the town property, she had always understood, was, in effect, hers. What new fraudulence was William plotting? And suddenly it dawned on her. Oh, dear God, she could see it, now. The trust he had set up for their first home – seemingly as an act of benevolence in the event of his death – could not be enforced against him. So long as William was alive, she, as his legal wife, could not hold any property in her name alone.

He threw her a nod. 'The boys we'll discuss later.'

She could hear the hollowness of her words as she cried, 'You would try to divest me of what is rightfully mine? Wheedle everything I own … what kind of husband would do that?'

He let out a chilly laugh. 'A very generous one, I should think.'

No sooner had she unleashed her protest than the boys came rushing in through the back door.

'Ah, there you are!' William drew them together and affably ruffled their hair. 'You'll be coming with me soon enough. I'm going to build us a brand new cottage at Greenleaf. Eh, my beauties? Now run along. I'll be back later.'

From the kitchen window, she watched him unharness Kitty. After fixing the halter and nosebag, he sauntered off down the laneway in the direction of the nearest hotel.

The boys! Whatever her faults, she had always been a careful and devoted mother, taken care of their bodies and souls. It was the grossest cruelty – locking her out; worse still, denying them her love. The law gave him her children. She knew it did, but the law did no more. It did not compel her to have to endure separation from them.

William returned a few hours later, flushed with grog. He banged his fist on the table and lurched at her. 'Where are the boys?'

'You and your bush law. Unless you tear them from me by force, William, they stay with me.' If he murdered her, she no longer cared. She wrenched open the windows for all to hear so they could be her witness.

He came at her. 'Tell me, woman, or I will have you put in a madhouse.'

She edged away, both hands braced against the door. Something snapped inside her. She raised her chin and drew her body as tall as she could.

'Yes, you are the father of my children and your presence I must brook if only for them, but as to your latest indignity I declare here and now I am no longer your wife.'

'Who would want you?' He almost spat the words. 'You with your fire, piss and vinegar. It is the boys I want. Where are they? They need to know what's what around here.'

'What need they know? That their father is not a fit father?'

'Fit enough to know what's good for them. Boarding school.'

'You come here to tell me that?' She was trying to read the drift of his kelp-coloured eyes, searching for the slightest twitch, any lightning-fast movement of the mouth that might betray his motives. 'And where, pray tell?' She reeled backwards from the brandy on his breath. 'Oh yes, Geelong is nice and close, but completely out of the question, at least until they are older.'

'Geelong is not far enough away, as far as I'm concerned.'

'I can teach them all they need to know, William. You dismiss the level of my education. I would have gone to university had they seen fit to admit a woman.'

He gave her one of his stony stares. 'Boys need to be away from their mother's apron strings. The further the better. As far as a ship can take them.'

'I forbid you to send them away. Besides, think of the cost.' Her voice remained low and steady but she knew she was clutching at straws.

William went over to the chiffonier and began sifting randomly through her pile of unopened mail. He looked up, patting his palm with her silver letter opener. 'My mother has agreed to pay,' he said. 'And go they shall.'

'No!'

'P&O have started up a school near Southampton for the sons of their officers. They take them young and prepare them early.' He thrust at her a crumpled prospectus from out of his pocket – a new school set up in Hampshire by the name of Bannister Court.

There are two divisions of education. The Classical, as one would expect, run along the lines of the great Public Schools. And in the Modern, we prepare pupils for the Military and Civil Services, and for Mercantile and Nautical Pursuits.

She stood mute, letting the paper fall from her hands.

'The latter should suit well,' he said. 'As for Austin, he'll follow on once he's lost his milk teeth.'

'I will not have you subject my sons to such a life.' She dashed at William. Pulled at his sleeve. 'They need their mother, can't you see?'

He sneered, looking down at her with contempt. 'Have no fear, Madam. They can go to their grandmother or aunts, if they are ever in want of female company.'

'I implore you. 'Tis too far away.'

'Phaff! Think of all those Anglo-Indians. They would send a boy of five away to England without turning a hair.' He pointed his finger at her, listing for a moment, before finding his way back out to the laneway.

The boys? Her heart took flight. She dashed back down the path to the Swan Ponds, searched the shores high and low, only to find the three of them dangling from the boughs of an old sheoak. Relieved, she let them be and collapsed into the shell grit, weeping into her knees with naught but shadows of paperbarks wrapped around her. The thought of her boys, sent away to England like little Anglo-Indians, their mothers left languishing in isolated hill stations, bereft of love and purpose.

She knew something of their sorrow, their cycles of hope and dejection. Before coming to Australia, she had travelled through India, putting up at hill stations while Junius was off chronicling his adventures. Side-by-side these lilywhite ladies, she was eyewitness to the sadness of their superficial lives.

She remembered being woken up each morning by a bird. Oh, how it exasperated her, that bird. Would it never let up? Luring, yet also lonesome in its isolation. It was the mating call of the male koel, she had been told, the culprit who kept breaking her peace. Its call would return again late afternoon, on and on, accentuating the long drawn-out mournfulness of its sound. *Koel? Koel?* Where are you? Soft and swift, each time like a question, waiting for an answer. Where are you, Junius? Where are you? Her eyes travelling up the strangling roots of the banyan trees, searching canopies of lacquered leaves and the weep of jungle vines above. So mysterious, the bird's wail, so elusive; never once was she graced with a sighting. To have fallen with child, only then to experience the misery of disappointment, with not a soul to tell but a servant. When those first fat splotches wet the flagstone in herald of the downpour, her heart had cried with them.

And now her nest would soon be bare. Through the watery blur, she could make out the black ruffled outline of the swans, the drift of their lazy circles and their home from home, the dark-fringed island frowning back at her from across the mudflats.

Panic began to grip her again. For a moment, she thought she might choke. She attempted to get up, but her body went to jelly, feet bound in the sand. She flapped her hands and let out a cry.

The boys, who were now paddling in the water, looked up startled. They carried the canoe and wedged it high into the beach and came running amid silvery flicks of water. What swans were left scattered. From the open battery on the Bluff, she could hear the boom of cannons. On the very dot they were. You could set your pocket watch by them.

◡

Nothing wore Henrietta out, body and soul, more than fear and anger. William, true to his word, had come back and taken the boys. What happened had happened by stealth by end of summer. One minute they were playing cricket happily in the laneway, and the next they had vanished. Could the imps be hiding? She stood on the road, waving her arms, hearing nothing but the high-pitched hollowness of her calls, her throat squeezing, emaciating their names one by one, *Einnim! Carlie! Austin!* until her voice was reduced to nothing.

Her neighbour, Mr Behan, came out from his house and said he had seen William driving off erratically with the boys in a buggy.

No sign or sound since, her letters and messages unanswered. Who in this world could she trust? Servants could not be expected to exchange such information for any small favour that might come their way. William, she knew, would have his spies. The only person she could confide in was Sarah Harding.

Some weeks later, Henrietta bumped into her faithful friend coming out of the post office. Together they walked for a while on the Bluff, and Sarah told her, in guarded tones, that William was now living at Greenleaf with a woman, his new young housekeeper, no less.

'I told him I do not approve,' said Sarah.

Once Henrietta was alone at home, the full horror finally hit her, slamming hard into her chest. To have her children ripped from her bosom and put in the care of a paid helper – a stranger in place of their rightful mother. What morality could there possibly be in that? It was a grief beyond all proportion, fuelled by fury that left her on the brink of exhaustion.

Sarah dropped by one day during an early winter storm.

'I just wanted to see if everything is alright. I don't like to think of you here on your own.'

'I am utterly devastated,' Henrietta said, wiping a tear from her eye. 'What makes it even more excruciating, I was not even able to kiss my boys goodbye.' She sniffed. 'And now, as if that is not enough, William, the weasel, has been contriving to have the deeds to Greenleaf and Stevens Street adjusted – to my great disadvantage, I might add.' Her carefully written proviso, she feared, had not stood the test. Why had she ever thought otherwise?

'Surely not!' Sarah looked at her in dismay.

In the brutal eye of the law, it was simple. Henrietta tried to explain in lay terms that a married woman was merely the adjunct or property or the servant of her husband, and she had the legal duty of yielding and employing her body to her husband's will and bidding in all his domestic relations. However much goodwill she had expected him to show – whatever trust or arrangement – she could not enforce it against him or third parties, since a married man could neither grant anything to his wife nor enter into a covenant with her, for the grant would be to suppose her a separate existence, and to covenant with her would be to covenant only with himself.

William had studied the law of cruelty and applied it as suited, she said. Proof that a married man could take whatever property was in his wife's name and use it to barter with her, or even give it back to her, if he should so wish, in a patronising act of sham generosity.

The next time she was in town, Sarah called again, this time with a hamper of produce – fresh fruit and vegetables, ham, cheese, pickles and pies.

'How kind and thoughtful, Sarah. Come in.' Henrietta shut the door quickly behind them. 'I'm badly in need of company.'

'That wind is coming straight from the Heads.' Sarah put her basket down on the dining table and went to comfort her friend. 'Goodness me, Henrie, your hands, they're like ice.' She reached forward and touched her hollow cheek. 'Oh my goodness, dear, you're wasting away.'

Henrietta broke down as she tried to explain her current circumstances.

Both conveyances were sworn on 10 June 1868 in Geelong 'for the purpose of effectuating agreement and in consideration of the premises'. Simultaneously, the block next door and the cottage where she was currently living were released from the dower trust and amalgamated with the original Stevens Street property, upon William's undertaking not to make any further claim on property or rental in her name. Her real and personal property thus was for the first time hers, albeit subject to William not revoking his undertaking. No longer one flesh, one person, she had come out of this 'settlement' very much the loser. The termagant wife.

The Married Women's Property Bill was being debated in the House of Commons, but whatever reform it might bring for Victorians, it was too late. William had got in first.

'But he has not taken everything, I see, ' said Sarah, casting her eyes around the room.

To all appearances, nothing much had changed. Henrietta's small private world otherwise presented in much the same way, with pieces William had since released to her: her precious piano, her desk and the oak refectory table with its matching set of chairs.

'No,' she said. 'But my soul, Sarah, my soul, like my nest, is empty. I think of the children constantly, I can't stop pacing around. I try to console myself that at least they are healthy and strong and well brought-up to the best of my intentions.'

Sarah stood up and studied her with concern. 'Has he mentioned the boys?'

'Not since they left. Many times I have written seeking some arrangements, but all I get is silence.'

Sarah gripped Henrietta's hand, faltering for the right words. 'Then I am sorry to have to be the one to tell you, dear. According to John, Einnim and Carl have already sailed for Southampton. They are to be put in boarding school. Home schooling has done them no favours, William has let it be known. What they need, he said, is a bit of toughening up.'

Henrietta's eyes began to swim, searching the room for anything that might block out her feelings of desolation. And now her birdies had flown. Little Austin already set to follow suit. She had suffered all the more humiliation, being the last in town to know.

Chapter 10

Thirteen thousand miles. Such a long journey. Such a long way from home. She unfolded the map. Noted how the land curled around Port Phillip Bay like a mother reaching out to embrace a child to her bosom. The waters dividing Henrietta and her boys were so interminably wide. She felt unendingly giddy, waves of grief sweeping over her, engulfing her, taking away her raison d'être.

The pain in her chest swelled to the point where she thought her heart would truly break. Unable to stand it any longer, she took the morning ferry to Melbourne. It was nigh impossible for a married woman to sue her husband – that much she knew – just as she could not sign a contract, make a valid will, or herself be sued. The little she could do was seek the counsel of young Mr Lynch on the morrow and hear him out.

Discreet enquiries revealed that Mr Johnson was now employed by Mr Lynch's law firm, doing clerical work by day and studying by night. She could hardly front up to Mr Lynch's offices without first addressing Mr Johnson in private. Aside from her own feelings of loss, she was aggrieved that William had coerced the young man into selling back his parcel of land at Greenleaf for a trifle. Mr Johnson had been disadvantaged, dispossessed, as well. She wanted to let it be known that she had had no say in the matter. She wanted to commiserate, somehow make good by divorcing herself from William's deceit. It being a Sunday, she must call on Mr Johnson, who, she had heard, was living apart from his family in Camberwell – a short train journey from the city to nearby Hawthorn.

From Hawthorn, she hailed a cab, which dropped her outside an old timber dwelling in Moloney's Road. Hearing the plaintive velvety strains of a violin, Henrietta knocked once, twice, and he stood before her, embracing fiddle and bow with a look of bewilderment.

'Mr Johnson, I have come to apologise.' She spoke very softly, sorrowfully. 'I would have come much earlier, had I been able.'

He quickly ushered her inside, sat her down, and placed his violin beside his bow. She waited uncomfortably, agonisingly shy, as he crouched over the open fireplace, scraping the few remaining coals together to heat the kettle. A small vestige of hospitality but the intimacy was humbling – this young man making her a cup of tea and a buttered crumpet.

'My husband … his behaviour was boorish, unforgivable. I fear you have been badly short-changed.'

'My dear Mrs Dugdale, you must not worry on my account. It is you I fear for. Your, if I may say, parlous state. Is it wise for you to be alone in my company?'

She lifted her dark grey eyes.

'He has taken the boys.' She gave an audible gulp; her mouth quivered. 'And my property. He has annexed everything valuable that belonged to me.'

Mr Johnson looked deep into his cup. Carefully he put it down on its saucer and stood beside her.

'Words escape me, Mrs Dugdale.' His jaw began to droop, his face downcast. 'I cannot imagine the pain you must be feeling.' He fiddled uneasily with his beard for a few seconds, then sought her eyes. 'Forgive me – if I have been improper, in any way to blame.'

'No, no, Mr Johnson … there is nothing to forgive.'

The pain of late had changed. She put her fingers to her throat. What remained was an emptiness in the centre of her chest.

Conscious of a severe headache coming on, she reached up, took out her hairpins and eased off her hat, which Mr Johnson hung on the stand near the door. Having adjusted her hair, she hurriedly put her thumbs to her temples. 'I must send a message to Mr Lynch. I fear I will be in no frame of mind to discuss the finer points of law tomorrow.'

Mr Johnson took her hand, gazing into her face. As she closed her eyes, tears began to ooze between the lids.

'Pray, Mrs Dugdale, you must rest,' he said in his deep musical voice. 'Allow me to play for you a little Beethoven so you can lie back and gather your thoughts.'

Back home in Queenscliff, she could hear the haunting sound of steamers groaning across the bay. Their horns and their constant comings and goings depressed her even more. For each vessel berthing and each one departing only drew attention to what was missing.

Henrietta swore to herself that she had never had favourites, but she pined for her middle child, Carl. She pictured her boy as she had seen him last, his skinny freckled arm interlaced through the verandah balustrade, a smile of wonderment playing on his face as he admired up close the intricate wrought-iron inlay of Australian flora and fauna. The creative light in his eye. Such an intelligent, thoughtful, inquisitive child. Always drawn to nature's beauty and pointing it out to others.

Einnim, twelve, was almost a stripling now, fast growing into manhood. As for her baby, Austin, barely seven, he was still living with William. She had seen her little darling once in the street, called out to him, but his father spirited him away before she could do a thing. William made no provision for her to see her son. He continued to obstruct any form of intervention, preferring to see her suffer.

She found herself in a prolonged state of fatigue, the waiting, day in, day out, waiting for resolve to return. The constant struggle, having to fight the unpardonable – swimming against the current, her state of affairs fast drawing to ruin. Somehow she held out in this scattered way of living, a bitter existence of nightly tears and anguish.

The advice from Mr Lynch, when she eventually saw him in Melbourne a few days later, had been short and simple: 'possession is nine points of the law.' By removing the children without warning and sending the older two abroad, William had jumped the gun. A pre-emptive strike against her, which Mr Lynch said would seriously weaken her position in their coming battles. It made William virtually impregnable. In law, the children were in his custody and he could deny her access to them, and even to their whereabouts, should he choose so to do. Mr Lynch believed it was high time the law was changed. 'Write to your local member, Mrs Dugdale,' he said, 'and I will try and lobby mine – my old friend and foe, George Higinbotham.'

Further tidings were to come when Sarah Harding called on Henrietta when she got back.

'I came straight here from the haberdasher. I do not like gossip, as you know, but I could not help overhearing your name spoken in vain.'

'What are they saying about me now? Tell me.'

Sarah reached for her hand. 'William has been telling people that you had a lover. That he would not be made a cuckold.'

'Nonsense!' Henrietta snatched away her fist. 'You, of all people, know that is not true. Face-saving, that's what it is. You, my dearest friend, please, you must set things straight in this town.'

Without waiting for her friend's response, she marched across the room and pretended to tidy the chiffonier. The stink of sham, the foul hypocrisy, hung in the air and it revolted her. She spun around. 'The man is mean and vicious,' she cried, her voice cracking. 'A nasty, miserable rake. He would put around such a monstrous lie, yet have no scruples about the kind of sordid life he chooses to lead. Why has the law no pity in my defence? Why should *my* reputation be on trial? Here, I cannot even walk down the street with respect. If looks could kill, they would put me to death.'

'Forgive me, but better I be silent. John is still William's friend.'

Henrietta knew she was asking the impossible, hoping Sarah could contain the whisperings, and yet …

'John will be waiting. I'm afraid I must go.' Sarah was about to turn.

'Wait!' Henrietta grabbed a clean sheet of notepaper from her writing compendium and dashed off a message in her large bold hand: the simplest of words.

'Give this to Austin. Tell him, once read, to burn it. I would not trust another soul but you, Sarah.'

'Rest assured, Henrie, dear, I will find a way to place it safely in his hands.'

'Thank you, and give him a kiss from me.'

It was such a thing for a woman to be estranged from her husband and children – a woman, mind, who didn't go to church. Well, they could talk, for all she cared. She would walk the street like any other respectable woman, head high, eyes straight ahead.

The idea of a feme sole, a married woman financially independent of her husband, had become a topic of much fascination. The town of Queenscliff was abuzz. Not just idle gossip but *oohs* and *ahhs* and quiet remonstrations. Newspapers from the Old Country were full of the news, and now Victoria, as well. Unmentionable subjects like divorce bills, women's rights, marriage contracts – subjects Henrietta had been bursting to talk about for years. It wasn't just Barbara Bodichon, John Stuart Mill, who had presented Bodichon's women's suffrage petition to Parliament, and his good wife Harriet Taylor; so many brave people were coming out of the woodwork. Professor Henry Fawcett speaking out in England, and in Melbourne, their very own Mr Higinbotham, the member for Brighton.

When Christmas arrived, families came flocking to the seaside town, their joyfulness trailing through her windows in the breeze. By early morning the next day, boys of all ages were out and about, canoeing and dragging nets in the shallows of Swan Bay.

Alone, at nightfall, she could hear the sound of the sea breaking around her. Henrietta tossed and turned, padded about in her nightdress, looking out the window at the dead moon. Persona non grata, how could she exist in this town? But then again, had she ever truly belonged?

The idea of leaving Queenscliff both pulled and pushed at her, adding to her lethargy. What to take? What not to take? Where to go? And what she would be leaving behind, the grinding guilt of abandonment.

⌒

Part 2

1 8 6 9 – 1 8 7 7

Chapter 11

*C*rying was all very well, as Mama used to say, but to do nothing was a sin. Once she had secured new leases on the adjoining Queenscliff properties, Henrietta made the move to Melbourne. Here, in the old part of Brighton, she found a humble one-bedroomed terrace house of uncertain age to rent, barely a few streets from Bombala, the Lynches' bayside home. Mrs Lynch's patronage was wide and varied and she welcomed Henrietta with open arms.

Faith in the growing metropolis began to stave off her heartbreak. It was a privilege to be socialising with the cream of youth, all yearning for fame as artists, poets and novelists, scientists and philosophers, budding jurists and politicians. To enjoy the camaraderie, to test her brain within this galaxy of talent, was as if she had been thrown back into the Athens of old. Mr Lynch was among other freethinkers such as George Higinbotham and Henry Turner, current president of the new Eclectic Society.

The monthly debates of the Eclectics were hot topics of conversation. Once invited, Henrietta had taken to making notes and commentary, which invariably gave way to further discussion. Thick on current affairs, she at last felt free to write and speak without fear of scrutiny. To earn her daily bread, she gave piano and singing lessons. In between, she attended meetings, lectures and debates on every kind of philosophical issue, notebook in hand. Any spare minutes she filled with reading – books and newspapers and journals.

Here in Melbourne, women of advanced views, like Mrs Carrie Lynch, were making their drawing rooms informal forums for women, in order to meet men on their own ground. Things that their grandmothers and mothers went to the grave in ignorance of were being discussed in the light of day.

In the dulling of wounds, Henrietta's heart began to beat with a sense of impending triumph. Lady Anna Gore Langton, daughter of the late Duke of Buckingham, had signed a petition in London for women's suffrage. Since more had followed suit, Henrietta knew it would surely happen: the old laws of coverture would change and pave the way for women's rights.

Even so, the deprivation of her children was agonising. Salt to her wounds were the general everyday critics claiming that women had no rights since they had no souls and, being less holy than men, would only sully themselves in the dirty world of politics. These were deliberate ploys to ridicule and diminish women, maddening tosh that made her blood boil, and she would think of William, his burly face, his bullishness. Her heart would turn in on itself and she would feel yet again the painful pump of anger. She had no lever. Though they lived in separation, there had been no talk of a divorce – a costly affair – two hundred pounds plus the added pain of a public exhibition in the newspapers. William, as her husband, could divorce her; as his wife, the only 'divorce' she could obtain was permission to reside alone – married to his name. Rather than have his home truths aired, William had arbitrarily settled things out of court to suit himself, should the law ever change in her favour.

Yet, the children, her beloved children, would, under present circumstances, never be settled, however much she pressed on with life. Even as plaintiff, there would be no remedy, whatever her charge. In seeking to bring him down – his respectability – she risked bringing down her own; her reputation was unfairly tainted as it was.

Oh, for the day when she would feel safe enough to strike out and put her own name in print. Henrietta could only remain alert, mindful of that ungrateful soulless curmudgeon. William.

It was not until Easter that she heard from Einnim and Carl. They had arrived safely in Southampton and were now installed in Bannister Court. She treasured their occasional notes, hastily written scraps, riddled with misspellings and ink blots and not always in the King's best English. She would read them and re-read them, for they kept her alive, and for a few secret moments her sad heart would sing.

~

Among freethinkers, Henrietta had noticed the growing custom of men calling each other by their Christian names. It was endearing to hear Mr Lynch now call Mr Johnson 'Freddie'.

'So, is that what they call you at home, Mr Johnson?' she ventured to ask one day, for invariably they ran into each other at the same gatherings. 'Freddie?'

'Yes,' he said. 'Freddie.'

She knew he found her forwardness, her candour, attractive, especially in the presence of other men.

'Then may I?' A faint twinkle came into her eye. 'At least, occasionally.'

'I have such respect, I would grant you anything, Mrs Dugdale.'

'Well, so long as you don't consider it a breach of etiquette.' She could see he was touched. 'You have become such a good, dear friend, I should not for one minute like to cause you distress.'

There was great novelty in having articulated his name in person for the first time. It signalled an instant development in their relationship, a mutually recognisable warming. She began to pet him, and, having used his name once, could not utter it enough. What silly games one plays, she reflected gladly when later alone. *If we dispensed with half of society's conventions, we would be far better off.*

At least a Married Women's Property Bill was being openly discussed in Victoria. Mr Mill's publication *The Subjection of Women* had taken the country by storm. Oh, what an uproar! As much as she admired Mr Higinbotham and supported his Married Women's Property Bill, for her it had come too late and did not go anywhere near far enough. She had spoken openly and forcefully about it, and the need for women's equality, at various informal meetings and social gatherings. Those detractors who believed the Bill was going too far – the kind who would write to the editor of the *Argus* to ask *Are all women to be trusted with such sums?* – must suffer riposte. Write she would to the *Argus*, requesting anonymity of the press.

AN APPEAL TO MR HIGINBOTHAM

Sir, At best the bill to secure property to married women is but a poor and partial remedy for a great and crying evil. It is, of course, highly proper to prevent wicked men from squandering the means of their wives, and throwing them a burden on society. But can society do nothing more than that? If a man is unfit to take care of his property, is he unfit to take care of his wife? And if he is totally unable or unwilling to love, cherish, and protect her, is it possible that she can love, honour, and obey him? Is the marriage bond not a perfect sham under such circumstances? If so, why does not Mr Higinbotham lay the axe to the root of the tree? If the marriage tie is a contract based on certain conditions, why is one party to be held bound if the other violates these conditions? I know, and no doubt so do you, Sir, cases in which women have been deserted by their husbands, and husbands by their wives, under circumstances which give them no relief, as the law stands at present. But there they are, bound by an invisible tie to some person they have not seen for years, whom they may never see again, who may be on the other side of the world altogether, and yet by an abominable legal fiction, for it is no reality, this person is deemed to sufficiently sustain the most intimate human relationship, and the injured and deserted party is bound by the strong arm of law to remain an isolated individual. This is a piece of the grossest injustice, and being unjust, the consequences can only be evil. In the case of a young woman so deserted it is three to one but she either falls victim to some vile seducer, and ultimately ends her shortened career in Bourke-street or the River Yarra, or she forms some other connection which may or may not turn out happy, but which, under the best conditions, the law does not recognise. If it be a man who is deserted, how can he help feeling that society makes no provision for his occupying an honourable relationship towards the female sex, and, with a deep sense of injustice, he throws himself into a whirlpool of licentiousness.

Sir, I do not send my name because my letter contains no statements requiring to be sustained, and the anonymity of the press may be properly extended to me; but I sincerely hope that you will not merely insert this letter, and then let the matter drop into oblivion. Please bring your own powerful pen to bear on the subject, and, if you have any influence with Mr Higinbotham, try and induce him to take a wider view of the married relationship, and make his remedy complete. Yours,

ADA

The law was a silly ass. Fickle and prejudicial beyond all reason. Mr Higinbotham must get to the root of the problem – the doctrine of unity of spouses – and force open the iron gates of the law which continued to lock out justice.

∿

Over and over they discussed it as they came to the end of the decade. Already Freddie had made much enquiry on Henrietta's behalf to see if there was any possible way around the law; any little chestnuts that could be picked up and reinterpreted. Could the courts exercising their equitable jurisdiction ever provide any relief under equity in certain circumstances? Freddie, so eager and innocent, kept poring over the famous Norton Case by candlelight. Caroline Norton was an illustration, hers was the cause of all women, and the personal experiences of this English writer and campaigner bore so many similarities to her own. But whichever way Henrietta and Freddie looked at the law, its principle seemed to keep coming back to the same old thing: the doctrine of unity of spouses, which controlled a woman's rights to real property during her marriage. This doctrine was now a rule of law, having had its origins in the common law doctrine of coverture.

Freddie wanted so badly to help. A burning sense of justice had overtaken his shyness. He was beyond forthcoming, tantalisingly loyal and full of generous advice. So refreshing in every way: his simplicity, his quiet energy, his incorruptible honesty and depth of devotion to her.

As they pored over case after case, article after article, Henrietta jotting things down in her notebook, she could feel the heat of his body beside her – his hands, his fine head, his breath, his big heart all the time beating wildly.

Of course, one had to be discreet. Sometimes meeting at prearranged venues: cafes, libraries or bookshops, the Botanical Gardens, private homes, or, when the time was ripe, in her rooms. Putting her arm in his seemed so natural now.

In many ways, Freddie had missed out. His mother had found it a hard life. On the move, often in difficult, camp-like conditions. Imagine having to serve two masters, he said: bandmaster husband Henry, whose loyalty was to his commanding officer, and the British Army, whose reluctant patronage controlled their family's very existence.

Freddie did not want to follow his father. Though he struggled to free himself from the traditions of his upbringing, he admitted he was sincerely grateful to the army for his education and musical training.

'A life without music,' she agreed, 'would be unimaginable.'

But blind obedience, and the way music regulated a soldier's day, signalling him what to do, Freddie held in disdain. Garrison life, though socially privileged, could be an unhealthy one, even more so for a wife and family – no privacy, no sense of permanency.

Alone together in her little parlour, they played his favourite, Schubert's 'Serenade'.

'Once more,' she said, 'and then I will make you some tea.'

'I used to play it as a boy,' he told her, as he put away his violin and covered it tenderly with an old silk kerchief. 'No amount of repetition could satisfy my craving for it.'

She well understood. Its grace and beauty, its mournful strains, were enough to make her weep.

'What a lonely child you must have been.' She searched his kind, frank eyes.

'Yes,' he said, pressing her palm against his lips, 'but now, I do nothing but think of you.' His boyish intensity bespoke lovesickness. 'I have the utmost respect and admiration for you, Mrs Dugdale – my dearest, I am captivated. At last I have met a woman who is not afraid to think, whose rebellious spirit has taken me under her spell. You have given me a cause.'

His confession, finally out, was the declaration she needed. All she wanted to do was run her fingers through his thick wavy hair, feel the thrust of his body inside hers and love him completely as he deserved to be loved.

Cupping the curves of his soft-whiskered cheeks, she kissed his lips again and again. Sweet, sweet Freddie, old beyond his years, yet in so many other ways delightfully pure. Not once had she felt their thirteen-and-a-half-year age gap. It would suit them, this arrangement: she unattainable; he afraid to marry, with his unresolvable doubt as to what really constituted a 'good marriage' and a 'good wife'.

∽

The more she thought about it, the more Henrietta envisaged herself settling in Melbourne, Freddie beside her, ventilating her sense of injustice, her outrage. Rent, even in the old part of Brighton, was high. If she were to buy a humble dwelling of her own in Melbourne, it would mean having to sell her existing property in Queenscliff. Not that she was afraid of showing up in the town – she did so periodically, being well within her rights – but every return had been a slap in the face. Austin, ten years old, was still at Greenleaf, still under the arm of his father, who had repeatedly denied all her requests for access.

Yet the town of Queenscliff was booming – 'Queen of the watering places' – wealthy daytrippers and holidaymakers filling its hotels and guesthouses. Any property overlooking blue waters would fetch a pretty price. Henrietta was her father's daughter. She knew she must keep an eye on trends; to speculate, one had to be astute. What she could not envisage was a future without her three sons. To realise her Queenscliff assets would be to sell out on her children – to all appearances, abandon them. This, she knew, would only prejudice her side of the argument.

For now, she must remain a Queenscliff ratepayer on paper, and never give up hope. Soon enough, Austin would be sent off to boarding school in England, like his brothers.

To Carl and Einnim, she wrote back individually with everyday news. Were they warm enough? Were they getting enough to eat? Did their boots and stockings still fit?

'They are alive and well,' Freddie reminded her gently. 'Of course they miss you,' he said. 'But they will come back a little wiser for it, in spite of their father. If nothing else, they will have learned the art of resilience – and to be themselves.'

What did she remember about her schooling in Grenoble? Freddie wanted to know.

Not so much the spectacular snow-capped alps, which followed her throughout the day from every arched window, but the bell that punctuated the harsh routine. Struggling out of bed in the darkest hour, having to break ice in her urn in order to wash. Then, once dressed, taking a burning candle and, with her music books, finding her way along the long corridors with their smell of rising damp. There in a vaulted room, with not even a brazier or a heated brick, she would practise for an hour before breaking her fast. Scale after scale, arpeggio upon arpeggio, her hands dressed in only a pair of woollen glovettes. When her fingers, blue with chilblains, chose not to obey, having to blow on them, sit on them, or sometimes even bash them with her Bible. And when the blood flowed free, as it often did from under her fingernails, the relief intense.

At the time, she would have run away had there been a way out. Thinking about it now, though, some twenty-five years later, she would not have exchanged that experience for anything. The nuns had trained her well. To live sparsely without comfort and unnecessary distractions, disciplining mind and body through the daily rigours of selflessness and pain.

It was in her fifteenth year that her parents had sent her away, with the idea of staving off an untimely romance with Junius. It was for her own protection, she was told. She could not recall being particularly unhappy during her stay at Grenoble. She had strung out each term, knowing there was certainty to her life after finishing school, that it was just a matter of time. She was *affianced*, not a child, her body rippling on the breeze of love. She would soon be of age to marry, and nobody could take that love away.

Certain rituals, she remembered – not the Roman prayers and dirges muttered in solemn nonsensical repetition that were so foreign to her ear, but music, proper music – had made her imprisonment bearable. By aspiring to beauty through music, one was aspiring heavenward, or so the nuns would harp. When the choir burst into song, it was indeed sublime. Did it matter that melody and harmony brought forth ungodly thoughts as she played the hours away? How her heart throbbed and her voice quivered as she sang. If it were not the music, then it would have been the unspeakable dreamy silence that reached up through the valleys and the chain of mountains behind that gave her a sense of majesty, purity and overwhelming peace.

'"Finishing school", they called it, Freddie.'

'Finishing what?' Education, he said, was an ongoing lifelong journey, so far as he could see.

'Oh, I agree wholeheartedly.'

Once-vibrant images of France were now nothing more than a potpourri of passing experience: artworks, fragments fetched from inside a cathedral, the glimpse of a ruin or scenery snatched from the window of a rolling carriage – nothing catalogued, nothing more substantial than the fragrance floating from a dusty grove of orange trees.

Home had been barely a dream. In those days, there was no Gare de Grenoble. It was a long, arduous, convoluted expedition to the convent, which meant she became privy to things a properly brought-up young lady wouldn't otherwise see. Every so often would come the flicker of human flesh. Not from a painting in some famous gallery but in open fields, where women worked alongside men daily as their equals. Many a time had she seen them. 'Dirty, wretched importunate souls', her mother would call them. Empty bottles of wine, pieces of broken bread and dried-out butts of sausage lying discarded on crumpled calico cloths.

It aroused her to see the men with trousers loosened, their womenfolk uncorseted, bosoms half-exposed in siesta. Once walking through an avenue of walnut trees, she had spied a young couple running hand-in-hand. They had disappeared behind a nearby haystack, and she had watched open-mouthed as it wavered this way and that while fellow workers slumbered barely fifty yards away.

'Sorry, my sweet.' Freddie's voice followed her from the other side of the room. 'I missed what you said.' He was standing with his back to her, winding forward the clock.

'Oh! Just thinking aloud. They are far freer than the English, the French, far more in tune with nature and its functions. Don't you agree?'

In France she had found muscles she never knew existed. In France she had learned to stand on her own two feet, finding her earliest independence.

～

Music was for Henrietta a life habit; life without a piano was unimaginable. She set herself a daily schedule of gruelling self-discipline that enabled her to revive old skills with gratifying progression. Virtuosic pieces she had long forgotten. Hour upon hour, she played, her fingers retraining and retrieving, until every piece in her repertoire became intimately mastered. In such a way, she found she could temporarily forget her own sorrow and loss, everything except the beauty of the black and white keys before her.

Piano teaching proved more than a good standby. It drew her out of herself, moved her forward. Though her income was paltry, the reward of seeing her students' progress was twofold, since she was made party to their joy and satisfaction, as well. Teaching music revolved around various orders. Explaining these orders to young minds helped restore a sense of order and meaning to her life in turn. It was not just the theory. To understand the pianoforte, its wide-ranging effects – soft one end, loud the other – to know how to make love and war, was to know how to find peace and resolution. This remarkable instrument had given rise to so much beauty of thought and movement over the years, as had her precious chess set. 'My trusty old friends', she called them, their black and white patterns never varying. They challenged the mind but did not argue back. How to explain to her pupils this humbling experience of being taken out of oneself? She must remember to ask Freddie.

He arrived early one afternoon armed with a cold bottle of ginger beer. There was a delightful breeze coming through the open window, and beyond Brighton Beach were small craft, and white sails like the wings of seabirds soaring across the leaden-coloured water.

'"Music has charms to soothe a savage beast." Papa always said it for my benefit, old tease.'

'Ah, but you know, music is also a kind of asylum, isn't it?' said Freddie.

His eyes were soft with love. A vagrant lock had fallen across his forehead and his eyes gleamed like rich, dark honey. But he was right. Without music, she knew, without broader purpose in life, her mind might have turned. Teaching gave her solace. There was the constant chorus of students inside her head, giving rise for hope.

After work, he would occasionally call upon her and, like today, sit in on a lesson, only too happy to lend her his ear. Upon hearing a good performance, he would reward a parting pupil with bonbons drawn from his pocket.

She could tell that, deep down, Freddie ardently wished for children of his own. But that would never be, at least not on her account. She must treasure what little she had: Sunday letters from England, a stray button of Einnim's she'd found in her sewing box, strands of Carl's red-gold hair caught from a brush.

'Now, the boys,' she said. 'Let me find you their letters.' She said she hoped the regimentation of boarding school life would not kill the artistic streak in Carl. Undoubtedly, the formality of a joyless Christmas spent with Grandma Dugdale would dampen his spirits. 'Look what he's written.'

The woodlands are bare now – elm and birch, chestnut, rarely oak. Not much to see in the way of birds apart from the odd pair of raven – their untidy bowl of sticks and twigs stark atop the tallest branches. Oh Mama, how I pine for a good old gum tree and the smell of eucalypts and wattles. Yes, we get enough to eat – just – though I don't always like it – something horrible they call 'toad-in-the-hole'.

According to Carl, Einnim had been teased unmercifully because of his name. The news upset her deeply. Einnim was 'Minnie' backwards

– she had so wished for a girl – and hence the name in reverse held private meaning.

'Bullying is rampant,' she said. Einnim had alluded to scuffles with his tormentors and one prolonged fight with an older boy.

I let him know I had fists and knew how to use them. In the end, I won through with pluck and strength. Father would have been proud of me. But I did not like or enjoy what I had done, Mama. I much prefer to win at swimming or cricket than knock someone down.

'Imagine them,' she said, 'thrown into a strange country with its own laws and customs, for that's what an English public school really is, you know.' It would be painful and trying for them, not just new boys boarding in a public school but ones far from home on the other side of the world. Their colonial manners, their marked idiosyncrasies, which she knew so well, their sturdy independence as Australians – these would be open to the scrutiny of curious and often hostile eyes. To be singled out from their fellows as original or deviating from the normal, she feared, would expose them to ridicule.

Freddie tried to play it down. 'Oh yes, they will have a rough time of it, but I expect they are tough little blighters. Tougher than you think.'

She knew how resilient children could be. She had only to think of Joseph's daughters. Hattie, Emma and Fanny, she had discovered, were married and now producing themselves. How did they feel about their father bringing four more children into the world? The law made a father the natural protector of his children, no matter how he chose to treat them. Joseph, having served three measly months in prison in 1848, had been able to reclaim custody of children so young upon release – even when he was in no fit state of mind to do so – and allowed to take them to the other side of the world. What a cruel irony of the law. It made the loss of her own cherished sons more palpable.

Henrietta folded her arms and frowned. *I will not be jealous and small-minded*, she thought. *I will not. I will just have to get on with life.* But still the empty space was there. It echoed. Being a guest, being forced to sit within the domestic realms of others, being privy to their nests, their precious little darlings, could at times be acutely painful.

Sick of the insecurity of having to rent, she longed to live in a home of her own, a nest here in Melbourne, where she could welcome back her sons with open arms away from the intrusive eye of William.

Chapter 12

⁓

'Conveyancing is more an art than a science, Papa used to say. I tend to agree, Freddie.'

Henrietta had fallen in love with the russet-roofed weatherboard cottage that Freddie was renting as soon as she saw it. The little town of Camberwell, nine miles from Melbourne, was pleasantly countrified. It would suit them both. In 1872, she decided to make the owner of the cottage an offer to buy it freehold, an amount that she could comfortably afford with the security of keeping her Queenscliff property.

With Freddie as her witness, she carried out the transaction without need of an agent. The title was in her name, and in her name it would safely remain.

When confirmation finally came via the telegraph, she declared, 'What say "Telko" for a name?' She reached for Freddie's hand and, clasping his pointer finger, gave it a squeeze. They were fine strong hands. Musician's hands. The feel of his fingertips, the gliding silky sensation of rosin and the ridges where they pressed upon the strings of his violin.

At last they could live together, breathe deeply and easily away from the fine white city dust. The setting had a lyrical feel, the kind of dreamy, soft outlook one might long for – far enough distant from the church steeple and its stately line of poplars. There were areas of natural bushland where acacias and gum trees grew, but otherwise farmlets with small open paddocks and hawthorn hedges and the odd snowdrop or freesia to surprise in spring.

The garden, a rambling half acre, she gave over to her hens. Their talkativeness was a joy. Their chicks exuded vigour and brought new energy to her life. In the softer light of winter, she could look out and observe their movements, their plump frames, white and copper, picking their way systematically through the fruit trees and flowering kale. They laid eggs like clockwork. What was more, they kept the slugs down and they never got lost. At the end of the property was a blackberry hedge, the demarcation point for a neighbour's house cow, a sweet-faced black and white creature that lowed and tossed its head her way when she called. A newly installed net-wire fence surrounded the vegetable patch. Together, on weekends, they potted cuttings and seedlings. Freddie liked nothing better than filling a wheelbarrow with mulch and manure, or putting a match to a heap of dried leaves or prunings.

Freddie's family, the Johnsons, were all frowns right from the start. They did not approve of 'Mrs Dugdale', complaining she had brought nothing but disgrace to them all. Freddie, in turn, steered away, gradually estranging himself from his family.

Snubs only strengthened their resolve to flout convention. A wider, more accepting world was close at hand. And they were in good legal company. Mr Lynch, besides being a man of law, was also an amateur painter and broad-minded like his considerably older and outspoken other half. Mrs Carrie Lynch – the former Caroline Dexter – was a lively fifty-two; her legal spouse, twenty years her junior. The two couples could enjoy the mutuality and sanction of each other's company – further proof that custom was a fool.

Mrs Lynch did not suffer fools nor stand by custom. Twice married, the famous mesmerist, medico, lecturer, author and publisher was still encouraging women to throw away their petticoats and go beyond their domestic sphere for the moral betterment of humankind. But, after twenty years of continuous public life, she was content now to be a patroness, sharing her private art collection in her beautiful and peaceful happy home.

Mrs Lynch understood well the machinations of politics and the press, and how to grab attention. 'Never underestimate the value of self-advertising' was her advice. 'Have the courage of your convictions, Mrs Dugdale. Be defiant. Respect yourself and refuse to be ridiculed into silence. Remember, words are your arsenal.'

Having by now fully recovered her poise, Henrietta was able to circulate easily in society. She began to lobby those of influence – journalists and politicians. She wrote to Mr John Richardson, the Member for Geelong East, a colonist in the Bellarine she had long known from her earliest Queenscliff days, appealing to him to help pave the way for women's rights. She buttonholed Mr Higinbotham in person whenever she could.

'You are making a bit of a name for yourself, Mrs Dugdale,' laughed Mrs Lynch, 'and, my, what wit, what flair with a pen.'

It was Carrie Lynch who had originally suggested she start off using a pseudonym. 'At least it will open the door of a publisher and you will get a reading. I have done both and, may I say, a pen-name frees you up. There is sense in the old adage, *Who steals my purse steals trash ... but he who filches from me my good name ...*'

And with Mrs Lynch's words resounding clearly in her ears, Henrietta made her way into Collins Street to the offices of the *Daily Telegraph* for a meeting with the editor, Mr Howard Willoughby. The former Hansard reporter welcomed her and sat her opposite him in an oak swivel desk chair.

Henrietta folded her hands in her lap and faced him square on. 'I am led to believe your journal is a liberal one, Mr Willoughby, and you,' she said, noticing his prematurely balding head, 'a progressive young man?'

'Oh, you flatter me, Mrs Dugdale.' He gave her a half-smile and a twitch of his dark moustache. 'And how may I help you?'

From out of her satchel she drew a number of letters and placed them on his desk.

'These are letters written by your fair hand?'

'Yes, in the hope you might publish them.'

'And yet they have a nom de plume. "Eclectic".'

'And that is precisely why I have come to deliver them in person – in good faith, sir, as their creator.'

'I see,' said Mr Willoughby, 'and your subject is, I believe, "women's rights"?' His fine dark eyes looked at her with regard.

'Correct. There are whispers that Mr Higinbotham and Mr Richardson are banding together to propose a Bill for women's suffrage.'

'Well, it is news to me.'

'Indeed, good news, Mr Willoughby. We women have been waiting a long time.' She paused as he examined the letters. 'I hear you are newly married.'

'Indeed.'

'Then this will interest you, I am sure, as well as your good wife.'

Mr Willoughby's Roman nose gave him a stately air. 'I assure you, my good wife has no interest in the vote and I can't say I'm all for it, either. But I believe in freedom of speech, Mrs Dugdale, and I would be happy to take you on. Nothing excites readers more than a good spar.'

Henrietta thanked Mr Willoughby for his time and bid him goodbye. Joining the rush of businessmen, she made her way past the banks, the exchange, to the offices of barristers and solicitors to Lynch and MacDonald in Queen's Street, where she waited in reception for Freddie.

It was the quiet moments like this that affected her. However happy her life with Freddie, her pining for her children never dulled, it never lessened. But if she drew in gloomy thoughts, she knew how to ride them out. Her daily schedule – fitting in piano teaching between recitals and concerts, visiting the Picture Gallery, and attending plays at the Haymarket or the new Royal – was challenging and began to leave Freddie's behind. They would take the train or omnibus into the city and back, and by the time the cab dropped them at Telko, it was late. Within eight hours, the whole thing would start over again.

'Ah, there you are.' Freddie stood before her in hat, coat and gloves. 'Shall we go?' he said, offering her his arm.

'I just had a meeting with young Mr Willoughby,' she told him as soon as they had stepped out into the street.

'And ... how did you find the blighter?' he said, with a pat on her hand. 'They say he has a way of piercing to the heart of things. Cold and aloof.'

She gave him a droll smile. 'Well, he was courteous and cheery enough, but I suspect one would never know what he was really thinking. We shall see.'

～

One Sunday, it had broken dim, a mist still clinging to the bush-lined gully. From across the hill, the relentless come-hither of the matins bell, its sonority transporting her into the world of childhood. Each repeated peal struck her deepest intuition, reverberating throughout her soul. Something was wrong with the boys. The forlorn weekly letters from Southampton had come to an abrupt halt. The thought of having to contact William for news of them filled her with revulsion, yet the silence from across the seas and the absence of news were excruciating.

She was making the bed, folding back the coverlet, when she heard voices approaching the gate. Looking out the window, she spotted two grey figures clad in oilskins, making their way down the garden path. She felt her heart miss a beat. Her breath gave way. Could it be? Surely not. It was like a dream, as if the pair of them had materialised out of the mist.

'Freddie, Freddie, quick, the boys are here! I'm quite sure.' She lifted her skirt and ran to the door, and there they stood. Einnim and Carl.

'My darlings! Oh, my darlings!' She hugged them, laughing and crying at the same time. 'Come in, come in. Here, give me your things.'

Quickly she drew them into the kitchen before the fire and hung up their coats and rucksacks. Hungry and frozen and with no money, they had trudged through the night from the docks.

Within minutes, they had chirped up over cups of steaming sugary milk tea, though they were a little nonplussed to see Freddie. But with easy affection he shook their hands. 'You have done your mother proud.'

'You certainly have, my sweet sweet rebels!'

Not many a boy, she knew, would have the spunk to abscond from an English boarding school and stow away on a ship bound for Melbourne.

'Now then.' Face still rapt with joy, she bustled around, cracking eggs into a sizzling pan. Quickly she brought out a fresh pat of butter and bowls of jams and jellies – blackberry, marmalade, melon and lemon – from which they might choose, and her own freshly clotted cream.

Freddie toasted bread over the open fire – slices upon slices, no sooner browned than plucked from the rack and devoured until they could eat no more.

Rascals grown into young greyhounds, they were – so lean, all gristle and bone – and considerably taller than when she'd seen them last. Einnim, now sixteen, a little distant and flat. She hugged him regardless, praising him for looking after his fourteen-year-old brother so well. Not for one minute could she take her eyes off them both.

Einnim, head to his plate, did not give much away. It was Carl, sunburnt face bespattered with freckles, and scabby lips, who filled her in, though he was somewhat scant on detail. 'Einnim's idea, but between us, we kept abreast of the news. What ships were due in and what ones due out. We got a tip-off from the gardener. Gave the man two bob and took the chance while we had it. Not so very hard, once we had a mind to it.'

Carl's voice was breaking but, strangely, he had not lost his youthful rawness. His eyes shone clear as dawn when he related how they'd remained hidden while the ship was towed down Southampton Water, and were not found until the vessel was sailing well down the Channel.

The captain took pity on them in Lisbon. It suited him well enough to have two free pairs of hands on board.

Only then did Carl's eyes grow fearful as he described waves they'd seen, more than four storeys high. Einnim made light of the journey. The winds were not always fair, he admitted, and he was sure glad to be back on land.

Deep inside, her feelings poured one upon the other, a confusing mix of pain and pride. Einnim and Carl would have quickly made themselves useful aboard. She could easily imagine them, polishing the lamps, scrubbing the decks with holystone or holding a stay in high wind, but she winced to think of the rough life below and her beautifully mannered sons in the bilge, eating and sleeping with seadogs.

Freddie filled the bath and left them to soak. Having made them comfy in the spare room, Henrietta walked about the house, humming happily to herself. Sleep they did, uninterruptedly for fourteen hours. But they had yet to face their father. Carl's fidgety fingers, shiny red bitten-down quicks, and Einnim's unease had not passed her notice. Both boys would be feeling nervous, knowing they were more than likely in for a hiding.

The following morning, a cable arrived. William, having soon got wind of their return, spent several shillings making clear his demands.

Her voice went suddenly thin and reedy as she passed the telegram to Freddie.

'He is threatening me with a court order, the fiend.'

'Careful, love.' Freddie put a hand on her shoulder. 'Mind your p's and q's, if you ever wish to see your little rebels again.'

Henrietta cabled back immediately. *Einnim and Carl are happy and well. I beg you from the bottom of my heart please let them stay the week and I shall send them on at my expense.*

William's reply was chilling. If the boys were not returned on the morrow, he would have her up on a charge of abduction. His complete lack of concern for anything other than revenge incensed her and left

Einnim and Carl exhausted and bewildered. How to explain to her darlings that the law would take a father's side, no matter what?

Accompanying them to the docks was an agonising ordeal, and as the steamer executed a slow, wide turn, Henrietta watched them clambering past the lifeboats to the stern, all the time waving her wet handkerchief, helplessly kissing the air to the blow of the horn. The cold, gnawing ache had returned. Unable to face the journey back to an empty home, she would seek refuge in the Mechanics' Institute and wait for Freddie. In her mind, she could still see her darling pair paling into the blue. She stood on Princes Bridge, tearing William's telegram into infinitesimal strips, and watched numbly as they drifted downstream.

By evening, Einnim and Carl would be back with their father and Austin at Greenleaf. Fearful that William would intercept her letters, she would send them, like those to Austin, care of Sarah Harding. Even then, there was always the agonising risk of betrayal. At least the two older boys, in their new-gained worldliness, would be alert to their father's moles.

Self-sacrifice was not in Henrietta's nature. Her children had been brought up with certain liberty, not made to be silent or acquiesce in the presence of their elders. Their views were disputed politely, for a child should be made to observe and think, but in no way had she ever deferred to them. William liked to think he had moulded their independence, but woe betide if he'd been drinking: his freethinking quickly went to the wind. Yet she was loath to delve, knowing they would be reluctant to speak ill of their father. Dull loyalty was driven into them.

'Of course they're not happy,' she told Freddie, as the weeks slipped past. How could they possibly be? She could only picture their sorry faces, their father – or 'the old boy', as they secretly called him – berating them with that formidable look in his eyes. 'Snap to it, or I'll box your ears.'

The boys gave no account of what had happened upon their return, only Einnim's hasty note to indicate that things had settled down, and that William had put them to work forthwith and forbidden any further contact with their mother. At least she could take some gratification from those brief words, knowing William could never fully suppress their rebellious spirit.

⟋

One day, the following winter, Henrietta received an anonymous letter. She read it before passing it across the breakfast table to Freddie.

'Here,' she said, lost for words.

It is in your interest to know that your husband, William Dugdale, is a bigamist. He claims to have undergone a form of marriage in a Bendigo registry office with a young woman by the name of Mary Jane Pacey who is now sharing his bed.

Freddie jumped up. 'This is a criminal offence. He can be brought before the courts.'

Her hands by now were shaking violently. Inside, she could feel the fury, the torment and heartbreak rising all over again. After all she had gone through – to be made a pariah, cast out of her children's lives; they, like the rest of her property, stolen – and now to learn of this. To have to live with the fermenting image of William's paramour in the same house, caring for her own flesh and blood.

'We must tread lightly.' Freddie remained dubious. 'Could it be some kind of blackmail?'

'Nothing would surprise me about that man, nothing.' Henrietta crumpled the letter, let it fall to the floor.

'Dare you ask the boys to testify?'

'How could I put them through more stress, Fred? Either way, it is untenable. I never see them,' she cried. 'I never really know where they are.'

⟋

Another year passed by in separation, but as soon as Henrietta set eyes on Einnim, she could tell something was up. Just eighteen, he seemed strung-out, his eyes ever so slightly off-centre. He offered no excuse for his surprise visit, preferring to twiddle his thumbs. Stalling, no doubt. She waited, with gathering discomfort, for him to mention his father's bigamy. There had been no further developments, and Freddie still had some detective work to do.

'Presume you heard the news, Ma. Grandma Dugdale died.'

Henrietta's smile evaporated as she froze, teapot poised. 'Oh, I am sorry to hear that, dear, very sorry.' Thank goodness that was all.

'Pa's inheritance has come through. So … I'm going to live in New Zealand, Mama. See what it's like.'

'New Zealand?' Her face plummeted. She nearly dropped the teapot.

'Yes. I leave in a week by steamer.'

She began to grill him, her lips tightening.

'New Plymouth area,' he replied, with renewed energy. 'Waitara's a main port for river trade. The land is rich, you see, because of the volcano. Everything lush and green. Dairy farms by the plenty. Lovely sweeping surf beaches to the west.'

She poured out the tea, her mouth working furiously inside.

'But what about the trouble with the Maoris? The Taranaki wars. Hundreds killed.'

'Things have settled down, Ma, and the town has come along.'

He told her about the new freezing works, the makings of the future. He'd been reading up on it. Waitara was a vital, growing river port. Flourishing. Soon it would have a railway. 'Already there's a Harbour Board, two breweries …'

She cut him off. 'Please, Einnim, don't talk to me of frozen animals and breweries!'

'Well, then, two printing houses, if you prefer, and talk of a soap and candle factory, an iron foundry, a boatbuilding yard, a wool-scouring plant and a tannery. I would never be short of work in Waitara.'

She was barely listening. She looked out the window, watching Freddie digging in the garden, the slow, systematic movements, the moving hulk of his body. She let him fade, feeling a knot forming in her throat.

'It's just that sometimes I feel I'm not quite cut out for Queenscliff.' He wiped his forehead. 'Sometimes I feel I can't quite breathe in the town.'

Einnim had matured. Six months ago, a group of Queenscliff youths celebrating Guy Fawkes had burned an effigy opposite the cottage in Stevens Street. The object of ridicule was her tenant, the local headmaster, Mr Behan. Einnim, she had heard, had been implicated, and William had attempted to hush it up. Behan had brought it to court, but it was found the lads were only burning a guy.

Henrietta looked at her son. He had stopped growing and was filling out, a fine athletic specimen. Her heart swelled. He was wearing respectable attire, a clean collar and a well-fitting suit, and he showed all the attributes of a young man of the world, not some hobbledehoy picking hayseeds out of his jacket. He exuded confidence and self-respect. In his face, his bearing, in the cowlick swept back cleanly from his brow.

'And what does your father think of the idea?'

'He's all for it,' he said with growing confidence. 'Told me to go on ahead. Give the place the once-over. Actually, to tell you the truth, he's toying with the idea of joining me.'

'And your brothers?'

He nodded. 'Oh yes, Carl and Austin are keen as mustard.'

Einnim was intoxicated. She could see the glow on his face, unsullied vigour, that inner need to be out there, hauling in life. She gave a sigh and turned away as a big fat tear ran down her face. So that beast of a man still had the power to punish her.

Einnim, never one to show affection, put his hands on her shoulders and said gently, 'Greenleaf is on the market. I thought you should know.'

Early in 1875, Carl and Austin came to Camberwell to say their goodbyes, with the news that Greenleaf had been sold and everything auctioned off at a clearing sale. Her heart leaped into her throat, for it was six years since she had seen her youngest. She had everything arranged to perfection outside under the shady trellis – white-clothed table laden with special cakes, half-oranges with jelly and other dainty offerings. She wanted her lost baby to remember only the best in her as a loving, nurturing mother.

The boy stood stiffly as she squeezed him fervently against her breast.

'Oh, Austin, darling! Don't be shy.' She patted the chair. 'Here, come and sit beside me.' And all the while she sipped her tea, feasting her eyes on Austin's face, searching his adolescent features for something, something she could claim as her own. She kept wanting to smell him, touch him. Reaching again and again for him.

'Oh, how I've missed you, my precious!'

But she could sense his childish indifference. It seemed he could barely remember her as he disentangled himself. It struck on her nerves. She knew she should relish the few hours she had left with the boys, but felt so tense, so overwhelmingly tense, knowing she had failed to properly engage.

Her top lip began to twitch with the taste of her own venom. William, not only a monster but a bigamist to boot.

'Is he taking *her* with him?' There, it was out.

'It's not right, Mama,' Carl said. 'She is heavily with child and barely much older than Einnim.' He admitted he liked the young woman well enough. 'Mary Jane is kind, isn't she, Austin … and very pretty.' But clearly the situation distressed him. He folded his mother gently in his arms and held her close. 'Don't worry, Mama dearest. We won't forget. Whatever happens, wherever we are, you will always be our rightful mother.'

William, the coward, had already bolted.

Freddie had arranged a writ. Fat lot of good that was now. Once outside Australian waters, William was untouchable.

*12 March 1875. We have arrived in New Zealand, safe and sound,
Mama, and I am writing this letter under a roof that we can at last call
our own.*

They were in a place called 'Horseshoe Bend', dairy country east of
Waitara. Carl described the local scenery of the settlement, and Mount
Egmont in its solitary grandeur. *Some days it is covered with snow so far
appearing to us above the horizon.* He sounded upbeat. Coupled with
that peaceful image, the postscript that a half-brother, Cara, had been
safely born on board the crossing.

Henrietta tried to write to the boys without tears, without questions.
But then the screaming would start up, the screaming she could hear
between her ears. She dared not worry Freddie again. She had worried
him enough, as it was. So many attempts to write until blind anger
had finally taken over. And now look: her inkwell all but dry. Pen-nib
scorings deep into the paper. Pathetic screwed-up balls of nothing to be
thrown in the fire and burned. Blazing in her mind were the words of
that famous American woman, Dr Mary Walker:

*Some men love women as children love dolls, and, as a natural result, treat
them just as dolls are cared for. They dress them in all the finery they are
able to procure, pet and exhibit them until the clothes become old, and the
beautiful colour of the face is gone, and the eyes are contracted and dim,
and then, like worn out dolls, they are thrown aside for neighbours' dolls,
or for some beautiful images in the show windows of false society's market.
To be deprived of a divorce was like being shut up in a prison.*

But to be deprived of her boys made her situation worse. It was like
slowly dying in prison.

Henrietta put away her pen and closed the latches of her writing
compendium. A gift from Junius, it was a magnificent piece of Indian

craftsmanship, one of the few personal possessions she deeply treasured. But today it brought no pleasure, her eyes dull to its beauty, the delicate ivory inlay a mass of cloudy squiggles and scrolls. Even its silver failed to shine. Slowly, through the blur of tears, shapes came into relief, and her eyes were drawn to the centre: a single floral and leaf motif, part of a circular pattern, a pattern of release and enclosure. There it was, that ancient eastern spiritual symbol of Hinduism and Buddhism, the circle – the centre and the whole.

Many times she had found herself twisted in time, asking: *Where do things start and end in this world?* Freed of the Bible – a man's book, with its belittling depictions of Eve – the spiritual side of life remained a mystery to her. Even Mrs Carrie Lynch's occult theories were never quite convincing. Her seances brought mixed results. Once, as a test, Henrietta had asked her to call down Junius' spirit, but, try as she might, Junius would not be summoned.

The ideas of Mr Emerson were more substantial. Thought was that wordless, powerful prayer to the Infinite Mind, which was never without result. This was *real religion* – and Freddie agreed – religion not needing dungeons and red-hot pincers but born of reason and *real* reverence for the Great Mind – having sincerity for basis, with bright hope in the future for everyone.

She must try again. Having poured herself a cup of mint tea, she sat down to a clean sheet of her monogrammed notepaper. Without hesitation, she dipped pen in ink. 'My dearest, darling boy,' she said to herself, as she began to write in her bold upright hand.

Chapter 13

～

Even during her worst trials, Henrietta had never unburdened herself to her brother Joseph. Contact was sporadic. What remained between them was an enduring emotional deadness. Out of common courtesy, she had, at the time, written to her brother to inform him that she and William had had an almighty row and separated. Upon relocating to Camberwell, she had again written with her new address. His reply was brief and slating: 'Living in sin, I hear? Shame on you, Henrietta.'

That same year, Joseph was besieged with troubles of his own in relation to his new position as shire secretary, one of a number of positions he juggled in Mornington. Allegations were made that he had colluded with the shire president to defraud the Shire of Mornington. He had written a letter of self-defence to the *Argus*. With a dubious charge of forgery resting upon him, he could see the scandalous proceedings would in time hereafter be recorded as another 'vile blot' upon his character unless measures were taken to bring to justice the libeller or libellers.

Numerous newspaper reports had followed, then court hearings, but Joseph had threatened to take the matter into his own hands by filing a writ for defamation of character.

She had written to her brother – in spite of her general distrust of Joseph, for she was thinking more of his wife and children than him, and seeking the best outcome – asking if there was any way in which Freddie might provide counsel. As managing clerk, he could sound out Mr Lynch and get back to Joseph within the week.

'Do what you can, Freddie, there's a dear.'

The three men had met briefly, with Freddie reporting the upshot.

Mr Lynch had talked at length about *justification* and *fair comment* and how in the end it all came back to the *onus of truth*. 'Libel can be a damn difficult thing to prove. Easier said than done.' Mr Lynch's advice had been 'let it go to the keeper, Mr Worrell. Give it a year and everyone will have forgotten.' To take the matter further and serve notice would only add fuel to the fire.

But even the best of legal advice fell on deaf ears. Joseph, having had his day in court, then had to face not just the stigma of libel but the costs incurred, and the humiliation of finding himself, for the third time in his life, bankrupt.

Freddie had simply shrugged it off. 'Let him stew in his own juice.' But Henrietta knew that with Joseph, one imprudence invariably led to another – such had been the pattern of his life. And she could see it coming: from good to bad, from bad to worse.

For the past eighteen months, Henrietta had had no contact with Joseph. She refrained from writing to him, knowing he would have his hands full with the bankruptcy proceedings. To his credit, he was still gainfully employed as schoolmaster and shire secretary, so far as she knew. If he had done it twice before, she kept reassuring herself, he could do it again: start anew and manage on his income. But how long could he keep working? Joseph was not a young man. In two years he would be sixty.

Henrietta sighed – a long, vibrating sigh. Perhaps a little tea might see her through until Freddie came home, for she had not eaten since breakfast. This, the simplest of rituals, was known to help her settle. A few shavings of bread and butter beside the remaining heart of a lettuce would be sufficient. She took the tray out to the vestibule and poured from her Doulton pot, in the way she had been taught, with refinement of movement and control. The swirl of cream she stirred twice only, slowly and noiselessly as she mulled over what was left of the morning newspaper. She sipped at her tea, warm, comforting sips, her eyes scanning the various lists of notices in the *Argus*, through the Births, Marriages and Deaths, where they finally rested upon the very last in recoil. *WORRELL – On the 11th inst, at Schnapper Point, Margaret the beloved wife of Mr Joseph E. Worrell, aged 44.*

Henrietta could picture the torment in Joseph's face – a black sky before a storm. It was no good writing to him; he would be in no state to read. She must write at once to Emma.

An epidemic of measles had swept through Mornington, Margaret succumbing in hospital, with complications and pneumonia. Both families had been down with it, according to Emma. Henrietta folded her niece's letter and went to share the news with Freddie. The music he was practising – some Brahms – came floating down the hall. She felt at once the power of his playing, that wonderful fat, juicy sound he managed to extract – not one fear-soaked wobble – filled with strength and compassion.

Freddie set down fiddle and bow just so on the chiffonier.

'I'm so sorry,' she said, fidgeting with letter and paper knife. 'I've gone and interrupted you. How thoughtless. It sounded so beautiful, too.'

'No, no, not at all,' he said, tidying his sheets of music.

'Joseph is so distraught, he has had to close the school,' she sniffed. 'Emma assures me there is nothing I could have done.'

'Here, come and tell me all about it.' Within seconds he had taken her in his arms, and together they stayed like that as he rocked her back and forth with great tenderness.

She could smell his fresh, minty breath, and, through his whiskers, found his half-opened mouth. He drew back at last, inspecting her face with his finger, her wet eyes.

She pulled at her hands, knotting her fingers.

'I fear for Joseph's children – four youngsters, the eldest not yet twelve – without a mother.'

'Who is to care for them?'

'Margaret's younger sister – Miss Downward – their maiden aunt ...'

'Well, then, by all means support your brother. Providing the bairns are cared for, you don't have to step in.'

Freddie kissed each swollen eyelid in turn. 'Come.' He sat her down on the chaise longue and set about loosening her chignon, threading his fingers through her hair. Then, on one knee before her, he unbuttoned her boots, put a cushion under her feet and began massaging her soles, each of her toes in turn, paying special attention to her ankles. Ah, the release! As if an enormous wave had taken over. The throb gone, her veins running freely again, almost every muscle back in its rightful place. Through half-opened eyes, she could see the outline of his shoulders, his broad leonine chest hovering over her calves as he went on working upwards with his hands to the rhythmic tide of his breath.

Later that night in bed, she spoke more freely, giving some account of the strain of the past week. 'One thing is for certain,' she said, laying her head in the crook of his arm, 'I could never have been a doctor. In study, yes, but not in practice. Sickbeds make me weak and squeamish. Let me tell you a story, Freddie love. It was before you were born, 1838, the year of the fever.'

'Was it measles?'

'No. "Poor Man's Malady", they called it, for initially it found itself in poverty.' With all the workhouses and the hospitals next to overflowing and no means of isolation, the disease had combusted, spreading like a giant inferno from the hovels to the mansions. It brought with it no warning; neither did it discriminate, striking one hot summer's day in the very heart of Bloomsbury.

Her third brother, Edward, had woken up with a severe headache and stiffening of the neck. Over the hours, his fever had risen with the growing rash upon his torso. In and out of delirium he passed, breath hot and ragged. She, but a girl of eleven, had had to stand by and wipe rising vomit from his lips. Frothy green spew; she could see it now, slopping in a chipped enamel bowl. Teddy, back arched, head boring down into his pillow, so dangerously ill that light, even the presence of a candle burning, was for him a torture.

The awful hush, figures tiptoeing in and out of the darkened room. Poultices and leeches applied each in turn, only to be taken away and discarded. Her mother, crippled with backache, sitting helpless by his side as every minute fretted away. The hideous tremor and the downward deviation of the eyes as the doctor drew back his eyelids – whites bloodshot, almost devoid of pupils, half-mooned irises disappearing into the sockets of his eyes.

Gathering around, they had all kneeled and prayed that a miracle would happen. But come morning, her father had had to face the unbearable task of signing his own son's death certificate. Three days her father had sat in his office, his hair shot with grey. The portly register, she remembered, lay spread out on his desk, with every death and burial in the district recorded in copperplate. Poor Papa! Each of those names so painstakingly inscribed correlated to not just a number but a real human being – the majority, children or babies who had surrendered this world far too prematurely. This was one more child her father had seen put to rest and buried.

And yet, it was his job, and when, at some late hour, she had crept downstairs to ask her father why he worked so late into the night, he explained it was figures he was after. Medical statistics. From gathering mortality figures, comparative tables and studies could be made; recommendations and reports put forward to Parliament for the betterment of mankind. ''Tis figures,' he said. ''Tis figures will bring reform.'

'You know, Freddie, Papa was right. Where would we be without statistics? There would be no social surveillance. No proof. People would still be living by their old laissez-faire attitudes, always wanting to put the onus back on God.'

'But, then again,' Freddie said, holding her close, 'figures can also be so darned impersonal. The one thing they cannot measure is love and human suffering.'

～

It had been nearly two years since Margaret's death. Joseph had stopped writing. Henrietta knew it was not her call. However much he might need her help, he would draw short of asking her – a sister who had violated respectability and was living in impropriety – to have any influence over the upbringing of his children. More shame, he would prefer to draw on his young sister-in-law and have her living in the same house than see his sister set foot in town.

Early in 1877, another letter arrived from Emma.

Father is a mere shadow of himself. I fear he is going downhill fast. He cries and gibbers, wheezing like some ghostly machine. Some days he can barely walk. Please Aunty, please come if you possibly can.

'Will you go down, then?' said Freddie.

She looked away evasively, feeling the weight of duty. It disturbed her own private misery, stole from the dull longing for her own children that had never been resolved. She felt in some strange way manipulated by Joseph, crisis upon crisis consuming her life over the years. Had she been living a fool's blindest hope, that Joseph might rise up and give himself a good shaking? She made a pact with herself. She would not allow Joseph to elicit any more pity from her. The decision was not hard to rationalise, since he had shown none to her, ever. She eyed Freddie beneath drooping lids.

'Oh, pet, it would take all my strength. Perhaps best if I don't.'

Outside, the air was humid. The garden hung thick with fragrance, the blossom of a small Mexican tree that Freddie had planted as a house-warming present. Lack of rain had taken its toll on the rest of the garden. Poor Freddie. It distressed him. Everything so dry and scruffy. He had all but given up on his vegetable patch. Beds of agapanthus bowed their blue-and-white china heads, longing for the sound of the water cart. Nearby, the hens nestled in the dusty shade. Barely visible bees droned dizzily around rotting bunches of bird-pecked muscatels. Still as still, the smell of mock orange, and for a second its heaven-sent sweetness came as sickening.

How could things have fallen into such a terrible state of decline? She could bear it all herself, but she could not bear to think of Joseph's poor innocent children suffering by his bedside.

She dashed inside and scrawled a message: *Hold tight, Emma dear. Coming soonest. Aunty.*

It was far too hot in the day for walking, but Henrietta unhooked her straw hat from the hatstand, smoothing the magpie feathers against the brim with a mission.

'Where are you off to?' Freddie puckered his brow.

'If I hurry I will catch the mail.'

In barely a rustle and with ribbons tied in a stiff bow, she set out on the short footslog down the road to the post office.

∽

Thirty miles of water crossed the bay. By the time the ferry had tied up at the Mornington pier, the hot wind had lost its sting. An umbrella was as good as useless; it was sultry. The light dull, diffused, the sun too lazy even to move, let alone chase the shadows.

In hindsight, she thought, *I would have been far better off staying at one of the local hotels, where I could have been alone with my thoughts and come and gone as I pleased.*

Having sent the porter off with her luggage, Emma quickly grabbed her arm. 'If you don't mind, Aunty, I'll take you straight to Father.' Her telltale eyes frantic.

Through cabs and porters, they made their way down Main Street, past shops and hotels, hedges of oleanders and hibiscus and white picket fences, to Joseph's weatherboard house.

The only thing of colour, purple blooms of lantana trailing wild, and as Emma pushed open the wooden gate, the sharp, almost oily scent of sage followed them up the path.

Joseph's four youngsters, whose ages ranged from fourteen to eight, were waiting on the front verandah, half-hidden behind a flaky white-latticed screen. Thin and pale, they emerged and immediately fell upon Emma, their brown spaniel-like eyes melting her down.

Emma gathered them together. 'Remember Aunty? Where are your manners, now? Say, "How do you do?"'

The sight of the kiddies, their nerviness, their urgent whispers, softened her heart. The youngest was on her toes, flapping her hands.

The dark rooms were hot and curiously silent, everything permeated with salt air, sand, and a mix of medicinal smells. Miss Downward, Joseph's sister-in-law, led them to his bedside.

Emma pressed her lips against her father's cheek. 'Please.' She turned to the young woman. 'If you'll excuse us, dear. Mrs Dugdale and I would like to be left alone with Father. Do your best and keep the children outside.'

Joseph's eyes were closed, whiskers more salt than pepper, his skin the colour of camel-hide. Every few seconds, the drunken drone of a blowfly would start up at some unreachable height. With the blind three-quarters drawn, the room lay in semi-darkness. Either side of the open window, swathes of white muslin trembled at the slightest breath, while dark wooden architraves stood solemnly on guard.

A forbidding moroseness seemed to have overtaken all show of civility and common sense. Henrietta felt stiff and awkward, a stranger in her brother's house. She clasped and unclasped her hands, moistened her lips and looked back down at her boots again and again. She resorted to the obvious, the most inane, question she could possibly ask.

'How are you feeling, Joseph?'

He turned his head to one side and, drawing up his knees, clutched at his stomach.

'Where does it hurt, Father? Please, tell us,' whispered Emma.

'Everything hurts,' he groaned, and writhed, setting off a spate of coughing – mucousy froth that sent globs of blood spurting into a towel. When Emma tried to settle her father with spoonfuls of water, he threw off the coverlet in wild unrest and retched violently – dark yellowish stuff that gave off a disgusting faecal odour.

Henrietta began to sweat. 'I think I need some fresh air.' She staggered out to the front garden, finding refuge under a weeping pepper tree. Its pendant foliage a shroud, breaking the light. Shadows shifted about behind the lattice. In the thick stillness came strains of Miss Downward reading to the children from a prayer book. She waited before approaching her.

'How long has he been in this kind of pain?'

'He's had bouts before, Mrs Dugdale, frightful pain and fevers, though never as bad as this. Gallstones, you see, they come and go.'

'Thank you, dear. Now, be so good as to fetch me some ice.'

Later, sponging him down, Henrietta could see how much condition her brother had lost. His once-proud body now nothing but scrawny limbs and a sparrow's chest.

'Here, Father dear, suck on some ice.' What was left Emma made into an ice bag. 'Now try and clutch it to your belly to bring down the swelling.'

Joseph opened his lips and looked up with sunken eyes.

'Hattie? Is that you, Hattie?'

'No, Father, it's me, Emma.'

'Think I'm a goner,' he whispered, and drew up his wasted limbs.

'Oh, Father, dear, no, no, please hang on.'

Moths batted against the glass shield of the lamp, fighting for the light.

The only sustaining sign of life coming from Joseph's body was his teeth chattering and the rhythmic whistle of his moans. Was it the petrifying fever or death that he feared? For Henrietta, there was nothing more bloodcurdling than the clatter of bone against bone.

Emma, sensing the need to say something in her enduring loyalty, took his hand and squeezed it. 'What is it, Father?'

'You're a good girl.' His eyes began to wander, then closed one last time. 'God forgive me all of my sins.'

～

Hattie and Fanny had long forsaken their father. From their absence, their ongoing silence, they had honoured estrangement to the bitter end. As such, they would remain oblivious to the plight of their half-siblings.

But at least Emma could breathe easier, knowing provisions had been made for them to become wards of their Uncle Downward. For the moment, they would continue to be looked after by his youngest sister, their aunt.

As Emma's house guest, Henrietta had stayed on a few extra days following the funeral, drawn as a matter of course into the intimacy of daily family ritual. Observing the natural glow of Emma's children, their innocence eventually got the better of her. Jim, Emma's husband, was a man of gentle ways. He rallied the children and filled the hip bath from a line of steaming kettles. Stripped to their vests, Emma's kiddies hovered around the fire, hugging their arms, ready and waiting their turn. Oh, the sight of them. What a pang it caused, making her yearn for her own three boys. The struggle she used to have, getting the weekly baths done in winter. The water quickly got cold and the tub could only take one at a time.

She turned away, wanting to cry, aching with loneliness. She missed Freddie's love, his music and empathy, the tender red mark on his neck, the fiddler's corn where it grazed. The thought of him home alone, dear love, pacing about an empty house, hands behind his back. How her darling would love a child of his own. She could picture him, sitting in a better world by the fireside, his face radiating love and good humour, a clean contented child of his own on each knee.

Having steadied herself, she helped dry and dress the children after each had been washed. For here was Emma, too, guarding her memories with the task at hand. Black teardrops gathering in her deep-set eyes, her mouth a slim line of resilience. The way she mothered was admirable, making each child feel loved and important, without any fuss. Three girls buttoned-up alike in white flannel nightdresses, all shiny and clean. Children, like all of God's creatures, pick up on things – the transmission of human anxiety, the prevailing mood of a room – but rarely do they dwell in mourning.

'Now take the brush to Aunty, Louie.'

Henrietta drew her, Emma's eldest daughter, aged five, against her knee, lingering over her, petting as one would a favourite.

'What pretty hair, dear. Stand still while Aunty gets rid of the tinkers.'

Louie blinked her blue eyes, allowing her damp milky-white floss to be brushed, then finger-curled into ringlets.

'I wish I had a little girl like you,' said Henrietta as she planted a kiss on her forehead.

Chapter 14

Henrietta stood at the bay window of her drawing room at Telko and tightened her shawl. In her mind, she tried to focus on a final image of Joseph – a white marble headstone resting among the wattles and gums at Mornington Cemetery. Two months had passed. The heat and the dust had gone and the spoils of autumn were already upon them, gradually draining the sky of colour. Here in the cosseted quietness of Camberwell, with its leisurely daubs of whitewash and terracotta brick chimneys domesticating the landscape, the grey-green contours were otherwise in a state of flux. What inevitably drew her restive eye were the elms, oaks and poplars, yellowing, leaf by leaf, against the Gothic steeple of St John's.

She turned to Freddie, who was making pencil notations on some sheets of music. 'I keep telling myself I must write to brother Charles. Let him know of Joseph's passing.'

'Then what is stopping you? You have ample paper, pen and ink.'

'It is the past that stops me. Joseph's past.'

'We all make blunders. Forgive and forget, Mrs Dugdale. Find it in yourself. After all, the man was your brother.'

'Yes, but he was once a bad fellow – a very bad fellow – so much the worse for him. I would do well to forgive him, as well as forget the past. But I can't, because of the things he did.'

Even Papa and his own brothers had written Joseph off. But Freddie knew little about the black sheep of the family, the 'Remittance Man', the ne'er-do-well, the drunken wastrel whom Papa had had shipped out to Australia.

'Have you no atom of heart?'

'Yes, of course, I have a full heart, as well you know. But I can't make believe.'

Freddie threw a log on the fire and brushed his hands.

'Let's get you away from everything, eh?' he said. 'Go up the Yarra and stay a night or two at an inn.'

The following weekend they were in the real countryside: the air fresh and balmy, picnic hamper laden with leek tarts, mock chicken sandwiches, apple cake and bunches of the finest freshly picked table grapes. At the foot of the vineyard, the wide valley spread, fanlike, beyond the encircling hills and rows of gilded vines purpling in the sun. Across the hillocks she could just make out the pickers, some carrying baskets, and down the track a pair of fat horses dragging a loaded wagon to the press-house.

Since mid-morning they had walked and walked, admiring the vintage, yet still she struggled to work up an appetite. Fast looming was her fiftieth birthday. All very well for Freddie, three years the better side of forty. But as far as she was concerned, there would be nothing to celebrate next month.

Henrietta picked perfunctorily at a bunch of grapes. She had awoken before dawn. Outside a death-white mist creeping over the countryside obliterated all signs of civilisation – a frozen snow-like sea caping all but the black spurs and peaks of the distant mountains. When next she opened her eyes, it had vanished. She went to pour water to wash her face, and all she could see was a glum, grey figure looking back in the mirror.

To all appearances, she could live happily. Yet separation still felt like death as life's landmarks came and went. Time had in no way deadened the pain. The dull ache was still there. Its ripples never left entirely. It distorted her memories so that she tended to see the boys rather whimsically – her birdies roughly the same size as when they had been stolen away. Three personalities, as different from each other in every possible way, as she had been from each of her siblings, in her joys and jealousies, her growing quirks.

Her own was a childhood lived through the senses. Things were either sweet or sour, scalding or tepid, dingy or scarlet – no halftones or half-measures. A little girl forever craving fulfilment through what moved her physically and emotionally. Invariably, it came back to excess, the impulse of the moment. Never far away, her mother's voice, a constant damper: 'Too much sauce is neither polite nor healthy, dear. Do show some decorum.'

These days she far preferred to direct her passions to the impulses of the mind. In that way, body and mind could be in balance, united. Good health, she had come to believe, meant good diet and good manners, self-control and discipline.

She had tried most of all to be a good mother. Manners were not, as many people thought, inherited; they were learned from example. But the moderation of behaviour was quite another thing, and she would find herself banking on things her mother used to say. Little boys had to be taught how to be civilised: to eat one mouthful of vegetables to every one of meat, to chew slowly and put their knives and forks down in between. 'Let the food be taken to the mouth, dear, not the mouth to the food.'

The drifting aroma of roast meat coming from the kitchen of the inn that morning had wrought far-off memories of family rituals. Shining flatware on damask. The sound of knife sharpening against steel. Joseph standing up, waving the horn-handled carvers above the joint. 'Would you like me to do the honours?' Papa beaming. 'Go ahead, darling boy,' and Joseph looking so mightily pleased with himself.

Mutton gone grey and stringy, slices slipped surreptitiously under her chair for Toska, her tan and white terrier, who gobbled them up.

The English ate flesh with impunity, made a real show of it; vegetables were merely an afterthought, even then usually overcooked or maltreated in some perfunctory way. Other cultures managed to show due respect by making special some simple food-source from the ground.

Since leaving Queenscliff, she had given up meat entirely. The very thought of dead flesh, of tooth and claw, reminded her of William. The smell of a butcher shop or the sight of an abattoir with blood running down a drain brought back distressing memories of unwanted steers gone to the knife. William and his meat. William madly waving his arms, *hoy hoy hoying* the cattle. Typical that a man of bravado would pay a poor man to slaughter, yet boast all the trademarks of cruelty and aggression.

Life at Telko was simple. Entertaining kept to a minimum. She made no attempt at meat-mimicry for the sake of guests, being far more high-minded. Vegetarianism was enough, even for men. She looked down at Freddie, a picture of health, lying with his hands clasped loosely behind his head, his handsome face glowing in the autumnal sun. You wouldn't find a fitter, stronger man for one of his size. But he didn't parade it. Whatever else her darling consumed in clubs and cafés, she would rather not know. The fare on her table was plain. It satisfied the stomach but did not indulge it. Fillet of fish with some braised fennel was about as fancy as it got. Mulligatawny soup, her old favourite, pulses, milk, cheese, custards and curd were always good standbys. For milk and milk products, she had long known, had a calming effect both on the stomach and on the mind. To eat flesh, she believed, was to loosen one's morals. As for alcohol, there was none. A drop of sherry in a trifle or plum pudding goes a very long way. When dining out, she would push aside a perfectly clean crystal wine goblet with repugnance. 'Take it away, please. I shan't be needing that.'

Freddie, as always, was ravenous. He leaned over and rubbed her shoulder, and took a sip of his juleps. 'Still in the dumps, eh? If there was one thing you could change in this world, right now, my love, what would it be?'

'Male ignorance,' she said, her face still, her plate untouched. 'Imagine, Freddie, what men and women of the future will think. They'll look back in wonder at these curious people believing what the myth-men tell them: that the Bible and the Koran are the actual words of their God. Too bad about the interests of women and children.' She sought Freddie's hand and, smiling bleakly, gave it a squeeze. 'For more than two thousand years, men have knowingly been unjust to women.' Her eyes lit up with gratitude. 'It's only within the last half century that a few men, the likes of you, loyal heart, have become noble enough to recognise her rights. That in itself leaves room for hope.'

'And you, my dear, are in the vanguard.'

He reminded her of all that she had achieved since leaving Queenscliff, quietly but persistently agitating for women's rights. There was the ongoing debate with Mr Willoughby, editor of the *Daily Telegraph*. That and the lectures she had given for members and friends of the Eclectic Society had, for some years, been attracting considerable attention. 'Don't forget, you are a torchbearer.'

Women's rights always set her thinking about evolution and the evolution of human thought. If one looked upon it as having been, well, retarded, could the evolution of thought conversely be hastened in catch up?

'No change is abrupt.' Freddie gave a light-hearted shrug and munched on a Scotch egg, catching at falling crumbs and yolk. 'But at least minds are slowly changing.'

'In my head, you know, I see it, this ladder of life.'

Freddie propped himself up on his elbow and swallowed. 'A timeline, you mean?'

'Yes,' she said.

'Mr Darwin might beg to differ,' he said, before taking a final swig from his beaker.

She gave Freddie a wry smile. 'Either way, avoiding thought is just a habit, the worst of habits.' The effect of ignorance seemed to her balefully lasting. Men had allowed themselves to be ruled by habit, which in turn saved idle and lethargic people the trouble of acting for themselves. One could not be changed without the other. Even she could see that. While women appeared to be at a higher moral stage of evolution, they were just as much bound by custom as men. They must learn to think or sink. Therein was the rub.

'I see what you mean.' Freddie wiped his mouth on his napkin, stood up and stretched like a well-fed lion. 'Why don't you wait till we're home and you can write all of it down.'

When she and Freddie arrived back from their weekend away, it was waiting at the post office – a large package from New Zealand stencilled all over with the word 'fragile'.

'Hello, what have we here?' Freddie stood over her, peering into the wrappings.

'Oh, how ingenious.' She set the broadly bound case upon the table and opened the lid. 'A photograph album musical box.'

'How does it work?'

'Ah, I see. Look,' she said, 'the latch sets it off.'

The latest thing. Bound in tooled heavy leather, it must have cost the boys a small fortune, even with the three of them chipping in together. Inside were cream cardboard pages printed in gold with floral borders – a gallery of photographs of her own three sons, facsimiles granted. But it was somewhat disconcerting to see her dearest ones staring back at her, so still and silent. They had always been such lively boys. Now, not so much as a sparkle appeared to be radiating from their hearts. She hardly recognised her baby, Austin. At sixteen, he was leaner, lighter-framed, than the other two, and dark, very much a young man with the makings of a beard.

Several times a day, she went to the chiffonier to take a peek at her gift. Her darlings. Beautiful though their pictures were, she wished that she had something still more dear and lifelike to hold and look at than those stony likenesses. But it was their caring love that counted, and the music. The tune of 'On the Beautiful Blue Danube' – with the childish innocence of its bell-like chink – affected her so deeply, she thought her ears would bleed.

Carl had written:

A miserable week, Mama, blowing hard with a great deal of rain leaving everything saturated. To top it off, the nasty shock of waking up in the middle of the night to an earthquake – imagine a sharp jerking and plates and dishes rattling loudly. We all ran outside by the light of the moon to see water spilling over the top of the tank. The three of us still holding the fort for Pa. Can't wait to get back to Waitara.

Henrietta understood from Carl that William, having sailed for England the previous year with his young mistress in tow, was due back in New Zealand, but he made no mention of their little boy born out of wedlock. Carl was set on making himself a living. With all the project work going on in Waitara, the Harbour Board would be more than ready to take on smart, healthy young fellows like him and Austin.

Einnim was unsure of his plans. Dairying had its drawbacks, he wrote. Powdery ash from the volcano had been known to spoil the milk. Strange, since that was how she pictured it, the boiling white lava erupting out of a mountain like the bubbling, scalding froth of milk, to set cold as white marble.

Carl sent her some of his paintings. The New Zealand landscape was such a contrast to Australia.

Watercolours don't quite do it justice, the curtain of voluminous mist that sometimes surrounds Mount Taranaki, or Mount Egmont, as they now call it. But as much as I try I can never quite manage to convey the mystery and sublimity of the mountain.

It's not called a mighty beacon for nothing. Rising abruptly out of the plain, its snow-capped summit can be seen for a hundred miles over the Pacific. There are some wonderful legends too. The natives look upon it as sacred. They have a superstitious dread of approaching it and believe it to be the abode of Ngarara, a huge reptilian monster ... there are so many wonders to see. One day, Mama, I hope you will come and pay us a visit.

Henrietta felt her heart contract, then skip a beat. New Zealand, so near, yet so far-off and exotic. Forever searching through articles and journals, she was fast becoming an amateur expert in geology and geophysics. Australia was actually an old land, she had discovered, New Zealand relatively new. Carl was always happy to furnish her with sketches and detailed local descriptions. Volcanic rock, he said, could be found as far as a few miles north of Waitara. Clay marls had risen to form a broken range of hills, and abundant fossils could be found on the coast at the base of the White Cliffs. Now she could picture her boys: Carl, of a weekend, riding out with his brothers in the buggy to spend many an hour rummaging on the beach. Oh, how she wished she could fly over the ocean to join them.

Wintertime she invariably pictured them waking up to snow and gales. Then, in July, when she was outside one day picking the last of her jonquils, a letter arrived from Einnim. A tender ache swept through her. He felt it his duty, as her eldest child, to let her know that Mary Jane Pacey, his father's de facto, had died at Huirangi. Henrietta gripped the page.

A sad affair ... tragic her being so young ... and Cara, our half-brother, poor little devil, only two and half years old, running around not knowing what to do with himself.

The news otherwise sparked her out of her reverie. Henrietta picked up her pen, dipped the metal nib in ink and watched the blue liquid drip back slowly into the inkwell. She must thank Einnim, commend him for his show of common decency.

No, it was not exactly schadenfreude that she was feeling. That a young innocent boy should be left motherless was indeed a terrible fate, and she genuinely felt for the child, but the thought that William, that cold, callous monster of a man, might be suffering remained a private one that only gave rise to strength.

～

Emma had written to say she was again with child and would Aunty care to pay her a visit. Bolstered by the first bright forecast, Henrietta arrived in Mornington, keen to make an excursion to nearby Fossil Beach. From all accounts it was a treasure trove – one of the best examples of fossilisation beds in Port Phillip Bay – and she was eager to compare notes with Carl.

The next morning, Jim drove Henrietta, Emma and the children out in the dray. It was not hard to spot the big clay kiln for it towered like an orange cone from the cliffside. Below, the secluded beach where Emma, in her delicate state, could picnic out of public gaze.

'Be back by three, mind.' Emma waved Jim off.

Picnic baskets deposited in the cool of the stone ruins, they made their way down the path to the cove. Spiky seed-balls cartwheeled across the shore from the silvery green spinifex. Oh, to feel it again, the beneficent power of the beach. The way it soothed and purified. The calm surface of the water stretched out pale turquoise to Tyrian purple, and the sand enfolded its warmth on her toes.

The little girls tucked their skirts into their drawers and tiptoed tentatively hand-in-hand, their white legs marbling in the flush of midday sun. They looked so free and healthy as they paddled in the rock pools, painting the wash with colour, with the soft, silent drift of the clouds above keeping a distant guard.

Even children this young could see how the clays that formed this protected little beach were filled richly with shells of all shapes and sizes. Every so often, one or another of the children would stoop to pick up a piece of driftwood, a bottle, a washed-up cork or whalebone. A paradise where little ones and big ones could fossick to their hearts' content.

'What better education,' Henrietta remarked to Emma. Empirical evidence at one's fingertips, combined with the art of practical explanation, provided a free and seamless introduction to the theory of evolution.

Young Willie let out a whoop as he held up a shark's tooth. Louie, not to be outdone, ran up beside him. 'Look, Will, a conch shell.'

Holding bunches of white-gold windswept hair, the little girl pressed the shell against her ear, then gave it to her mother before running off after her brother.

'In India, you know, a conch shell is considered sacred,' said Henrietta. 'Holy men blow in them in a calling to prayer. Its shape resembles an ear.'

'The fishermen say you can talk into them, too,' replied Emma. 'Bring back the dead. Heathen talk, I call it, but there are times when I think I can hear the dead.'

'Your father's spirit, dear?'

Emma shook her head. She described how visitations of her baby sister, Annie, returned from time to time, through no rhyme or reason. The black-veiled brim of Emma's bonnet gave a flutter, flashes of sunlight bringing out the freckles on her wrinkled nose. 'Jim tells me not to be silly. When you're gone you're gone, that's what he believes. But I'm not so sure, Aunty.'

Emma held her back for a minute, easing herself down on a rock. She wore that thin, pinched look, her pallor striking against the dark cobalt of her smocked tunic.

Conversation turned to the old days before steamers. The hardships endured. As it happened, Emma could remember little of the journey out in the year of 1849. Only the foul stench from below, she said, and the relief brought by the smell of eucalypts as the *Abberton* made a tilt for the land.

And the thirst, with no fresh water sometimes for days, and then, when the rains eventually fell, the taste of tar tainting every drop that was salvaged. 'By the time we disembarked in Melbourne, baby Annie was weak and struggling to eat. Hattie tried her utmost, we all did – that I can vouch for. Dipping pieces of bread in milk, plying open her mouth, pleading with her, to no avail. Sniffs and sniffles; everything cold and dank. Fanny sucking, between whimpers, always sucking away on that old rag doll. Makes me feel sick, the thought of that soggy thing and the sound of her sucking on her own dried spit. I remember the odd potato rotting in a crate, but rarely anything to eat.' Emma paused, her eyes searching seawards.

'One day, Father brought home an orange, at great expense, thinking Annie might fancy a quarter-piece, that it might give the poor mite a much-needed boost. I don't think I'd ever seen an orange before, Aunty, let alone tasted one.'

The solemn expression had melted, and a look of something childlike came into Emma's face. Even now, in the wash of time, that event remained vivid to her senses.

'The way he curled away the peel, carefully segmenting the fruit for us all to share. At the time, there seemed a special art to it, an act of great deliberation, as he picked meticulously at strands of pith, being the finicky man he was, to then offer a piece to us each in turn, so generous, like Father were trying to offset his sins. Oh, Aunty, the tang of that first rush of juice has stayed with me this long, and those tiny globes like pent-up tears inside.'

'Does your baby sister still rest heavily in your mind, dear?'

'Oh, sweet pet she was, a favourite in the orphanage. Being the sickly one, Annie got to sit on Matron's knee.'

'Orphanage, you say?'

'Oh yes, Aunty. Did Father not tell you?'

It was as if something had suddenly lodged in her chest. 'Pray, do go on, dear.'

'Well, you see, it was not long after we landed in Melbourne. Father was, as they say, "certified", taken away and committed. In dire straits, we were, us four kiddies, scared stiff, near starving down in Flinders Lane. When Father came for us eighteen months later on his way to the goldfields, he only took three of us, Hattie, Fanny and me. 'Twas the last we saw of little Annie.'

Henrietta opened her arms to Emma, stifling pain as she held her. 'How extraordinary,' she said calmly, for in some ways, she was not really surprised. 'I shall make some enquiries upon my return.'

∿

Once back in the everyday hub of Emma's home, Henrietta was instantly swept into the present. With five little kiddies keeping her amused and busy, she felt a growing sense of attachment and responsibility. She wished Freddie could join her in Mornington. But, unendorsed, her mate had yet to be invited to Emma's house. More's the pity. Freddie had a knack of being able to quickly form friends with young people, the young rarely being judgemental. He was always happy to bestow his affection on the offspring of others.

But with Emma's children, he was missing out. Young Willie, her eldest, now nine, was a natural performer and not afraid of fanfare. The cornet he blew as freely and easily as he could sing. There was maturity, a mellow purity, to his playing. For one so young, he extracted a lovely buttery tone. Not a strident note escaped.

Shepherding Louie and her two little sisters into the drawing room, Henrietta sat them on the sofa beside her, with toddler, James, quietly on her knee.

'Bravo, Willie, bravo!' Henrietta's eyes lit up as she clapped with gusto.

Willie was practising a tortuous little phrase, his sunburnt cheeks popping, his mischievous blue eyes rolling to check if she was listening.

Jim waved an arm at him. 'Take it outside on the woodheap, son, there's a good boy, and not too loud, otherwise you'll break a blood vessel.'

Wriggling out of her grasp, the children scampered off after Willie.

'Where do they get all that energy?' said Henrietta, joining Emma in the kitchen.

'Oh, they'll be getting tired and tetchy and hungry soon enough. Worst time of the day.'

So it was, with the growing smell of tripe and onions beginning to overrun the house. Emma, rushing around amid the rumpus, lit the lamps, her eyes like a pair of acorns tucked beneath her brow. 'Best you leave us to it for a while, Aunty,' she said, throwing rashers of bacon in a frypan.

'Why don't you sneak down to the point while you can, Mrs Dugdale, and watch the sunset,' said Jim.

Taking up Jim's suggestion, Henrietta left the house, with her hat and cape. Head bowed, and at last alone with her thoughts, she walked briskly in and out of the shop verandah posts in the twilight, Annie's fate haunting her with awkward questions. *Might I have taken the little one? Might I have taken all four?* But it was no good berating herself. There had been neither hide nor hair of Joseph or the children when she had arrived in the colony, and, anyway, had she known, what could she have done, freshly a widow, herself in desperate need of asylum? Irrespective of their state – or her brother's – it would have come back to the same law. No woman had any claim over a natural father's.

In spite of her sorrow, she could hear it beckoning, the minor sound of the sea she craved. The quay was bereft of people as she climbed the rocks to the point. There was something deeply poignant about being part of the land, yet part of the sea, waiting, watching time drift in its cycle. To sit here, listening to the soft monotonous plash, the creak and sway of the fishing boats and the restless tide beating the rocks below. Mothers' Beach, over there, still bathing in the last warm tones of solitude, and the long, dark finger of the promontory showing the way to the Heads. Then to look back and see the cliff so deeply green above the orange scar of overhang, and not so very far away the faint shell of a moon. In that single blinding instant, the sun struck the scarp. It glowed like a furnace, its molten colours startling, fevered, intensifying the outline of the bay.

Part 3

1878 – 1890

Chapter 15

⌒

On a winter night in 1879, Henrietta stood looking out of the window of her living room at Camberwell. It was past sunset, and in the cool of evening she began to shiver with the beginnings of a bold idea. She had stood by long enough, thinking, reading, writing, discussing Owenism, socialism, Darwinism, debating abstractions until the small hours of the morn. Through all this, the strand of enlightenment had always held strong. Her unshakeable belief that reason would be her guiding light.

Finally, Henrietta drew the blinds and lit the lamps. Lost in her fight for progress was her old sparring partner, Mr Howard Willoughby from the *Daily Telegraph*, now chief of staff and leader writer for the *Argus*. Lost with him, her numerous pen-names. A latent desire to write in her own right had outgrown her desire to read. Novels rarely slaked her thirst for knowledge and the search for truth; they were often disappointingly pale and wishy-washy. There were so few Australian women writers, apart from Catherine Spence, and, like Spence, she invariably found herself looking towards America for something fresh and sincere. Obviously, Australian society was not quite prepared for it. 'It' being 'the woman question', a question that had been plaguing her for as long as she could remember. Men, with more rights to education, had had every advantage over women in telling their story. With pens in their hands and printing presses at their disposal, the stories had been theirs to tell. She thought, without malice, of her brother, John, a published poet, now a priest in Canada. Well, the hour cometh. She must tell her story, in her own voice and name, and of her own free will, expressing herself from the depths of her soul.

Having spent the last thirty minutes reflecting, Henrietta reached for her large marble-covered journal marked 'Thoughts', to christen a fresh blank page.

I write not for myself. Man's tyrannical laws are powerless to wound me more. My suffering has been borne. No alteration of laws could now benefit me; but there are thousands enduring the pain I have experienced through man's injustice, and thousands to follow, until there be just legislation. For those — for the progress of all humankind — I strive, and will continue to do so while power be left me to speak or hold my pen.

'Soon you'll be typing faster than you can write,' Freddie said, chuckling.

Two years on and the power to write was just as strong, but in a different mode. Her darling had bought for her one of those new American writing contraptions. A bulky, ugly-looking thing, made to look pretty by floral ornamentation, it sat before her on a kind of wooden sewing stand with elegant turned legs. But once she got the hang of it, her fingers fell as naturally on the keyboard as on the ivories of any piano she had ever played, and quickly found their way.

'It's legible, less messy than writing.'

'True, but your own fair hand is round and generous, my sweet, and gloriously free. None of those horrid spider-legs to frighten a man.'

The machine was otherwise a cross between a piano and a clock. The rhythmic click never interfered with her flow of thought. Rather, it acted as a positive spur, urging her on. She knew she had control of every strike.

Beside her, a reference journal overflowing with hastily scribbled quotes, and an amassment of cuttings from magazines and newspapers, with passages heavily underscored in pencil. Her study otherwise displayed notable orderliness. Her physical comforts in writing remained spartan. No letters or papers lay around unsorted or in temporary confusion. Not even a nearby workbox to cause her guilt.

Time was her only adversary in writing. Time could well be a 'he', not an 'it', as the Mad Hatter maintained. Either way, she felt continually troubled by time, the uneasy feeling it was slipping away. If only she could conquer time, arrange it to suit.

The March of Progress went hand-in-hand with the march of the imagination. Once in hand, time, she understood, could free a writer as much as any writer could free time – and her thoughts drifted from Plato to Eliot and Verne. Well, dream she would, invent her own afterlife, a dream she could make real by challenging what existed. She would have to hurry. The wildest dreams and air castles of the past were being realised and surpassed with astonishing speed. Scarcely a day went by when there was not some new invention and patent lodged. And soon Melbourne would be hosting the longed-for International Exhibition of 1880.

Within the first week of the International Exhibition, Henrietta and Freddie had already done the rounds of Exhibition Hall numerous times. Equipped with notebook and pencil, she pretty well knew her way around every gallery by now. Freddie, having proudly played with the fiddles in the big Australian Band for the opening concert, had nigh exhausted himself. What an honour – it made Henrietta swell – for only the best in the land could audition. But nothing would have thrilled her more as a mother than to have been able to accompany her own dear children, exchanging commentary, as they promenaded the galleries of this hallowed hall of learning.

Sadly, that was not to be. Waitara, according to Carl, was humming with plenty of work around the waterside. William, dairyman turned publican, had recently been made a member of the Waitara Harbour Board, his sights set on becoming pilot master. So long as he wasn't putting her boys to work in the Inglewood Hotel, she had no objection. So long as their work was honest, her sons need not ride on the tails of the Dugdale name.

She would have much to report to them in their absence. Since the crowds would be less between the 'Cup' and Christmas, she suggested to Emma that she and Jim might like to join her for the day at Carlton Gardens to visit the great exposition.

'Oh, it really is like a palace!' said Emma, as they stepped into the main entrance.

They hovered around the transept. Emma held tight the ribbons of her cap-like bonnet, looking up into the soaring blue dome. 'Almost like being in heaven!'

And to think it had all been nightsoil once. Henrietta rolled her eyes.

The Fine Arts galleries were the chief attractions and, since there were plenty of chairs, they could take their time. Having directed them to the great artworks, she stood contemplating a series of Turner seascapes.

'Darned if I can see how a fellow could do it – make it so lifelike,' said Jim at last.

'Well,' she explained, 'the painter is believed to have asked a sailor to lash him against a mast so he could record it – a storm at sea.'

Emma remained, head to one side. 'I see nothing but soapsuds and whitewash.' She said she saw more beauty from her own back door, blessed with a sunset as well.

Jim had come with a mission. It was the steam engines and new inventions in machinery he wanted to see first. As a young man, he had been studying engineering up until the gold rush struck. Many an hour he had spent at the Mechanics' Institute, keeping himself informed. Jim was no ordinary blacksmith. He was an artisan, forever scribbling down bright ideas, designing newfangled coaches, steam tractors, spring tooth harrows and other farm tools and equipment.

But Emma was urging Jim to set up a foundry in fancy decorative iron lace; it was all the rage in Melbourne.

'World's all going the way of steel,' said Jim. 'No going back.'

'Rather like the human mind.' Henrietta's eyes came to rest on Emma. 'Warm it to a concept and one's whole perspective on life can open up to all kinds of possibilities.'

'It excites me, Mrs Dugdale. If a man only had the time and money,' Jim said, 'there'd be no end to what he could do.'

They strolled out on to the balcony, admiring the view of the city and the well laid-out gardens. Emma, in an olive-tinted robe, pressed against the balustrade. Her cheeks pink, auburn hair frizzled around her bonnet. 'Feel like a birdie up here, Jim.'

'Indeed. Won't be long. Mr Edison says that the flying machine is the next big thing in science. Apparently, he's been making a few tests with a machine worked by electricity. Too amazing to even contemplate.'

'What young Willie will say when we get home. Eyes out on stalks at the stories we'll have to tell.'

After a late luncheon, they walked downstairs and, joining the promenaders, said their goodbyes. With her inner need to educate sated for the day, Henrietta remained, basking on a garden bench. The People's Palace in Carlton Gardens bore little resemblance to the famous Crystal Palace – the Great Exhibition of thirty years ago in London's Hyde Park. She had seen it at dusk from atop an omnibus, like something out of *The Arabian Nights* – a palace of glass glittering above the trees.

The displays and curiosities she remembered as splendid and varied. Monstrous works of art finished in gold, bronze and silver, some studded with gems; samples of exotic foods and produce; and a diversity of magnificent inventions. Her young eyes were agog. But for all the extravaganza, what lingered were simple impressions – among these, the rhythmic ticking sounds of a telegraph machine, the two young men demonstrating how speedily coded impulses could transmit communications across the world. Now the telegraph was the norm.

Yet another memory was the curious sight of young women strolling around the Crystal Palace in trousers tied in at the ankles, and with short stuck-out skirts like ballet dancers. 'The Bloomers', as they called them, were a singular exhibition in themselves. There, for the world to see, were women with real legs, gracing the floors in soft grey boots. They had later taken to the streets of London with passion, and she would have run off and joined them had she dared.

Here, the tall, stately stone hall and the courtyards of the gardens, with their radiating gravel walkways, had all but emptied, while inside, gallery after gallery was bursting with the future. And yet, thought Henrietta, for all the promises and advancements in the world, it sometimes felt like human rights had barely moved. What had happened to all those freethinking Bloomer ladies? The crinolines of yesteryear had been replaced by the hobble skirts of today. Close-fitting cloth with ties hidden behind the knees still hampered woman's movement. One had only to watch how slow they were, their mincing little steps. All the pleasure in healthy walking gone; the fatigue of battling every few paces. What hope had these women of travelling, let alone travelling in time?

By now, the sun had virtually fallen behind the city. Blocks of shadow were cast over the lanes and thoroughfares. As darkness gathered in its last dying shapes, the soft yellow glimmer of gaslights beckoned like barley sugars.

Henrietta rose stiffly. Dampness from the ornamental lake, or was it the first few drops of dew? Smoothing the folds of her skirt, she stretched her legs discreetly. Waddling ducks scurried out of her way towards the lily pads as she gathered her pace. She and Freddie were due to meet up at the Masonic Hall with fellow members of the Eclectic Society, and there was no-one more punctual than Freddie, her old pet.

As the cab clattered on its way down the hill, she took one last look at the Carlton Gardens. The great rococo building was lit up from top to bottom like a wedding cake. Silver frosting, ganache in between. Behind, streaks of leftover light playing havoc in the sky. Through the big glass dome, she could see the clouds moving, the swift drift of silver leaving the face of the moon.

She would have to make it quite plain at the meeting. She was a sceptic, not a psychic. Carrie Lynch's efforts to mesmerise her into the occult over the years had been to no avail. To her mind, the spirit rapping, the clever jugglery, all those pamphlets and paraphernalia being foisted upon them by the spirit circles only clouded the real issues of social concern. It surprised her that other members – Henry Turner and that precocious young lawyer, Alfred Deakin, lovely chap though he was – still remained caught up in it, while she had grown old and wary. This current craze had gone too far, she felt, and would only distract and undermine her seriousness of purpose.

And yet, as Freddie had reminded her, they were, after all, an eclectic bunch, and one was entitled to be a psychic – air one's views and test phenomena. In this day and age, one never knew what new piece of intelligence would prove its predecessor wrong.

∽

Again and again over the summer months, she returned to the galleries, each time finding them even more scintillating than before. By evening, she would be back in her well-lit study, her mind charged with new ideas and new understandings, and an energy that was nothing short of electric.

Her story was becoming clearer. That great hall of education in Carlton would be a physical and symbolic structure, the entry point from which to tell her story. Words began to flow without hesitation or a nervous glance of fear. The past, like a springboard, releasing itself in the future projection of some far-off age. It was only natural she should want to situate herself in this story.

I stand in the doorway of an immense building, which appears to be devoted to the display of antiquities. Many people are entering, although the morning is young. A magnificent scene is before me.

At last I see a city in which are combined grandeur, cleanliness, order and picturesque loveliness. Between this one and those of the nineteenth century exists a difference as great, if not greater, than between the latter and the loathsome lairs of our cannibal progenitors reeking with refuse of human remains. My mind power has so widened that I know more than can be here told …

The doors of the exhibition had opened her head, her heart, the very key to her imagination. The daily writing, the nightly talking, week after week, month after month. Nothing, she said, would induce her to write drivel for dishonest money or fawn like some writers or take the middle ground. By using her own name, not a pseudonym, by refusing to shield herself from ridicule, she knew she would be putting herself on the line.

One night she noticed Freddie giving her the occasional dubious glance as he sat humming to himself on the sofa by her desk. At last he spoke.

'So, what's it all about?'

'Well, it's a place called "Alethia" in a far-off age. A vantage point from which to look back at the evils of our day.'

'Go on, then, tell me. How do you create a future in this phantasmagoria?' His eyes appeared to mock. 'Without being dubbed a silly soothsayer.'

'It is not hard to envisage how I'd like the world to be. A world that is true and just, where reason rules instead of cruelty and violence.'

'Ah, but how do you create a sense of verisimilitude? Reality and truth are not always the same thing, as well we know.'

'It will be more than obvious it's a utopia.' She told him how reality lay in the past and the evidence left behind, archaeological and scientific relics displayed in an enormous museum – not unlike the International Exhibition – where the young, instructed by their mothers or their aunts, could pass through the ages and learn of humankind's progress by means of analytical comparison and evolutionary example. 'Faithful and accurate observation of science,' she said, 'being the foundation of realism.'

'Of course, people will think it is autobiographical. That it's you. A *roman à clef.*'

'Yes, well, in a sense it is. The "I" being the narrator, you see. I interrupt to comment, shedding light on the past, but mostly I remain carefully in the background, the quiet all-seeing observer, gliding in and out of the galleries, following a perfect mother as she lectures or remarks on observations made through the intelligent eyes of her children.'

'There is a Carl in it, you say?'

'Yes.' She explained how he symbolised the young generation around them, to whom the idea of evolution had been the intellectual milk on which they were nourished.

'And what about this Frederick, eh? Where does he fit in to the scheme of things?'

'Oh, angel!' Her eyebrows gave way. 'Do you mind if I borrow your name? It's so very dear to me.'

Freddie shrugged. 'Then, do as you must,' he said, with a gentle touch on her shoulder.

The quiet smile on her face faded as she fell into silence, contemplating again the course of the mighty past into the aching hearts of her own century – 'The Christian Era', or the 'Age of Blood', she thought she would call it. How could she describe the momentousness of what she was trying to create? That it was no different from any other grand invention showing at the exhibition that would have seemed preposterous at some earlier point in time.

From her study, she could hear Freddie on his violin, practising the little motif he'd been humming, over and over, faster and faster, fingers skittering over the fingerboard. She wondered if she had piqued him. But there it was, what was done was done.

Chapter 16

Once started, Henrietta could not stop. She clicked and clacked on her new machine, drawing breath with every pause and punctuation mark.

It all came back to dogma, and on no account would she write delicately about dogma. It was Mother Eve who had caused the first trouble. In such a way, men had framed religion with doctrines for continuing the humiliation of women, blaming them for all their manly sins. Women were slaves in all but the name.

In administering the sacred oaths, clergymen had knowingly assisted in the perpetration of a crime. The husband – so the man was named, meaning master – vowed to the Infinite that he would endow his wife – old name for slave – with all his 'worldly goods' and that he would 'cherish' and 'love' her. Except in rare cases, not only did the endowment end in nothing but he annexed everything valuable that belonged to her, under the miserable pretext similar to others men used in all their acts of unjust dealing with women – that woman's brain was inadequate for the care of her own property. With the same foolish logic, they asserted that her strength was insufficient for the various light situations monopolised by man, including those of learned professions. So she generally performed the menial work, which was heavy, so heavy she frequently died from the effects, lamed, hands distorted, in her heroic efforts to fulfil duties imposed upon her by the ape cunning of men. The husband frequently proved his superior intellect by the rapidity with which he squandered his wife's property and reduced her to hardships she never would have known had his sense or conscientiousness equalled hers. As to loving and cherishing – alas!

In the late summer of 1882, it was too hot to do anything, let alone write or type. Exhausted, she lay outside in the shade on the cane day bed, enjoying the sweet pungency of gumleaves and freshly cut grass. The Christmas present she had given Freddie – a spiral-bladed lawnmower from the exhibition – added a distinctive new sound to their weekends. Not that he had ever complained. Bending down, scything the grass, he believed, brought him closer to nature. If the great Tolstoy could do it, so could he.

Stockings and boots abandoned, she lay in a state of *déshabillé*, dangling her white feet over the side, waiting for the breeze to find its way up to Camberwell. A black and tan lacquered tray laden with a crumpled cloth and leftover tea things lay on the wicker table beside her.

Looking out on the close-cropped lawn had a soothing effect, smooth swards extending past the agapanthus, up to the potting shed and the tall, shady lemon-scented gums beyond.

'Perhaps I should try my hand with the lawnmower,' she said.

Freddie, who was sitting on the other side of the table, set his napkin down on his plate and flicked away the flies.

'Why would you choose to do tedious men's work? All that pushing and pulling?'

'No more tedious than washing bed linen, and far less like heavy work, and yet you let me do that.'

He threw up his hands. 'Send it out. By all means, send it out. I keep telling you but you will not listen. Have six girls in, if you like.'

'No, I'm not listening. I'm thinking about all the unnecessary yards of fabric women have had to wash over the years. How it could be minimised very simply and easily.'

Lady Harberton had for some years been trumpeting her new Rational Dress Society in London. There were other rebels abroad. The American abolitionist and Civil War surgeon Dr Mary Walker, with her standard dress of long tunic, waistcoat, watch chain and dark pantalettes, who had long ago earned herself a Congressional Medal of Honour.

'And these are our models, Freddie. They are not afraid.'

Though Henrietta would shy from being a surgeon on a battlefield, she was passionate about the abolition of slavery. It was a convoluted family connection, a distant and dubious one, according to Papa, but it sickened her that the Worrells of Barbados and Prince Edward Island had made their fortunes out of slaves. And to think that one of her brothers might have profited from that past connection.

As for Dr Walker, her ethics were unquestionable, her all-round useful advice relevant the world over, the height of advancement. Female dress, its bearings on health and the management of children, should be the concerns of all women. And now, fancy, Dr Walker was standing as a candidate for the United States Senate.

Henrietta's bosom rose amid the trickle of perspiration. She loosened her kimono. The gorgeous simplicity of Japanese silk – blue wisteria, ibis, cloud and a sprinkling of soft orange. Exotic, erotic, even democratic, since in Japan both men and women wore kimonos – though Japanese society was not entirely democratic.

She unhooked the fold of her sleeve, which had caught on a shred of cane, and reached for her fan. As it waved to and fro with vigour, her thoughts were drawn again to the immediacy of dress reform. Even in a kimono, one could never stand before an open fire. How many women must yearly be sacrificed, suffer the appalling agony of their clothes catching alight near open-flamed candles or fireplaces, burned to death through conforming to a senseless custom? For two years now, she had been collating news cuttings – sickening accounts daily. Fifty-one martyrs, from young girls to old women, cremated alive as a result of being compelled to wear dangerous clothing. That was in Australia alone.

'What we need, Freddie, are rational clothes.' She threw aside her fan and sat herself upright. 'When all's said and done, it could simply be a modification of the ones our mamas used to wear when they were young.'

Not a day went past when she did not encounter dearest Mama in in some form or other: her various mementos and objets d'art. *Mama, look at me*, she wanted to say as she passed the portrait of that familiar young woman wearing a 'Josephine dress'. But Mama, of course, was framed forever, face turned away in profile, one eye looking along the whitewashed wall, back to another time.

⌒

Henrietta's prevailing interest in the chains of women's dress made her alert to new developments from overseas.

'Listen to this, Fred,' she exclaimed one morning over breakfast, finger jabbing a page of the *Australasian*. It was one of a number of reports of an exhibition of rational and hygienic dress in London, showcasing how gracefully dress could follow the natural movements of the body uncorseted. Excellent articles she had read, one illustrated by the *Australasian*, an engraving of the 'Greek dress', otherwise known as a 'perfectly plain Princess dress' – a compromise between the Athenian lady twenty centuries ago and that of modern London or Paris.

Freddie peered over her shoulder, as he shook himself into his heavy winter coat.

'I see,' he said. 'Reinventing the past.'

After waving him off to work, Henrietta sat down at her desk and composed a letter to the newspaper's women's columnist:

RATIONAL DRESS

To 'Humming Bee' – Dear Madam, Enclosed are envelope and stamps for pattern of divided skirt, according to your directions. Kindly also let me know Lady Harberton's address. Being myself the rara avis, a woman not having worn stays, or the remotest semblance thereof,

*since irresponsible girlhood (40 years since) I think that lady would
like to know some particulars from me. Ever since my thoughts began
approaching cohesion and direction, the improvement of women's
position in the world has occupied them deeply and tenderly, not, as
some men pretend to believe, from paltry jealousy of or wish to wrench
from them the very many advantages they have so cleverly usurped
to themselves; but simply and purely as an influence on the growth
of higher nature in the whole of mankind. Remote as the apparently
trivial matter of stays-wearing appears in connection with so important
an attainment, 45 years of reflection have taught me that the two are
closely connected. Any one who has considered the subject impartially
will acknowledge that no great number of noble men can appear in
the world without noble women to give them birth; and it is equally
certain no woman can become noble who fritters away her beautiful
brain-power by suffering from head-aches, back-weakness, indigestion,
and dozens of other ailments, resulting from compressing all the delicate
organs it is absolutely necessary should enjoy full freedom to give health
to body and mind. When I see these fools – for whatever they may have
been born, they are nothing higher now – getting along, one cannot call
it walking, on their deformed feet as if carved out of a straight piece of
wood, having unsightly shapeless lumps above and below, I ask myself
how many more ages must pass away before woman will fully join in
the much desired work of her redemption from the nothingness state
assigned to her in the era of childish traditions and monkey ignorance.
With pain I reflect it is not surprising so many millions of humans are
born before an Emerson, a Rosa Bonheur, Darwin, or Carlyle appear?
Millions of distorted beings, who eat, sleep, if they can, reduce their
brains proportionally with their waists, and idiotically squeeze out their
poor little silly lives leaving no nobler record than did the ganoids and
trilobites of the far-off past. And as I watch such fools, I am humbly
compelled to own that much I used to wholly blame men for was chiefly
due to stays.*

Pardon if my loved topic has exacted too much of your time or patience.

With kindly admiration for your many sensible contributions to the Australasian,

I am etc.

H. A. DUGDALE

Telko, Camberwell

⌁

Henrietta was sitting having tea and cucumber sandwiches at Bombala. It was a lovely room for a Saturday afternoon tea party – even in July. 'My garden salon', Mrs Carrie Lynch called it, an entire wall of French windows opening up onto a conservatory. Ruched maroon-striped blinds had been half-raised to show off the kentia palms and terracotta urns in the fernery outside. Its effect was both restive and exotic – a holiday feel. Cool, shady fronds that lent themselves to intimacy and seclusion as much as to intellectual discussion, away from the sea breeze.

Carrie Lynch, with her vast knowledge of art, not surprisingly had a natural eye for decor.

The best of the Lynches' great art collection – Romneys, Reynolds and Turners – was reserved for the front rooms of the house, where they could be shown off in appropriate grandeur. Here, though, was a sunny, cheerful room. No need for undue ceremony; the lush green outlook was sufficient in itself. A soft-hued shabby carpet graced oak parquetry. An oval tea table had been draped rather haphazardly with a square of white linen and silver tea service. Comfortable cane chairs with plump cushions in varying shades of plum, apricot and cream invited guests to sit back and relax. Next to the window, a day bed in salmon-pink linen reclined, catching long pencils of light.

But with tea now finished, it was time to stand. Henrietta smoothed the folds of her new grey costume, a style of rational dress featuring a divided skirt. Never would she sell her soul to the demon of fashion, but here was a garment that was undeniably a step towards health, comfort, convenience and decency in women's dress. With an air of natural dignity, she moved about the room, modelling her own workmanship.

'We've all been admiring your new creation, Mrs Dugdale.' Drawing her into the fold, Mrs Lynch introduced Henrietta to a couple of newcomers, a Mr and Mrs Lowe.

'Now, turn around, so we can all see,' said Mrs Lynch.

Henrietta turned about with pride, all eyes following her.

'See, it fits snug around the stomach, and the weight is evenly borne, without straining the hipbones,' she said, 'and, because it is sleek and light, any fashionable simpleton might hang twenty or thirty pounds of glass beads about her, without feeling much inconvenience.' Here, she paused, waiting until the last titter had died. 'I stress, one need only tailor to suit. Women need to ask themselves, *Why should a wrong be continued because it has been long in force?* They must follow their conscience.' She waved with an outswept hand. 'Educated women like us have a moral duty to wear the divided skirt and go out and help our more timid sisters free themselves from custom.'

Having set the room buzzing with discussion, Henrietta sat down.

'Now, where did you say you are from, Mrs Lowe? Which part of the country?'

'I was brought up on the Hawkesbury.' Mrs Lowe rearranged her excuse of a bustle and smiled with pride. 'Third generation.'

Taken with the warm, breezy manner of this woman, Henrietta knew instantly she had found in her a future friend and ally.

Mrs Lowe saw things very clearly. Her fresh attitude to life was reflected in her simple costume, a loose lettuce-green affair with white trim and a sunflower buttonhole. She leaned forward with her cup and saucer, and said confidentially, 'We were taught that what was good for boys was equally right for girls.'

'Really! Do tell.'

'Oh, nobody thought anything of it. If there were not enough side-saddles for the girls, we were allowed to ride astride – sometimes bareback.' Mrs Lowe chuckled. She explained how, as a young bride, she had been taken to live outback in Queensland, hundreds of miles from the nearest white people, and there she had borne her husband several children. From there they had long since returned to Sydney and were now living in Melbourne. 'But I never felt out of touch, Mrs Dugdale. I always knew what was going on in the world. Politics was day-to-day dinner-talk when I was a child. We were always encouraged to have our say.'

'Likewise, Mrs Lowe.' Henrietta could see they had much in common, though their early lives were worlds apart. 'Mercifully, my parents were not entirely bound by custom. Mama was a bit of a bluestocking who'd been brought up on French cream. Thanks to her, I was au fait with Literature, Music, History, Philosophy and Art. Accomplishments were all very well, I was taught, but women should not make love their profession – what they needed was knowledge and skills. Otherwise their only option in penury was to marry, stitch, die or do worse, as the saying goes. Papa had no quibbles about teaching me vulgar fractions and equations, the principles of business accounting, and the game of chess.'

Mr Lynch, having just joined them, drew up a chocolate studded-leather armchair but remained standing. 'Do you reason any better for that, Mrs Dugdale?'

'Dare say I do.'

They talked about liberal views and home rule for Ireland, but when eventually they got on to women's rights again, Mr Lynch excused himself and, together with Mr Lowe, went out into the conservatory to join Freddie.

Bird-of-paradise blooms craned either side of the men, the orange set off by the brilliant blue petal and purple beak. Henrietta narrowed her eyes. How very clever of Carrie Lynch, for the strelitzia was a work of art in itself – the striking shape of a bird in flight.

'My father once stood as a candidate,' said Mrs Lowe. 'He supported suffrage for all men, not just those who owned property.'

'How inspiring. My dear old Papa, always an active campaigner, switched parties. I always remember him as a compassionate man – a Liberal wolf in sheep's clothing – who sympathised with the Chartists.'

'As I see it, Mrs Dugdale, the same arguments can be applied equally to men or women.'

'Exactly! No doubt you have heard of Miss Helen Hart, women's rights campaigner from New Zealand, who is now lecturing in Victoria? She herself has spoken of the need for women's clubs where women can freely discuss ideas. That in itself would be a novel advancement and help women's isolation and open their minds, but what I have in mind is far more specific – a women's suffrage society.'

Mrs Lowe nodded eagerly. 'What an excellent idea.'

'We will just be following on from the others – George Eliot, Harriet Martineau and Mrs Somerville – those valiant enlightened ladies of yore. What we must do, Mrs Lowe, is band together and form a women's suffrage society made up of both male and female advocates. All it requires is a little derring-do.'

Henrietta looked up to find the room was empty and they were being summoned.

Together she and Mrs Lowe joined the crush of skirts as they made their way down the hall to the front reception room. She felt a tap on the shoulder. Their hostess whispering in her ear.

'Will you play for us, Henrie dear?'

'Of course, of course.'

Henrietta was a little rusty, her writing having taken over from the making of music. But who could refuse the charming Carrie Lynch? Who would pass up the opportunity of playing her magnificent Broadwood grand piano? Henrietta leaned forward and adjusted the stool so as to sit higher and firmer than was normally expected of a woman. She checked, as she always did, that her feet could work the pedals and that the pedals worked, all the while thinking, *Now, what shall I play?* The dark lacquered woodwork reflected obliquely those standing behind her. Any movements caught, light colours in particular: whites of eyes, even teeth when people smiled. The room was unbearably hot. In the mounting tension, she felt overcome by the smell of face powder, sherry and hot shellac. 'Sonata Pathétique', she decided in a hurry.

'Is everything quite to your liking, Mrs Dugdale?' Mrs Lynch murmured in her ear. 'Would you like me to bring some music?'

Henrietta shook her head. Terraces of milky-white flounce shimmied to the crackle of silk. Silence gave way to muffled whispers, a creaking stay. What seemed like minutes was only seconds. Once settled, Henrietta reached out her arms to the keyboard and began, *grave*. The rocket theme swept her away, and despite all distractions she fell victim to the beauty of Beethoven. From violence and illusion to the slow movement, a liberal *rubato*, and just the right amount of rhythmic fluidity building it, sublime and songlike, and then, almost without break, the finale, lightning fast. Throughout the entire nineteen-minute recital, she did not look up until the very last note had been played. She rose, bowed her head, floating in the afterglow of applause.

'A wonderful accomplishment,' somebody murmured.

It used to mystify her, the things people said, as if it were some outward gilding. 'Suits woman's sphere, the piano, don't it?' Or, 'A good play on the piano often takes the place of a good cry upstairs.' Comments like that made her bristle. Performance was in her blood. She could have pursued a concert career, with her parents' blessing. At the time, it was thought improper for a lady to be skilled enough to play professionally – very few could be Clara Schumann – let alone forsake the realms of domesticity. Henrietta knew she could have played chess, too, at the highest level, had she wanted – only one did not play chess with body, soul and mind in the way one did the piano, especially a grand piano.

She remembered once being accused of playing to men's heads, as would a man – making a spectacle of herself. She was told that any woman calling herself a lady would confine her piano playing to the limits of a drawing room and exercise a little more delicacy and restraint. That, or stick to the flute, or sing. It was alright for a man to battle this great beast of an instrument, but not a woman. It was far too gladiatorial. A lady was meant to be demure.

'Nonsense!' Freddie was adamant. 'In America, they would love you. Your playing has technique, energy, and fire that can just as quickly be dampened by your lovely liquid touch. It is as much the music of brains as emotion. Don't let anyone tell you otherwise.'

But even here, among a sympathetic audience, still she must put up with it. For what had changed? The English came out with their insular whims and prejudice, and here they stayed so that fools could judge.

'*Bravissimo*, Mrs Dugdale!' A newcomer to Australia had taken her hand. 'My word. Those *tremolos*, and fancy, you can barely reach an octave. Your poor little wrist must be sore as sore.' He kissed the tips of her fingers. 'I suggest you jolly well ask to have the black notes lowered to suit in future.'

Swiftly she retrieved her hand. 'Never you mind my small wrists, sir; of more concern to women are small waists.'

∽

By winter's end, women were finally beginning to question the point of prison corsets. After all, the Greeks – those models of perfection – had been innocent of them. Yet some women correspondents remained concerned about the so-called health aspects, fearing loss of comfort and the support they believed requisite for vigorous exercise and horseriding.

Here was Henrietta's cue. She sat, pencil to her lips, composing a letter of response to the national illustrated weekly, the *Australasian*:

For eleven years, with the exception of a few months, I was daily in the saddle for three or four hours, and often twice that time – not a Hyde-Park riding school sort of a ride, but over uncleared land, where fallen trees, stumps, and similar obstructions abounded – after uncivilised horses, and cattle of a species called scrubbers, possessing superb trotting qualities, and unflagging energy for getting into almost inaccessible places; where the rider must have a firm seat and strength of nerve quite impossible to ladies whose highest ambition appears to be the displacement of their ribs. When your correspondent reflects it was during those years my children were born, and that they are now powerful men, healthy in mind and body, she will understand the thoroughness of the test. Conventional, wooden-looking lady riders always cause me a thrill of pain. Save a few notable examples, they add nothing to the 'poetry of motion', feel none of the true enjoyments of equitation, and would have had their poor little heads cracked open long ago but for the superior intelligence and benevolence of the graceful animals in charge of them. Let 'N. E. A.' burn her corsets, substitute a cloth garment, fitting comfortably from neck to below hips, and remove the third pommel from her saddle – a device for pinning the leg in a fall. Thus equipped, she will feel the elasticity and freedom of muscles necessary to make her at one with her horse's movements. Their minds will be in accord, and she will realise the delight of riding. Horses prefer ladies without corsets – mine told me so quite distinctly.

One day I lent my favourite mare to a friend. After having gone about 100 yards the clever beast (is it needful to say I refer to the horse?) became so refractory that the corset wearer was obliged to alight, and mount one of much inferior intellect. It is cheering to observe some of your readers fearlessly evincing a partiality for common sense. It gives one a peep into the future of woman, towards the improvement of whom, all our actions should tend. 'N. E. A.' comments rightly upon the follies of our dear old grandmothers – not to imitate them is duty to coming generations, and assists in no small degree to spread of God's intelligence; which exists in all of us, to be used at will for emancipating ourselves from pitiful shame, and every other untruthfulness. When women become sufficiently courageous and religious for the observance of Nature's wise laws in preference to the absurdities of fashion, numerous, righteous, and beneficial changes will appear. Then will men, the majority of whom are now in the arrogance of ignorance, increase in understanding and justice until they acquire sufficient to acknowledge, by merciful thought and deed, that the earth belongs equally to woman as to man.

    I am etc.

    H.A. Dugdale

    Camberwell

~

Henrietta, keen to renew her acquaintance with Mrs Lowe, sent a message, inviting her to join her at one of the popular afternoon concerts in October.

Coming out of the Athenaeum, the two women made their way into the new warm leafy light.

'You'll have no trouble finding your way around Melbourne. It's a gridiron. Giants could play chess on it,' Henrietta said, chuckling.

At the corner of Collins and Russell streets, she stopped, pausing to show Mrs Lowe the famous monument of Burke and Wills.

'Poor devils,' said Mrs Lowe, her eyes misting for a moment.

'I often wonder what Wills is reading.' Henrietta nodded, her bonnet gesturing to the open book in his lap.

'Whatever would give him hope and strength, I suppose.' Mrs Lowe understood, having experienced firsthand the wilderness, and as they strolled, she began to reminisce again about her early life in the outback. 'Of course, this' – she gave a sweep of her hand – 'this is a far cry from a cattle station.'

'The "New Athens", they call it. Now, what other sites would you like to see?'

'Do you know, Mrs Dugdale, I'm dying for a cup of tea.'

'There is a place nearby, come.' Taking Mrs Lowe's arm, Henrietta directed her into a small but comfortable rest house with narrow upstairs dining space.

'Have you settled in, then?' Henrietta wanted to know, as they nestled around a small table and two pots of freshly made tea.

'We've bought a house in St Kilda,' said Mrs Lowe in her quick, warm voice. 'It will do us well, I think. The children are more than glad to be so close to the seaside.'

'You'll find it quite safe there and the salt water will do them good.'

'Already my daughter can swim and ride and she is only six.'

'That is how it should be. Girls need to grow up healthful and capable. There's no reason why feebleness should still be considered a feminine charm.' Henrietta offered Mrs Lowe some more bread and jam.

'And you, Mrs Dugdale? I've been following your letters avidly in the newspapers – so plentiful. I admire you for your impudence and courage.'

Henrietta's face lit up, her voice assured. 'I try to lead by example,' she said, gesturing to her fern-green woollen gown. 'My style of dress is unfashionably simple and free-flowing. It assists my body and mind. As to my writing …' Her eyes gave a twinkle. 'I promise, there is more in store.'

She looked down at her watch as she reached for her gloves. 'Can I walk you to the station? I have to be at Lynch and MacDonald by five.'

Chapter 17

~

Among the many legal reforms which came into effect at the beginning of 1883 was the long-awaited *Married Women's Property Act* of 1882. Both Henrietta and Freddie knew it would have an enormous effect on society. The position of a husband and wife living apart would be materially altered, as if they were strangers. They could take criminal proceedings against each other for the protection of their separate property, and give evidence against each other.

The new Act would take away all the old maxims of the common law that had become sacred, the root of society's problems.

A significant shift towards equality, it crystallised Henrietta's vision of a far-off age. Once forgotten scribblings found their way into her storyline. Chapters and page numbers materialised. Notations and 'xxxings' enriching first, then second and third drafts, until her manuscript was finally complete.

Freddie, so wise and insightful, was enthusiastic when he read her final draft, and in every way supportive. With the summer holidays drawing to a close, he would be back at the office and she could attend to the final edits.

A small, sympathetic firm in Flinders Lane, McCarron Bird & Co., had agreed to print her work. The result, *A Few Hours in a Far-Off Age*, was a slim volume, little over one hundred pages.

With great gratitude, Henrietta had dedicated it to *Justice George Higinbotham in earnest admiration for the brave attacks he had made upon what had been, during all known ages, the greatest obstacle to human advancement, the most irrational, fiercest, and most powerful of the world's monsters, the only devil: male ignorance.* The judge had himself already delivered a slashing tirade against those effete and noxious institutions – the churches of the day. This good man, originator of free education for the young, was endeavouring to obtain from the other legislators partial recognition of women's rights.

Henrietta braced herself for the onslaught of censure. Freddie was worried that her satire might, to a great extent, miss its aim by manner of its exaggeration of statement and fierceness of attack. There was always the risk it could put people offside. Of course, it was radical, just as it was fanciful, the present time and place preserved as archaeological curiosities. Never mind that. To educate people, to have any impact, she reminded him, one had to be brave and bold.

Already she taken the liberty of pre-ordering her own printed cards – not the kind to be put on a silver tray when calling, but those with which to promote oneself and one's professional services.

And now, the time was ripe to launch her book. She had been following a new group of freethinkers, the Australasian Secular Association, with avid interest. She was one of a few women among the sixty people who had attended the inaugural meeting six months before, a spirited social evening held in the Athenaeum Hall – songs, duets, trios, choruses and dancing interspersed with free discussion. She had since involved herself at Sunday meetings, gaining the support of their debating society. When asked by the president to prepare a paper on 'Women's Position in the World', she was jubilant.

Her lecture at the Masonic Hall in Lonsdale Street had been advertised well and provided a platform from which to launch her new book. Being a free lecture, it had brought people from all walks of life. So crowded that many were left standing.

To test the intelligence of the audience, she began with woman's position when humans were learning to walk with only two legs, and from there her argument evolved. She knew it was a severe and dangerous test – because the more brute there was in people, the less they liked to hear of their progenitors.

She urged her audience to form a suffrage society. Her defence for woman's right to equality amounted to tit for tat. If the Bible said one thing, it might equally say another, yet on the subject of equality it was quite definite. If we are *all his children*, as St Paul says, we are neither Jew nor Greek, there is neither bond nor free, male nor female; we must therefore in Jesus' eyes all be equal.

It was not simply a mother's duty to bear children and suckle fools. It was an ongoing responsibility for her to oversee her children's education, their advancement towards a self-supporting vocation in life, as equally for her daughters as for her sons. People went on about love when in fact work was the great beautifier. Of heart, brain and limb, of health and good looks, work was of more lasting value, for when love faded, as so often it did, what then had one left?

Nor was it a question of woman against man. The women's movement concerned the advancement of the whole species. Both sexes must face the ages yet to come side-by-side – no following by either. There could be no real unity upon any other terms. Equality was the only sure path for progress and happiness in all humankind.

Yet out of this jam-packed assemblage, only four poor shocked persons left. The rest, nearly half women, listened and approved in a manner most encouraging, and, to her great joy, several personally offered their hearty thanks.

Out of the six men who bothered to raise questions at the end of the lecture, not one differed from what she had said respecting the tyrannical law relating to mother and child, and only two were averse to women in politics; but their arguments were utterly untenable, for the simple reason that there could be no just argument against equal rights. And that was all women were asking for.

At the end of the evening, Henrietta assembled herself at a trestle table in the supper room, signing her book; Freddie sat beside her with a toffee tin, collecting two shillings per copy. The book sold well – more than expected – and copies had been distributed to the principal booksellers.

～

She asked on the weekend, when they were together pottering in the garden, 'Did I go on for too long?'

'No, dear.' Freddie snipped the dead agapanthus spikes with his shears and snip-snipped again.

'Was I being bombastic?' she asked, loading armfuls of rotting leaves and seeding blooms into the wheelbarrow.

'Of course not.'

'Freddie?' Henrietta looked up to see him coming out the vestibule door in his felt hat. Women needed work for all the same reasons men needed work. She breathed out hard, resting for a moment on her spade, before bending down again to hack her way through the thick fibrous mat of bulbs that had been choking each other for want of water. Blessed things did take over so.

She handed Freddie the spade, feeling tightness in her back.

So far she had managed to ward off the creep of rheumatism. The culprit was the petticoat, according to newfound scientific theory. Not only did the petticoat spread disease, she believed, it absorbed dampness, one unavoidable cause of rheumatic pains in the knees, hips, loins and back.

'I'm not too old for you, am I, love? I do feel we're a good match and we work very well as a team. But it's your choice.'

She knew he didn't like her talking like this, sowing doubts in his mind.

'Don't be silly.' He took off his gloves and gave her a little side hug, his long fingers reaching for the nape of her neck. 'How many times do I have to say it? I cannot imagine life without you. You are the most extraordinary woman I have ever met. Gifted in every way: clever, strong-willed, yet playful and loving. You make me laugh. Your spirit invigorates me. You are full of surprises. Your wit scintillates, and I never quite know what you are going to come out with next. Yet I always feel at ease when I am by your side.'

'Ah!' She looked up at him and felt a warm surge ripple through body as he drew her close. Just his touch, the prolonged gaze of his warm brown eyes were enough to reassure her.

Preaching to Freddie was preaching to the converted. More than once he had stood up for all her sex to say that in his experience of women, chiefly gained from observation in the course of his occupation in a law office, they were more business-like, intelligent, conscientious, moral and reliable than their brethren.

She decided to plant him some pansies, dear little heart's ease *pensées*, the wild variety, with their rich, velvety colours and their sweet but spicy fragrance, leaning forward in summer in free thought. If thought could materialise, there was hardly a more pleasing form it could take than 'ladies' delight'.

At the back of her mind, another face kept popping its head up. The man with the dignified demeanour who had said after her lecture at the Masonic Hall that the apathy of women would prove a greater obstacle than the antipathy of men. No mistake, it was Mr Charles Edwin Jones, editor of the new radical *People's Tribune*.

'It is *you* who must take the lead and form a suffrage society, Mrs Dugdale. There is much movement abroad.'

∽

Henrietta shut the front door and, with curiosity, inspected the flat brown paper parcel freshly delivered by the postman. Quickly she cut the string and broke it open. It was not some new journals she had recently ordered but Reverend Cresswell's review, in defence of the clergy, of Judge Higinbotham's *Lecture on Science & Religion*. The pamphlet came with the compliments of the author. The very nerve of the man! She had no desire to hurt anyone, even those who had wounded her in the past. But this was a red rag, for the local vicar of St John's knew full well that she shared Higinbotham's views on religion. Very well, then, she would take his missive as a challenge – in all courtesy and with great satisfaction, because only by the conflict of minds could truth be revealed and become a general peacemaker.

A lengthy visit to the reading room at the Athenaeum was what was needed. Here, the following day, amid hushed steps and whispers, she spent a good three hours trawling through journals and books, checking the latest facts on geological science – evidence of bones and skulls found in 200,000-year-old Pliocene deposits. From her readings on the antiquity of man and his origins, she was able to cite a number of leading naturalists, Professors Huxley, Whitney and Denton, as to the origins of mankind. She even managed to obtain on loan a drawing of the Calaveras Skull, its brutal appearance still haunting – very different from the ideal first humans that Reverend Cresswell's forgetfulness would place on the earth only six thousand years ago.

But since the reverend reviewer had gone to the Bible for proof, she would give a little of the same. Expose the indelible lines of hypocrisy – ignorant expoundings by incompetent teachers – of one of the most valuable books in the world's library. Crude lessons she had received from clerics in her young years had nearly deprived her of understanding the marvellous truth to be drawn from those old writings. Whenever she had remarked on any verse or passage, they told her, with much didactic solemnity, that it meant quite something other, often the very opposite to the words before her eyes.

Yet viewed by the light of common sense, the Bible was a most fascinating instructor. She could so equally turn around and point to, among others, Esau, Leviticus and Job, the latter having said, 'His breasts are full of milk', confirming Darwin's theory that at some remote time men suckled their children.

183

The Bible was too strong a meat for babes. To understand its true value required the light of matured thought, which showed it to be at the same time appalling, interesting, and the most conclusive proof of evolution that had ever been written.

Now, armed with ample references, all she had to do was to get out a typed copy of her eight-page pamphlet and post it off to the printers in Elizabeth Street, and that would be that. A blessed gift at the price of threepence. For Reverend Cresswell, a copy gratis. Morality was not the sole preserve of theism, and the clergy needed to learn that.

The tramp of horses' hooves and barking dogs amid the rush rose to greet her. She stepped out on to Collins Street and blinked. The sky was fractured by the outline of a young plane tree just beginning to shoot. Baubles on twigs hung stark and gold against the dazzle of blue. A dappled trunk rooted within the confines of a black wrought-iron tree guard. But one swallow does not make a summer. No, she thought. Nor do a few large-minded clergymen like the Reverend Doctor Bromby, the canon of St Paul's Cathedral, make all the clergy large-minded.

Better, far better, had the majority of humans been always deists: their history would not then have been stained with the dreadful records of thousands burned at the stake, or tortured to death by other fiendish means – *for the love of Christ*. All honour to Judge Higinbotham for his courageous honesty in promoting the reconciliation of science and religion – the key to human salvation.

⁓

Judge Higinbotham's attack on clerical tradition had provoked a spate of brochures, lectures and sermons, and though advertised and well distributed, she knew her pamphlet, 'Science and Religion: Judge Higinbotham's Admirable Lecture Defended', was only one among many.

Henrietta stepped off the train at the new Camberwell station. With the recent extension of the Hawthorn line, the town was a rising suburb. After the bustling city and a packed carriage, the short walk home to

Telko was an utter joy. The picturesque flow of farms and flourishing gardens cleared her mind. Higinbotham's lecture was a penetrating ray of light. She would continue to support this good man as he had supported her in his vain attempt to present a Bill on women's suffrage ten years ago, against much ridicule.

Still, there was the echo of a heckler: 'God-fearing women never say anything about rights.' Women need fear nothing that is right, Henrietta would argue. The common argument was that if woman were permitted to go beyond her sphere, domestic duties would be neglected; that the granting of franchise would only make her unwomanly. Good gracious. A woman was more than a broom or an incubator. Women were made unwomanly when men put more children in their houses than could be wholesomely and nobly reared. There were other silly, shallow objections. If voting or reflecting upon whom to vote for interfered with duties, then by their own ruling it would be far more likely to do so with men, because they assert that their occupations require more thought than those of women. Since most of woman's work, at present, required only pretty strong muscles and patience, she therefore had more time for thinking about the world's economy than men did, and as a result would often think more deeply than men.

Walking briskly, Henrietta could feel such promise and energy, the air pregnant with the future. To be out at this time of the year was to witness nature's tenderest, most unimaginable smile. Bursting out of the rich chocolate loam were blue hyacinths. Drifting all around was the fragrance of the hawthorn hedges so reminiscent of May Day, and down the laneway, the humble little tumbledown cottage embowered in creeper, its garden full of lilies and laurustinus bushes. Like Judge Higinbotham, she would give equal voice to the poor, for in them lay the heart of democracy.

Here at Telko, she liked to think it was all work and fare alike – a classless society. Freddie pitched in whenever he could, tea towel draped over his shoulder, putting away cups and saucers, scrubbing a blackened pot. Only once in sixteen years had she had to employ labour, then only during illness, and her house had not an unwholesome corner in it.

And still men found reason to complain. One recent critic said that women should stay at home and reform servants. Surely this class of workers suffered enough, as it was. Little did people know what might be their harsh circumstances. Bending down, she lifted the cowhide from under her cane chair in the vestibule, took it outside, gave it a good beating and let what was left of the sun do the rest. From corner to corner, she swept and dusted and rubbed until everything in the house was clean and smelling of beeswax.

It was a good smell, thought Henrietta. As it wafted through her senses, it brought back images of her Bloomsbury home in Hunter Street, and a dark-haired young woman, in cap and apron, sleeves rolled up, going about her duties with otherworldly calm. Henrietta had first come upon her one day while walking with a friend in London. The woman had been then in a wretched state, her expression one of genuine sorrow, and had piteously tried to sell Henrietta something. On being questioned, she described how her husband had drunk all her money and deserted her. Henrietta had asked Mama and Papa to allow her to bring the woman into their house as a domestic servant. Acquaintances said it would never do – an Irishwoman and a Roman Catholic, too, *Oh, impossible!* – but Henrietta prevailed. Catherine Fitzgerald was with them for years and never gave her cause for regret. Her religion was gratitude – her fault was that she considered herself so much indebted to Henrietta that her attachment became that of a faithful dog, ever ready to do more than her strength would have borne.

Life at Telko was a far simpler one. What had to be done took little enough time. Henrietta knew she could be more a saviour to women standing on a platform than worrying about employing a maid. It was easy enough to keep things in order, both of them being home so little. She peered into the tall dried arrangement adorning the living room. Almost a year old. Her artistry she heaved, dust and all, outside onto Freddie's compost heap. Ordinary everyday things could be quite beautiful. One need only open one's eyes. Armed with her straw hat and her pair of shears, she slipped back down Riversdale Road, returning with a handful of pampas grass, some wild barley and a large switch of gumnuts covered in lichen. The lot she bundled into her freshly polished copper urn, the one moulded with the lions, and, with a tweak here and there, set it back on display. It was unpretentious. So little time or thought, yet it gave immense satisfaction. At any time of night or day, she could turn to this show of soft natural beauty for inspiration, and there find harmony, grace and goodness of soul.

Doilies served no earthly purpose, so there were none in the house. Otherwise, what drapes, cloths or curtains could be boiled she bundled into the copper. Then, the silverware. With toothpick and gauze and lint, she systematically worked at every dark crevice until she had brought up a patina so shiny she could almost see the smile on her mother's face. The indigo tablecloth she washed carefully by hand and replaced on the table without aid of a hot-iron. While waiting for the rest of the washing to dry, she went outside and broke off some sprays of wattle and set the globular yellow puffs in a sea-green glazed stoneware vase. By evening, the heady, honey-laden scent of the acacia filled the house like the odour of the very moon herself.

༄

Henrietta had been wearing the divided skirt for more than a year before it took Melbourne by storm. Never would she return to petticoats, even now it was winter. It gave her so much of physical and moral comfort. Knickerbockers worn underneath – made of silk or wool in the cooler months, calico in summer – were a far more practical kind of underclothing than petticoats by the plenty. Length of garment was another advancement. She found that wearing a dress three or four inches shorter than normal was so very pleasant that she often felt inclined to throw aside the dignity of her years and grey hairs, and jump about in the delight of free movement. Such a dress, she knew, would – must – be the costume of the future.

She thought nothing nowadays of wearing only knickerbockers while labouring at home in private. And with the winter frosts behind them, she had taken to wearing them outside too. Freddie had no objection. Whereas William … A decade ago, a lady would never have dreamed of talking about such things, least of all with her husband. Of course, what went on in the privacy of one's own bedroom was quite another thing. Often there was no respect. She thought of William with loathing and disgust, his drunken demands that 'the gates of paradise be left open, ready and waiting'. Knickerbockers for William would have been an impost to conjugal rights. Oh, if only that had been all.

One day in early spring, she was in the garden planting some Jerusalem artichokes. She sat on her haunches, resting comfortably forward on her kneeling cushion, hands gloved and a bucketful of cut-up tubers beside her, sowing them one by one; they were simplicity itself to grow. Having finished her task, she stood up, brushing some soil off her new blue-striped flannel home-made 'britches'; her stockinged ankles were still surprisingly trim above her buttoned boots.

She put the bucket away in the potting shed and drew off her gloves. Her heart pummelled her ribs. Even spending time in her precious garden could not take her mind from the latest indignity. William, the fraud, the infernal bigamist, had done it again. Three years ago, according to Carl, shamelessly before a Taranaki registrar. It was a heaping of insult upon injustice.

The law was complicit in making her suffer – in having no choice but to live with Freddie outside that law – whereas William had no qualms, took the law into his own hands. Whatever her rights of late, little could be done to bring him to account; so long as William remained in New Zealand, he was unassailable. The boys, all of them now grown men, had for whatever reason chosen to remain there. They did not need her. No. Nor did they need William. For her, it was the principle that mattered. She had saddled her hobbyhorse and was ready to go.

When she learned that the Member for Normandy, Mr William Shiels, intended, as a private member, to carry an amendment to the *Marriage and Matrimonial Causes Act*, she wrote to *The Age*.

MR SHIELS'S JUST DIVORCE CLAUSE

Sir, Men are perpetually vaunting their 'abstract justice and abstract reason'. How do they show the basis of those faculties by advocating the retention of a barbarous law which gives immunity to the man and degradation to the woman for precisely the same offence? And more than that; for whether she or he be guilty, the punishment now falls only on her, because where she commits the offence she is hounded to death, infamy or insanity by the esoteric good and 'pious', where her husband is the offender, her injured body and mind lead also to similar result.

One of our wise legislators showed what amount of abstract reasoning is his when in stating why Mr Shiels's just cause should not be passed, he conclusively proved the great necessity for it. We learn from him that if it became law 200 women will be enabled to liberate themselves from the most revolting sickening life any woman could be condemned to endure. Another honourable member said no public demand had been made for this justice. What wonderful reasoning! It is well known to men of even ordinary understanding and observation that those most deprived of justice are exactly the ones that dare not cry for it. That same fallacious argument was used to keep the poor Africans in slavery; and they were denied the power of refuting it, as women are at the present time in some quarters. The women suffering under the demoralising tyranny engendered by our present divorce laws have had so little experience of nobility in man that they dread the inevitable insults from weak-brained males which generally follow any claims from women for justice. Then such legislators claim 'here is no need of reform'. But happily, there are also men like Mr Shiels, who are blessed with both intellect and

189

benevolence. The truth is, men cannot legislate for women. They have tried it ever since they gave themselves divine authority for so doing, and debasingly to all concerned.

It is fortunate for manhood's honour that such men as Shiels, Higinbotham, Strong, etc. are endeavouring to efface the disgrace their predecessors have brought upon their sex, and to raise woman to the position of a human being.

Yours etc.

H. A. Dugdale

Telko, Camberwell

To have the proprietor of *The Age*, Mr David Syme, take up women's cause was heartening. Enfranchisement, he agreed, was the reform from which all others would stem.

<p>

There was nothing Henrietta was not prepared to talk about or write. Alcohol, in particular, and the 'Repressive Legislation for Intoxicating Drink' were the topic of her second address to the Australasian Secular Association. What better way to start the year.

She rose at five and sat at her desk, wrapped in thought. Silence lay deep around her. Finally she raised the wick of the lamp and put a few main points on paper. In her heart, she knew what she had to say. Alcohol was a deadly poison swallowed by people to reduce their mental power until they became something other than themselves – some like young children in understanding, some idiotic, some resembling wild beasts, and others committing acts worse than any beast was ever known to descend to. For those who obtained wealth through such ignoble means, there could be only degradation. Invariably, it was families – women and children – who suffered the most. What she couldn't say was that she had seen the damage firsthand: Joseph promising, time after time, never to touch that vile beverage again.

She looked out the window and, through the effervescence of dawn, watched the shadows draining away like some dark brown bitter brew. How many men relied on drunkenness to stave off their fear?

Sailors were among the worst. Fools, she remembered, with their rum or whisky, slopping jugs of musty porter.

Henrietta drew up the window sash to clear the room of her thoughts. Immediately the sound of a butcherbird broke the air, rich and sweet and clear. She could see it now, this master of deception. Perched on the rim of the bird bath, still wet, feathers fluffed, it looked around with its fierce stare, and its strong hooked beak, waiting for its prey. Suddenly it swooped down upon its breakfast.

Chapter 18

⁓

Henrietta liked to think that the idea of a female suffrage society was hers and hers alone. A decade and a half of agitating virtually single-handedly had earned her this privilege. But one could not stand alone in advocacy.

Further advice from Mr Charles Edwin Jones, the newspaper editor, was that she needed the backing of a good committee, on which he would be only too happy to serve. Mrs Lowe, she knew, would be ideal; so would Freddie. Miss Helen Hart, the veteran activist from New Zealand, would be invaluable, though the travelling lecturer was hard to pin down.

One evening at a Royal Society meeting, Henrietta chanced to meet another likely candidate, an Elizabeth Rennick – a fine-boned, comely, graceful Englishwoman – along with her husband, Charles.

'Spendid, splendid,' said Henrietta when she heard they were freethinkers and new members of the Eclectic and Secular societies. Here was another fellow advocate of women's rights. 'I am thinking of forming a suffrage club, and I can tell you are just the type I need, Mrs Rennick.'

She gave her one of her printed cards and proposed they organise a get-together. 'Where, now …?'

'Where other than Adjmere?'

Mrs Rennick's kind offer of her private home in Shipley Street provided the perfect venue, South Yarra being convenient to all, and the date was set.

'Oh, and we shall need some more men, otherwise it will not seem at all fair or balanced. Mr Charles Jones and Mr Johnson will come, you can be sure of that, and I know of a number of other good ones to ask, including a young Scot by the name of John Brunton who is fresh off a ship. Do what you can, Mrs Rennick, and Mrs Lowe and I will do the rest.'

Adjmere was a gracious home. The room they met in was large and well proportioned, with freshly gathered flowers and other refinements adorning throughout. Henrietta clasped her hands, heartened by the mid-afternoon sun streaming through the long French windows, and the outlook. Amid clouds of turning leaves were glimpses of beautifully smooth green lawn and broken borders of bright, well-kept flowerbeds, a tiny verandah facing north, and a perfect conservatory of fresh green ferns.

Chairs had been arranged in rows facing a white-clothed dining table well stocked with writing material.

Mrs Rennick rang her brass tea bell. They were all set, having been given their roles in advance. Henrietta placed herself strategically at the table and waited, feeling the run of the velvet cloth, smooth one way and rough the other. She toyed in anticipation with its long silken tassels, for the first suffrage society in Australia was about to be inaugurated.

Once everyone was seated, she took the chair.

The purposes of the meeting having been declared, it was determined that the association should be called the Victorian Women's Suffrage Society. It was agreed and set forth:

1st. The object of the Society is to obtain parliamentary franchise for women.

2nd. The Society seeks to achieve this object by acting as a centre for the collection of a diffusion of information with regard to the progress of the movement in all parts of the Empire.

3rd. By the holding of public meetings to agitate the subject and educate public opinion thereon.

4th. By the publication of pamphlets, leaflets, and other literature bearing upon the subject.

Upon Mrs Lowe's proposal, it was resolved that all the ladies and gentlemen present should form a general committee, with power to add to their number. Once the executive committee had been appointed, a subcommittee was appointed to draw up a constitution and by-laws for the society. Henrietta was on both committees, doubling her feelings of privilege.

What a thrill to see the formation of the society duly reported in all the newspapers. It made it even more official.

The five-shilling subscription Henrietta had suggested would cover necessary printing of pamphlets. Advertising would obviously have to be paid for, but she would need to keep the momentum flowing, starting with a letter to Mr Syme of *The Age*.

WOMAN SUFFRAGE

Sir, I hope you will permit me to publicly thank you for all that is large minded and just to women in your article on 'The Victorian Women's Suffrage Society'. Usurpers of power are naturally the last to understand the iniquity of the usurpation, therefore I am always grateful to those men who are honest enough to admit the injustice on women's position, and brave the taunts of noodles by aiding to ameliorate it. We certainly do not expect to succeed immediately, for there are not sufficient thinking men in power. We are prepared for uphill work, and have well weighed the fact that there is much before us, for we know there is nothing more difficult to overcome than the obtuseness and prejudice of male ignorance. We know, also, we have work to do with some of our own sex, for man's cunning has reared them in such apathy on these important subjects that many only awake to their humiliating

position when the pangs of male law are rending their hearts. I cannot
join in your apprehension that 'giving votes to women would increase
clerical ascendency everywhere'. There is a growing yearning in the
human mind to join in great public good. To women's cramped energy
the priestly paddock is a world for action, but enlarge their powers by
giving them their rights as human beings, and in proportion as they
would feel their freedom much time that is now worse than wasted
over the unknowable or the ephemeral would be more nobly turned
to humanitarianism, which, after all, whatever the future may be,
is the best preparative. To be just is right; but, in any case, to act
unjustly – and on a mere assumption, too – is contemptible. Injustice
to woman is a culpable retardation to progress in the whole of human
kind; it is a wrong which rebounds from the oppressed to the oppressor,
and acts as a continual force for retrogression, periodically swamping
civilisation with ever emulating generations of fools, hypocrites and all
other rogues – a bitter truth to be read in the present insignificance of
once powerful nations, and the almost total extinction of others. The
student of human nature knows that injustice to woman is the most
illogical of all man's illogicalities excepting, perhaps, his defence of it
by an assumption. Men of Victoria have already stepped out of ancient
ignorance to aid woman, and, I foresee, will not be arrested in this, the
only march to prosperity, by boyish sillinesses, or puny old men's tales of
fancied evils.

   Yours etc.

H. A. DUGDALE
Telko, Camberwell

⌣

The Victorian Women's Suffrage Society was summonsed to assemble
at the Melbourne Coffee Palace in Bourke Street on Monday 23 June
1884 for their first general meeting. Henrietta looked around eagerly,
nodding variously at familiar faces. Mrs Rennick introduced her to a

newly arrived Englishwoman, Mrs Sarah Parker; they had both been members of the women's suffrage movement in London.

But where oh where were the Lynches? It was most unlike Carrie to be malingering from her recent illness.

What a great turnout it was. At a glance, Henrietta counted not less than sixty people, including numerous men – thanks to their incumbent chairman. The Reverend Dr Bromby was well known, a man of wit and easy balance who, like Judge Higinbotham, could reconcile Darwin and the Bible, yet speak out vociferously against the poisonous weeds of society – gambling and alcohol. If only this snowy-haired man could be the lawmaker of the universe.

In introducing the topic of suffrage, Dr Bromby made reference to the last prohibition of the Ten Commandments, the one about the coveting of neighbour's property, the one from which that nefarious law of the unity of spouses was drawn. Originally, the house had been placed first, and the wife second, he said, but when the Decalogue was published a second time, in the book of Deuteronomy, the position was reversed, the wife being placed first and the house second, and that arrangement had been acknowledged by Christians and Mahometans alike up to the present day.

It mattered little. Either way, it implied a wife was represented as man's property, along with his slave, his house, his oxen, his ass, or any other material possession. This generic lumping together should be held to account. Society variously fed off it, the prevailing objection being that females had plenty to do in their own houses, and should not interfere with public political matters.

Dr Bromby trusted that when the ladies obtained suffrage, they would secure better representation from the males, and not feel obliged to vote accordingly with their husbands. Henrietta's heart lifted to know that Dr Bromby was warmly encouraging revolt in his search for truth.

She felt honoured to have been asked to move the first resolution. Later, she kept going back over it, word for word, each time breathing in with a little flair of her nostrils, trying to recapture the thrill of stepping up on the podium.

Firstly, she had tendered the thanks of the society to *The Age*, which had not only helped to initiate the society but continued to support it.

For the past fifteen years, she had advocated the giving of votes to women; that there could not exist in a free state one law for the male and no law for the female on this question of political rights. Did not the women pay taxation equal to the men? Did they not have to obey the laws the same as men? Then why, if they were called upon to pay and obey, should they be voiceless and powerless in matters political? Before attempting to move the motion, she reiterated the platform of the society, simply: To obtain the same political privileges for women as now possessed by male voters, with the restriction of an educational test by the candidate writing legibly their name upon the ballot paper.

The franchise must not stop at the ratepayers' roll, as some members presently suggested. According to the Office of the Government Statistician, the current number of women ratepayers would only give rise to 17,000 votes, leaving 197,000 women without votes. To leave it at that was an insult. The ratepayers' suffrage might be sufficient for the women of England but it was not for the women of Victoria. They must go honestly to the Parliament and demand their rights. 'We must, we shall, have female suffrage.'

The idea that women, if given equal political privileges with men, would be too conservative was nonsense. It was men who were the conservatives, and women the democrats. And in support of this, she pointed out that it was the conservatism of men which made them averse to giving up the privilege of burning women for witchcraft, and which had endeavoured to bar her entrance to the universities.

She trusted that the resolution would be carried and sent on to the Parliament, and if the House threw it out, what matter! Parliament did not last forever. It was a grand democratic measure, and nobler sons were being born, and in the course of time there would not be sufficient men mean enough to oppose it.

The motion was passed with an overwhelming majority and the applause that followed was loud and long.

The Governor, Sir Henry Loch, and Alfred Deakin and David Syme were among the growing number of just-minded men who had seen fit to support their cause. But what really set her abuzz was the knowledge that her dear Judge Higinbotham, or the 'Little Doctor', as he was known, had joined the society unsolicited. Here was further proof that a great mind could exist without great animal size and strength, and that a great body gave no guarantee of a large mind. What an advertisement to have her friend and ally in their club. What a coup. And a handsome donation to boot.

⌀

Carl had written to say he was coming over from New Zealand, to share her success. Then why did she keep dreaming of falling stars? Carrie Lynch, of course, was no longer here to ask. She of the mediums and seances, sibyls and priestesses, had gone to the other side.

Carrie's death in August had affected them all, the coterie on whom this extraordinary woman had generously bestowed her time and affections. Not just old friends like her and Freddie – there were so many – but poor down-at-heel writers and artists who needed bringing out in the world. And now Carrie had gone to join them – journalist and novelist Marcus Clarke and the poet Henry Kendall – people whom she had grown to love and patronise.

Henrietta was devastated. For the former Caroline Dexter to appear lukewarm about the newly inaugurated Suffrage Society was a tragedy in itself. But now Henrietta knew why. Carrie had not wanted her friends to know she was dying. The last thing this famous sixty-five-year-old woman would have wanted was pity. She was a giver, not a taker, though she never gave herself away entirely. At times, Carrie could be intensely private and secretive, as she was at the end. Without Carrie, being a guest at Bombala wouldn't be the same – no 'at homes', no scintillating salon, no tete-a-tetes, no fellow support. Oh, how she would miss her brilliant, kind-hearted friend.

William Lynch, in his bereavement, leaning heavily on Freddie, both at home and at work; Freddie in turn felt duty-bound, when he should just as rightfully have been backing her up, leaving him torn betwixt loyalties.

Her friend and mentor had gone, but once Carl arrived Henrietta was overcome. Oh, the joy, the joy! What a fine man he'd grown into. Carl was happy enough to tag along to her various events and commitments; she, so proud to be showing him off – *may I present my son Carl, all the way from New Zealand*. But she could only have him to herself a few hours here, a few there. Poor darling probably wished he'd never come.

But Carl was in awe of Marvellous Melbourne.

'Can't get over the scale of things. A chap could as well be in any major city in Europe. The size of the metropolis, Ma – half a million people. The size of the buildings, too, so many five storeys high.'

Carl was never short of something to do. Happy to make his way into the city to Spencer Street station each day with Freddie, with a list of great wonders he wanted to see.

Freddie, with foresight, had directed him to an exhibition of amateur photographers showing at the Royal Society's Hall near his office. Each day Carl returned to Telko enthralled, having attended yet another instructive lecture showing the rise and progress of this growing artform. And when her son sailed off for New Zealand with a new light in his eye, she knew he would be back before too long.

⌁

Being chairwoman of committees was time-consuming, and the day following Carl's departure, Henrietta spent in the city, following up on matters for action. It was late by the time she arrived back at Telko. From the smell of woodsmoke and the flicker of lamps, she could tell Freddie was already home. Henrietta opened the door, her cape flapping in a blast of arctic wind. Swept up in the emotion of saying goodbye to Carl, she had missed what Mrs Lowe described as some subtle manoeuvring in the inner workings of their new society, or 'club', as she called it. Already Mrs Rennick's English friend, Sarah Parker, had been asserting herself.

Henrietta took off her hat and gloves, updating Freddie as she went about the kitchen preparing them a light supper.

'She's barely been in the country a few months. No sooner off the ship and she is wanting to take control.' Henrietta laid out the food: leftover mushroom pudding, which she had quickly heated up, a witlof and walnut salad, plus some bread and cheese.

'Rubs me up the wrong way, I'm afraid,' said Freddie, cutting hungrily into his pie. 'She's a little too high and mighty for my liking.'

Once they had finished the meal and cleared things away, Henrietta showed him Mrs Parker's letter to the *Herald*.

'To be so critical – especially after the kindness shown to her by so many of our lady members, Mrs Rennick included. Then broadcasting her claim that we are going about things entirely the wrong way. She cherry-picks from the newspapers, highlighting sordid real-life individual cases of injustice to women, claiming this is the only way to achieve our aim, as if the rest of us have no pity or are simply in disregard. Then, to go so far as to say: *Will the women's suffrage society seize the cases published or are its lady members too 'nice' to touch such vital questions?* Too nice? Heaven forbid, what an insult!'

'It's self-interest,' said Freddie. 'Her aim is to side-track, while putting herself in the limelight. And to hell with unity. If she has a bone to pick, then she should pick it face-to-face with the committee and the rest of the members, not go rushing off deviously to the papers to share her concerns with the public at large.' He turned to Henrietta. 'I think we would be better off without her, but as she's paid her subscription, I suppose we are stuck with her.'

'I cannot sleep, Fred, until I have written. She must be brought into line.' And she went to her desk at once, dashing off a letter to the editor of the *Herald*.

Sir, With all respect to Mrs Parker as a lady, and herself a suffragist, I beg to remind her that in her letter published in this evening's Herald, she appears to have forgotten that the sole object of the Victorian Women's Suffrage Society is to obtain the Parliamentary Franchise for Women. This is the one result for which we organised, and aught else is quite outside the functions of the society as a society. Instead of crouching to a Chief Secretary with a petition for justice in single instances, we are working to obtain the right to ensure justice for all women. Far from having 'gone to sleep', I can affirm that since the start of the society those constituting its Executive have cheerfully given up many hours of sleep in working towards obtaining the object of our organisation, sometimes after a day passed in the performance of excessive toil in home or office. In one respect I think many besides suffragists will cordially agree with Mrs Parker. Honour to the Herald for its help to the defenceless.

H. A. DUGDALE
Chairwoman of Committees V.W.S.S.
Telko, Camberwell

'Will you write a letter, then?' she asked the next morning before Freddie went off to work.

'Yes, tonight.'

'We must hold ground.'

'Know thy enemy, as my father used to say.' Freddie bent down and gave her a kiss.

That night after dinner, he put his thoughts on paper.

Sir, With your permission a few words in reply to the double-barrelled discharge by Mrs Sarah Parker. The V.W.S.S., as a society, has no more

*to do with the questions of wife-beating and seduction than it has with
the prevention of the spread of smallpox. The society has but one aim – to
procure votes for women. As citizens, its members, in common with
the rest of the community, 'as in duty-bound', interest themselves in the
proper administration of our laws, including of course those affecting the
questions referred to by your correspondent, and endeavour by agitating
to procure their amendment where defective. One of the direct means
to that end they adopt by appealing for permission to take part in the
making of those laws. To my knowledge several of the lady members of the
executive of the society have let slip no opportunity of years past of giving
points similar to those mentioned by Mrs Parker through the press on the
platform and by every other available method. The effort to obtain the
franchise for women is more widely philanthropic than the opponents of
the movement, and even some of its friends, are able to realise.*
    FRED JOHNSON
    Member of Committee V.W.S.S.
    Camberwell

The odd backbiting was to be expected. But as the week progressed,
it soon became apparent that Mrs Sarah Parker was in league with Mrs
Rennick.

Henrietta and Freddie sat side-by-side in the rush-hour train as the
carriage swayed this way and that.

'Have you seen the *Herald*?'

'Not yet.' Freddie looked straight ahead.

'They have interviewed Mrs Rennick about the aims of the society,'
she said under her breath.

Freddie held on to his bowler hat as the train came grinding to a stop.
Once at Camberwell, they got off and walked to Telko, arm-in-arm in
the evening dusk, as Henrietta expounded.

'Most of her views I share, in respect to women's health, children's
education, and religion. But she has gone too far, as if making out to

speak for us all – she has been saying the most outrageous things – outright admitting she does not care whom she shocks. Says shamelessly that she does not believe in "asylums for incurables" – it is a cruel kindness and she would rather have them put out of the way altogether. That is nothing short of murder!'

'I fear you are being undermined, love,' said Freddie.

'Mrs Elliott is horrified and is protesting most strongly. I have yet to find out what the others think. We must reassure all and sundry that Mrs Rennick is not the spokeswoman for the society. Otherwise her opinions will turn people away.'

Putting heads together that evening, they again penned tandem ripostes to the *Herald*, with a terse reminder that aside from personal views, the single platform of the Victorian Women's Suffrage Society was to procure votes for women. Their sympathy was only in connection with the object of the society, outside of which it was not their duty, or incumbent upon them in any way, to be guided or influenced by the opinions of anyone.

Mrs Rennick was quick to point out that she had been misrepresented by the *Herald*, while her partner-in-crime, the interloper Mrs Parker, raced to her defence, saying it was all a ridiculous storm in teacup.

Mrs Rennick, whose views had seemed so in tune with Henrietta's when the two first met back in April, had turned out to be a Malthusian, who would have the infirm and incurable pitilessly put down. There was no end to the despicable things that a woman like that would do. There was no alternative but for the society to disassociate itself from this voluble, flighty lady and her views. Henrietta would have to ask her to resign.

Mrs Rennick, however, did not give in without a fight.

VICTORIAN WOMEN'S SUFFRAGE SOCIETY

Sir, Mrs Dugdale takes great pains to inform through your columns that – 'Mrs Rennick is not a type of our suffragists. I beg to assure one need not mourn over the thought of her being leader of the V.W.S.S.

The lady is simply our hon. Secretary and Treasurer. In no sense is she a leader.' I enclose extracts from two letters from that lady to myself – one, this next day after the initiatory meeting of the Society convened by me, and held at my residence, 7th May: the other a few days after.

Yours etc.

E. H. RENNICK

Ex Hon Secretary and Treasurer

South Yarra, 14 October, 1884

Resignation sent in yesterday, 13th inst.

––––––––––

[Copy]

8 May 1884

Had I been a man yesterday, I should have inevitably fallen deeply in love with you. You remain in my memory a perfect marvel of graceful earnest energy and bright intelligence. To watch you moving ca and la was to me a pleasure like that derived from looking at a pretty picture set in motion. How well I read you at that Royal Society gathering! If we do not succeed it will not be for want of a competent leader.

Yours very sincerely

H. A. Dugdale

––––––––––

[Copy]

14 May 1884

Dear Mrs Rennick,

Mr Johnson has been consulting with me on the subject of Byelaws, etc. etc. Remember I have only given you invited opinion without a possibility of my ever taking offence at anything in your own decisions.

I have only, and most disinterestedly, the cause at heart: therefore act as your greater experience in necessary details teaches you.

 Yours sincerely

 H. A. Dugdale

'Now look what she's done. We cannot let it pass, Fred. You must respond at once, show your support as a founding member of the society.'

'Sorry, love, I have already written two letters. I have a crust to earn.'

The only thing Henrietta could do was let it blow over. Perhaps she might have been too effusive, she mused later, too impulsive. But a couple of thank-you notes hastily scribbled to the Hon. Sec. were hardly brevet for rank. Freddie agreed it was sheer hubris.

'But what should I do, dear?'

'Nothing,' he said. 'In my experience, silence often holds a stronger power.'

Somehow, the matter escaped the notice of the major newspapers. Henrietta resolved to attend the usual fortnightly meeting at 30 Russell Street. Even so, her words had been taken out of context, grossly misinterpreted. It was vile and vindictive. It did nothing for the suffrage cause and only opened a mine of fun for the public.

Chapter 19

⁓

If not the Athenaeum, the Art Gallery or the Public Library, it was the Coffee Palace where Henrietta now spent much of her time. She liked to get there early for their fortnightly meetings, reserve her usual place at the table and take possession of herself before proceedings got under way. From the upper floor of this grand stucco building, she could look out past the bright city lamps to the dark seaside suburbs and see ship lights quivering around the bay.

It was nearly March 1885, and another year was rolling by. They had distributed well over five thousand pamphlets setting out John Stuart Mill's advocacy for woman's suffrage. The executive committee had met last night, with her presiding. Henrietta had woken, her mind on matters arising. Arrangements needed to be made for a public meeting to be held in Richmond – time, date and venue set, and advertisements placed. Still to be formalised were their upcoming winter campaign and her yearly report in time for the first annual general meeting at the end of June.

Where to start? Henrietta opened her file, sifting through an assortment of pamphlets, letters and newspaper clippings. The last year had been a lot of hard work and not much headway. A groundswell of hostility and what she could only describe as scarring ribaldry had put their mission in part-eclipse. They had been called everything from the 'Noble Army of

She-Beasts' to the 'Prurient Prudes' to 'Petticoat Power' – silly, insulting names with no purpose other than to demoralise and wound.

The expression 'shrieking sisterhood' had been around for some years. Now it was almost common parlance among the society's rudest objectors, and a test of her patience and wit. If these men had but a grain of sense, they would see that she attacked principles, not individuals. What sustained her day after day was the joy of seeing more great men change their reasoning in so short a time.

'We do not want to be men,' she had explained countless times. 'Nor do we hate them. All we really want is suffrage.'

In fact, she readily enjoyed the society of freethinking men, because the most of them – the greatest thinkers among them – were freed from deadening conceit, fostered by the cryptic doctrines of those ancient pious rogues. She wished someone would find an old record proving God a she!

So far, woman had not been tried in legislatures; man had, and had proved himself lamentably a failure. Even towards his fellow man, he was unjust, imprisoned in the past. She had spoken out about this recently, protesting against the treatment of workers, their long hours and conditions. Men themselves would never know true freedom until the reign of political equality, when women would no more permit the oppression of their husbands, sons, fathers and brothers than allow the statutes to be disgraced by the continuance of those old-time, ignorantly unjust laws which degraded men by placing women little above the level of slaves.

Years spent running a dairy farm, Henrietta supposed – up at some ungodly hour, separating and churning and making cheeses – had forced her to survive on minimal sleep. Now, it seemed, she thrived on it. There was even a suggestion of moral superiority in rising early, with the added advantage of having one's letters catch the first post, there being so many to write in a day.

Already she had baked the bread, composed a couple of letters and it was not yet seven. Busyness and toil were virtues, she told herself.

Furthermore, they helped stave off unnecessary criticism, there being enough as it was.

I hope you have a couple of good girls looking after you now that you're famous, Sarah Harding wanted to know in her recent letter. She was still able to do for herself was Henrietta's proud reply. Delegating took time that could otherwise be spent doing something productive. Staying busy, she believed, was the way to be on top of it, this pressure, this constant feeling that, as a suffragist, one had to keep house better than one's friends who were not. And the silly assumption by people that she should somehow have an undying duty to be kinder, more caring, of her mate than otherwise, for fear he might walk out on her and leave.

Don't you feel at risk, dear? Sarah Harding had once asked.

Not at all! There was no more risk or reason why two domestic partners who were comrades, mutually acknowledging a pleasant equality, should separate than there was for the separation of two people condemned to live together who were striving to maintain an inequality.

Sarah was far more broad-minded than she let on. It was true, the observation made by Mrs Lowe that women up-country read widely. In their isolation, they thought about questions and were often more accepting. Country people in general were rarely rude to a woman speaker, even if they disagreed. Often, they appeared to have better manners than those in the metropolis.

The worst offenders were the faceless ones, like Melbourne's *Punch*, a magazine mimicking its London counterpart. Looking back on the yearly record of events in her file, Henrietta could see that her wit had lost the freshness, the playfulness, with which she had countered the jibes of 'Mr Punch' only a year before:

MRS H.A. DUGDALE IN REPLY

1. 'Is she prepared to walk the baby about at night?' I would have no baby walked about at night on any platform, especially not on one belonging to a railway, because it demoralises both baby and walker.

When women and men have equal rights, fretfulness will gradually vanish from the world, and their wise babies will sleep at night.

2. 'Will she get outside a 'bus in the rain to oblige a man?' I have never allowed a man to get outside a 'bus to oblige me, and can't see why voting power should propel me there; but if that man be PUNCH I would certainly oblige him – even if it rained with Presbyterian Assembly violence.

4. 'Is she prepared to smoke or chew?' If smoking and chewing are the results of suffrage for men, I should say, Take it away at once and give it all to women, who would make far better use of it.

5. 'Will she put the hired girl out of the house when necessary, and fling her boxes after her?' That is an expediency that could never arise in my house, for 'hired girls,' I always find, 'do as they are done by.'

6. 'Will she be a policeman and a soldier?' Certainly. Both at once – if dear PUNCH will!

7. 'Will she consent to have her hair pulled out and flatirons thrown at her?' I never before knew that the franchise placed male darlings in such danger. Surely it is only your own light and airy view of matters; but, truthfully, I would just as soon consent to have 'flat' as round irons thrown at me.

8. 'Will she ride a bicycle?' Decidedly not. Equality being my aim, I prefer a cycle which would carry two.

9. 'Will she discard the side saddle?' I have already discarded all saddles, including saddles of mutton.

10. 'Will she grow beard and moustache?' This one is really the only puzzling question, for I would as soon think of committing the highest of treason as accuse PUNCH of being illogical; yet, I often see men who vote, who have no beard and moustache, and numerous others who carefully shave them off. Now either such hair is a necessary qualification for voting, or it is not! If beard and moustache are necessary, why are some men without? Why do men shave them off? And why are not all such unqualified men disfranchised?

*11. 'Will she learn to go up ladders and throw stones?' I have learned
to go up one ladder already; but I don't approve of throwing stones. So
many people live in glass houses, and they are not all fully insured.*

*12. 'Will she discover some way of stopping her sex looking dreadfully
ridiculous when they put on men's unmentionables?' In this I do think
you are a little too hypothetical. Don't you know we have only skirted the
subject as yet, and have only arrived at a 'divided' or 'dual' opinion.*

*Deeming No. 3 to be the most momentous question of all, I have
reserved it for the last: — 'Will she raise her bonnet when she passes a
male acquaintance?' If the acquaintance be you, very dear Mr PUNCH,
that I will, bonnet, hat or cap.*

Yours admiringly

H. A. DUGDALE

Chairman of Committees V.W.S.S.

Telko, Camberwell

[You do us proud, madam. – Ed. Punch]

Did Mr Punch never tire of asking silly questions? Henrietta reached
for notebook and pencil to suppress another flare of irritation.

The best way to deal with Mr Punch, she had come to realise, was
to toss a few questions at him, and with a loud scratch of her pen, she
dotted her 'i's and crossed her 't's and threw back her head. Ah, one
more letter crossed off her letters pending list, just as the clock struck
seven. Opening the door gently, she peeped in. Freddie's slippers were
beside the bed ready. Such a stickler for routine, her dear mate. She,
not much better.

'Just the early bird,' she chirped. 'Breakfast ready when you are, dear.
Don't forget we have a debate tonight. Be there early, if you can.'

Freddie sat up in his nightshirt, swung his great white limbs to the
edge of the bed, bug-eyed and cranky. 'We're out every other night of
the week. Meetings, lectures, debates. Never mind attending a damned
good play or a concert once in a while. How many letters to the

newspapers have you written over the past few years alone? Hundreds, or is it thousands? Do you never, never stop writing letters? Not a minute of the day do you rest, and you are exhausting yourself. And when you exhaust yourself, you become tiresome and exhaust those around you.'

Freddie, gone quiet, slumped back into his shell. Where was her hero? He used to be a formidable debater, accompanying her to meetings. Happily airing his defiance of custom, everything to the wind. What was wrong with her mate? Where was the fun? In all the time she had known him, never had she seen him so boorish and immature. Almost playing the devil's advocate just to annoy.

He stood up and tied the silk cord of his gown into a crisp knot. 'We go out of an evening, and invariably I have to sit and watch you pit yourself against some hot-headed, hot-handed fool. Enough is enough!' Finally he turned to face her. 'I will support you to the end in the Suffrage Society. But do not ask me to accompany you again to any more public meetings.'

ᔧ

That evening, they ate their supper in silence.

'For all that,' she said, clearing away the dishes, 'I may as well have gone to the blessed debate as stay home and talk to myself.'

Freddie put down the tea towel and left the room without reply. Having tuned his violin, he began playing through scales, warming up, by force of habit, but even in those boring scales and exercises she could hear him colouring a different shape, and in each and every one giving free rein to all his emotions. Not a quick, close *tremolo* but broad oscillations, now wild and woolly and full of impurities, and the irate, almost ferocious style of bowing. No. She would not be moved. She stood at the door, not daring to look, mindful of his hard brown eyes following her from over the bridge as he played, pacing about the room.

'A violin is not a drum, dear,' she said gently, when it was finally over.

Freddie had never shown any desire to control her – the very opposite, always appreciative of her independence. She had never been financially reliant on him, having built successfully on her holdings; in effect, she gave him exactly what he wanted – his own sense of freedom.

Freddie was a far harder master of himself. But he was right. A holiday might slow her down.

～

What a busy life you must lead, Henrie. Come and pay us a visit when you get sick of it all.

Henrietta toyed with the idea. She hadn't seen her old friends, the Hardings, since they'd left Queenscliff for the Riverina eight years ago to manage a sheep station.

Moira, the station, was just as Sarah had described. An oasis. Lush and verdant; islands of river-reed and a lake-like lagoon. Shimmering beyond, the hot, dry plain rising red out of the saltbush. And as the buggy pulled up outside the old wide-verandahed homestead, with its faded orange bricks, Sarah was there to greet her. Seven years her senior, she had visibly aged.

'John and the young ones will be back directly. Now come and tell me all about your club.' Having poured some iced tea, Sarah smiled and listened as they sat in the shady courtyard.

'Hello Mrs Dugdale!' Sarah's daughter, Alice, stood before her in navy-blue riding habit.

Later, as they walked about the grounds, Henrietta and Alice were able to talk more openly in private about the women's movement. Alice was surprisingly up-to-date. There were no frills on Alice; cuffs and collar of her white shirt crisp against her cutaway jacket, and what looked like breeches under her riding skirt.

'And you say you have heard the famous Miss Helen Hart fresh from New Zealand speak on the suffrage?'

'Yes,' said Alice, 'in Echuca. Most impressive.'

'Indeed. Miss Hart certainly travels around. Mind you, she likes to work alone. But any woman, I believe, has a right to work how and where she wants.'

'Well, I for one much prefer to be out in the open air. Come and I'll show you the rams.' Alice led her out of the garden past the outhouses to the pens.

Back in the early days, John Harding wouldn't have a bar of merinos. Now the merino was king, filling the Riverina plains thousands to the flock.

Alfred, Alice's brother, saw them coming and opened the gate. 'Handsome beasts, aren't they?'

Henrietta had to agree. They were indeed majestic beings – their noble heads and the size of their horns. What she could see was disdain, their eyes looking down their noses at her over colossal woolly folds.

The woolshed was deserted. Pigeons cooed among the rafters. Slats of sunlight striped the empty boards. There was a strange feeling of abandonment about the place, a kind of ghostliness. In the hot, dry, dusty stillness came the agonising creak of the iron roof contracting, and everywhere the distant scream of cicadas mingling in the haze.

Every now and then a rabbit would pop its head up out of the summer-brown grass. And as they passed the meat-house beneath a mantle of pepper trees, the smell of clotting blood and sawdust floated from the gauze-wire screens.

'Enough.' Henrietta steered away. 'Now, show me a vegetable garden, Alice, or an orchard, please.'

⁓

Figures in white caps and aprons drifted inconspicuously in and out of the dark rooms throughout the day. Henrietta knew she couldn't live this sort of life. An army of staff to supervise inside and out, one's home always open to inspection and a never-ending array of passing visitors and 'sundowners', as they were known. But Henrietta knew that Sarah, so kind and hospitable, would never send away empty-handed a man with a swag or a native – those most in need.

'And your little book, Henrie? Was it well received?' asked Sarah during the evening meal.

'Only two reviews,' said Henrietta. 'Critical but encouraging.' She gave a laugh. 'Henry Gyles Turner called me a "high-toned, impulsive theorist". Apart from that, there's been nothing in the press – much to my disappointment – but according to my friends, my little book has not gone unnoticed. Tongues are wagging, I'm told, and sales speak for themselves. I believe there are still some copies to be had by postal order from Mr Charles Edwin Jones of the *People's Tribune*. One shilling, going for a song.'

'An interesting book,' said Sarah with a thoughtful pause. 'Alice read it too, didn't you, dear?'

Alice looked up. 'Oh yes, I was most intrigued.'

'Dashed if I could make head nor tail of this never-never land of yours,' said John. Having finished a final mouthful, he put knife and fork together. 'Too odd by half. But then again, I'm only a mere male.'

After dinner, the three women retreated to the broad verandah. Through French windows came the click and muted pop of billiard balls. Together with Sarah and Alice, Henrietta sat watching the gradual transformation of the evening. The dust had settled. Half-submerged logs and red-gums silhouetted, their reflection stark across the still waters. So many different types of waterbirds up high, roosting among the dead branches; a plumed egret standing white among the reeds; a cockatoo pooling ripples of its own reflection. Silence thickening in the shadows. Here life stood in isolation, ageless. In contrast, the long, dark Christian era – 'the Age of Blood and Malevolence' – seemed all the more potent. As burning as it was, as exquisitely poetic this summer twilight in the Australian bush, it was the coming light of the truth she craved. If only she could in some way hasten the progress, the old ethos waning and a new one evolving.

'You seem rather out of sorts, Henrie dear,' said Sarah at length. 'I had no idea you were so set against the eating of meat. Never mind. We shall catch you some fish tomorrow. There are plenty of cod and perch out there, if that's more to your liking.'

Henrietta slapped at a mosquito. 'Oh, I wouldn't dream of it. The fish are not hurting anyone, Sarah, let them be.'

'And Einnim, Carl and Austin, how are your boys?'

'Carl is talking about coming to Melbourne again later this year.' She smiled at Sarah. 'I live in hope.'

From out of the darkness came the tap-tap-tapping of John's walking stick on the timber boards. 'I say,' he coughed, 'are those trousers you are wearing, Henrie?'

'It's a divided skirt, Father,' said Alice. 'And fancy, I now have the pattern.'

After a long day, Henrietta was more than ready for bed. 'Men were very wise when they cast off their stays, their long hair and their petticoats.' With straight back, she rose and walked out of her chair. 'Why on earth, John, should two legs be clothed as if one simply because they are a woman's?'

A cat came out of the hydrangeas and stropped against her ankles. Little red tongue out, panting like a dog. She would have picked it up, but John shooed it away. Said not to encourage it. There was plenty of water and plenty of rats.

⌇

The coolest place was out on the lagoon. The next afternoon, floating on the pontoon, surrounded by rippling spirals, she and Sarah found themselves reminiscing about their Queenscliff days, picnics at Point Lonsdale, and the benefits for youngsters growing up by the sea.

'Neither of mine looks like marrying,' Sarah lamented. 'John and I have just about given up hope.'

'So long as they are happy, Sarah, that is the main thing. You wouldn't want them to end up like some poor couples, would you, just for the sake of convenience?'

Henrietta rolled her eyes sideways. But Sarah had fallen asleep. Beyond, she could see Alice mounted astride, her grey gelding splashing confidently through the shallows into a stand of trees.

How she missed her old horses, their stomach-butting for titbits, their snorts, their warm, breathy smell. The feeling of running muscles beneath her, of being woman and horse at one.

Dozing amid the birdsong and the purple-blue blur of dragonflies, she opened her eyes to see a pod of pelicans, their sails wind-filled as they hit and sank upon the water.

How silly it was, both she and Sarah doing their best to navigate the conversation around pleasantries. Neither daring to utter William's name, fearing the mutual discomfort of digging up the past. Better to stick to literature or music, deferring to things they had in common. Small talk could be exhausting. She much preferred in-depth discussions. With Alice so busy, and the newspapers more than a week old, Henrietta began to feel she had been unable to fully stretch her mind. But Sarah, she knew, would send her back in far better spirits, boasting hampers full of jams and pickles, seeds for Freddie and the rest of nature's bounty.

Freddie was quite a different person of late. Gone into himself in his growlery. Her once ardent supporter would now come home and do nothing but grunt and grump. Playing music so dark and thorny. How to penetrate it, this amour of irony and coldness? For, try as she might, she could not hear the great warm heart beating behind it. But she would win him back. Her old spell was not yet broken.

Chapter 20

ᔋ

The first annual general meeting had been and gone, with Mr Charles Jones at the helm. During the very busy lead-up, Henrietta had made the difficult decision to stand down from the committee, with Freddie quick in following suit. Most of the original executive committee had fallen away. Mrs Derham had replaced Dr Bromby, who was now vice-president, and it was reassuring to know that there were ample good women like Mrs Brettana Smyth, Mrs Parker, Mrs Elliott and Misses Hart and Simmons, as well as very capable men, to follow in their footsteps.

By now, Henrietta's name was synonymous with women's rights, her reputation 'prodigious', veering towards 'heroic', as one journalist liked to put it. But increasingly, hecklers left her miffed. If only they would understand. She was not just for women, she was for the equality of all humankind – a utilitarian. Attached to the art of notoriety was a touch of self-gratification, although at times she felt like a snake eating its own tail – all her energies spent continually defending one and the same against the old tried tactic. That in effect brought far more pain than pleasure. Innuendo could be such a hurtful, devastating tool. There was no more brutal method of stopping a woman's mouth than by accusing her of want of delicacy. Both what she had said and written about men over the last four years had been maliciously represented and construed by every newspaper and magazine across the country.

Cold had descended upon Melbourne. The city's streets, as usual, had run to mud and swamp. Henrietta had woken from a long midwinter night with the thought that she would be better off staying at home than having to spend the day wading around the city block in sopping wet boots, just for the sake of a concert.

Having dressed hurriedly behind her bedroom screen, she twisted her hair up angrily in a knot and pinned it firm. Was she really as vinegary and unattractive as they made out? She reached for the beautiful magenta shawl that Freddie had recently bought her and, looking over her shoulder, consulted the mirror. Greying hair swept back elegantly into a Grecian roll, her forehead exposed, the lines of her face had taken on a noble, sculptured look and the dull shine of old alabaster. Hardly the sharp-featured, short-sighted termagant depicted in recent cartoons. Freddie would be the first to pooh-pooh that idea, but against all her better judgement, the odd worming doubt began to niggle her – that vile implication she had lost 'the most precious thing a woman could have' – her feminine charm.

Fiddlesticks! To suggest that the effect of speaking in public would imprint a masculine look on her features, or that political activity would in any way make her less of a woman – to suggest that the polling booth would contaminate the delicacy, the purity, the refinement, the elevation of her own nature and make her into a 'manly woman' – was the common ploy of her attackers; the tyranny of custom that had kept women in the same humiliating position. Whatever was said, Henrietta refused to be intimidated by baiting and harassment. She would continue to rebut in the belief that the power of justice would prevail. People had accused her of being all kinds of things: a truculent haranguer, a *she-man*, even a *she-devil*. Though ludicrous, such imputations were cruel, and sometimes, in a quiet moment alone, she would find herself thinking about them and dwelling on the downside of feminine fame.

Not all newspapers were unkind, she must remind herself. Some, like *The Age*, the *Herald* and the new *Liberator*, even took her seriously. And now one nice chappie from the Sydney *Bulletin* had called her *the champion advocate of women's rights in Australia. Mrs Dugdale has a large heart, a large head, abundance of time, an active pen, and a supple tongue.*

And there it was, her *supple tongue*, secretly giving her cause for concern.

Freddie had taken a look at it and said he couldn't see a darned thing. 'Must be your imagination.' He licked a finger and starting creating little spit curls around her temples. 'There! Put out of mind.'

But she could feel it, a soft, jelly-like protrusion. Once found, her supple tongue wouldn't let it go. The very tip bending over backwards, flicking side to side, checking on it, wobbling it, worrying it with the question *Is it cancer I have?*

It set off her nerves, that lump, being so painfully sore. In her mind, the far-off glint became sharper: the surgeon's knife she had so vigorously proposed for rapists.

She heard the vestibule door close. It was Freddie, returning with a bunch of freesias he had picked from the bottom of the garden. 'Here. Now, for crying out aloud, leave it alone.' He pressed the posy in her lap.

'You have no idea, Freddie. It drives me to distraction.'

Other things began to worry her, floating pains throughout her body. Her 'nemesis', as she called this all-pervasive malady – whatever it was – had now shifted its quarters from her limbs to her chest and tummy. Overriding all else was her tongue. Even a second visit from the doctor failed to allay her misgivings.

'You simply must slow down, Mrs Dugdale. It is well known,' he said, 'that educated women like yourself can end up with a mixture of troubles – uterine disease, hysteria and other derangements of the nervous system – among them neuralgia, which is what I believe you have. So, six weeks in bed without any work, reading or social life. Oh, and no more letter-writing.'

The man was a tyrant, not a doctor. As soon as the front door had closed, she squeezed her eyes and felt a hot, angry tear roll onto her cheek. Far be it for medical theory to rest on fact. Fifty years ago, one death out of every one hundred was due to cancer. Now it was one out of every twenty-two. She looked out the window. Everything was blanched and still. Little to intrigue other than the strange rudimentary outline of a bare-branched frangipani and some frostbitten kale.

'Oh, Freddie. I feel cramped and unsure. I still live in dread that what I have cannot be cured. That I will end up like poor Mama.'

'There, there.' He gave her a pat. 'Come now. Things will turn.'

She shrank into his arms, softening as he began to stroke her hair, circling the pulsating veins in her temples, seeking out the still delicate wedge of skin behind her ears that he knew so well. Freddie, the anchor in her life. There beneath the surface.

⌒

Sunbeams burst through the bay window, saturating the room with a pool of warm light. Outside, arms of ivy and creeper waved wildly this way and that. Freddie's tweed-clad figure emerged, hovering on a ladder, amid falling leaves.

'Shouldn't you be in bed?' His frown said it all.

Six weeks was an eternity. Reducing the amount of tea she drank had stemmed her palpitations and cleared her head. The lump under her tongue, aided by frequent sluicing with a mouth-wash of thymol, borax and boiled water, gradually began to disappear. Apart from the distraction of the odd wave of pain, she could now sit at her desk. The society, she accepted, would have to wait. Her first duty would be to address the mounting pile of personal correspondence from both here and abroad.

Upon opening Einnim's letter, Henrietta began to read, her face double-edged with emotion. Oh Lord! She closed her eyes, his words swimming in the darksome silence.

'No surprise you've been ailing.' Freddie came inside, flung open the window and stood softly whistling, his hands in his pockets, balancing himself on his toes. 'We've been living in a house of dampness far too long.'

Dazed, she tilted her head at him, her eyes lit up and a small smile swelled from within. 'Forget about me, Freddie. It's Einnim!'

'Good heavens, what's happened?' Freddie spun around.

'All's well, dear, but what a frightful experience. Apparently he and his survey team were taking soundings at the mouth of the Mokau River.' She elaborated on how the survey boat got swamped about a quarter of a mile out to sea. Einnim had swum ashore through the surf, but on seeing one of the others in trouble, he had stripped and re-entered the water, at considerable personal risk, and saved the man. For this gallant effort, he had earned himself a bronze medal and a certificate from the Royal Humane Society of Australasia, presented at a special ceremony in Waitara.

The news of Einnim's award, the recognition of his outstanding bravery, his integrity, would be inspirational to others. For Henrietta, it was the tonic she needed – an instant injection of humanism, health and wellbeing.

Billows of blue rhododendrons appeared to float for a minute, clusters of colour bursting in the breeze. The window would need a jolly good clean, but at least the vista was clear.

I sincerely hope I will never be placed in similar unpleasant circumstances again. But if I should be, I trust I would be actuated by the same feelings. I wish to say that though the medal is mine through circumstances the honour is due to all my comrades who could not have behaved in a braver more selfless manner, considering the danger they were in. I desire also to thank our friends, the Maoris for their assistance for without them some of us would have fared badly ... I wish to call attention to the fact that if I had not been taught to swim when I was young I should not have the lasting pleasure of saving another fellow creature's life.

'Well, I never …' Freddie shook his head in disbelief as he read the enclosed newspaper report of the ceremony and Einnim's words of thanks. 'Einnim, eh? Heroism of that nature rarely springs from great deliberation.' He rubbed at his beard. 'Humble, that's the sign of a real hero. What a sterling young man of yours.'

'Not so young,' she said. 'Thirty next year.' But in her mind, she would be forever keeping vigilance from the Queenscliff jetty – his sinewy little body spinning through the shallows like a minnow.

So sorry to hear of your illness. Come out to St Kilda and indulge yourself in the hot sea baths, wrote Mrs Lowe. The healing powers of the seawater and its minerals were nothing new to Henrietta, and, with her hair now like a shorn lamb's, the easy excursion soon became a thrice-weekly habit through the summer months. Five minutes' walk from the terminus to the baths, and she could call upon Mrs Lowe in the one round trip.

Arm in arm, the two friends strolled along the esplanade one Sunday afternoon in January 1886, discussing the progress of the society and the year ahead.

'Presumably your husband is still happy to be our auditor?'

'Oh yes,' said Mrs Lowe. 'We've almost three hundred members, I believe.'

'It heartens me, Annie. I feel born again. I can't wait to get back.'

The south breeze was fresh and bracing as they wove their way through thick bands of promenaders. Midway at the grassy square, they stopped to take in the ragbag of colours and whites shimmering on the open blue waters. Henrietta steadied her parasol, eyes scanning beyond the pier. Masts stood forest-like at Sandridge. Black hulls and spars at Williamstown, their stark outlines dissolving into the steely dock waters.

Drifting in the wind amid squealing seagulls, the strains of a brass band – the Salvation Army songsters they had seen around the flagstaff.

'What harm are they doing? If they save a few souls here, well and good, but I dare say they would be better off concentrating their efforts in the grog-houses.'

'And fancy' – Mrs Lowe's eyes began to crinkle – 'they even see fit to put a woman in the pulpit. Some of their best men are women, I'm told!'

The two women chuckled between themselves, before settling on the topic of Sunday entertainment.

'Isn't it ridiculous?' said Henrietta. She related how she and Freddie had been regular attendees at Joseph Symes's Sunday lectures at the Hall of Science, and she had ended up having recently been called upon as a defence witness after Symes, a fellow secularist, had been charged in the Supreme Court for creating a disturbance. 'Surely, if a church can be open on a Sunday, so too can a library, a museum or other venues of instruction. We should be more concerned about legislating for early closing and the day-to-day sale of alcohol, for the damage it does.'

A debate on 'The Heredity of Alcohol' was coming up at the Secular Association in December, and she would have much to say about that. She pulled at a glove. There were many other injustices she wished to see fixed. Placing a limit on the opening hours of all shops was one, which she had let be known at a recent public meeting at the Richmond Town Hall.

Leaving the esplanade, the two women passed a mixture of handsome stone mansions, hotels, terrace houses and pretty wooden cottages with verandahs, until they came to Mrs Lowe's house.

Once inside, Mrs Lowe took off her hat and gloves and gave a passing glance in the hall mirror. Henrietta was pleased to see her friend had followed suit in cropping her hair. Shortly curled, it showed off her fresh complexion and plump cheeks, making her look years younger, almost like an untidy schoolboy.

'Now sit back, Mrs D., and let me go and see about some tea.'

The drawing room was simply furnished with a piano, and a collection of old colonial pieces made from cedar. Grey walls were relieved by a white marble fireplace and panels with gold beading and delicate sprays of hand-painted Australian blossom. It was a room where one could as easily entertain or quietly reflect.

'Ah, good afternoon, Mrs Dugdale.' Mr Lowe entered in white flannel trousers, followed by his wife and young daughter of about nine or ten years old, carrying tea trays.

'There. You may pour, if you are careful.' Mrs Lowe bent down and fondled the girl's chin affectionately. 'And when you've done that, dear, you can offer Mrs Dugdale some of those lovely dainties, then pass them to Father.'

The child's sunny face was a junior replica of her mother's. After doing as she was told, the girl sat herself opposite, her licorice-stockinged legs scissoring under her short-skirted sailor suit, as she nibbled contentedly, biscuit concealed in either hand.

'May I say, Mrs Dugdale, you look fresher than paint?'

'Thank you, Mr Lowe. I'm so excited. Your good wife has just been telling me a new development could well bring things forward for our club and the promise of more support.'

'Oh?' he said, looking at her with interest. 'Go on.'

'Yes, the recently inaugurated National Liberal League of Victoria claims among other things to stand for the protection of women and children. There is talk women's suffrage will be a new plank in their platform.'

⁓

A blue sky rising and it was not yet six. Already Henrietta could feel the intense heat, the bright striped light almost vibrating against the whitewashed walls. The thought of climbing aboard one of Camberwell's one hundred and thirty screeching, dirty iron horses per day in a February heatwave was abhorrent. She would dress to suit – a simple, loose cornflower-coloured costume she had recently styled out of Liberty silk, which would see her through the better part of the day and into the evening. Better to go earlier than later, rest up at the Coffee Palace under the new ceiling fans, have a light tea, before heading off to Temperance Hall in Russell Street, where the central branch of the National Liberal League would be gathering to formally consider its platform proposals.

Henrietta and Mrs Lowe each paid a shilling at the door and joined Mrs Elliott and Mrs Parker, a warm draught following them to their seats. Henrietta waved her fan and smiled and nodded. Five rows of women – about twenty in all, she counted.

With the meeting finally under way, one of their own, Mrs King, moved that 'women's suffrage' be added to the plank. Everything was proceeding smoothly. Both she and Mrs Lowe were among those who spoke strenuously in favour of the motion, backing it with much point and emphasis. Against strong objection from some quarters, the motion, by a small majority, was voted in. There was a sudden scuffle at the door and the meeting turned rowdy. Everyone talking over the top of each other, nobody willing to give way. Mrs Lowe stood up.

'Gentlemen, please, the confusion is such that I cannot hear what is being done. At our meetings, we allow one to speak at a time.'

Craning her neck, Henrietta saw a crowd fighting its way into the hall, refusing to leave amid further havoc.

'Savages of Melbourne, order!' the chairman roared, addressing the gatecrashers. Amid much farcical confusion, the gaslights went off, the police were called, and the league was forced to resume the meeting in the quieter quarters of the Coffee Palace.

Barely a few weeks on, Mr Punch was still having a go at the plank of women's suffrage, calling it 'a rotten plank with a hell yawning before them'. Oh, craven Mr Punch, up to his old tricks again. Daring her to throw down the gauntlet, to 'step up'.

'NOW, MRS DUGDALE, STEP UP!'

Noble Mr Punch – You invite me to 'step up', though the plank, you imply is rotten? Where can I upper step than where I am? Beloved of the Argus and Punch's friend!! There is no higher step!

*That the holy Father Campion should have found our planks rotten
is more than perplexing, considering that they were made to bear just
the exact weight of honest men – particularly the women's suffrage
plank ... I think so much of men that all I desire is equality with
them; and my dreams are of future facts, when men and women will
be such dear friends and equals that man's boots will be used solely
for the feet, pokers for the fire, axe-handles for the axe-heads only,
and many other beautiful things I see in that future when your efforts
and those of the Women's Suffrage Society shall have worked out their
humanitarian aims.*

*Always, dear Mr Punch, whether you have a Bullet-in, or not, your
same old friend,*

HENRIETTA DUGDALE

Telko, Camberwell

Every time Punch tried to ridicule her, Henrietta fretted. It infuriated
her; it sapped her, took away precious time and energy she could put to
better use.

'He's a bully boy,' she muttered. 'Forever taunting me, making me
the butt of every insult. Now I suppose I'll have to go and write yet
another letter.'

Freddie pinched his eyes and raised a warning finger. 'Don't let him
get off lightly, love, but whatever you do, keep him as your friend.'

Henrietta stood watching him leave for work, turn at the gate, his
routine wave and air kiss. She hugged her arms in the cold pure air,
feeling the creep of defeat. Either side of the portico, what remained of
the wisteria for company; great knots and a series of snake-like snarls
struggling to breathe in brown and silent gasps.

How to advance the society and its cause? There was only one way left
she could see. If some member of the government could not be induced
to introduce a Bill to legalise women's suffrage, then the society should

ask a private member to do so, with the object of moving it annually until the Bill became law. Who best to appeal to?

Quickly she closed the door and returned to her desk, opening the *Argus*. Her eyes froze, coming across a report of her June address at Secular Hall, 'Advanced Women on Customs and Costumes', and she winced. The reporter had taken everything she had said completely out of context.

It was a lengthy speech in which she had again attacked principles, not people. She had denounced the monarchy, the church, and the Legislative Council. She had gone on to condemn unsparingly the customs of drinking and smoking, and the customs of dress, which she had so often spoken and written about before. She pointed to the silliness and prejudice that came of custom, before finally turning to the custom of kissing. Her words had been quite clear. 'Gentlemen and ladies, do not feel alarmed,' she had reassured her audience. 'I would NOT, save with two exceptions, abolish that custom, old as I am.' These exceptions were kissing children and kissing Bibles in court, since new scientific evidence from America had shown the dangers of cross-infection to those most vulnerable.

What had she done to deserve such vilification – this horrible hastily and petulantly drawn sketch of her published in the *Argus*? The reporter was low enough to attack her attitude and demeanour, and to speculate as to what manner of man the speaker's husband must be, if yet alive.

Freddie was fuming that night when he read it. He stretched his neck from his high white collar. 'I will not let this pass.'

She had never seen him so provoked and fiery. It thrilled her to know that he was still on her side no matter what. And yet, though he would stand proudly to defend her honour in the name of love, it seemed a perilous dance – since her humiliation was his – and she wondered how much longer he would be able to take it.

'Is there anything I can get you, dear?'

'Cooking sherry, if there is some, and a fresh nib.' He glowered. 'By Jove, I'll give them something to talk about!'

Freddie took to his desk, where he laboured until late in a great shroud of darkness. When he had finished his letter, he took off his boots and removed the dust; then, with a soft brush, he spread them with Mason's blacking, and buffed them up to a spit-shine.

The next morning, she went over to his desk and lifted the paperweight – a prized headless sphinx – so as to dust. She drew in her breath at the very thought of touching his neatly stacked notes. Already her cheeks were aglow. She reached for her brow, half-shielding her downcast eyes. It was wrong to pry – a sin made worse by knowing one would only have to make a secret of one's shame. And yet … she smiled inwardly, her guilt enhancing her pleasure. What a fitting response to the *Argus*. In no uncertain terms, Freddie was wanting to let it be known, in black and white, that after twenty years of the closest relationship, he knew 'this lady' better than any other, and 'this lady' was obviously her.

A face of such benevolence – a character and manner so gentle that, brought within its influence the confidence and love of children, animals and all in trouble are instantly secured. A mind of such honest and high purposes and of such absolute purity that the offer of a Golconda weighed against a grain of truth would not possess an atom of temptation. A heart filled with such kindly sympathies for all animated nature, but especially for the weak and defenceless, that no effort of body or intellect is spared or grudged to alleviate any ills of their condition – a courage so great that the formerly frequent, but now happily less frequent, tortures of an enduring and painful disease produced no relaxation of endeavour to help forward … all the subject of injustice hardship or cruelty – a philanthropy so wide spreading and impartial as to embrace … even men! Of habits so domestic that nothing is left undone on her part (and almost unaided) to make her home what it is – a model of cleanliness, order, comfort – a place of rest.

Each morning, Henrietta rushed to open the *Argus* in search of Freddie's letter. By the end of July, it was obvious the editor had chosen not to publish it. Then, to her surprise, the letter appeared in the weekly *Liberator* at the beginning of August, thanks to Joseph Symes, the editor.

Freddie! Her darling Freddie, tender, wise and valiant, almost verging on quixotic. But for him to paint her as a paragon was really far more than she deserved.

⁓

The more Henrietta's notoriety grew, the greater curiosity it seemed to attract about her personal life – both her past and present situations. Awkward questions that made her prickle she managed to dodge or obfuscate with an enigmatic smile.

If it wasn't questions, it was accusations and cartoons. Now Punch, the old devil, continuing his insults into the following year, depicted her as a cruel ogress terrifying the life out of a man who had his back to her and not a stitch on. She, the thief, clutching his stolen clothes.

Punch, she suspected, was in league with the devil-cum-publisher Mr Willoughby of the *Daily Telegraph*, who had recently reproached her – in her quest for the vote – of wanting everything else a man had.

As soon as she saw the cartoon, Henrietta sat down and wrote off a rambunctious reply. But that evening, without the armour of her pen, she failed to hide her anger. Freddie gave her a hug, did his best to humour her. 'Don't worry, my sweet. Beat him at his own game.' Off he went the next morning, whistling his flutey notes upon the breeze.

But she knew that, like her, he would still feel acutely every hostile taunt. Brave though he was, deep down he would be feeling isolated, ostracised, with the bank of male judgement against him. Who would not face the mirth of a mob without some of it getting under one's hide?

Since she could not fight with muscle, she resolved to fight with her wits.

Once open, the floodgates of controversy were hard to close. It distressed the boys to see their mother being mocked in every broadsheet across Australasia. The matter was as embarrassing as it was intensely personal, for her children had been ripped from her bosom and, like her, had suffered under the laws that sanctioned their father's behaviour.

How it lifted her heart to have Carl publicly express his support for her in a letter to the *Herald* in May. He did not hold back, showing how much he cared for her in the face of all her detractors.

Women's Suffrage has for many years been championed in Melbourne by my mother … I feel a deep interest in it as a man knowing the injustice is on the side of my sex. Who is to determine the sphere of any one? What right has any law to lay down the sphere of a woman any more than of a man. To be prohibited from entering into any occupation that one's nature fits one for, and which is perfectly moral and just only because of the accident of birth – then it is a misfortune to be a woman. There never will be perfect laws until women take part in their formation. The influence of women in Parliament is as necessary as in the home or any other sphere. Let women follow whatsoever occupation they please and their nature permits, and receive the same wage for the same work as men, and it will be found that they will command more respect instead of less – they will make better wives and mothers because of their increased knowledge and ability, and they will also be more independent in making their own choice of a husband, and will not be driven into alliance with some unworthy object through the eagerness of parents to get them off their hands, as now is too often the case.

Carl, bless him, could see to a better future.

Chapter 21

~

There was no such thing as a discreet or docile suffragist, Henrietta had long ago decided. Now, 1887 – the year of the Queen's Golden Jubilee – was the time to make their pitch, to put a deputation to the Premier and point out that strange paradox. For if Her Majesty the Queen was considered fit to rule the entire British Empire, how could she not be considered capable of exercising the franchise? As it stood, the argument that women were intellectually inferior to men was about exhausted.

But at the third annual general meeting of the Victorian Women's Suffrage Society, Henrietta could already hear rumblings of discontent. Numbers were down; the society was waning. A dog by any other name would bark as loud, but Brettana Smyth, their stalwart, was now talking about starting up her own group. Mrs Smyth's motto was delivered with a towering presence: *know thyself, thy body, as the first step towards democracy.* Henrietta was quick to agree; a woman had a right to birth control. There was nothing obscene or scandalous about it, as some members suggested, and for Mrs Smyth, it was even more important than the suffrage.

The editor of the *Argus* pounced upon their differences, claiming the Suffrage Society didn't seem to have a clear idea of what they wanted and should make up their minds.

Surely, she thought, we have laid our purposes very clearly before the public. They were a band – a little band – of eccentric people, if the editor chose to call them so, but they had been stimulated to action by faith in a great principle of truth: freedom. They had always been united on one point: women's right to take part in the choice of a legislature. In legislation, there were many things that concerned women equally with men, and there were parts to be played in political life that women were particularly suited to fill. Their influence would correct many evils. The *Argus* spoke of the mean, hardening influence of politics as a reason why women should be held aloof from them. What pettiness this line of reasoning was. If women deserved such credit as was assigned to them for virtue, for modesty, for right feeling and right action, then this was a God-given power they possessed, and if it was a God-given power, it would bear the trial and test it would be subjected to in the political arena.

What a pity Freddie had been off-colour and missed the meeting. But he too could see that despite a united goal, side issues were a distracting and often divisive force. Whether it be contraceptives, child-raising, physical freedom, education, temperance, church or secular, some things just didn't go down well with some members. Associated members of the Secular Association, like Freddie and herself, were from all stripes. Humanitarians with a hostility to church and state. Some just wanted the suffrage, others total anarchy. But, as she knew from experience, divisiveness would only bring self-destruction.

They were all more or less still up against the same archenemies: those from the Old Country. Conservatives – so-called men of letters – who failed to understand or accept science. Prigs and pedants who could never really understand Darwin. Egotists, born with perverted notions of mine and thine. Some made her laugh. One recent assailant at a public meeting reminded her of a turkey cock, feathers puffed up, fanning and strutting, babbling the same weary inanities that he had heard his father and grandfather constantly dinning into the ears of his hen-relatives.

But now it was time to take stock. Freddie had appeared so solid; she, too busy fending off the enemy – Punch and his gloating army of admirers – to have noticed his decline.

'What's wrong, love?'

'Darned dyspepsia again.' Freddie sat up in bed, his breathing short and fluttery.

The attack had come on overnight, and she had been woken by his restlessness and grinding moans. Distressed to see him in such a state, she called for the doctor at once. She drew the Chinese screen around the bed, allowing a peephole for herself. With every prod and poke, Freddie gripped his belly. Questions like 'Any passing of blood?' sent her into further waves of alarm. Clearly, Freddie was very unwell. Greenish tinges crossed the pallor of his cheeks, shadowing his pain.

Gripped in a chill of fear, she retreated to the window, the *pound-pound-pound* of her heart excruciating, her mind wild with all kinds of sinister findings.

The doctor, who had been serenely silent, put away his stethoscope and snapped shut his bag.

'Well, Mrs Dugdale …'

She held her breath, trying to prepare herself for the worst.

'It's not his heart, you'll be pleased to know.'

'Oh, Doctor.' She exhaled sharply. 'Tell me, then, what is it?'

'Could be the beginnings of a stomach ulcer.'

'An ulcer? But Freddie is young.'

'Overwork, dietetic excesses, impoverished food …'

Well, it's certainly not dietetic excess, Doctor, we eat only good plain food in this house. Pulses and vegetables – no meat – only fresh milk, cheese and eggs.'

'Very wise, Mrs Dugdale. But you and Mr Johnson have been very busy over recent years, have you not? Publicity is not always kind to those in fame. It can be very stressful.'

Bodies were breaking up. There was pressure from all directions. First the Secular Association. Now their own Victorian Women's Suffrage Society.

But Freddie, poor darling. She nipped at her lips. How could she have been so complacent? So negligent? Taken her ascendancy of suffering for granted. She shuddered, envisaging leeches and enemas. Somehow she maintained a sober voice.

'Now, Doctor, as to the treatment?'

'Rest and good nursing are what Mr Johnson needs.' He hurriedly jotted something down. 'We prefer to fast the patient these days. So ice-cold milk to be given six times a day for the first twenty-four hours. Gradually increase day to day, then perhaps try some eggnog. Need I say, not a drop of alcohol.' He nudged his wire-rimmed spectacles up his nose and gave her what she took to be a sneer. 'You must be pleased, Mrs Dugdale. I believe the temperance movement is going stronger than ever.'

She caught his glassy eye and held it. 'Yes, Doctor, and so, too, I believe, is the medical profession. That, in the year 1887, the female medical faculty of Melbourne will be represented by one woman will be looked back on in years to come as something truly astonishing.' She pulled back her lip. 'In America, you see, women are princesses of science and are here to stay.' Thousands had gained the coveted knowledge, many practising prosperously in both medicine and law; over there, she told him, women even sat as jurors.

Duty was duty. Henrietta tended the sickbed, making nutritious broths and blancmanges. Fussed as she had never fussed before while Freddie's illness took its course. Rather than have him stew or stare all day at a dead wall, she found ways to excite his sensitivities, as well as her own. Music. She played for him all of his favourites. Beethoven by the hour; Schubert, Schumann, Brahms. There were times he was so sleepy that she had to resort to colour. Fresh poppies. A rose on his breakfast tray. Light, in itself, she knew, could be enough to relieve one's state of nerves. The craved return of a day.

It was a lingering malady, but by year's end Freddie claimed he was fit enough to go back to work. By then, Henrietta was hankering to know what had been going on inside the inner sanctums of their little club, and the general state of affairs. However, her absence, according to Mrs Lowe, had been neither here nor there; the Women's Suffrage Society had dissolved through natural attrition.

In May the following year, a carton of women's magazines, the first of a Sydney issue called *The Dawn*, arrived on Henrietta's doorstep. She had heard only good things about the editress, Mrs Lawson, a remarkable, brave countrywoman, and her latest success.

Opening the box, she savoured the crispness, the smell, of fresh printer ink on paper. Here was something to be grateful for.

As she distributed copies to fellow suffrage supporters, each day brought more surprises. Mrs Smyth, true to her promise, had formed her own Australian Women's Suffrage Society. Another group, the Woman's Christian Temperance Union, was growing daily. There was also talk of Dr William Maloney, the newly elected Member for West Melbourne, putting a Bill for women's suffrage to the assembly next year.

Freddie, still weak on optimism, had wearied of interest. 'Fluff in the pan', he called it.

Months of nursing Freddie through convalescence had given Henrietta rise for reflection. Had she neglected him, been too self-centred, too wrapped up in the cause? She dared not decide, for he was still not himself.

Coming home late from the office one night, he looked fed up and frazzled.

'I must either leave it till later,' he grumbled, 'or suffer.' All he wanted, he said, was a seat in a train that would take him from the turmoil of the city to the quietude of his suburban home, without having to plunge into the pandemonium of the station.

Freddie was not exaggerating. With the suburbs growing exponentially, the transport system could not keep up. The ordeal at rush hour was as he described: engines belching volumes of black smoke and flavours of cooked oil, escaping steam frizzling, locomotives whistling in every key known to music. But add to all that the confusion of men hurrying to and fro amid the crowd, with blazing trucks loaded with lamps that must be fixed in a train of eleven carriages, and only three minutes in which to do it.

Then to have to inhale the acrid, suffocating odours of dying oil lamps, being pushed and shoved and told to get out of the way.

Henrietta sympathised. But it was just as bad for everyone travelling by train as it was for the 'jaded businessman', as Freddie called himself. Not all Freddie's miseries could be blamed on the railway. It was obvious he was being overworked. The law firm blood-sucked, and for paltry compensation. He would never be made a partner; never be admitted to the Bar. He had the knowledge, all the prerequisites. But lacking in judgement, whisper would have it. Because of her? Hardly a case for safeguarding the image of the legal profession, with its shysters and pettifoggers and inebriated old men with false hair. There was no more moral man on earth than Frederick Johnson – and yet his good name and public standing were in question simply because he and she lived together as man and wife.

In truth, they had both been so diabolically busy that they had drifted apart. Looking back at the merry-go-round of events, there'd been little time for each other, little time too for old friends, true friends, whom over the years one had come to value above all others, let alone what she had left of family. How oft had Emma written? *Aunty, come and see our new house. We've called it 'Austin Villa'.*

And what about Sarah Harding? Sarah's letters lay fading in folds. According to Alice, her mother had become lost in her frailty. Due to old age and injury, her father had retired from station work, and Alice and her brother, Alfred, were now running their own family property in Moama.

When Alice arrived early in the new year, she came determined to enjoy the last few weeks of the world fair – Melbourne's second

International Exhibition. Arm in arm, she and Henrietta joined the grey, lilac and lavender hues streaming through Carlton Gardens to the main entrance of the People's Palace.

Alice was keen to see some of the agricultural displays. Bypassing bale after bale of different classes of wool, she finally stopped at the merino sign, took off a glove and parted a fleece with the side of her palm. 'Feel that, Henrie.'

It was truly the finest, most lustrous wool of all.

Alice was interested to hear about the contributions made by other countrywomen in the care and rearing of livestock.

'The famous Mrs Lawson is a model of inspiration,' said Henrietta.

Alice thanked her for the two copies of *The Dawn*. 'You'll be pleased to know I'm now an ardent fan of Mrs Lawson.'

'Good to hear, Alice. She's not afraid to tackle any subject. Nothing's too sacred.'

What a hard life this brave, resourceful widow had had in the bush. Not only could Mrs Lawson fatten cattle and drive a four-in-hand, she had since given the world a journal and mouthpiece for all women: a club and a platform for the message of enfranchisement. The rising sun of a new beginning.

Henrietta went on to talk about women's education and equality of opportunity between the sexes. 'Give a girl a chance and see how far she'll go. Fancy, Alice, seven young women admitted to Melbourne Medical School. We'll be running our own hospital soon.'

After doing the rounds of the painting galleries, Henrietta took Alice's arm and directed her towards the lake, with its various illustrations of Aboriginal life, before going on to the Maori whares and idols in the New Zealand Court.

'And how are the boys?'

'Oh, pretty good, thanks. Of course, you realise they are grown men now – bachelors still, all three. I'm long due a visit.' Her gaze rested upon her friend as she asked, 'Are you happy with your lot,

Alice? Tell me, do you hanker for anything, being stuck up there in the bush?'

Alice pondered and gave her a whimsical smile, as if reading her thoughts. 'The seaside.'

The next day, being perfect, they took the tram to Brighton. They talked variously about the land boom and the banks, tomorrow's weather, and ended up back on the subject of women's rights.

'Do you ever think about marriage, dear?' Presumably Alice had since got over the embarrassment of a broken engagement to some long-lost cad of a beau.

'I used to say there was plenty of time. Remember? Now I tell people I have enough men to look after, what with a middle-aged brother and invalid parents, plus a farm – where would I be with a husband as well?'

Alice was just the sort of daughter-in-law to long for. It was not entirely out of the question. Einnim, eight years her junior, was too remote and obsessed with boats. No, it was Carl she was thinking of. Was it too late? Alice was forty-two. The trim, plump promise of youth had somewhat relaxed.

Henrietta squinted through her veil. Across the sand, a row of bathing-huts stood, shimmering gaudy blocks.

'I never knew women could duel,' said Alice, her mind still fresh with the daring French paintings they had seen at the Exhibition that day of a pair of half-clad women in action before a crowd of spectators. 'I should have thought that even women of that class would have sufficient regard for their health to cover their upper halves. What a stir they caused.'

'Oh, that?' Henrietta dismissed it with a *pff*. 'The French and their facetiousness – free play of the limbs. To an artist, nudity is perfectly natural, Alice. As to duelling and whatever honour means – that is quite another thing.'

The discipline of art and skill was good for body and mind. Young actresses in the Conservatory of Music and Declamation in Paris were being taught the art of fencing in costumes unrestricted. What a curious coincidence that two of the best lady fencers on record had retained their youth and beauty until very late in life.

'Are you coming in?' Henrietta dipped a toe in the water. Even at her age, stripping down into woollen navy-blue *breeks* brought frissons of delight. That feeling of taking the plunge, head down to break the surface, sips of air carefully expended in the cold aftershock. To linger underneath again and again, the water's silence, calm and sublime, was to be at one with Junius. In the black blur of solitude, to conjure his presence: Junius looking up at her body from his ocean bed. Once so clear, the image had changed shape over the years, now smaller and fuzzy around the edges.

Thank heavens for good health and her early rebellion against the wearing of stays. One had only to look around at the various states of womanhood on the beach. Grossly deformed figures and bent ribs; sides from armpit to hip forming a right angle. A carpenter's square would fit exactly.

She shook her pearly wet curls and gave them a towelling. Not many sixty-three-year-old women were as fit or as adventurous. She could run and swim with thorough pleasure, stoop or bend in any direction without the inevitable grunt usually heard from elderly persons. Her back straight and free from pain, as it had been in childhood, she could do garden work, nearly all that was needed in the house, and generally walk two or three miles daily – sometimes double that distance – in comfort, too, because her boots were made to fit her feet instead of her fitting her feet into boots.

Henrietta looked around. The pretence of modesty and confinement had always baffled her – women having to swim in pairs when the beach was already well-roped to separate the sexes. Men, lucky things, were free to swim anywhere, anytime – at night, naked or alone.

'You know, Alice,' she sighed, 'one day men and women will be taking their swims together and they'll look back at us with laughing pity.'

After they had changed out of their wet swimsuits, the two women sat sheltered by a shady grove of tea-trees. Here, there was nothing to do but sit back and follow the pleasure-seekers, the beauty of the coast against the city and the gentle floating lines – figures in whites drifting past the jagged outlines of the reef; the quivering brightness and the easy *lip-lap* soporific.

'Drop more, Alice dear?' Together they sipped cold tea, which she had flavoured with a little lemon and honey. 'Now, promise me you'll stay down for the final Centennial concert. Beethoven's 5th. And do you like Wagner? *Tristan und Isolde.* Oh, I can't wait. It's so enthralling!' In her mind, the 'love death' could never be played too often.

Henrietta opened the wicker basket and unwrapped rounds of walnut, celery and cottage cheese sandwiches, and thin slices of pound cake, which she offered to Alice in turn.

'Wake me in half an hour, would you?' she said when they had eaten. 'I like to be home before Freddie, half past four at the latest.' Hat over face, she stretched out against an old clinker-boat and closed her eyes.

⁓

By late winter, Sarah, her darling confidante of thirty-seven years ago, was dead. Looking back, their periodic rendezvous in Melbourne had been far too few. She should have gone and paid Sarah another visit, or at least have written more often. She had been meaning to. Always meaning to. But the intensity of her letter-writing and her compulsion for public speaking had worn her thin. There seemed never to be enough time, never quite enough love to go around.

Sarah's funeral sadly had been and gone. Henrietta penned a note to Alice, expressing her deepest sorrow and promising she would come at the end of spring.

⁓

Best take the train to Echuca, she thought, there being only the one change, and stay the night in town so as to arrive at the Harding property the following day, fully rested. A short excursion upriver to break the journey. Clear blue skies and sunshine were just what she needed.

And yet, as the paddle steamer left the wharf in Echuca, it kept haunting her – her earliest association with Sarah in Queenscliff.

Had she ever thought to pay Sarah that kindness back? To enquire more frequently and sincerely as to her health? Here she was, trying to save the world from injustice, and her dearest friend, one of the most beautiful, caring women in the world, had slipped away without notice.

Henrietta sank back into her canvas deckchair. There was an air of exhaustion about the narrow part of the river, its body filled with mood and introspection. Her shoulders began to sag with pain and defeat. As the grey-green waters slopped against the silver river beaches, the spray-rooted rivergums bowed and beckoned beyond. Any rocking motion was barely perceptible. Eyes half-closed, she fell into a kind of torpor. Besides the accompanying birdsong, she could detect a peculiar bush music, the soft chug a steady continuum behind the churning of paddles. One two three four, one two three four, slowing down for corners or natural obstructions.

Leaden leaves shivered above. In between slivers of sky of the deepest blue penetrated the naked white limbs of the rivergums, sending the water into rippling reflections, and in the ghostly rhythms and all their shades of sorrow she felt a strange sense of belonging, a sense that she might reach out and find her friend.

But as soon as she tried to cling to that moment, reality jarred. Pink and grey galahs swarmed and circled above like gulls at sea, serving to warn of oncoming traffic. Then the inevitable ear-splitting horn as they idled. Otherwise the water was bereft, a graveyard of rotting bark, fallen leaves and branches. Its course unclear, unpredictable, broken by shifting shadows. All too often would come the sickening sound of snags dragging under the flat-bottomed hull, and the holding of breath. On one occasion, everything stopped dead and a petrifying hush fell across the river.

Henrietta undid her top button and patted the sweat from her brow. 'How long back to Echuca?' she asked the captain.

'Five more minutes, Ma'am.'

Then the brilliance as light came crashing through. Dried-out pylons loomed, a mishmash of heads, hands and a raucous hail as a fat rope spun out from above.

∽

The drive was relatively short, the homestead half-hidden behind the curve of a palm-shaded driveway. Through the golden dusty light, she could make out the horizontal patterns of a garden. Ripening valencias on rows of glossy trees. To the north, the monotony of endless kangaroo-coloured plains, with saltbush and pine ridge and the glassy line beyond.

As soon as she arrived, the pups erupted from their dustbowls, squiggling and squirming around her feet. She bent down and tickled them, smelling their peculiar puppy smell as they licked her hands and slipped over her boots in topsy-turvy. It set them all off.

'Down, Buster! Down, pups!'

Oh, what a joy to see them dancing and gyrating on the end of their chains. White teeth gleaming at her; their yips, their smiles.

Henrietta, hearing a whistle, looked up. John Harding limped out and gave her a wave of his walking stick.

The air was hot and dry, and tea was taken outside on the croquet lawn. From here, Henrietta could restfully survey her surroundings: the rambling weatherboard house and its gingerbread fretwork gables swathed by tall, shady gums and the relief of wetland verdure.

'My one great wish is to visit your mother's grave before I leave.'

'Best in the cool of day,' said Alice. 'What about first thing tomorrow morning?'

Alice accompanied her to the cemetery. They began picking their way among the pepper trees, with their weeping foliage and dark, undulating shadows, to Sarah's resting place. Here and there, a fresh glint of sun lit up a headstone or the rust on a wrought-iron surround.

'I'm afraid it's only temporary,' whispered Alice as they came to a standstill. 'The stonemason's running late.'

Henrietta bowed her head. For all that, Sarah's grave was just an anonymous wooden cross marking a sandy mound. How inadequate and empty it made her feel. She kneeled down and placed a twig of pink peppercorns before the cross. For a while, she remained bound in stillness, taking in the sweet, lingering fragrance of the berries. Not far away, she could hear the riverboats, and the waterfowl honking around the levee banks, and in the early-morning light came the realisation that while Sarah may be dead, yet she shall live.

Chapter 22

⌒

As the year turned with the decade, Henrietta was torn between going to New Zealand for a holiday and staying home and keeping an eye on Freddie. His daily commute was the last straw, compelling him to write a letter of complaint to the *Herald*.

RAILWAY FREAKS

Sir, Can mortal man give a reasonable solution of the following enigma? The 5.15 train from town to Camberwell is always so rushed that unless one is on the platform awaiting its arrival, the obtaining of even standing room is problematical. You would think that in the face of the loud and continuous complaints of overcrowding which have assailed the department for years past, it would gladly welcome any means to relieve the pressure of the traffic. Not so, however, as in the mysterious language of the 'Family Herald', 'the sequel will show.'

The train leaving for Lilydale at 5.12 makes the first stop at Camberwell, and numerous residents in the latter suburb, including myself, have for months past been accustomed to travel by it. It is always half empty. I have rarely had as companions in my compartment more than two, generally one; sometimes I have been the sole occupant. For which reason, and the nearness of the second-class carriages to the exit

gate at Camberwell I have, although a first-class yearly ticket-holder,
invariably ridden second-class, consequently have felt that while
consulting my own comfort I was at the same time conferring a benefit
on the Commissioners by leaving a cranny in the always too compactly
loaded Camberwell train available for one other unfortunate, and thus
doing my little toward relieving the difficulty.

Now for my conundrum. In the last week, the harassed
Camberwellian has been autocratically ejected from the nearly empty
Lilydale train and relegated to the woolpack like pressure of the other.
I had as usual taken my seat in the first-named when a porter demanded
inspection of tickets. After scrutinising mine, he said, 'This train doesn't
stop at Camberwell.'

'Pardon me, I have ridden in it for months past.'

'Well, it doesn't stop to put down passengers, only to take them up.'

'Ah, my friend,' I reflected, 'there you are wrong. The policy of your
superiors – in an official position, of course, I meant – is to put down
passengers at every available opportunity, not only to put down, but to
keep down and sit upon them.'

From the calmness of moral elevation, induced by a few months
travel in comparative comfort, I was able to reason with that porter,
and in the end was 'put down' but at Prince's Bridge station, not in my
home suburb. And then after wriggling painfully into an interstice in a
Camberwell train, I was duly sat upon. Presently the two trains left the
station together, the one sliding, slowing and groaning under its load of
suffering humans, the other merrily bobbing along, so scantily weighted
by its light-hearted occupants, as to be barely able to keep the metals.

In my garden is a very prolific vine, its crop being chiefly caterpillars.
After spending an hour in gathering them in a tin-billy, the entangled
squirming mass so painfully reminds me of the Camberwell 5.15 train,
that I hastened to bury my harvest out of sight. If I gave expression to my
feelings, those of some highly paid – I have even heard them called too
highly paid – officials might be hurt, and surely rather than that should

*happen, it is more endurable that some few thousands of the gentle
public should daily be compressed, parboiled and infuriated, and that
without apparent prospect of relief.*

*So I simply and pathetically enquire: of two trains leaving
Melbourne for the same suburb at the same time, one thronged, the other
nearly empty, why should I, a yearly ticket-holder, be forced into the
packed one?*

Yours etc.

FRED JOHNSON

Telko, Camberwell

Having aired his grievances, Freddie was able to enjoy the Christmas
break and seemed in far better spirits to face his daily commute in the
coming year. Now might have been her chance to visit the boys and safely
avoid William. The Old Weasel was enjoying a prolonged visit to England
and in no hurry to come home. But for Einnim, Carl and Austin, it would
now be a case of passing ships, for they were hoping to join him for a short
holiday, each in turn. Since each intended stopping off in Melbourne en
route, there seemed no point now in her going to New Zealand.

Carl arrived in Melbourne in April, laden with the latest photographic
equipment from London.

'State of the art, Mama.' He told her about his ambition to set up a
photographic studio.

She eyed him up and down, his waxed moustache and goatee beard.

'Yes, dear, cutting edge.' No doubt Carl had been shopping in Bond
Street, by the look of his new grey sack linen suit and yellow bow tie.

Later he showed off his travel albums. 'All taken with this portable
device and a flexible roll of film. Feel like a bit of a spy at times.'

Snapshots, he called them, taken on the go without a tripod.
Astonishingly candid. There were portraits, as well – ovular vignettes
which captured a mood – artistic studies of friends and family. Her
eyes instinctively singled out the boy, a clean-cut youngster of about

fourteen, clad in school blazer. So this was Cara, their half-brother, whom William had enrolled at Bannister Court School.

'Oh, sweet young thing, and that blond, blond hair. Butter wouldn't melt, I suspect. And who, pray, is this?' Henrietta's head jerked backwards in surprise. It was as if someone had stuck a needle in her back. Such poise and dark elegance, such natural beauty. Which of her three sons had implicated himself with this striking young woman?

'Oh Mama, forgive me.' Carl quickly turned the page, and then another. 'That's ... actually, that's Cara's mother, Mary Jane. Pa had a photo of her redeveloped in London after ...'

'After what, my son?'

'Lucy What's-her-name – the one after Mary Jane. Aunt Dugdale refused to have her in the house. She took off and hasn't been seen since.'

'Well, then, nothing lost.' Henrietta rubbed her hands briskly and found him a smile. 'You have done well, dear, and you say you have taken all these photographs yourself?'

'Yes. Keep what you want, since I can make more from the negatives. Can't wait to show them to Austin. Wonderful scientific mind he has. That's the difference, you see. Einnim's of a more practical nature, better with his hands. He can read the water, seems to feel it in his blood.' Carl turned the page. 'But look at this, Mama. The Eiffel Tower. What an engineering marvel.'

And there he was, her own Carlie, posing on those famous iron steps, top hat and all. She smiled. 'I imagine Austin will be itching to see it firsthand.'

Carl spoke continually about the mechanical eye. 'The principal enemy is dust. Might not be visible to the naked eye, yet it can settle on the plates.' Cinematography, he said, was the next big thing. Moving photographs. A man called Goodwin had filed a patent. New flexible medium known as cellulose roll film. Transparent, tough, yet flexible. 'Think of it, Mama. A moving picture combined with sounds, music, traffic, eh? The thud of horses' hooves on turf, the striking of ball, all the elements of human speech including crying. We're not that far away. As Austin says, synchronisation of sound and sight. In the end, it all comes down to mechanism.'

~

'Scientific reconnaissance', he called it. Austin had taken the opportunity to stop off in Melbourne in May en route, rather than upon return. No longer the callow lad who waved her goodbye for New Zealand, her youngest son was now a fully-fledged marine engineer working at the Waitara Freezing Works. The news of his accreditation she had embraced with much pride, but not his current line of business. Boasting, he was, about how every major port in the North Island now had a freezing works. How meat would become the cornerstone of New Zealand's economy.

'Europe's a pretty big market, you know. Miles ahead of Australia.'

Freddie looked up and put his head to one side. 'So tell me, how do they do it, Austin?'

'Well, it's like this. Ships can have their own steam-driven plants on board, but it's an expensive business keeping meat frozen all that time in transit. New Zealand's further away than Australia, don't forget.'

What was needed, he said, was a cheaper mode of producing cold, or chemicals that would arrest the decay of the meat, yet still leave it wholesome for human consumption. A new American process had been tried and trialled in Victoria. Now it was about to be made public, and if it proved correct, it would revolutionise things. Austin wanted to be first in. Make his fortune. So far as he could see, though, Australia didn't seem to be much in the know.

It was a little off-putting, thought Henrietta. Austin had not asked them anything about themselves. He was far too full of himself. And he had a rude habit of either cutting Freddie out when he spoke or cutting him short.

'Australia not good enough, eh?' Freddie stood up. 'Now, if you'll excuse me, I'm off to bed.'

Henrietta pinned her lips. Melbourne – after London, the biggest city in the British Empire – was at the height of the boom, and the boom had run its course. To be bullish at such a time would be rash. But for a son of hers to stoop to make his living out of dead animals she took as a personal slight. The very thought of raw carcasses jam-packed head to tail in ice repulsed her. She had a good mind to give Austin a lecture there and then.

'I shall bring your buttermilk directly, Fred,' she called. 'Shan't be long.' She went into the kitchen, set a tray with jug, tumbler and an oatmeal biscuit, and took it in to Freddie. Closing the bedroom door gently behind her, she whispered, 'Not quite back to his old self. On top of that, his mother recently died.'

'How sad.' Austin was staring at her, a quirk in his brow, and for an awful moment, he looked just like his father.

'Is something wrong, dear?'

'Nothing, only you've … well, I only just noticed, actually, Ma. You've cut your hair.'

She stiffened. 'It should look no shorter than when you saw it last, drawn back in a topknot. My ears, my wrinkle-ridden neck, do they offend your critical young eyes?'

Since Austin was stuck for a reply, she asked: 'Whether my hair is short or not, I am still the same mother inside as out, am I not?'

'Of course you are.' He blew her a perfunctory kiss. 'Well, then, think I'll be off, too,' he said. 'Night-night.'

'For goodness sake, Austin, take that supercilious look off your face. Do you know what it is to have to wash long hair, to have it sitting wet hour after hour, middle of winter, to have it bring on rheumatism or a nasty chill? A man does not have to suffer that, so why, pray, should a woman?'

⁓

Henrietta stood outside Spencer Street station, looking sadly upon the swollen Yarra. When each son sailed from Melbourne, the bitter ache returned, each time a reminder of how she'd been robbed. Austin showed no heart. Having been stolen from her at such a tender age, he had grown into a selfish, somewhat haughty man. He seemed to lack the innate egalitarian sentiments, the humanity, she had instilled into his brothers. She had fought to foster attachment by sending weekly letters and parcels and plum puddings to each of the boys, and had left the post office feeling a little better for it, all the time never knowing whether such tokens would ever reach their goal, such was William's bitter denial.

A little thoughtfulness, reciprocity, might have counted. But Austin struggled to relate to her, or express love and affection, since unlike his brothers he had never been sent to England for schooling and thus never been free of his father. Carl kept up a regular interchange, forwarding newspaper cuttings of articles of interest – especially on politics, 'the woman question' and a future Australasian federation.

Henrietta picked up her skirt, sidestepping the slush and mud. Rather than return home, she would take a tram down Collins Street and seek cover in her latest haunt, a relatively new tea house where she could get lunch, write a handful of letters or skim the daily papers – all within an hour or two in a quiet, cosy room in the heart of the city. Here she could catch up with old friends, play a game of chess or simply rest or take tea before a lunchtime choral concert.

Today no amount of tea would lift her spirits. The depression in trade was worsening. The newspapers were full of it. Already Melbourne had experienced a major strike. Bread and milk prices were up. The world was collapsing around them, further proof that women should voice their concerns and take control.

Feeling so moved, she wrote to the *New Zealand Observer*.

A WAR AGAINST WOMEN

*Sir, My son, Carl T. Dugdale, has sent me copies of your Observer,
in which the surprising intelligence re the Auckland Typographical
Association and their ignoble attempt to deprive women of the power*

*to support themselves by the very suitable work of typesetting. My
principal object in addressing you is to offer my heartfelt congratulations
on the manly and just stand taken by the Observer in this disgraceful
transaction.*

*It has been suggested the Typ. Ass. and other asses (is the plural
permissible?) contain some members having Solomonic proclivities, who
fear that by allowing women to earn their living respectably, the ranks
of the 'unfortunate class' will become too thin, and in time, disappear
altogether, a not unlikely contingency; for there can be no doubt that by
the increased independency, for their entering what trades they may be
fitted for, there will be a great decrease of legal or illegal prostitution, as
you wisely word it.*

*From the Dawn, a journal conducted entirely by women, I had
previously heard of the Sydney Typ. Ass stupidity, but thought it confined
to a few indigenous idiots; now having imparted their shameful rule to
kindred asses, they are becoming dangerous bars to progress.*

*My sympathy has always been with the world's workers, and I have
exerted any power of mine to promoting their advancement … believing
'Union' meant the union of workers of both sexes, having championed
the movement in every possible direction; for woman is quite as much
the raison d'etre of all trades as is man; therefore, is equally entitled to
earn her living in the various employments created by trade. But if her
unionism means casting women adrift in order to fill their places with
cheap boy labour, then my sympathy can exist no longer for a movement
thus proving itself so meanly selfish and cowardly. By such acts, I, one of
the Union's strongest defenders, am thereby driven to rejoice at the great
blow it has received through the insane conduct of the recent strike; a
strike which would have settled long ago honourably, and without the
misery that has been brought into so many homes, if women's common
sense and tact had a proper share in the affairs of the Trades Hall.*

*Accompanying this I send copy of the Dawn, by which you will
learn that the Sydney Typ Ass. tried to throw women compositors out of*

*employment because they consider the work of type-setting too hard for
my sex. Is it not minded that such generous-minded fellows don't get up
a society for relieving women of the truly hard labour of rubbing and
scrubbing. There would be real humanity, for I knew two women who
died from strangulated rupture caused by lifting over washing; and I also
know of several who have received internal injuries over other laborious
housework, while the husbands were performing some of the various
light duties they grandly call 'men's sphere'. I should like to have said
something about the women's suffrage but fear my letter is already too
long, so will only wish your brave journal success, and repeat my thanks
for its honourable and powerful shield in this 'war against women'.*

> *Yours gratefully*
> *H. A. Dugdale*
> *Telko, Camberwell, Victoria*

With that out of the way, she could finish her weekly epistle to Alice.

'Oh my dear,' she wanted to say, 'you have no idea the damage done
all those years ago. When Austin came to visit, I felt I hardly knew my
own son.' That barbarous law must be repealed. The one dealing with
mother and child.

Her breast rose and fell. What could be gained from spoiling the
buoyancy of a private letter? It was not fair to Alice. She would reserve
her protests and write once again, publicly, powerfully, about that law.
It made great pretensions to justice but it remained a two-edged weapon
for the use of bad men.

Save in the rare cases of rife immorality, no good man would use
so demoniacal a power. No good husband would risk the life of the
one and unity of the other by separating an infant from its mother. A
man had no moral right to dispose of children without their mother's
consent; no right to legislate upon either without women's cooperation.
Goodness, to think she had had no say over these precious bits of her
own body, grown and introduced to the world under such a terrible

ordeal – nurtured with her blood. In all her studies and observations in natural history, she was yet to find beast, reptile or vermin low enough to rob the mother of her young. Of all the multitudinous beings on this earth, it was man, yes, man, who had reached the lowest depths of cruelty.

Her eyes quickly scanned the *Herald*.

And now some fool had written to ask, *Why there is this inclination to resist legitimate authority in an otherwise charming and almost perfect sex, we do not know?'*

She picked up her pen again and, turning to a new sheet of paper, wrote:

If you will allow me, I will tell you why. It is for the same reason that woman resists the wonderful 'legitimate authority' to beat her 'with a stick' (a law not yet repealed) and for the same reason she will resist the most recent of disgraceful 'legitimate authority', that which empowers a man to commit adultery three times. But it is rather late to discuss Mr Shiels's Amended Divorce Act. Thank God it has become law. What an interminable blessing.

Part 4

1891–1899

Chapter 23

I t was well over twenty years since Henrietta had seen Hattie. To learn by telegram in early 1891 that her niece and namesake was implicated in the death of her husband, Martin Walsh, turned her pale.

'Poor girl. I must leave for Benalla posthaste.'

'Chloral poisoning, eh?' Freddie had given her a shake of his head and a sorry frown. 'Nasty. An inquest can be very taxing.'

Henrietta settled herself in the railway carriage, heavy and duty-bound. She was, after all, matriarch of the family, and she did know something about the law. While Hattie had always fiercely valued her independence, courts could be intimidating; being cross-examined under duress had a way of drawing things out. That nasty thing, the truth.

If only the rolling ranges could speak. As they changed to misty-blue, deepening into a shadowy violet, Henrietta could sense her tension building. The morning temperature already unforgiving, the iron horse steamed on north to Benalla, through dense scrub and stands of timber, dried-up swamps and ponds and pastureland, following the endless line of telegraph poles. Jam-packed in her boiling dogbox, Henrietta adjusted the window blind and closed her eyes.

In the monotonous swaying to and fro, she tried to picture Hattie as she'd seen her last, white neck and dark springy curls and her figure, a shapely swirl of cerise. Hattie's face, all but lost in the frantic shuffle of memory, suddenly flipped before her, young, proud and defiant, with fire in her eyes.

Hattie, before she married Martin Walsh, had had her own thriving fruit shop in Benalla. But it was a hotel she'd really set her heart on. Henrietta had tried to warn her niece against the idea. Back then, Hattie was all flair and gloss. Child after child she had borne Martin – nine in all.

Henrietta lurched as the train let out an unearthly shriek to the growing sound of churning pistons. Quickly, she flung up the blind to a seething blue sky and trails of vapour. Where were they? Metal squealed against metal amid high-pitched rushes of air and clunking jolts of carriages coupling. She had arrived in Benalla.

~

When Henrietta stepped into the Vineyard Hotel, there he was – Martin – hanging in the saloon lounge, framed in gold. Little lopsided smile and those loose dark curls which gave him a rather pretty appearance. Looked more like a poet, really, than a publican.

Hattie's eldest daughter, Mary, led her upstairs and showed her her room.

Hattie, her hair now gunmetal with a pure white flash, swept back in mourning ribbons, was waiting for her in her private parlour. Her children – seven remaining – gathered solemnly around.

Later, in private, Henrietta poured her niece a cup of tea, added cream and two heaped spoonfuls of sugar. 'Drink it up, Hattie dear,' she said. 'You'll need to stay strong to give your deposition at the inquest. Now, get your thoughts in order and try and imagine you are standing in front of a court.'

Hattie's high black lace collar framed her pale face, as she sniffed repeatedly. 'Well, you see, Aunty, Martin had been drinking heavily for about ten days – a debilitating spree, with awful retching bouts – but refused to let me call a doctor. On Thursday night, he was up and about; in fact, he served some drinks in the bar, though very unwell, his eyes standing out in a frightening way. He played a game of billiards with a friend about ten o'clock. Since he asked for a sleeping draught – as he often did – I gave him one and put him to bed. Later I checked ... 'pon my word, Aunty, try as I might, I couldn't find his pulse.'

The following day, Hattie shed tears during the entire inquest, shivering in fear of the findings. When the case was brought to an end, there was shown to be fibroid degeneration of the liver and kidneys, the result of heavy drinking.

Emma's cable was unexpected. *I send you my love Hattie and I will come if you want.* But when Emma arrived later that afternoon, the strain between the sisters was palpable as they sat in Hattie's parlour.

Henrietta ran her eyes uncomfortably around the cornices and the ornate ceiling rose. The air was hot and breathless, odours rising up the stairwell, and it felt like there was no escape, surrounded as she was by sickly wallpaper – a repeated running vine of bloated curves and flourishes in orange and putrid sulphur and bunches of purple grapes.

In demanding loyalty and obedience from his children, Joseph had pitted them against each other, determined to guard his secrets. For thirty years, Emma and Hattie had had no contact, not even when their father or their sister, Fanny, had died.

And the old tensions started up again, like a toothache.

It appeared that Emma had resented having to care for their father alone, after Hattie and Fanny had run away during the move to Mornington, refusing to be his scapegoat any longer.

Hattie flung her sister a look. 'But Emma, you liked being the golden girl. Whereas the rest of us were never good enough.'

Emma could remember nothing about the Old Country and their tragic past. Now she kept harking back, deeper and deeper, desperate to get to the heart of it, her eyes so darkly brown, they were almost black. 'Go on, Aunty, tell us – where was Father when we children stayed with you in London?'

How could she use that cold, hard word, 'prison'?

'Was it the workhouse?' Emma was wanting to know. 'Is that where we ended up before coming to Australia?'

Henrietta felt sick. She knew not where to start, before or after he went to prison. She could picture the poor kiddies, in the dull, brothy light, the long row of beds and flock-filled sacks, and the drift of ammonia. Four little girls huddled together beneath thin grey blankets that prickled their scabs and weeping sores. Their aching shudders, sobs convulsing deep inside their silence; their fate lying with the powers-that-be. Papa had pulled some strings with the Board of Guardians so he could act as their temporary ward during Joseph's imprisonment. Upon his release, Joseph had turned up at their Bloomsbury house, holier-than-thou, demanding the return of his four little girls. 'I'm a free man,' he said, 'I'm within my legal rights.' Grabbing their arms and bundling them one by one into a waiting cab.

Within weeks, Joseph had admitted himself to the workhouse in an unfit state, the children again wards of the workhouse. Papa intervened once more, this time with a final solution – emigration and exile.

'Remember, Emma?' Hattie leaned forward in her readiness to answer. 'We were made to dress in identical brown smocks. Taken to a refectory of sorts, given tin porringers of gruel, like little Oliver Twists. Years on, Father denied we were ever in such a place. Denied he had been in prison. He ranted and raged, all spit and splutter. Told me I didn't know what I was talking about – 'twas nothing but evil nonsense.'

'Oh Hattie!' Emma let out a choking half-sob. 'Don't you remember him saying, *Never, never, say anything bad about anyone in the family*?'

So ready to mollify her father, the little dove had made a habit out of forgetting. Fine-framed Emma, with her crimped red hair, side-by-side her sister, so singularly dark and striking. No wonder Emma was drawing a blank on the unfixable past. Hattie, with a good eighteen months' seniority, had the authority of memory plus the art of conviction. With her natural presence, Hattie knew how to hold sway.

'Hattie is right, Emma,' said Henrietta at last. 'Sadly, your father did spend time in prison, but better we talk about the workhouse another time.'

Hattie took out a fresh handkerchief and blew her nose. 'Now, tell us about our uncles and aunts,' she said, blinking away tears. 'Do, Aunty, for I have often wondered about them. And then I shall order some tea.'

'Well, dear.' Henrietta adjusted her cuffs. 'Like me, they are all getting on; Maria, my sister, the eldest, eighty-six. Deaf, poor soul, and living in care.' Otherwise, it was a world of men. She began ticking off each sibling on her fingers. Brother John had long lived in Canada – now a reverend canon in the church, he had written her off years ago. The middle two, Edward and William, like Joseph, had died, which left her younger two, Thomas and Charles.

''Tis Charles who keeps in touch.' He who had followed in Papa's footsteps: Registrar, then later Chief of Works for the parish of St Pancras. A huge undertaking. Half of Somers Town carved up by the railways. *Three new termini. Wouldn't recognise the place*, he wrote, *St Pancras station, a Gothic masterpiece. Our Gateway to the North.*

'Whatever I might say about my brothers, all have worked hard and done remarkably well.'

It had been drummed into them, the Nobility of Work, Papa's everyday gospel. What did they dread the most? Fire and brimstone? No. The terror of not succeeding, of not making money, of losing money. How clever of her brother Thomas to turn around and become Chief Clerk of the London Bankruptcy Court.

Both Joseph and Papa, as his reluctant guarantor, had had to face the wrath of their creditors in the year of 1841, Joseph absconding to Canada, leaving Papa to the harrows and saws of the bankruptcy court and its protracted terms of settlement. Others, she remembered, did not survive. From one to another, it was like a pack of cards falling through the parish.

More important was moral bankruptcy, spiritual death, which Joseph had had to face after he sneaked through the back doors of England with his family five years later. Not only did he lose his poor wife upon arrival, he lost all pride: the shame of penury, of being in prison, followed by the workhouse. With work came salvation. Hadn't she seen it, how Joseph, the chastened hero, would rise up, struggling with his whole soul to escape this living hell to start his life afresh?

Coins jingled as Emma, fumbling in her reticule, drew out a photograph.

'Here, Hattie, keep it if you like, 'tis Father in his better days.'

A uniform has a strange way of enlarging a man's notions of himself, be it military or naval dress or the fine linen frocks of the church. In a uniform, a man could do no wrong. Here was Joseph in full masonic regalia: white apron and collar over black evening dress. Admittedly, it sat well on him. He had the general bearing of a man long accustomed to wearing such apparel, a man who loved nothing more than a little pomp and ceremony. And what could be more fitting than his installation as Grand Master of the Mornington Lodge?

In his hand, he held the square, presumably to square his actions; the compass, to circumscribe and keep him within bounds of all mankind. What, Henrietta wondered, would the all-seeing eye of Osiris, the creator, think about all this?

It was mystifying. The photograph of Joseph still seemed to stimulate pride in Emma, who had only ever preferred to see the good in her father.

And now, Hattie, amid all her prevailing stresses, wanting to get in touch with her uncles, who had all but forgotten her.

'Charles is a busy man, dear, but a very humane one. I'm sure he'd be pleased to hear from you.'

Hattie, who would write a letter to a virtual stranger, yet had no time to read. Forever busy, the never-ending tasks of stocktaking, keeping the ledgers up-to-date, checking the till, delegating to either servants or children, ensuring the bringing in of custom so that business went on as usual.

Henrietta could not understand how Hattie, given her family history, could live with alcohol every day; could make money out of this evil poison, tolerate the rough-and-tumble, the nightly bawdiness, could have her offspring running around offstage. Her niece's occupation went against all Henrietta's deepest values. It broke families apart, and often took them to ruin. It was a travesty, and she wanted to rage against it.

For there in her memory, her child's eye could still behold Joseph's undoing. The British Queen had been a fine, salubrious place, a coffee house with spirits and wine vaults, where he, Joseph, as stakeholder and joint licensee with Papa, could drop in and play the convivial host. Scholars and gentlemen could partake of food and beverages, read a newspaper or journal. The British Queen also catered for private dinners and political meetings and, her father's passion of all passions, the playing of chess. Joseph, cock-a-hoop – hobnobbing at all hours – blind to the costs and the forthcoming Bankruptcy Court. Fifty years on, the smell of his cigar and the orange glow were for Henrietta as bitter as the smell of spirits. Joseph, head back, feet up, steeling his eyes at his smoke-rings, watching his artwork float before dissolving.

～

Having endured the long Catholic mass the previous day, Henrietta knew she could suffer anything. The five-minute walk from the Vineyard Hotel to the ticket office in the searing midday sun was almost liberating. Benalla railway station – for all its handsome red brickwork and fancy white trim – was no cooler in the waiting room than on the platform. The train had pulled in and was waiting, the engine enveloped in thick billowing clouds dissipating up into the black cast-iron girders. The porter had already gone on ahead with her boxes.

Perspiration dripped. Henrietta waved her fan a little faster, heat radiating from every direction. She squeezed her eyes. Beyond the yards, sets of iron rails converged, shimmering into the distance.

The stationmaster was standing, flags at the ready. She gave one final glance at the clock on the belltower, then cleared her throat for her parting words.

'What are your plans, Hattie, dear? Is it wise to keep living off the sale of alcohol?' Squeezing her hand, she looked into her eyes long and deep. 'Think what it did to Martin. Think what it did to your father.'

Hattie hurriedly drew the children together. 'Aunty, I have a family to feed. This is my livelihood. I have a thousand pound mortgage at ten per cent hanging over my head. Give me five years and I'll pay it off and be free of the brewery. I know I can clear twelve pounds a hogshead. So long as I can get the licence transferred to my name, I'll make the business pay.'

Ahead in the engine, the menacing glow of red – a dragon, a demon, no less, belching sparks and smoke from its nostrils. Nothing but fire and filth and smuts – worse than Dante's hell. Henrietta dabbed her smarting eyes yet again with her handkerchief.

'Well, then, my girl, I'd better be off.' They stood in one final embrace. 'Look after yourself, won't you, dear, and don't forget to write. Promise?'

Henrietta climbed the ladder into the carriage and, without looking back, sank into the padded leather seat. The door locked with a clunk. The last bell rang.

The train slid forward along the platform amid a flurry of faces.

By rights, she should have been travelling second-class like everybody else, making do with a hard wooden seat. She folded her hands in her lap: what a relief. Egalitarian principle for once cast aside, she could settle back, uninterrupted in her thoughts, in a compartment by herself.

But the heavy breathing had begun. She gripped the armrests as the carriage swung from side to side. The engine jerked and pulled. It puffed and panted, picking up amid foul exhalations. She had to block her ears as the whistle screamed through every hamlet. Straps of red-gum and yellow box and stringybark periodically beat at the windows in rapid succession, only to give way to dried-up creek beds and burning dust. Yonder, ranges etched in melancholy, their cold blue shadows stealing the light.

She thought of the loss of the youngest, Annie, who could still be alive goodness knows where. All her enquiries had led to nowhere. And still she grieved for Fanny – so colourless and remote, her short, sad life spent in oblivion. Fanny, as a small child, she remembered, had for a time stopped talking altogether.

Upon opening a book one day, she had found one of Fanny's pale white locks pressed between the pages. To her horror, the child had been hair-pulling.

'Why, Fanny, do you feel no pain?'

That shrug, that vapid look. All her life, it had been one calamity after another. Then to die in childbed.

What a shocking waste of humanity. Women having to risk their lives, their wellbeing and their babies' lives, reproducing time and again like human machines. If a woman could not control her body, what hope had she of controlling her life, especially while having to contend with a drunkard husband?

Alone in her compartment, Henrietta fell captive, condemned to the past. When men took to the bottle, it was their womenfolk and families who suffered the most. 'A five-pound loaf of bread contains more food than twenty-seven barrels of beer.' As a longstanding member of the temperance movement, she had made that point time and time again. Alcoholic drink was one of the most degrading drawbacks of progress that humankind ever suffered. It was a disease.

Chapter 24

~

O nce back at Telko, Henrietta threw her arms around Freddie and pressed her mouth into his chest. Every time she thought about her niece, she felt a shaft of pain.

'Hattie will end up insolvent, just like her father. Oh dear God, and all those children.'

'Here, sit down, my dear girl, and I'll make you some tea.' Freddie put the kettle on, and opened the flue.

After several cups of tea came a surge of energy; an inner need for her to be at her desk, tidying up the past. Years ago, Freddie had shown her how to keep her affairs in order by sewing papers and private documents together, as per legal tradition. With her naturally tidy mind, she had quickly taken to the ritual, the categorising of subject material, punching holes and threading with different coloured ribbons. But there had always been that horrid backlog from her Queenscliff days that she couldn't bear to touch.

Freddie frowned as she began rifling through her mother's tea caddy, spilling things onto the table.

'What is it you're after?'

'Charles's address. Ah, here it is. I promised Hattie I would send it to her. I shall write at once, see if I can persuade her to give up the hotel once and for all.'

'It is her life, Henrie. Don't interfere. Let her do as she sees fit.' Freddie scooped up a pile of old newspaper cuttings from the floor. 'Is this rubbish? If so, I'll throw it in the fire.'

'Oh, no, no! Those I need.' She seized the papers from his hands. 'They're to remind me of what her father did.'

'Still not forgiven your brother? There are far worse sins in life than bankruptcy, my dear girl.'

'Yes.' She could not look him in the eye. 'Things of a barbarous nature.'

Freddie spun around. 'What?

She tossed him an article from *The Times*. 'Very well, then, read for yourself.'

MIDDLESEX SESSIONS, *Friday 13 October 1848*

Before Mr Serjeant Adams, Assistant-Judge, and a Bench of Magistrates

J. E. WORRELL, who pleaded guilty at these sessions on Wednesday, the indictment charging him with a cruel assault upon four of his children, was this morning called up to receive judgement.

Mr PRENDERGAST, who appeared for the prosecution, which was at the instance of the authorities of the parish of St Luke, said that this was a most painful and lamentable case, for these poor children had been found in such a wretched state that had they not been discovered and taken away, death must have put an end to their sufferings. The children had been carried to the workhouse in the most filthy condition, and at that time they were completely covered in vermin, whilst the eldest child was covered with bruises. He was quite free to admit that the defendant was in extremely bad circumstances which might to a certain extent perhaps have operated upon his mind, and that in that state he might have been guilty of these gross acts of cruelty. The defendant, he understood, was living with the sister of his deceased wife, and the children were under her care.

MR BALLANTINE – Yes, that was in consequence of the present state of the law as to marriage, and this was one only of almost numberless similar instances of its results.

The learned JUDGE remarked that as the law at present stood these parties could not legally marry. Where was the elder girl, who appeared by the depositions to have been so much beaten?

Mr PRENDERGAST – The girl was in the workhouse where she would be well provided for. Indeed, all the children were under the charge and care of the parish authorities, and such had been the barbarous treatment the poor creatures had received from their father that they could not permit him to have care of them.

Mr BALLANTINE said he had but few observations to offer on behalf of the defendant, nor would he in any way attempt to palliate or excuse his conduct towards these children. In the first instance he must be permitted to state that his instructions had been that the defendant intended to plead guilty, and that in truth he had no defence to make in answer to the charge. He could not lament more deeply what had occurred, but at the same time was greatly rejoiced to find that the parochial authorities of St Luke's were not blind to the distresses of their poorer neighbours, and that they appeared ever ready, as is the present case, to afford them protection. As he had already stated, the defendant offered no defence. He was the son of persons of the highest respectability, and had been himself in a respectable line of life; but some time since he had gone over to Canada, and from which country he was that day charged …

3 months imprisonment

'Papa saw to it, you see. Nothing but the best defence for his son and heir. Ballantine – local barrister, a formidable cross-examiner. Knew all the right people – Dickens, Thackeray, Trollope – got himself several famous cases. Three months was a soft sentence, far too soft; even Papa agreed it was criminal.'

268

'Talk about defending the indefensible.' Freddie tossed aside the clippings.

'But you have only read the trial. Do you not want to know the rest of the story, the lead-up, the witness statements, the preliminary hearings? It is all there.'

'Much of the same, I suspect.'

Word by word, the evidence rose from the recesses of her mind – as real as any Dickens. A police constable, upon passing Garden Row in Clerkenwell, witnessed a crowd of between three and four hundred people gathered, and, upon asking their common purpose, was duly informed that a woman was ill-using and strangling some children upstairs. A ladder was procured to gain access to the first-floor window. Joseph was inside, wielding a piece of wood, threatening to kill anyone who dared enter his place. *Blow out his bloomin' brains* with a pistol.

The four children, one of whom was first believed to be dead, were rescued and safely delivered to the workhouse; Joseph and his sister-in-law taken into custody. There was a bed and bedsteads on which the two of them had slept, while the little ones had only the bare boards and nothing to cover them. In an open drawer was a package, 'arsenic-poison' penned upon it in his own handwriting.

Hattie cried convulsively throughout all of the questioning, exciting great sympathy. Intelligent little creature, little more than seven, she said artlessly that her father beat her for lying and thieving. Her aunt also beat her sometimes. Slapped her for missing 'messages'.

Joseph shed tears and questioned her with a view to showing that he beat her for stealing and telling lies while she was his servant. 'Have I not sent you into the streets with a paper on your back, with thief and liar written upon it, in order to shame you?' So incensed were the audience that they hissed and groaned until checked by the Bench.

When asked if he had anything to say to the charge, Joseph said he was an accountant, thirty-one years of age, and had formerly an office in the parish of St Pancras for seven years. He had been in America, and returned two years ago to Liverpool, where he held a situation as clerk. His wife died, he lost his situation, and his wife's sister undertook care of his family, and they eventually lived together. He was driven to distress, and would not degrade himself by applying for parish relief; and had frequently lain in bed for days without food, to afford his children sustenance. He was subject to aberrations in his mind, that extreme poverty and wretchedness had sometimes driven him to insanity.

Freddie stood with his back to her, facing the wall. He placed a painting back into alignment, stood back, then turned around and moistened his lips.

'You and your huggermugger. Why did you never think to tell me? All these years together, darn it. Did you not trust me?' he growled. 'Is that what it is?'

A deep flush came over her. 'I dreaded even thinking about it.' She looked away, blinking furiously. 'Makes me feel sick in the pit of my stomach. Time and again, I would try and put it out of my mind … and now …'

'You could have shared your shame with me, surely, since we share everything else in this house, including our bed. It might have helped to unload your secret burden. Instead of that, you let it fester for years until it bursts open like some nasty carbuncle.'

He gave a grunt and began to pace about, backwards and forwards, with a slight bear-like stoop of the wounded.

She swung around and shot him a scalding glance.

'It was not for myself. Not my secret. I was trying to protect the girls. I did what I could, but I had their reputations to consider. What do you think I have been fighting for all these years? My suffering has been borne. It is for others, can't you understand? Fighting for all wives and daughters.'

She could see them in the distant gallery of her mind, mere skeletons attired in the workhouse costume, heads shaven, a mass of bruises, scabs and festering sores, bones literally protruding through their skin, scarce able to stand on their legs.

Poor, poor little beggars. Hattie with her two black eyes, her stomach in such a weak condition that it would not retain any food. Emma and Fanny and even baby Annie, two years and one month old, emaciated and covered with marks of abuse.

'I still can't believe it happened. Joseph, the cur, had been living off his dead wife's sister, who at the time had been reduced to living an abandoned life.' Henrietta threw herself against Freddie's shoulder. Her eyes swept open, wild and wet. 'Ho, yes, they were in the habit of living well themselves, the two of them, and having eggs and bacon for breakfast, while they starved the children. Joseph, by night, regaling himself over his pipe with gin and water at the Macclesfield Arms.'

They stood together in each other's arms.

'I'm sorry, love,' said Freddie, at length. 'Bit of a shock. To think it was through him I met you, remember? How could it be the same man?'

～

Many a man would just as easily sell his wife or children as sell his vote for a pint of beer. When women were enfranchised, they would change the laws. There would be no misery and turmoil and slum houses, where women tended to large families, suffering violence and abuse at the hands of drunken husbands while babies starved and children resorted to petty crime.

Mrs Brettana Smyth was right. If men could not control themselves, women needed to take control for the moral and physical improvement of society. Henrietta slid a handful of pamphlets into her satchel, put up her umbrella and made her way from the North Melbourne Town Hall through the drizzle and piles of rotting leaves to the tram stop. She had just attended one of Mrs Smyth's medical lectures. There was nothing suggestive or scandalous about it. Far from forbidden knowledge, the information, she felt, should be made accessible to males and females alike, albeit at separate times. *I only wish there had been a 'Mrs Smyth' around in my younger time*, she thought. Someone brave enough to speak about women's health, and birth control, while selling the means openly from her shop.

Once aboard the tram, Henrietta sat herself down and smiled. It was no surprise to learn that the Australian Women's Suffrage Society, which Mrs Smyth had founded, was finally banding together in crusade with the temperance movement. For the drink evil was only going to get worse. With the widespread failure of banks and building societies giving rise to private and personal bankruptcies, unemployment, disease, hunger and fear, the country was all but doomed.

Where was the justice? When one half of the nation could arrogate to itself by 'positive legislation' the right to deprive the other half of a voice in the making of laws by which they were to be governed. When the voiceless half was the most law-abiding.

Henrietta contemplated the frosted window and formless grey buildings, as the tram rattled its way down Victoria Street. Mrs Bessie Lee, one of the temperance members, had led a deputation to the new Premier. Mr Munro, being a temperance man himself, was sympathetic to their cause, and said if the temperance movement could demonstrate that ordinary women wanted the vote, he would bring in a Bill for the franchise for women ratepayers.

Give them half the bread would make him twice a fool. All women wanted was justice for human beings, not only for ratepayers. Heavens! She had paid rates for many years, but it hadn't made her superior to other women. How silly of the male brain to think otherwise.

Henrietta stepped down into Elizabeth Street, negotiating an onslaught of gushing roads and gutters before finding sanctuary in the Athenaeum.

'How are you, Mrs D.?' Mrs Lowe's eyes were sparkling as she whispered. 'There is to be a monster petition. Has anyone been in touch? Here, take some copies.'

Mrs Goldstein, a recent campaigner and social advocate, and her daughter Vida – a tall, articulate young woman and the toast of Melbourne

– were planning to collect signatures for the Women's Suffrage Petition. Mrs Goldstein and her merry band intended campaigning one side of the country to the other, following the railway lines. Twelve weeks they had given themselves to accomplish this great mission.

'So it's not just a rumour. I'm thrilled to bits, Mrs Lowe,' said Henrietta, as the two women retreated to a quiet corner.

'Bessie Lee is quite the Queen of Orators, isn't she?'

'Most impressive. I have the utmost respect for Marie Kirk, too.' Mrs Kirk, she who had founded the Woman's Christian Temperance Union some years back, was a wonderful organiser, a down-to-earth woman. 'And if anyone knows how to get things done, it is Mrs Kirk, for she has in her heart a commitment to home protection.' Inevitably, it came back to one and the same – the rights of women and children.

'I've been ever so tied up over the last six months with personal affairs,' said Mrs Lowe, 'but to know the baton is in good hands is enough in itself.'

Creed – whatever one's ideology – was of little consequence, they agreed. People from high circles were rallying and rapidly finding power in common ground.

Henrietta welcomed the hot new surge in her heart. *Wait till I tell Freddie*, she thought, jotting names down in her notebook. She would have until 20 August to round up a list of signees and return her copy of the petition.

After Mrs Lowe had left, she wrote to as many people as she could, including Hattie and Emma, pressing for them and any of their older girls to sign. She also dashed off a quick note to Alice, who was still grieving over the death of her father. Every name would count. But Henrietta knew that any Bill proposed must yet be put to a vote, and in the end, the arithmetic of Parliament would rule.

As the due date closed in, so, too, did the weather, doing everything in its power to obstruct. Rain hammered down non-stop – nearly five inches in less than two days – followed by a flood of extraordinary magnitude that swept down the Yarra valley. Bridges fell away. Houses were taken downstream. With everything awash, and tram and traffic at a standstill, Melbourne was in chaos.

Either side of Telko was cut off. The Boroondara boatshed floated down the Yarra and, like many of the boats on moorings, very soon fell to pieces. Freddie, unable to get home, had been prevailing on the hospitality of William Lynch and his young wife. Powerless and alone in her isolation, Henrietta could not so much as visit a local tea house. The damage, the mopping up, the cost to the Victorian economy. The land boom was over. The banks had crashed. The government was desperately trying to rush through new legislation. What would become of their monster petition?

～

Six weeks later, despite all the gods being against them, the petition was amassed and ready to be presented to the Assembly. If she could bottle and sell an emotion, it would be pure nervous excitement. Having hardly slept the night before, she was feeling dreamy, giddy, and by mid-afternoon she was getting ahead of herself, all the time imagining what it would be like, looking back in time at the start of this new destination, when women could have a say in making the laws that controlled their lives.

She took Mrs Lowe's arm and joined the crowd of women congregating in front of Parliament House. Every now and then, she had to slow herself to catch her thoughts. The scene inside the main entrance and the grand hall was unusually buoyant. Members talked together in private groups. Messengers flew around like Mercuries in every direction. Today's atmosphere was distinct. The higher, lighter hum of women's voices rose, alive and expectant amid the rustling of dresses and softer shuffle of boots.

Eventually, the doors of the Chamber opened. Henrietta stood back as people streamed through, waited patiently till the rush was over before making her way with great dignity into the galleries. Looking up, she could see tier upon tier of bonnets and scores of eager faces, smiling and nodding fervently to members below. Mrs Lowe, half-standing, gave her a little wave to say she had saved her a seat. Throughout the preliminary proceedings, they sat taking it all in – the splendour, the ornamental plasterwork, the stencilling and gilt.

Henrietta leaned forward and pressed her hands upon her knees. For there it was at last, without ceremony, without so much as a wave of a gaudy mace. Upon the table, a huge roll of paper on a cardboard spindle almost hid the clerk, and remained an enigma till the Premier rose. He put his hand upon the spindled roll and said he had the honour to present a petition with the names of thirty thousand women from all over Victoria. The sheer size of this roll had to be seen to be believed, 330 yards in length, she was told, written forms glued onto linen in an endless line of patchwork. What a lot of work for the organisers, whom she could see dotted around the galleries: Marie Kirk, the Goldsteins, Annette Bear-Crawford, Mrs Lee. New names and old – not just those from the women's leagues, but ordinary women, others of social prominence: Mrs Higinbotham and the Premier's wife, Jane Munro, who had given her pledge. Added to these, she knew, were the names of many men.

And the energy it emanated, rows of women, hands linked, hearts beating hard, and again and again, with each squeeze of a palm, the rising power of solidarity. It was a defining moment.

The Assembly was in shock. The petition was presented and a Bill brought straightaway, the same day. A lively debate had ensued. Mr Munro's heart, clearly, was in the Bill. His words, emphatic and eloquent. 'The whole thing,' he said, 'was a scandalous disgrace.'

Yes, it was indeed a disgrace that it had come to this, that a few dedicated women should have to go door-to-door across the country to petition for what was, after all, only women's right, and they had done this often under duress. There had been scurrilous reports of standover tactics, according to Mrs Lowe. Forms returned with names erased, and at the foot, a note: *these names were erased by order of the husbands.* Such was the position of the mothers of the nation, sighed Henrietta.

No, the Bill did not get through. But as she said that night to Freddie, they would not be disillusioned. The very sight of that big spindle on the desk said a lot in itself: there, in black and white, was spelled out the enormous effort, the determination, the numbers and diversification of supporters. It was not just a few radical suffragists agitating for the vote but a formidable united force. She knew it would have an impact.

Chapter 25

～

A sickening sombreness shrouded the Mornington harbour with each surge of spray. Henrietta fastened her mackintosh cape and gripped tight the railings as the ferry docked, bumping and bouncing against the pylons of the pier with almighty thuds.

The telegram from Emma's husband, Jim, had been short on detail. *Fearing the worst. Our darling Willie perished at sea.* The rest of the news Henrietta had gleaned from the *Argus*.

SHOCKING DISASTER IN THE BAY

A FISHING YAWL SUNK.

A FOOTBALL TEAM ON BOARD.

ALL HANDS DROWNED.

FIFTEEN LIVES LOST.

DISTRESSING SCENES IN MORNINGTON.

A terrible boating calamity happened on Saturday evening in Port Phillip Bay about four and a half miles from Mornington. The fishing yawl 'Process', having on board three fishermen and 12 members of the Mornington Football Club, capsized, and went down with all hands. At the time of the disaster the boat was returning from Mordialloc, where a football match had been played in the afternoon, and as the wind was favourable and the sea not particularly high, there was no reason to expect anything but a speedy and comfortable trip. Under such conditions of wind and weather the 'Process' should have reached the Mornington jetty at between 8 and 9 o'clock, but when midnight came without sign of the missing boat, her absence began to cause serious alarm, and search parties were sent out to examine the beach, but without result.

The *Process* had been found off Pelican's Reef late Sunday morning, only a few hundred yards from shore, along with the body of a naked man trapped inside by rigging. The body was identified and the boat bailed and towed back to shore. There, strung up beside the fishing-boat jetty for all to see, was the heavily gouged hull minus its mainsail and what remained of the rigging – the sound of its sorry emptiness crying in the wind, and the ocean, looking on, so cold and cruel and livid.

Large groups stood clustered about the pier, atop the red cliffs and lighthouse hill. Still out scanning the beaches were the last of the search parties. For Henrietta, each twist of angst began to spiral. In her mind, she could picture the morning prior – mothers, wives and sisters, poor tormented souls, rushing forward, sick with worry, each wanting to see with her own eyes if that corpse was her loved one, then the distress having to watch it being loaded from a stretcher into the waiting mail coach. In front, encapsulating the mood, the dark outline of despair: a pair of blinkered horses standing heads bowed, backs to the weather.

She knew only too well what it was like to run each time a wave slapped against the rocks, only to find nothing. Then to wait, teeth chattering, knees knocking, eyes straining through the darkness, seawater sucking at her boots, slopping around her skirts and long-wet stockings. Oh and how brutal it was and bitter, the sting of salt, sand, and the wind moaning madly, the throb in her ears and the churn eating her insides away.

Even alongside the pier, it was a battle to be heard above the creaking and whistling, an eerie, ominous rustling through the riggings, and faraway thunder in the offing.

Carefully she made her way down the bobbling gangplank, followed by authorities and what looked like a pack of newspaper reporters in wool gabardines. Weaving through the crowd, she spotted Jim and the girls, and rushed towards them, her eyes craving to read their expressions.

'Go on ahead, if you would, Mrs Dugdale.' Jim put on a brave front. 'Take the girls home to their mother. She's not slept a wink.'

Arm in arm, they trudged up the path from the point, she sensitive to the fearfulness of their sorrow – knowing in their hearts, yet not knowing for certain. In ragged sobs, Louie struggled to give some account of what had happened. Everyone was out searching, waving torches over the shallows – all bar her seventeen-year-old brother, James, who was heavily down with the fever – huddling together, with only the glow of flares and beach-fire keeping alive their hopes.

Looking down Main Street from the post office, Henrietta thought it could, at first take, have been a Sunday – shops and shutters closed up, blinds and curtains drawn out of respect – were it not for sounds of weeping and pitiful enquiry at every turn. Such was the torture of their waiting.

'This way, Aunty.' Louie led her to Austin Villa, a neat weatherboard house with a lace-trimmed verandah. The front door flew open, whereupon Emma staggered into her arms, knees about to buckle, so distraught she could barely utter a word.

'There, there, Emma, love.' Gently Henrietta laid her niece upon the sofa and sat stroking her temples while the girls went off to make some tea.

Shortly after, Jim walked in, lugging a bucketful of wet clothes.

A whiff of stale squid rose from out of the brininess as he extracted a flannel undershirt and a black military greatcoat that had been found washed up on the beach.

'Willie's, no mistake, Mrs Dugdale. He … he was a corporal with the Rangers.' Jim choked and stuttered, seeking refuge in his handkerchief. 'Ah, my dear poor wife.'

Emma sat up and gathered the dark, slimy garments, dripping, to her breast. It was heart-wrenching to witness a mother so broken, near demented, clutching, pressing the sopping mess against her cheek, her lips; taking in the cloying smell of damp wool and whatever else for even the feeblest trace of her son.

Henrietta gently relieved her of the load.

'Dear, dear, you've wet your costume. Come, Emma, let us bathe you and put you to bed.'

When Captain Dugdale had broken the news about Junius that godforsaken day almost forty years ago, she had gone into a flap, like an injured gull beating itself into a frenzy. Her heart would not let up, nor the lump in her throat. As much as she tried to swallow, that lump kept swallowing her back. The lantern, she remembered, bumping against her legs, absorbing the black void as she ran and ran and ran, trying to get her breath. Ears aching, eyes watering from the wind. The rock-strewn sand, spewed with slimy kelp. A numbness set in as, limb by limb, the chill and the shock began to paralyse; her clothes, stiff from salt and sweat, the only things holding her upright. For days she kept watch, seeming to float in her emptiness amid masses of heaving grey.

In the shared intimacy of grief, she began to feel protectively at one with this family. The next day, Jim came rushing home to say that Willie's trunk and cornet had been found. Everyone gathered around, and as he broke open the waterlogged case, there surfaced in her mind an image of the boy wonder that was – silver instrument pressed against his lips, now with the dark brush of manhood, red cheeks a-dimple, his eyebrows shaping every note. In the silence came the faint waft of Willie's lament, so wildly prophetic, 'The Ship that Never Returned'.

Jim took the instrument and, after examining the crook, gave it a good shake. 'I shall take it to pieces directly. Polish it till it shines like it's never shone before.' He walked off, wiping his eyes on his sleeve.

Young James fell back upon his pillows, sobbing and shaking. 'Oh Lord, oh Lord,' he howled, 'why wasn't it me?'

The pain of seeing others suffering both pinched and pulled at Henrietta's heart. Football was a vile, brutal game, in her mind, but it drew on natural skills. Willie, light of body and limb, strong of heart, according to Jim, and, yes, she could well believe it. Jim was a good father and husband and rightly proud of his sons. Willie was said to be one of the best in the team. James, near as good, would have played, too, had he not been ill.

By the hour, they all trod in fear amid whisperings of typhoid, the ongoing danger that God might take their second son as well. With James's moans reaching every room, and a fever fuelled by the guilt of being spared, all the young fellow wanted, it seemed, was to curl up and die.

Emma could cry no longer; her eyes were exhausted wells. 'My whole body aches, Aunty. My head, my heart, my limbs like lead.'

Once Emma had finally succumbed to sleep, Henrietta took Willie's greatcoat and placed it outside to dry in the wind.

Would the chilling cry 'man overboard' have made it real? So oft she had tried to imagine Junius' last moments – the terror, the chaos, every moment seeming to be an hour, yet all the while rushing towards the inevitable. First the *shwhack*, the gasping, spluttering, floundering, only to be pounded and pulped time and again, lungs rising up up up, brain bursting, blood and bubbles and bits of flesh in the desperate chase for light. Suddenly to find oneself in a pool of calm, life events passing in a floating emerald silence. Then the darkness, the slow, hideous submerging into nothingness.

It would not necessarily have been a violent, painful death. In reality, the process might have lasted only a heartbeat. But for those young men, on a dark, cold night, fatigued, frozen to the bone in the black waves, with not so much as a swinging lantern to go by, it would surely have been one of the most terrifying deaths of all.

⌒

Over the days, it was Louie who came to the fore, directing her family courageously and tirelessly, with father and sisters in tow. James, still poorly, took things hardest. After a week of fevers and rigours, the young fellow came staggering out at first light to find Louie in the washhouse, poling at a copper full of black dye. Dumb, he stood in his dressing-gown, his Adam's apple rising and falling, as his sisters prodded and poked, poked and prodded, in an effort to free their pain. Back and forth they stirred and shunted until they had exploded every single dye-seed into the inky swirl. Louie, busily sorting through every piece of their womanly apparel – everything except their corsets – stopped every so often to dab rising moisture from her eyes.

Oh, horrible! Henrietta drew back. Why this deadening of colour to a matchless black? It served no earthly purpose. The old code of mourning for women was cruel and unfair: home behind closed doors, without society, having to suffer alone. Men got off more lightly. Back in early colonial years, the rituals of death had gone to the wind.

Yet still it was there, that familiar ache for Junius. It rose, it fell.

No, she told herself. Let us do, not dwell. There was comfort in stoking the fire, in baking. In those daily rhythms one did without thinking: kneading and rolling, punching, pounding, the simple sensations of sieving and, with lightest white finger-tips, feeling the softness of flour, folding the dough thick and snug like a child's eiderdown. Food could express love when words failed to help. The smell of scones cooking might help draw them from their grief.

With fire roaring and kettles on the boil, she gathered another bucketful of wood. Outside she could hear the autumn leaves rustling, preparing themselves, turning their backs on the bay. Winter was here, all right. There'd be no hope now. But in the rising swells and in the froth and bubbles, she would see the returning blur of a face.

⁓

Three long months had passed since the boating accident. When Henrietta next returned to Mornington, she took the day excursion on the ferry.

Washed of the winter squalls, the bay stood out with remarkable clarity. The quince-coloured sun, the wind sighing as softly as an infant's breathing, the water stretched out iridescent. The sort of conditions she knew that could just as easily falsify distances and objects, magnify them grotesquely into Fata Morganas. She herself had seen ships hanging upside down in the air, and now the Heads were appearing on the horizon, despite there being eighteen nautical miles in distance and that great expanse of seawater, so gentle, so disarming, as if nothing at all had happened.

Were they all still praying? Henrietta wondered as they docked. That poor wretched soul, God's servant, the Reverend Caldwell, who had lost three of his sons in the boating tragedy – did he still believe in prayer?

Emma, in the same black high-buttoned bombazine mourning dress, eased off her black bonnet and veil. She appeared to have shrunk. Mercifully, she had rid herself of that damp, musty greatcoat.

'One day I took to it with a pair of scissors,' she quietly confessed, 'saved what I could.' The epaulettes, brass buttons and corporal's stripes now lay in the safekeeping of her petticoat pocket.

There was talk, Jim said, of a memorial being erected at the end of Main Street, overlooking the jetty. 'Not as good as a grave, Mrs Dugdale, but I think it'd help heal the town.'

Mornington was akin to Queenscliff – a town supposedly without class, everyone thrown into the mix. Fishermen, like sailors, were a rummy lot. Being always at the mercy of the sea, they clung to their own peculiar fatalism, fearing the curse of watery spirits. Most of the team were otherwise from educated families. Either way, a death at sea was not a good Christian death; not a good death at all. Emma, like other townsfolk, believed that without a body to bury, there could be no burial – let alone a burial at sea in a grave with no earth.

A sense of painful reverence lingered on at Austin Villa, with its hushed tones, still noticeably shy of music. After the midday meal had been cleared away and the dishes washed and dried, Louie whispered, 'Would you care to play for us, Aunty? Something gentle for Mother … as if our Willie were here.'

'Of course, dear.'

Henrietta was left to ponder while Louie gathered the others around. There flared in her mind one of the most haunting melodies ever written – a nocturne by Borodin which Freddie played in his string quartet now and then – and as she set her fingers upon the keys, she closed her eyes, drawing out both the rich, sweet lyrical air and the dark struggle, all the inner voices, and the pauses like a breath taken by a singer. The piece seemed to exert a loving grip on the room. Such was its power and poignancy, it brought release to their grief, as each family member then rose in turn to contribute in the mutual making of music: piano, flute, violin and song.

It was later, with such a feeling of togetherness, that the family walked her back down to the pier. Ever vigilant along the clifftop, the spindly tea-trees with their sad grey-green droopy needles and tight white floral balls, their contorted trunks joining forces in a first show of blossom.

Having bid Emma and her family goodbye, Henrietta made her way to the ferry, through the porters and trolleys, back up the gangplank. Lighter of heart, she climbed the companionway to the upper deck and stood, taking in the sweep of the bay. Fishing boats swung easily from their moorings. Beneath the scarp, gulls bedded down in black banks of kelp. Tidal pools flushed in the tide. There, tight in the crowd, the enduring image of Emma waving a handkerchief, her veiled face a mask of resigned sadness.

Slowly the paddles began to turn, the warm throb of the engine, the thump, thump, thump as they brought in the lines. Yes, life must go on, and yet the dredge of memory sometimes was so powerful, it could retrieve the most poignant, heartbreaking moments as if they were only yesterday. So often the smell of brine and weed brought the backwash of that fateful day in the winter of 1852. Dark, slimy strands seeming to separate, changing with the wind and the currents and the colours of the sky. Somewhere entwined in all this murkiness was a Neptune-like shadow. Henrietta searched the horizon. Was she grieving for young Willie or for a husband lost forty years ago, whom she had never been allowed to grieve?

'There's no God in blue waters,' William used to say, boasting he'd given up God long ago.

The ocean rose and in the dark silence, Henrietta's emptiness welled. She steadied herself as the ferry rocked and rolled, and looked out at the dim stars, which seemed to be pitching about in confusion. Unlike Emma, she felt no need to pray. That Emma did so made her pity her all the more. Compassion surely was what she was feeling. Compassion sprung from the very depths of one's heart, a painful human throb. Christ remained otherwise a terrible anomaly in reason. For her, the Promised Land resided more arguably in her own *far-off age*.

Whatever doubts she might entertain, she was right to do without dogma. By the time Henrietta arrived back at Telko, it was with a much clearer head. Her upcoming address to the Eclectic Society, as a pioneer member of twenty-five years, she knew would be her last. She may have lost some of the dramatic power of her voice, but she was still pretty good on her feet. Shakespeare or Darwin? Which was the greater teacher? She would discuss it with Freddie. What it came down to, she supposed, was 'literature or science'. A light lit up inside. Her work would be cut out for her on this one. Mr Darwin, the same Mr Darwin whom she had met all those years ago in Bloomsbury when she was little more than a girl. Surely Mr Darwin would have to come out victorious. Yet he too had admired the great mentor and master for his understanding of the human mind. The Great Bard, with his amalgamation of truths and myths, demonstrated time and again that the language of the body was a universal one, accessible to all, regardless of birthright or education.

Crying was one of the most truthful expressions. Darwin believed it could be neither repressed nor generated by an act of will. Only with the aid of onions could one feign tears. But if one had suffered enough oneself, one could easily cry for others.

Chapter 26

꒰

Willing her boys away was one thing, but William had never succeeded in poisoning them against Henrietta. Their isolated sojourns – all too brief – had initially been difficult and strained. As Freddie put it, half the time she was overwrought with the joy of their return and the other half, miserable in anticipation of their departure. They never really knew her in her normal state. Yet, with time, there had grown between them mutual trust and acceptance. Each still kept in contact, paying her the occasional visit from across the seas.

In turn, she had followed their lives with keen interest. Travel abroad had done them good, opening their hearts and minds. Einnim, dark horse that he was, had taken a shine to public speaking. In a mock debate at the Waitara Institute, he had spoken to a full house arguing in favour of women's suffrage. Bless him, her own dear Einnim, so watchful and removed. What he loved most was the sea. The wind. Feeling in tune with both. The precision of navigating. Checking and counting. Weathercocks, mastheads, portholes, buttons, beacons. Signals and codes, sightings and sounds. As a child, he would remember the name of every blessed ship that came into port. Faces meant nothing to him. Yet here he was, publicly batting for women.

But it was Carl's belated decision to settle back in Australia the same year as the Mornington boating tragedy that came as sweetest surprise. His voyage to England had been the crossroads. Travelling alone brought space, new associations and independence. His back-turning on his father she saw as a coming home to the fold.

'Thinking of going bush,' he had announced upon his arrival at Telko. 'Outback. Funny how you don't appreciate something until you've been away from it.' As a native born and bred, he wanted to get to know the real Australia that people were writing about. Boldrewood, with his Captain Starlight country, had been the rage of London. 'Not exactly sure where I belong in this world, but one thing's for sure, I was out of place in England,' Carl told her. 'Anyone without an English accent can't be ranked; they don't count. Fellows like Paterson and Lawson make a chap feel proud and progressive to be Australian and not the British of one's parents' stock. All this talk about Federation makes good sense, Ma. Thing is, though, New Zealand thinks it's a cut above the rest. Wants to go it alone.'

At thirty-five, Carl was beginning to bald. His forehead growing taller, taking over his rusty curls.

'But why Narrandera, dear?' she had asked, noting his crumpled brow.

'Squatter country. Wool, wheat and grain, water and now timber: natural pine and wealth.' Narrandera, he explained, was the most highly industrialised town in the Riverina, a river port and junction. 'Good place to set up a studio. You see, Ma, the real border lies with the Murrumbidgee, not the Murray.'

In his letters, Carl talked about the birdlife, the red plains and the waterways, and the old rivalry between the states. The Tasman Sea no longer divided them. Instead, he was three hundred and seventy miles away in New South Wales. The railway was a long connection through Albury, but knowing Carl could come down to visit her at short notice made her feel so much closer to him.

No man is an island, she had heard it said. The need for affection and affiliation was only human when searching for one's place in the world. Next time Carl was back in town, she would introduce him to his cousins. Louie had grown into a bright, capable girl. She did everything commonly expected of an eldest daughter. She played the piano and sang well, had even taken on a few budding pupils. Thanks to elocution lessons, she could also recite at a moment's call and, like her sisters, was much in demand to perform. She swam, she ran. She was not afraid of hitting a tennis ball in front of a man; not at all shy or demure. But Henrietta was convinced there was a lot more to Louie than that.

Last Christmas holidays, she had gathered Louie and her sisters together at Austin Villa for some informal lessons on Beethoven. Louie, with her good ear, had been quick on the uptake. For Emma, it was uplifting to see her daughters aspire. To mark Louie's birthday in February, Henrietta had given her a gift: *Days with the Great Composers*, an imaginatively rendered account of the lives of the three great masters, Beethoven, Mendelssohn and Schubert, with captivating colour plates.

'Remember, Louie. Music cannot paint. It is on a different plane of time. A painting must leap to the eye, but a musical piece unfolds itself slowly, rather like a story.'

She had come to know Louie well, had begun to think of her as one might a surrogate daughter. Little flashes of dignity, that would-be air of *je ne sais quoi*, set her apart from the others – a latent fire that made Henrietta think, what can I do for this girl? Awaken her.

Bit by bit, she began to brief her on the background of the women's movement and the unedifying nature of politics. Goodness, it was almost a decade since she and her fellow suffragists had launched Australia's first women's suffrage society, the tender nursling of a newborn hope. The dissent and prevailing brick wall of Victorian conservatism they had encountered.

When Henrietta returned to Mornington in spring, Louie was looking poised and eager for more. Going off to sleep to the sound of distant waves in the bay, Henrietta knew she had a convert, and for Louie there was something higher in store.

So often, during her visit, dinnertime conversation at Austin Villa found its way to the Depression and the girls and their future spheres. These days, women outnumbered men. The sex imbalance posed even more of a problem in Mornington, since the town was still in mourning. Young James, now the sole breadwinner for the family, could pick and choose with love, while his sisters chanced their luck.

⁓

When Henrietta met Carl at Spencer Street station a few months later, he appeared lacklustre. Too long in the bush, she suspected. What her son needed for Christmas was love, and a liberal dose of sea salt – a good old plunge and let the warm, stinging fluid lap him round.

'Why don't I take you to Mornington so you can pay your respects?'

They took the earliest Saturday Bay steamer, with the help of a fair wind. It was good to feel the lift and fall on the swell. Riding the waves a boost to the spirits, spray flying across the bow – for Carl, the best two-shilling tonic there was. Downstairs, ripples of opalescent light danced on the pine-panelled ceiling. Through the portholes, she could see them waiting at the pier, Emma in respectful black, the rest of them a nice neat line of cream – the girls, four modern misses decked out in seersucker, with straw boaters perched on their heads, and the two Jameses, senior and junior, alike in their ducks. The younger man was on his toes, waving his hat at her, his forehead shining in the sun.

Barely had they been welcomed ashore when James gave Carl a clap on the shoulder. 'We'll be playing lawn tennis.'

'I'm more a cricket man myself.' Carl nodded with a sideways grin. 'But I'll give it a shot.'

From the shade of the wooden rotunda, it was quite a study, one of the purest and most elegant forms of human movement Henrietta had ever witnessed. Pop upon pop – she looked on in approval. Free-flowing figures and leg-of-mutton sleeves; girls who had room to move, and moved as God meant them to move, so graceful and prettily daring. Carl, having arrived immaculate in striped blazer, had stripped down to his waistcoat. Beside, Louie, bold bands of navy-blue braid waving this way and that with every swish of her skirt.

Tea was followed by a quick game of cricket in the backyard.

'James is a devil of a batsman.' Louie's laugh tinkled through the warm evening air. 'See if you can't get him out, Carl.'

It was good to see Carl carefree, infected with the buoyancy of youth. It rubbed off on Henrietta, in turn, hearing the crack of leather on willow, the dull plop or thud as it bounced off the weatherboard to cries of applause.

When the last of the light had fallen behind the peninsula, they came inside and gathered around the piano. When it was Carl's turn to perform, he returned to his favourite, Beethoven's 'Adelaide' – 'if you would accompany me, please, Mama?' Her heart nearly burst, for in an outpouring of yearning came the love song of all time – the last word of a noble and ennobling passion.

 ∽

The following morning, it was arranged that Carl would be staying on for the week. Henrietta, not wanting to be in the way, insisted upon returning as planned on the Sunday afternoon steamer.

'Are you coming to church now?' Louie reached for Carl's hand. 'We're all in the choir.'

'Oh Lord, I wouldn't know what to do. All double-dutch to me.'

Louie smacked him playfully on the wrist with her fan. 'Oh, Carlie, don't tell fibs. You're having us on.'

Emma remained pensive, unable to share in the fun. That dent between her eyebrows, the nervous twitching around her mouth.

'What is it, Emma, dear?' Henrietta asked when the others were out of earshot. 'You seem out of sorts.' That eye with the slight cast in it, looking up at her, a black drip of despondency.

'Nothing, Aunty. Only this came. A letter, from London.'

10 Argyle Square,
Kings Cross,
W.C. London
4 September 1893

My dear Niece,
Having heard from your sister Hattie of your living near her, I trust
this letter to her care, thinking you might like to hear from your
youngest uncle – now an old man. As I came to 'man's estate' and got
children of my own I often thought over my boyhood life with you. I
realise now I did not treat you with that kindness or conduct that I
ought to have (though I was a boy) and have often desired to ask your
forgiveness. If you have any pleasant recollections of me – there may be
some as I was always fond of children – pray console me with any thing
you remember and accept my sorrow for anything wherein I was faulty.
With the enclosed buy some little keepsake – I wish I could afford to
make it a better one. For many years past I have devoted my spare time
and means to assisting orphan girls about which I send you a print.
This not as any atonement for I have none but that great one on the
Cross of our Lord for all my sins, but as in obedience to His injunction
to care for them.
*   I expect you recollect 'Aunt Henrie' – your sister will tell you what I*
have said about her.
*   My boyhood life was unhappy and bad and before I was 20 I realised*
it all and repented with scalding secret tears until I found peace with
God through his Son and I have at times felt the promised comfort of the
Holy Spirit but I shall never cease to regret the past of my sinful early
years. I have 5 daughters and 2 sons and have been blessed with them
all, good, loving more than I deserved, but I tried to train them as such
and God has granted me success. One, the eldest, is married (May) and

the rest are at home with me, and we have one drawback and that is for the most part they are not of robust health.

If you have a little girl, send me her photo as a remembrance of you. You promised to be like your Mother, who I remember looking on in the year 1840 with childlike admiration and love – she was a very sweet, affectionate creature. I did not see her after she came back from America and died in Liverpool. Oh how sad is the past and my heart aches in going over it!

I hope your later life has been brighter and happier and will continue to be so. Tell me about your husband – I hope he is a good one. Your Uncle William died about 6 years ago. Your Uncle Thomas who was 2 years older than I am lives at Ventnor on the Isle of Wight. He was a boy with us in Hunter Street when you were there. He has 3 daughters in Australia. I do not know their names as they are all married. They have all stayed with me. I think they love their uncle for they have lost their mother and I tried to be kind to them.

Now goodbye my dear niece and may God bless you and yours is the prayer of your loving,

Uncle Chas. Worrell.

PS Do you remember they used to call me 'Carrot-tops' or Carlos?

Henrietta passed the letter back to Emma. A throb of intense pity began to palpitate in her chest. Poor little girls.

As for Charles, she could see him as if it were yesterday. Standing at the window, the effect of the architrave partly framing his face into a kind of portrait. Morning light traced his profile, soft, unbroken, a line of white chalk stroking all of the nuances of youth. He looked exquisite, gold-spun hair curling upon his temple. It was the light, of course, the way it fell at that precise moment. But as everybody knows, boys eventually grow into young men. In the passing of seconds, his features appeared to coarsen, became more bony and masculine. His complexion dull, almost pasty, beneath a growing colony of pimples. There was something else about his face that was completely out of character. A churlishness around the mouth. His voice too was beginning to change, crackling and beeping at the most awkward times. The accompanying flushes of embarrassment only accentuated his sensitive colouring. Gangly limbs tripping over each other like a newborn colt's, a sudden gaucheness of face and bearing. Fourteen is a horrible age; the awkwardness of feeling not quite one thing nor the other.

'Charlie! Surely you're not jealous?'

A fine layer of golden down glistened above his upper lip. 'Jealous? Why should you think me jealous?'

'Simply by your countenance, my dear brother, that sweet but troubled brow ... that tender curling lip of yours. Admit it! You're downright smouldering with resentment that our house is in disorder because of four poor little girls.'

Somewhere at the back of her mind, she could see Emma, or was it Hattie, poking her tongue out at him, then screaming merry hell as he gave her a Chinese burn.

Chapter 27

For twenty years, Henrietta had been yearning to go to New Zealand. After all this time, she was beginning to feel she had missed her chance. Even the long tortuous trip north over the border to visit Carl in Narrandera was unthinkable. Her health was erratic. She had been suffering terribly from piles. Summer had been and gone without her usual dose of sea salt.

The better part of this morning she had spent reading in Carlton Gardens. From one of the wooden benches, she had watched them, children plying hoops and balls in the fallen leaves. Cosseted little darlings. Children need to breathe. Hers, she was pleased to say, no longer had to pander to their father. They had taken to wandering afar, which in turn had brought them closer to her.

Filthy pigeons flapped about her hands and feet as she pressed on down Collins Street, past the churches, the brass doorplates and the Melbourne Club.

Once at her favourite tea house, she put in her order – a pot of tea and some little dainty – before dashing off a couple of letters to the boys. Einnim, with his taste for independence, had simply followed his nose – as commander of his own coaster, trading around the North Island of New Zealand and up into the deepest wilds of the Mokau River.

Einnim was in hot demand by settlers and contractors alike, bringing fencing material, culvert pipes, machinery and all manner of goods. A lonely existence for him, but he was a welcome sight for remote settlers.

Austin, little so-and-so, she had not heard from for a while. Her thoughts turned more easily to Carl and his quiet achievements. It had been a risky undertaking, starting up a new business so far away from family and friends. But she couldn't have been more thrilled. Already Carl was making a name for himself. Portraiture was his specialty, and the local clubs and newspapers, as well as his private studio, were keeping him busy. Carl's personal attributes suited him well to the profession. The precise, methodical way he went about his artistry. His intelligence, his gentle charm, endeared him to others, enabling him to put his sitters at ease.

But Carl had been very quiet of late. Was he lonely in his aloneness, living in Narrandera? Carl was a thirty-six-year-old bachelor. If he was avoiding marriage, then so too were his two brothers. Whatever model her sons had inherited was through no fault of hers.

Despite years of separation, she felt she knew Carl like the back of her hand: all of his weaknesses and silly insecurities, imagined or otherwise. She felt his pain and his joy, essentially what she saw as the artist in her son. She understood only too well that while he could rise to unexpected heights, he would just as easily waste good time worrying that at any moment he might come tumbling down. That Carl was capable of love went without saying – there had been attachments from time to time, it was implied – and she, as his mother, had been left to presume that concealed in his heart was a vague but fervent longing for some sweet unknown.

༄

It was no secret that Carl and Louie had been writing to each other. During that time, Henrietta had seen much of Louie, who had entrusted her with the idea, the possibility, of a marriage. Why, then, had Carl not confided likewise?

'Do you think he will ask me, Aunty?'

She had come away confident that, given time, a suitable outcome would eventuate. She had gone so far as to tell Louie she had only two reservations about the marriage. The first was Carl's age, eleven and a half years being the difference.

Louie had answered with the most angelically sweet look. 'Oh, Aunty, I have always said I should love to marry a man a great deal older than myself. If I like Carl, I'm going to marry him.'

'I see. Well, be that as it may, dear, allow me to voice my second objection. Carl is an atheist but you, Louie, are pious, and I am certain he would not marry a pious woman.'

To that, Louie had said, 'But, Aunty, I am not pious. I go to church because we have always gone, but I never listen to anything; I go to see the fashion. And, besides, I should never let religion come between us; I should always go with my husband in such matters.'

Henrietta smiled dryly to herself. True love required a certain level of relinquishment of self on both sides, in her opinion, but as to how much of herself Louie would relinquish, she remained dubious. She began to blame herself. Hadn't she impressed upon her niece early that every young woman should be guardian of her own will?

On her visits they had talked, talked earnestly, about the advancement of women. The path had been cleared. Women in New Zealand were now enfranchised and had voted for the first time last November.

'So, you see, Louie dear, the women in New Zealand are now the real torchbearers of the world, followed by South Australians. With Mary Lee as their driving force and their big petition, they're expecting to get a Bill through before year's end. Whereas we Victorians, while we might have started the suffrage movement in Australia, we are being left behind.'

Louie blinked her bright periwinkle eyes. 'Some say a girl must not vote, otherwise she will quarrel with her brothers and degrade her home, but I don't quite go along with that, Aunty. I say what I think.'

'That's the spirit, Louie. Think of it this way: every man has the right to a free mother, wife and sister, and they can't have that until they have the suffrage.'

In time she would introduce Louie to Vida Goldstein. But Louie kept pestering her. Could Aunty come again to Mornington, perhaps make a long weekend of it?

At Christmas time, she again had to excuse herself politely: 'Health not permitting, dear, on account of *the usual.*'

'My commiserations, Aunty, do get better soon. See if you can't persuade Carl to spare a week next time he's in Melbourne and come and entertain his cousins.'

Perhaps Carl was busy entertaining second thoughts. The very idea was unsettling and not helping her health. Oh why, oh why, must one couch *piles* in such delicate terms? Foul, beastly disease. It had become her morning dread and the pain was excruciating, overbearing and exhausting.

By early that evening, Henrietta was doubled over in pain.

'Oh, good God!' Her cries brought Freddie rushing to her side.

'I swear I am losing flesh and can feel some deep excavatory fissure or ulcer. It's not just a fit of the vapours,' she gasped. 'What is to become of me?' The thought of surgery was utterly intolerable.

'You say doctors can be prejudiced about women's diseases. Sometimes, they can be just plain wrong, my dear girl. Wouldn't you be better off getting a second opinion?'

A few weeks later, she discussed the matter privately with her fellow suffragist, Brettana Smyth, now a well-known women's medico, only to be told, 'It is the pressures of pregnancy and childbirth catching up with you, Mrs Dugdale. You must rest. Elevate the feet at every opportunity.'

⁓

Carl, at such inconvenience to his business, came down to see her. She suspected that someone, almost certainly Freddie, must have told him her life was in danger. A sacrificial act on Carl's part, which made her love him all the more, since only a week earlier he had suggested a cure: epsom salts in cold water an hour before breakfast, sulphur when needed, tannin wash and witch hazel. It was simple and had miraculously begun to take effect.

Upon his arrival, she sat up in bed, arms wide, her heart radiating love and gratitude.

'How can I thank you, my darling boy?' She searched his troubled face. 'Now, what about you? Are you keeping something from your old Mama?'

'What do you mean?'

'Anxiety and overwork, eh? Is that what ails you, son?' Since he did not answer, she went on. 'Setting up your own business, I know, can be stressful – collecting your dues in a country town the most odious job of all. The wealthy, from my experience, are often the worst.'

'No, to tell you the truth, Ma, I've more work than I can possibly handle.'

'Louie knows you're here, of course. Quite taken with you, I believe.'

'Really?' Carl's face broke into a sudden smile.

'Yes, she's been pressing for you to come again. Do say yes, dear. Best time of the year is now.'

When Carl returned from Mornington some weeks later, Louie came also, to Henrietta's satisfaction. It was arranged with Emma that she keep Louie at Telko and have Carl sleep at their neighbours, the Rodmans'.

Louie greeted her with a peck and a nervous giggle. 'Oh, Aunty, those navy-blue knickerbockers are so exactly right for you!'

The room fell silent for a few seconds, but when Carl finally gathered Louie to his side with a little pre-emptive cough, it was to everyone's great relief.

'Well, you'll be pleased to know, Ma, I've popped the question.'

However much anticipated, the news left her old ear buzzing. That Carlie was going to give her such a kind, compliant daughter-in-law was cause for celebration.

Alas, they were only in the house together half an hour when she could see plainly that Louie had no wifely affection for Carl. Henrietta, wanting to share in their happiness, had been keeping a sharp eye on the couple. But it was the very smallest of slights she noticed. Louie's strange behaviour – averting her eyes, licking her lips, her body rigid – and surely not out of shyness. Every time Carl went to take her hand, Louie would discreetly pull away.

Louie, it seemed, was an actress in disguise, her voice momentarily like laughing water, her laugh ringing silver, but as to what she was feeling inside, Henrietta suspected it was no more than a spot of joy.

She waited until she and Freddie were alone outside in the garden. 'Look, Fred, look at the awkward way she's standing, and at such a distance. It worries me,' she whispered hoarsely. 'Marriage without love is nothing higher than prostitution.' It was not so much the lie itself; it was what the lie brought with it. And now, Louie's pretence pressed on old wounds and the sham of her marriage to William. Unable to sit still, Henrietta rubbed at her forearms and elbows. 'Why is she going to marry Carl, if she does not love him? I need to have it out with her, for Carl's sake.'

'You read too much into things,' said Freddie, hacking off arms of ivy and creeper. 'When you get too close to people, you exert yourself too thoroughly, become too involved, too excited. Let them be, love. Let things unfold.'

But Louie's manner, too, had changed; she had become more assertive. Altogether, the few days the new lovers had passed at Camberwell prior to Carl's leaving made her unaccountably ill at ease. And then came the final awakening. They were in the cab taking Carl to the station, when Henrietta remarked, 'The next time we drive from Telko I hope will be to the Registrar.'

Louie turned, looking sidewise from over her pink silk puffed sleeve. 'Oh, no, Aunty. The wedding will be at home – Austin Villa.'

'What?' She glared at Louie, but Louie's eyes barely flickered.

'You see, Carl refused my wish to be married in church, but he did promise me a Christian marriage, didn't you, Carlie?' Louie inched her chin above her lace-trimmed collar.

But Carl failed to hear her. They were already at the station. The wheels had stopped rolling, the horses standing, blowing through their noses, the sound of jingling bits amid the stir of luggage being unloaded, and she could smell sweaty leather and fresh droppings of manure as she sat there, everything in a blur, wanting to be sick but prevented from doing anything by a feeling of overwhelming paralysis.

Carl ducked his head back into the cab and planted a kiss on Louie's lips. 'Well, I'll be off now, Mama. Aren't you going to wish me goodbye?'

As soon as he had gone, she rolled the window right down in her hunger for air. Gasped at the fresh chill, pulled her cloak around her, tight, and began to shiver as the horses gathered speed. Having spent the past week watching on in a state of heightened suspense, she felt utterly duped. Now came the fatigue, the exhaustion of powers, the want of rest, all the time fighting the fierce restlessness, the fury working itself up inside, as she paced about in her absent son's defence.

Even when they were back at Telko, Henrietta could not look at the girl, those cool blue eyes so overriding in their clarity: 'It's all been decided, Aunty.'

～

I must put a stop to it, she decided. Deceitful little minx.

'What have you done with her?' Freddie looked around when he came home from work the next day.

'She's gone out to a party. When she comes in, I shall buttonhole her once and for all. I will not stand by and allow ...'

'Stand by? You need only stand back.'

She drew short, detecting the dryness in his voice, the telltale tightening of the lips, the tone and tongue of a good lawyer.

'Stop going on so!'

'Very well, then,' she sniffed. 'If you will not allow me to confront my own niece in my own home, then I shall direct her to leave by telegram without delay. Once I've done that, I'm off to bed. I'm far from well and feel a chill coming on.'

A tense sepulchral silence followed. Freddie took a deep breath, lifted his violin to his chin, and, without warning, executed a series of double stops with such force, purity and precision that she was stopped dead in her tracks. Freddie inspected his violin, blowing rosin from around the f-holes.

'Why must you insist on being so overbearing? You have no right, no right at all, to interfere. Can you not see that?'

He tapped his bow on the table and took her to task. 'What did you expect?' He twisted a dark eyebrow at her. 'All your wants and desires at the expense of all else? If you're always having to shoehorn matters, something is wrong.' Once started, he grew pitilessly lucid. 'You expect them to fall into line with you,' he said. 'I remember my father being exactly the same about us. If I had listened to him, where would I be now?'

She flung a hand over her mouth, smothering an inward gasp. 'Oh, how could you?'

But his face revealed little. A look that said, more or less, *leave me alone and don't bother me again with such trifles.*

Door shut, and half-dressed, she hurled herself upon the brass bed. There she lay, arms folded across her bosom and hands clenched. But, rolling her head, she could just make it out, a Bach *partita*; the delicate *tremolo*, the teeniest hills and valleys shaping every phrase, the pure, tragic restraint of his playing. Between his wall and hers, she was picturing him, the way his head dipped respectfully with every discord. Sorrow contending with pain, blending into a mood of profound resignation, his playing echoed the magnitude of her aloneness, her loss – and even more importantly, Carl's – both the result of Louie's deceit.

Now Freddie had deserted her. Alice would understand. She pulled up the eiderdown, burying her head in the pillows. The following day,

Henrietta was bed-bound. She scrawled a quick note to Alice, too feeble to unleash her troubles. There was no stopping it. Fever raged, with the onset of a fiery red skin eruption all over her body.

∽

It was several months before Henrietta could write to Alice again.

29 August 1895

As usual ALICE dear, have been GOING to write EVERY day;- and have not succeeded. Also, intended to send a book; but, perhaps, it would be better to ask if you already possess it. Its name is 'COO-EE'; a lovely name, – I DO love the word – and has some very pleasant little sketches. (Tales of Australian Life by Australian Ladies (c1890) edited in England by Harriette Anne Martin.)

No, dear, we have not read the one by ZOLA, you kindly offer, and should be pleased to read it.

We are jogging along quietly, my dear Mate's health pretty good and my own fast improving. Never before, for so long a period as FOUR MONTHS, have I been so free from piles. It was a marvellous cure; for I was in such a lamentable condition of weakness that life would have been impossible for many days longer. Only within the last week have I known the comfort of being without the wearying throbbing of the whole body. That began about a month after the bleeding had set about its devilish work; so, there was SIX months of that torment. No doubt, I should have quite mastered it sooner, but for an unfortunate bit of trouble which came most unexpectedly upon me; and to which I could only refer in my last letter to you;- it was so great a sore upon my heart that I had pain in even referring to it.

You will remember me explaining to you my reservations about the match, though happy when Carl and Louie eventually became engaged. It was what followed that brought upon me the greatest trouble of all.

Louie, unbeknown to me, had made Carl promise to have a Christian marriage. He refused to be married in Church, as she wished; and the cunning ANGEL had altered it to taking place in her father's house; Carl, who knows nothing of Christian mummery, thinking that would free him from the religious part of it. After all she had said to me, of which I have not time to tell you even half – led CARL into such a false position – to kneel to a god that he feels to be only a solar myth – and knowing my great pride in his truthful life – Oh, it was a cruel act; and such a blow that I had an illness, resulting from nervous shock, which seemed to poison my blood. I had a very narrow escape of ERYSPELAS. The nightly itching was maddening; I had to apply lotion six or seven times before morning, for weeks, and it is not quite well yet. I was lightheaded, night after night, thinking of her perfidy. There are very few who can conceive the excessive grief it caused me. NEVER again will I give my love to ANGELS. I tried to conceal my grief from her, so ill that the truth was the shortest. The day after CARL left, she went to a party and I telegraphed to her not to return. She tried to see me, but we have not met since – and I have no wish that we should. Indeed, we have decided to give up our family acquaintance. I am too old to run the risk of any more trouble.

That is, we have given up all but 'BEETHOVEN', our love in common. She is very straightforward, as I was with her. Freddie was always averse to having anything to do with relatives, either mine or his own; and I regret not having earlier fallen with his views.

Letters from CARL inform me that LOUIE has thrown off the mask and declared her piety; so CARL has broken the engagement. Of course, we are exceedingly pleased for there would have been no happiness – with such wide difference of religious opinion CARL says he begins to think that some one 'more staid' would suit him better. And so we think. May he soon find the one.

I am always ashamed of my hurried letters, after your well-written, orderly ones; it often amazes me that you can turn out such splendid epistles.

Your affectionate friend
HENRIE
Telko

⁓

'What's wrong, pet?'

Freddie was out in the garden, pruning, but she could tell he'd been weeping. She thrust out her arms in the sudden realisation that she had for the better part of the year been totally absorbed with her own wellbeing and Carl's. 'Still cross with me?'

'No, no, of course not …' He took off his gardening gloves, reached in his pocket for his handkerchief and blew his nose hard, encasing it in neatly ironed creases. 'It's just that … my father died.'

'Oh Freddie, love, when?'

'A month or so back.'

'Why didn't you tell me?'

'I didn't like to mention it, you being so ill.'

It was true. Any more distressing news would have taken her to the brink.

Father and son had never been an easy relationship for the Johnsons – Freddie a lifelong disappointment to his father, who had wanted him to follow in his regimental footsteps. She had been cast the villain, the virago, the older woman seductress leading Freddie astray, filling his clever young mind with revolutionary ideas, bringing shame on the Johnson name. Whereas her Freddie was a man of independent mind who would not be told how to think.

'Poor darling. Come.' She brought him into the vestibule and steered him onto the chaise longue, where they remained together enfolded. With his mother gone five years past, he was now, like her, an orphan.

'What an ass you must think me,' he said, finally breaking away, pulping his wet handkerchief in his palm.

'I always had the greatest admiration for your father.' She stroked his arm backwards and forwards. 'A wonderful musician, a popular man, a man of the people.'

Bright drops hung in his whiskers, his voice sad and halting.

'Popular, yes, but he was never a family man. I hardly ever saw him, as a child. He was the Leader and the Band always came first.'

'But you were right, Freddie. Had you listened to him, where would we be now?'

Freddie put his hand in his pocket and drew out a gold watch. 'Look. Father honoured his promise. It was all I ever wanted as a child.'

He unclipped the fob chain and pressed it into her hand.

'Eighteen carat,' he said.

'Obviously very special.' The detailed mechanism, the precision. The measured *tick, tick*. How like Freddie, she thought, passing it back. Set ten minutes fast, of course, in sync with every other timepiece in the house.

Wrapped in each other's arms, it seemed that nothing, nothing but time, could come between her and her old mate.

Chapter 28

It was like a pattern, a cycle. The way one financial boom had come to an end and another taken its place. The opportunities of a lifetime now lay on the other side of the country, as they had in Victoria over forty years ago.

There was a range of employment in the West Australian goldfields besides mining works and services, plus a desert scarce of water. Mr Forrest, the Premier, was building an enormous pipeline from Perth to Kalgoorlie. Time was of the essence, and communications systems in desperate need of upgrade. Young James, having applied to the Colonial Office as a telegraphy operator, had been posted far west to Israelite Bay.

'The whole family are thinking of joining the rush.'

'Oh?' said Freddie, raising an eyebrow. 'Lucky devils.'

The sky had darkened, with light drizzle, just the sort of Sunday afternoon for a cosy huddle. Henrietta brought the gate-leg table before the fire and set up the chessboard, before wheeling in the tea trolley from the kitchen.

'Are you ready?'

Freddie sat down, rubbing his hands as she poured the tea and cut into her freshly made ginger cake.

'You go first,' she said, knowing his propensity to wolf. 'I'm just going to settle back and have a look at Emma's letter again.' She would reply in due course – she could hardly punish her niece for Louie's behaviour.

Between sips of tea, Henrietta nibbled at a curried-egg and cucumber sandwich, leaving Freddie to make his opening gambit.

Emma, from the sound of her letter, was missing her only son.

We've booked our passage, Aunty. We're going to have a look-see. Gold's certainly put Westralia on the map. Fifteen men in no-man's-land save for occasional boats and ships calling in for mail and supplies. The Telegraph Station keeps a very hospitable camp. Gloriously long pristine beaches. Lots of fishing, even the sharks have a look in. Fine days reserved for football or cricket. The rest of their spare time, they play chess over the telegraph line.

Telegraphy chess had been around some fifty years. Young women of her time were only allowed to play competition chess by correspondence. Wasn't the same. It shielded, suppressed. Papa used to say a born performer always rises to an audience. There was nothing quite like the live drama of being witnessed. Win or lose, one had to be gracious.

Papa liked nothing better than making friend out of foe and would open his house to the best: Saint-Amant, Löwenthal, Horwitz – like Papa, among the champion chess masters in the world. Game over, he would take them out and, after showing them the sights of London, bring them home to dine.

She remembered one guest, a Frenchman, seemingly gay behind a miasma of brandy fumes. She had taken objection to his sudden rudeness of manner, his licentious asides made out of earshot in French. Refusing to blush, she feigned the coquette. 'Pray, monsieur, will you honour me by playing a game of chess with me?' Silly fool had insisted there and then. But the laugh was on him when she checkmated him in a matter of minutes.

Freddie, bless him, was a very good player, albeit a slow one. But oh, how she wished he wouldn't dither. At around twelve moves an hour, their chess games did drag on so. Hardly an even playing field. She slipped back out to the kitchen, busying herself for as long as she could. With lamps lit and fire stoked, she resumed her place, to find Freddie still playing with the same black knight.

She drummed her fingers on the table. Akin to law, chess demanded rational and critical thought, but in chess one also needed a good visual memory. Freddie, it seemed, could not visually process patterns and positions with quite the alacrity as she. Stumped, he would invariably sit staring at the chessboard with that frown of his until presumably the black squares appeared white and the white squares black.

The relationship between chess and freemasonry was as old as the Goths. Chess mimicked warfare, Papa pointed out, while masonry stood for peace and goodwill to all mankind. Either way, he said, demonstrated that the key to victory lay in clear-headedness and staying power, not brute force and bloodshed.

Henrietta folded her hands in forbearance. Life, in reality, was not so cut and dried. Freddie often remarked on ambiguity and paradoxes, the unbearable poignancies of life that she had somehow failed to see.

There were very few marriages where ability was equally balanced – in some, the woman's was greater; in some, the man's. She looked at her mate, as she always did, without servility. Theirs had only ever been a relationship of love and respect. Any bond as honourable should rightfully stand within the law.

She glanced at the clock. The fire, she noticed, had burned itself down. The curtains begging to be drawn. From somewhere outside came the wailing whistle of a curlew. Huddled in her cashmere shawl, she went to the window. The pane pressed back cold against her forehead, her eyes straining. In the clear black winter sky she could see faraway stars radiating stillness; their silence intense, unbroken, calling from a far-off age.

Suddenly, the clatter of wood on wood made her jump.

Freddie, fallen asleep, dear love. Knocked the board with his knee. 'Never mind. Shall we call it a day?'

What was left over she covered and put in the food-safe, then rinsed the blue and white crockery, quickly dried the pieces and placed them back on the dresser.

'Louie's still not found herself a husband, you know,' she said once they had climbed into bed.

That awful Mornington business she thought she had put to rest. The photos Carl had taken of Louie to mark their engagement, all destroyed. Yet still Louie's face persisted in resurrecting itself, its tilt and intent, and all its different guises. Often it was the one of her looking sylph-like up at Carl, her smile, her eyes blue as forget-me-nots, golden hair coming so prettily adrift, and the sway of her body as she sang 'Road to the Moon'. With Freddie accompanying on his violin and yours truly on the piano, it had sounded, oh, sublime. At the most poignant part of the song, Henrietta had just happened to look up from the keyboard and in that split second had felt excluded, of little import.

Jealousy was not in the realms of her emotional spectrum. She had discussed the matter with Freddie a number of times. Had she been too rash, too harsh in her dealings with the girl? Had she placed undue pressure on her own dear son? After all, Louie had been so young and impressionable. With time and maturity, perhaps things might have been different. Had age really been an issue? Emma and Jim had a twelve-year gap, and as for she and Freddie … Was it religion, then? Freddie would be quick to remind her that scepticism was open to inquiry as much as any religion, since it too was a form of dogma. Then again, she could have been a little overly sensitive.

Spooning her body against his, she tried to draw some bodily comfort. 'Perhaps Louie might have made Carlie happy. Should I be blaming myself?'

'Not at all,' said Freddie, stifling a yawn. 'It would never have worked. Stop playing the gadfly.'

$\sim$

It was unmistakable, the little spring in her steps. Women everywhere in Melbourne were upbeat, active and prominent in the forthcoming celebrations of the Queen's Diamond Jubilee in the capital city she had named. Though Henrietta would not give the Queen the time of day, the verve and spirit of the Jubilee movement were nonetheless contagious, a unifying force. What more deserving cause than the 'shilling fund' set up on Her Majesty's behalf for the building of a Women's Hospital in Melbourne for women patients, women doctors and women medical students? The Queen Victoria Hospital.

How sadly surprised she was to hear that that great promoter of women's health, Brettana Smyth, had recently died of overwork. A bold and original thinker, she had departed the world far too soon. South Australia's Catherine Spence had recently stood as a candidate for the Australian Federal Convention, to be the first female political representative in Australia. Though she did not win a seat, it was a step up – a public gesture that elevated women that bit more.

In the toing and froing to Jubilee events, travelling by train, Henrietta was drawn to looking back as much as forward, and how the world had changed in her lifetime.

'Did you notice the number of women out and about in the city this afternoon?' she said to Freddie on arriving home from an afternoon recital at the Athenaeum. 'I suppose we women can partly thank science for our advancement. A woman can travel anywhere now on a train without need of a chaperone.' She stripped off her hat, gloves and boots and placed them on the stand. 'To think, I've been doing it for thirty years.' She gave a proud smile.

'And don't forget the bicycle,' said Freddie, as he crouched down in front of the fireplace. 'It's done much to give women a new sphere, independence and direction in life.'

Henrietta curled herself up on the sofa, snuggled up in her cashmere cape. Her eyes were following Freddie's every movement, the painstaking way he went about constructing a neat framework of kindling, placing the sticks over twists of paper, bigger sticks still, before creating a draught hole with the poker. By the time he had finished, it was quite a work of engineering.

'Of course, the bicycle, in itself, has demanded a more practical mode of dress,' she said.

Freddie struck a match and held it, waiting for the flame to catch. 'Remember that race?' He stood up and chuckled. 'What a champion you were. First woman in Australia to ride a Boneshaker. A man's one at that!' Brushing his hands, he came and gave her a hug. 'I was so proud of you, love.'

'I couldn't have done it without your encouragement, dear heart. What a sight we must have been, me wobbling along, determined to win, you running along beside me, giving me the odd push. "Gently, gently, mind the flag. Now's your time!"'

Back around the end of the 1860s, that event had seemed of little import. A welcome lark, a moment's relief from a harrowing marital breakdown.

'I remember setting my teeth and saying to myself, "Head down, knees in." Rather like attempting to master a particularly vicious and unmanageable young horse, only I quickly decided I far preferred the horse.'

Strength and balance were the trick, she recalled.

'Well,' said Freddie, 'you got to the finish line and won without so much as losing a hairpin.'

Whereas the road to enfranchisement had been long and hard and bumpy; full of potholes and obstructions – more of an obstacle race. At times, there had seemed no end in sight, just the roar of people clapping her on.

Now enfranchisement was on their very doorstep. For the first time in the history of Australia, women – those from South Australia – had equal rights to vote with men. The whole nation, indeed the whole world, would be watching. For here, in the southern hemisphere, were models in the lead.

Mrs Lowe, who remained closely connected to the movement, regularly kept her informed by post. *Dozens of meetings are held from month to month in drawing rooms as well as halls, Mrs D., but rarely are they reported in the papers.*

In Victoria, and in New South Wales, two or more sessions, she hoped, would see it through. And with the new century nearly upon them, women's status would never be the same again.

Everyone, everywhere, was talking about the New Woman, the Twentieth Century Girl and a new upcoming Women's Bible. Yet as the date of the Jubilee celebration in June approached, visions of the New Woman were clouded by the veneration of the past. Henrietta could see herself all of ten years and irrepressible, knees jigging, snow-white pantalettes pumping backwards and forwards under the dinner table. Ready to pitch her voice above the others, pure and fresh, bursting like soda water out of a bottle. 'The King is dead! And little Queen *Victorie* is not much older than me!'

Sixty years later to the day in June, Henrietta ended up spending the occasion quietly at home, fires stoked. For her sixty years in office, what exactly had the Queen done for women? Only antagonise them.

If the Queen had had her way, women like Henrietta would have got a good whipping. To think she had been her yardstick as a girl. She remembered the day of the coronation quite clearly. It was 1838, the week after Teddy had died, for their house was deep in mourning. The blast at the break of dawn, followed by carillon from every church tower in London, tumbling over each other, clinging and clashing for what seemed hours. The lull outside so charged, clocks of St Pancras ready to chime. Their street was empty, everyone having descended upon the West End, anywhere near St James's Park and the line of march from Buckingham Palace to Westminster Abbey. Like a massive thunderbolt, the fire of guns signalling the start of the procession. Even from Brunswick Square in Bloomsbury, the uproar was deafening. She could only imagine it; the pomp and splendour, gilded carriages and silver harnesses, clopping horses and trumpets and drums. Thousands of people surging forward, heads craning, hands and handkerchiefs waving in the air, their spirits so roused, so invested in hope. Oh, how desperately she had wanted to be part of that throng.

'Henrietta, come away from the window. Show some respect and decorum.'

How could a child be expected to have any understanding of the nature of mortality? At the grand old age of seventy, she was still none the wiser. Freddie, bless his soul, had done his best to keep her young.

As she sat perusing the London newspapers, glimmers of that day returned to tug at her heart. During the laying-out, her mother had asked for a lock of Edward's hair to be taken and set in gold as a keepsake. The locket. The locket she had barely looked at in years.

Henrietta slipped into the bedroom. Yes. Still there, coiled up in her mother's jewellery box. Lifting it out, she carefully opened the catch. Ran a finger over the delicate blond knot, her brother Edward's hair, and closed her eyes in remembrance. There was nothing in the darkness. Then slowly a shroud emerged and, with it, a face, white and waxen, with an unnatural, almost bluish tinge against his blistered lips and staring eyes.

Quickly she put the locket away and unhooked her gold-rimmed spectacles. No. She had never been one for adornment. All clothes were sham, more or less. Why be slave to fashion? Beauty lay in what was right and natural.

She folded her spectacles, carefully placed them in their tortoiseshell case and snapped it shut. The thought of wearing her mother's jewellery was unsettling; to bear the sorrow of the past, a burden. Old chattels by the tea chest had been shipped out to her: Mama's capes, shawls, scraps of fabric, letters, newspaper clippings, theatre programs and calling cards – nothing but family baggage. Of what use was this to a woman of advanced thought? She had never liked history, could never remember it – the hard, dry black line in which it had been taught war after war, king after king, generation after generation of slaughter and principal slaughterers – atrocities frequently committed under the cloak of religion. 'Noble victories', they called these murders, and myth-men in their churches thanked their God for them. As for the old Queen – fancy describing woman's right to vote as 'mad wicked folly'. What wicked folly and indeed hypocrisy.

ᔐ

Once the fastest thing on earth was a galloping horse. Now humankind was constantly mastering the speeds of sound and light. There was no limit to the human mind, thought Henrietta, yet still one had to carry the heavy torch of enlightenment. *Our greatest weakness lies in giving up,* Mr Edison had warned. *The most certain way to succeed is always to try just one more time.*

Then, surprise! Sir John Forrest, West Australian Premier, doggedly against women voting, had done a turnaround. Was it a deep political dodge, as Freddie suggested, or had his good wife shamed him into it? Lady Forrest and Mrs Edith Cowan, founding members of the Karrakatta Club – uniting with the women's temperance movement – had been long pushing for the Bill. By August 1899, one last try had seen it through.

Buoyed by their recent success, Henrietta set to and wrote a letter of encouragement to Mrs Vida Goldstein, expressing her pleasure at the strides the women's movement had made in Victoria. Her words were kindly acknowledged at a weekly meeting of the Women's Franchise League at the Trades Hall Council. Mention was made of her excellent work in pioneering the agitation for the franchise, and the accompanying hostility she had endured:

the sneers and jeers and insults of individuals unworthy of the name of men. It was, therefore, gratifying to know that, although the movement had not yet been successful, she had outlived the ignorance of her opponents, and that the seeds which she had sown many years ago were now bearing ripe fruit.

Soon enough the Centennial celebrations would be upon them, and for Henrietta and her successors the event was another marker in the march for justice. So often it had been within reach, the golden bar of enfranchisement. In her dreams at night, she would put out her hand to grasp that bar, but every time, someone seemed to have moved it a little higher and she would be left empty with disappointment and the floating scum of denigration.

Freddie all the time tried to jolly her along.

'Yes, but why is it, Freddie? New Zealanders have found it's led to no harm or inconvenience, and according to Einnim, even the Primate approves. They must be having a good old laugh over there, wondering why we're taking so long about it.'

'Wait and see,' he said. 'The pressure of the new federation, when it comes … Each state will automatically fall into line.'

John Forrest might push for suffrage, push for all his worth, but federation, Henrietta knew, was in no way a fait accompli.

'Only thing holding it up in the west,' said Freddie, 'is a bucketful of old fossils. Always antagonistic to everything hailing from the Eastern States – Victoria, in particular.' Younger sandgropers, he said, accepted the inevitable and were more prepared to haggle. 'I bet you ten to one the promise of a transcontinental railway would fetch them at once.'

Chapter 29

～

Journalists and reporters, in her experience, were all the same. They never let the truth stand in the way of a good story, dull facts not quite good enough. No doubt the owner/editor of *Table Talk*, Mr Brodzky, thought he knew her well enough to cobble together a few snippets about her life to publish in his Political Paragraphs column. After his recent mockery of anti-suffragist argument by the Legislative Council, she should have felt flattered to have even been remembered.

'Married at fourteen, eh?' Freddie pointed to the Melbourne social weekly over the breakfast table. 'First I've heard of it.'

MRS DUGDALE

At the age of 73 Mrs Dugdale who has fought in the foremost ranks of the women's rights party since 1870, can look back on many triumphs for her cause, though the franchise is not yet won in Victoria. Mrs Dugdale was born in London, and was first married at the age of fourteen. She and her husband emigrated to Australia, where he died; and she later married Mr Dugdale, the son of an English clergyman. In her youth Mrs Dugdale showed such skill at chess that her father hoped she would become a champion player, but even then she took more interest in public affairs, and has a vivid recollection of the Chartist riots at the beginning of the present reign. She took an active part in the agitation for the Married Woman's Property Act, of which mild measure it was predicted that 'it would shake to their foundations the pillars of society.' Later on she took to lecturing as well as writing and was elected president of the newly formed Woman's Suffrage Society. As a pioneer, some of the hardest work was hers, and now out of the din of the fight, though still taking a lively interest in its progress, she is enjoying well-earned rest.

'Fourteen?' She frowned at the article, a little puzzled. 'Ah, an editorial error,' she said airily. 'I can hardly take offence at that. Even so, the least the fellow could have done was come and interview me in person and I could have set him straight. And this old photograph? Where did they get that?'

'Don't ask me.' Freddie gave a shrug. 'I've been with you thirty darn years and I don't even rate a mention.'

Henrietta's eyes followed him out of the room. Unlike her, Freddie had never quite learned to grow skin. However much he might spurn convention, he could be exquisitely sensitive to the painful slights of life. It saddened him that their de facto relationship could never be fully sanctioned. So often he or she had been publicly isolated or snubbed because of social stigma.

Her eyes fell back to the article, and the accompanying portrait, obviously a copy of the one taken by Carl after the inauguration of the suffrage society in 1884. What she could see was an earlier version of herself, a very young-looking fifty-five-year-old – a woman of assurance and distinction – staring back at her. Clear skin. Hair smoothed neatly with walnut pomade. Loosely fashioned ivory silk tucker to soften her otherwise no-nonsense apparel. Draped elegantly across the waist of her tunic into the side pocket of her velveteen jacket, the chain of her silver watch. One gloved hand resting calmly against a large, high-backed wicker chair, potted aspidistra behind, and in the other hand, what looked like a scroll. Below, in flaring gores, the first of her divided skirts that had once rocked the nation. Nothing of the young girl betrothed at fourteen.

Henrietta stroked her hollowed cheeks. For a second, the bittersweet chord of memory vibrated.

'Cousin Junius! Come in.' Junius had shown up at their Bloomsbury house unannounced, after a year at sea. 'The others have gone to Brighton for the day, so apart from me and our old guest upstairs, it is an empty house you find.' Being the first time she had been alone with a man, she was so hot and feverish, she would have blushed in the dark.

'May I say, Henrietta, how pretty you've become.' Junius, as if by magic, drew out a yellowish lacquered box from beneath his cloak.

An intricately carved chess set, the likes of which she'd not seen before. 'A gift ... for me? Oh, how exquisite!' For here were kings and queens as elephants, bishops as camels, rooks as elephants, and pawns as horsemen to bewitch her, amid the heady smell of sandalwood. 'Let me light up the tea urn,' she said, 'and then we can start.'

To stave off Junius' long absences at sea, she had learned how to summon him up: his hands, his mouth, his smell, his dark melanic eyes, the crinkle of white lines where the sun did not reach. A passing glimpse of herself in a mirror would fetch his instant approval. Now it was like looking back through shards of smoked glass.

Six years she had waited in troth until she was of age. Directly the *Duke of Bedford* arrived back at East India docks midsummer of 1848, Junius was off to stake his claim. Joined in hand at last, they had stepped out of St John's Church to joyful prospects. Hyde Park, with its newly planted trees and gardens in full blossom, made the recent Chartist rallies seem but an empty rumour. Ten minutes by carriage and they were back breakfasting in Bloomsbury: aunts, cousins, along with the rest of her family. Papa, a short and clever speech, and Mama fussing unnecessarily over a cold collation and an assortment of sweetmeats spread out on the dining room table. She, the blushing bride, oblivious to all else but her new husband and his hand on her pointed waist. No doubt the usual rituals applied: the kissing, the crying, the cutting of the cake, the bridal excursion. There was little to evoke now of their leave-taking other than the flush of sherry and waking up the following morning to the rich pearl sheen of her wedding dress, all her scattered finery on the floor.

Well, then, she thought, having dried the breakfast dishes, since the twentieth century should rightfully turn with a clean, white page, she would write to the editor of *Table Talk* and correct the two inaccuracies in their recent account of her life. She went to her desk, picked up her pen, and with a firm hand, wrote:

Firstly, Married at 14. This may be regarded by my relatives as a reflection (of course, not intentional by your always courteous journal) upon my good parents, who were too wise to permit the marriage before I was 21, although older heads than mine had arranged the engagement in my 15th year.

Secondly, that I was President of the first Victorian Suffrage Society. In any of my efforts to aid the emancipation of woman, self-aggrandisement has had no place: so I could not be mean enough to accept credit for an honour which was never mine. The talented large-minded Dr Bromby was our President. My position was simply Chairwoman of the Executive Committee, until compelled by failing health to cease active work. So far has self been away from a service in this great cause that I should not have appeared before the public but for my intense hatred of all injustice: and especially contempt for that remnant of archaic male vanity, the impertinent and most ignorant interference with woman's happiness and progress by man-made laws, without even consulting her.

Although unable to join the energetic ladies now working to gain woman's enfranchisement, no increase of age, or decrease of health, or silly insults of unthinking persons could ever lessen my interest in their endeavours for right. One of my dearest hopes is that, before I die, the Legislative Council may number enough intellectual and honourable members to pass the Woman's Franchise Bill: a wise measure, which three times has fully testified to the superior intelligence and justice of what is called the Lower House.

Having sealed the letter, Henrietta joined Freddie, who was in the living room reading in his wingback chair. And as she sat down beside him in her usual armchair and looked into the empty hearth, her eyes seemed to glaze for a moment, taking on the soft green of the faïence tiles, with their muse on either side.

'People used to call me a radical,' she said. 'Not anymore. Nice to know I'm now widely accepted by other suffragists.'

'That's because you were the bravest.' Freddie reached over and pressed her hand. 'Always the leading light. What honour to have passed on the torch.'

When had it all started? She remembered the thought dawning on her very early in life that boys were natural, girls artificial. Boys played outside; girls belonged inside, near hearth and home. It had seemed like some silly game one had to play. She, always pressing the issue: 'Why, Papa, why is the king the most important piece in chess, since the queen does all of the work? Why this world of men?'

'Because that is the way it is, my love, the nature of the game. An ancient noble game. But now, in the modern game, the queen, as you well know, has power and mobility. A king, while more powerful, is restricted in every direction.'

And in his usual clever way, Papa would turn it around and it didn't seem half so bad.

∿

Carl, who arrived in Melbourne by early sleeper some days later, came straight to the point. 'What's this nonsense I've been reading about you, Mama?'

She drew away, feeling herself stiffen.

'I say, Ma dear, you've gone awful quiet.'

As soon as they had waved Freddie off at the front gate, she pressed her straw hat on her head. 'Come, Carlie,' she said, 'let me show you my rosarium. Freddie only grafted the stocks last autumn. Now the blessed things are bursting out of their little hearts.'

Carl followed her out the back to the potting shed. She gave him the secateurs to hold while she thrust her hands into a pair of shabby tan leather gloves. 'Best picked first thing in the morning, I always think. Lovely. Lovely.' Here a snip, there a snip. Together mother and son ambled about the garden. 'Hmm. Belle de Crécy. Divine.' Deep cerise turning to soft parma violet, each cut bloom still fresh with dew she put to her nose before passing to Carl.

'Married at fourteen, Mama? That's a bit rich.'

'Engaged, my dear son.'

Taking the bunch of roses, she plunged them into a bucket of water and carried them inside to arrange.

Over the years, she had released selective drips and drops of her younger life only as she thought fit and appropriate for her son's age; Carl's visits being so infrequent, there had seemed never quite the right moment for this.

'Did I never tell you? Oh, my darling boy ...' She turned to him, discomforted by the gaze of his grey-green eyes. 'Well, you see, Carl ... well, the thing is, I married your father a widow.'

'A widow?'

'Yes,' she said crisply.

Out it came, once and for all. But she clammed up, as she had with Freddie, as to how at fourteen she had found herself alone with her first cousin, Junius. A game of chess that went on far too long, even for cousins. The playful dillydallying, neither willing to checkmate the other.

'Why did you never tell me, Mama, since I have a right to know about my cousin-removed?'

Carl pulled at his ear. She could tell he was miffed.

'Self-preservation, I suppose. Your father was always a very possessive man. As fate would have it, he and Junius were fellow officers on the *Duke of Bedford*; good friends and, only later I came to realise, the worst of rivals.'

'But engaged at fourteen?'

'Arranged marriages, sadly, were still fashionable in those days, and not always at the quest of one's parents.' With Mama and Papa abroad, she had, in their absence, unwittingly become the ward of her brother John. Having come home and caught her alone with Junius in a compromising position, he had considered it his rightful duty to extract a proposal from Junius as a way of restoring her honour.

Six years Junius had waited for her – testament of his love and constancy – by which time he was a very worldly thirty-two. Only now, with the benefit of time, she could see how she had been long on romance but short on the understanding of men, matrimony, mariners and sex.

'It was wrong, very wrong, for a girl to be bound at such a young and tender age.' She reached for Carl's hand. 'Mama and Papa did their best to protect me; wise old Papa, warning of the ways of mariners, made me wait.'

Henrietta blinked away a tear. 'I was so young, you see, so naive and vulnerable. I had known Cousin Junius since early childhood ... I had always thought him the dearest of dears.'

At the time, it had been like wine in her blood. She believed it was love – as love it was – and, being headstrong, had gone along with it, too. But now, as a woman of advanced age, she could not overlook her principles, having actively canvassed for the age of consent to be raised to sixteen, and since seen the law so amended for the purpose of child protection. How can a fourteen-year-old girl be mature enough to lodge her consent?

P a r t 5

⌒

1 9 0 0 – 1 9 0 3

Chapter 30

‿

‘O rdinary Wife-Beatings’ were not a very pleasant way to start the new century, but since the case in question had been drawn to her attention, Henrietta had felt compelled to put ink to paper in protest. She wrote to the editor of *Table Talk* in February 1900 to set things straight:

> *Sir, In last Saturday's Argus report of petitions for dissolution of marriage, occurs the following:—*
>
> *The petitioner having given evidence of the alleged acts of cruelty, Mr Justice Hood said that the law intended something more serious than ordinary acts of wife-beating, and he would therefore dismiss the petition.*
>
> *Is this really the law? If so, the sooner women have power to alter such a barbarous statute the better for the safety of wives; for all 'ordinary acts of wife-beating' are invariably of a murderous character. But perhaps, the law considers dissolution would be more fully accomplished by husbands' fists.*
>
> *H. A. Dugdale*
> *Telko, Camberwell*

And, as the year went on, there came more assaults. If not fist or foot, then cheap copy for newspapers. How it infuriated her: cartoons, articles and letters at women's expense. Portraying them as weak and unintelligent, disrupting parliamentary procedures by jumping on chairs in fear of a mouse or being distracted by a missing button fallen from a fellow member's clothing. Either that or playing on some curious moral element, how politics unsexed women, emasculated their husbands and made family life utterly miserable.

It seemed to make little difference that the country as a whole could come together in federation. The *Commonwealth of Australia Constitution Act* (UK) had been passed and the Royal Assent of the Queen given on 9 July for the founding of the Commonwealth. In developing a sense of nation, how more unifying than to extend suffrage across the board to man and woman alike.

Yet here, in their own state, a few antediluvians were stonewalling and holding the balance of power. What more could be done? Every constitutional means had been used in power. Bill after Bill put forward in the Victorian Parliament. The Victorian constituencies had twice at general elections and five times by the vote of their representatives in the Lower House declared their will on this question, and that will had four times been thwarted by the Legislative Council. Henrietta knew that if that body did not now pass the Bill, the women of Victoria would have no voice in electing the inaugural Federal Parliament, although women certainly in South and Western Australia and probably in New South Wales and Queensland would be consulted before the Commonwealth rulers were chosen.

What an impost that a majority of over two-thirds of the House of Representatives of Victoria had declared that the country wanted women's suffrage, and yet for the fifth time the unrepresentative Council was threatening to veto the will of the people.

It seemed there would always be some insidious circle working against them. And now, women – perish the thought – petitioning against the Women's Suffrage Bill!

Henrietta drew open the curtains. The air was cold and crisp; the promise of a fine day. There ready to greet her outside the long bay window, the changing backcloth of the front garden. Freddie's Japonicas – pulsating blood-red blooms against the sky so near yet so bitterly blue – had shed a carpet of petals upon the icy gravel.

Though she no longer attended suffrage society meetings, she could still rake up the old fire at home. To rise before dawn, force of habit; mornings were reserved for letter-writing, matters she would rather put off given first priority. Since her mind was set on the making out of her will – a resolution to mark the new century – she had made some preliminary points. Thank-yous and duty-bound letters, she decided, would have to wait today, oldest friends excepted.

Freddie was getting ready for work. She could hear him from her study – the splash of water; the clink-chink of razor-knife against porcelain; then the silence of cutthroat precision. Out he came, the city man, whistling softly in a waft of lavender soap and pomade. She went out to the kitchen and stoked the fire. The breakfast table as usual she had set the night before. Within minutes, she had the teapot filled and was dolloping out steaming rolled-oat porridge into a bowl. Sugar. Milk jug. Freshly clotted cream. Bread rolls and butter and her own cape gooseberry jam. Together they sat down. She poured his tea and then her own before unfolding her napkin, her mind, freshly occupied by her early-morning flurry of correspondence.

'"Anti-suffragists", they call themselves.' Never would she have believed that woman could be to her own sex so unkind and uncharitable.

Freddie nodded in sympathy but did not look up from his porridge.

Henrietta tore off a dainty piece of roll and popped it in her mouth before going on. 'I have no idea who these young women are, but I shall write to *The Age*. Anyone can tell, Fred, they're being urged on by narrow-minded men. If these harmless idiots do not wish to use the franchise themselves, they could leave it alone, and there end matters. But why act the dog-in-the-manger to those who do want to vote? To try and block the Bill is utterly scandalous.' She paused to draw breath. 'Freddie? Freddie? What about your bread and butter?'

Freddie was running late. She could hear him brushing his teeth with unnecessary vigour. Poor darling, they worked him far too hard. All at once he came tripping down the hallway, hurriedly buttoning his coat. By the time he reached the front door, she was ready, waiting, with his gloves and bowler hat.

'I cannot understand. What are they afraid of?' She waved her arms in frustration. 'Heavens. Women's enfranchisement is as harmless as a Persian prayer mat and as necessary as a family dinner.'

'They are the tools of politicians. Messrs Derham and Reid, who get their daughters to do their dirty work for them.' Freddie, directing the point of his umbrella, spiked a fallen leaf from the mat and flicked it in the garden.

Good God! Derham, the turncoat, had joined their own suffrage society back in 1885. His wife had even taken over as president from Dr Bromby. 'We must do something at once.'

'Sorry, love, have to dash.'

From the portico, she watched as Freddie strode off down the driveway and turned, as he did every morning, and blew her a kiss.

A rushed visit from Alice Harding in August had brought the enlivening news that her brother, Alfred, had joined the fray, adding to a hearty donation for the women's suffrage movement. The more support from men, the better – the more gravitas. Alfred's generosity was a fine example to promote. With renewed enthusiasm, Henrietta wrote to *The Age*, enclosing the five shillings from the Hardings with their request that the money be forwarded to David Syme, the editor, and a trustee of the Woman's Suffrage Fund. A radical liberal, Mr David Syme had been a loyal supporter of the suffrage movement for many years. She thanked her friend most heartily for the sincere, gentlemanly and firm tone in which he had always tried to awaken a feeling of justice through his editorial comments and what he chose to publish. It was a pleasant antidote to the various silly, illogical and discourteous arguments of those who were too selfish or thoughtless to understand the magnitude of national good and justice to the individual.

Henrietta had long given up on the *Argus*. So often they had declined to publish her offerings. But she knew their competitor, *The Age*, would be only too happy to put into print yet another of her letters.

THE LEGISLATIVE COUNCIL VERSUS BRAINS

Sir, 'To suppose that brains govern in politics would be absurd.' An unconscious prediction by the poor old 'Argus' (see its Tuesday's second article) most sadly verified in the Council's fifth rejection of the Woman Suffrage Bill – a measure of great importance to the welfare of the community. How much longer will our men of brains calmly bear this insultingly repeated defiance of their endeavor to obtain justice? Impertinent defiance by a few men, whose only necessary qualification for power in the Legislature is, not the possession of intelligence, but simply a certain monetary value of property. I trust their ignorant prejudice will never dishearten your efforts, which are always so earnestly given in every rightful cause.

 Yours etc.
H. A. DUGDALE
Telko, Camberwell

With spring finally under way, and fires burning only at night, she could venture outside for longer. Blessed with a goodly supply of newspapers, Henrietta potted cuttings in between keeping abreast of the news – ever mindful of the old 'hardy annual', women's suffrage, as it was known in the Legislative Council.

A demonstration for the extension of the suffrage held at the Melbourne Town Hall had brought great attendance and a stirring speech from Mrs Goldstein. What a relief to know that the anti-suffragist lobby, having been exposed to ridicule, was quashed. Otherwise there was much for an old lady to be grateful for. Within days, a lilac fringe of wisteria appeared, dangling from the eaves of her portico. The deepening blue of the sky beyond, and the play of light – the ochres, silvers and reds of trees, the subtle pink of the lemon-scented gumleaves at the back of her garden.

Before long, sparkles of sun began to find every new blade of grass or weed. Russet buds began bursting into green light, and in the fields and along the laneways came the first purple sprinklings of Paterson's curse. Everywhere, flowers springing up, the air teeming with bees, and the intermingling fragrances of wattle and hawthorn blossom. Soon there would be new potatoes and peas on the table for Freddie and the promise of an early supply of strawberries and white heart cherries. It was good to see him outside again and on the go, armed with her list of 'to do's'.

Inside took on a different look. Fresh light created new shapes and shadows, a sharper face on the clock. At this very moment, a fat warm ray of sunshine had settled itself across Freddie's wingback chair. Oh! Shame. Henrietta looked down, ran her hand along the armrest. Freddie had worked a hole in it, worrying the fabric with his forefinger.

Neither of them being a slave to convention, she and Freddie had collected what they pleased over the years. There was no 'right' or 'wrong'. Some of Carl's prize-winning photographs were mounted on display. Her Moorish 'cosy corner', with its hodgepodge of feathers, Japanese prints, planter chairs, French draperies and a few rugs scattered wall to wall. Things still came together in their own individual 'style'. A touch of floral or paisley here and there. Freddie preferred cool mineral shades, whereas she was drawn to mulberry, russet, a touch of clementine or India red to warm her up. Sparse but not austere, she liked to think.

A few years ago, she would have fixed Freddie's chair herself. Gone out, chosen a new print and set to with tacks and webbing, adding fresh flock and a set of new springs and checking over the joinery while she was at it. Now, why would she bother?

Like everything else about Telko, it was looking a little shabby and worse for wear, but doubtless would see them through.

⌇

October was promising to be a busy month, with her favourite, Carl, among her visitors. Lucky fellow had been commissioned to undertake a series of centennial portraits for a prominent Melbourne family. Excited he was about the prospect of employing a new method of portraiture using incandescent lamps so as to diffuse electric light and not blind the sitter. He had cabled to say he would be coming down by express train and making his way straight to Camberwell.

He arrived, dapper as usual, in a brown plaid suit, and stood holding something behind his back. He doffed his cap. Bent down and pressed his lips against her white curls before presenting her with a bunch of gillyflowers.

Oh, lovely! Intoxicated, Henrietta rolled her eyes, cooing over the sweet, spicy, clove-like scent.

'Meant to be medicinal,' said Carl.

'Be a love, will you, and hand me down that tall white jug from the dresser?' After filling it with water, she lowered the stems, allowing the coloured frills – white, lilac, mauve and deep purple – to fall where they liked.

'Now, Carlie, I've asked Freddie to prepare my will. Here …' And without further ado, she tossed a freshly typed draft on the table. 'Let me know if anything's amiss.'

'What, on a beautiful day like today? I can't be a witness, Ma, if that's what you want.'

So often duty goes hand-in-hand with guilt. She could detect it in his voice.

'No, no, dear, just read it. I want you to be quite clear about my testamentary dispositions. Alice is in town this week, so I shall be asking her to witness.' Henrietta realised she was scheming, working on the slim chance that Alice might land up at Telko anytime soon. 'Then, once I've set my house in order, I shall be ready to obey my summons to depart, fully aware of my unworthiness, of course.' She lifted her eyes heavenwards. 'And yet, not without hope.'

'Oh Mama, must you mock?' Carl gave her a searching look.

'As I keep telling Freddie, dear, I'm a respectable septuagenarian. Naturally, I'm banking on going first, but death doesn't always happen by design. Should anything happen to Freddie and me – we could both, or either, go anytime, a frightful rollover, a house fire or a runaway train – then you, my dearest son, will need to know what's what. Now bring me the tea caddy and let us not have any more pother.'

Carl pressed his hands upon the table.

'Come. Don't dillydally. After Freddie, you'll be informant. The Registrar will want to know, among other things, name of deceased's father and mother, number and names of spouse, children, nature, times and places of death, years in the colony… all those necessary details.'

'You are not dead yet, Ma.'

'It'll happen soon enough. You may as well be prepared, everything at your fingertips.'

Reluctantly, Carl returned with the tea caddy, gently rotating it, charmed by its rare decagonal shape. 'Ah, I remember this, Ma, you always kept it up high out of my reach.' His eyes settled wistfully on the deep green hue of the relic and its silver and ivory trim. 'Always wondered what was inside. Obviously not tea. So, what happened to the key?'

'Vanished,' she said. 'Thrown in the well. Go on, open it, son. My will be done!'

'Oh Lord, I feel like an evil prier, poking about in the past.'

Carl lifted out each compartment and began thumbing through old folded papers, many of which were brittle and in some cases falling apart. There, every so often, staring out of the typeface and the faded copperplate, in all its familiarity, her own signature – the big round generous hand, the exaggerated curl that personified her so well.

'Ah, so, what have we here?' Carl eased open a buff document covered in stains and blotches of red sealing wax. A quiver of angst registered. She knew exactly what it was – a certified copy of her first marriage certificate, no less.

'22 July 1848?' Carl squinted, then jerked his chin, pulling away in cold repulse. 'Sorry. Can't for one minute imagine you as "Mrs Davies",' he said. 'Can't come to grips with it, Ma. To think that if this cousin of mine had not come to grief, my brothers and I would never have been born.' Jealousy written all over him. The silent up and down of the shoulders, his breath audible through his nostrils. He swung around, and she saw his boyish sulk of a face. 'How did he die? This Davies cousin.'

It came in stops and starts. Junius and William – erstwhile shipmates always vying against each other. Who could have foreseen they should meet up again in Melbourne in June, the first year of gold fever in 1852? William, by then captain of the *Duke of Bedford*, was skint; his crew had deserted for the diggings, leaving him to bear the brunt of the costs. Junius, having signed off in London, was free to skipper his own boat, a cutter he had bought to supply the demand for short charter services in and beyond the bay.

The weather that day was boisterous, squally and thick. 'Why he had to go out in such conditions I will never understand.' Her bottom lip twisted and her voice began to quaver. 'I watched him for a while from Shortlands Bluff until I could watch no longer, for he was out there with no spare hand. A passing ship could easily have rammed him. Oh! It makes me sick to even think about it.' She closed her eyes as the turn of events unfolded. So dim the white glimmer in the grey fog, she recalled, so bitterly cold she had at once returned to the comfort of their lodgings.

William later claimed to have warned Junius against buying the cutter. Fast but, in his mind, defective. He told her later he had been observing from a jollyboat out of concern: Junius heading towards the Rip, approaching it in entirely the wrong manner and far too close for comfort. Fearing for his safety, William beached, scrambled to the Bluff to give the alert. With great horror, he saw the cutter strike the western reef and be carried away at full tilt, unmanageable, as if having lost her rudder. She then appeared to broach to with her head eastwards. Within ten minutes, the vessel had gone down, masts, sails, rigging and all.

'Was that it?' Carl looked at her, stunned. 'They found nothing?'

'Everything would have been broken up on the reef. With so much debris along the shores in those early days, it was hard to tell one piece of wreck from another – shards of wood, ropes, scraps of shredded sailcloth and halyards littered the beaches. As for a body, the only one found in the vicinity was around the bay, in Indented Heads. The authorities would not subject a lady to the horror of having to identify a corpse in such frightful condition. Instead they brought me a parcel of clothes they'd retrieved. A striped blue shirt, a silk waistcoat, a silk handkerchief, striped tweed trousers, flannel underclothing and worsted stockings. Gentlemen's clothes, clearly. But no, they were not Junius'. "May I see the body?" I pleaded with them, wanting to be sure there hadn't been some terrible mix-up.

'They refused. Half the face had been eaten away, and some of the front teeth were missing. "Is there any identifying feature on the rest of his body?" they asked. "Yes. My husband wore a ring," I told them, a signet ring worn on the little finger of his right hand, since he was left-handed. But as it happened, the right forearm of the corpse was missing.'

She swallowed, sniffed, looked out the window. Her eyes filled but she did not cry. Thirteen bodies had been washed up just in those few months alone, leading up to Christmas, mostly sailors jumping ship for the diggings. 'Ah, it was pandemonium. One more fool lost to gold fever meant nothing.'

And having explained things so far, she was left then to defend herself. 'I know what you are thinking, Carl, that if there was no body, if there was no proof, legally how could I marry your father? Presumption of death was sufficient for us to marry, and marry quickly we did.'

'Mama. Stop.' Carl raised a finger. 'Was that the doorbell?' He leapt to his feet and made off down the hall.

'Carl, how lovely to see you.'

It was Alice. Henrietta could hear her footsteps, the familiar sound of her gait on the floorboards.

'Speak of the devil.'

Henrietta stood up and smiled through her tears. 'Ah, Alice darling. What a surprise!' She embraced her old friend and pressed her against her breast.

'Did you not get my letter?' Alice, having released herself, stood back, rearranging her terracotta cashmere around her shoulders.

'Oh, yes, of course. It's just that I was ... well, never mind.'

'You look upset, Henrie dear. Now tell me, be honest. Would you rather I call another day? I'm in Melbourne the week, you know.'

'No, no, I won't hear of it. I insist.' Henrietta hastily stuffed the papers into the tea caddy and shut the horn-handled lid. 'Carl will take you back to the city late afternoon in a cab, won't you, Carlie.' She nodded at the green tortoiseshell box. 'Put it over there on the dresser, would you, dear? Now, Alice darling, let me offer you some refreshment. Good, good. Then you talk to Carlie, while I go and put the kettle on.'

Henrietta set about preparing a tray with a fresh cloth and set it down upon the vestibule table.

'Mama was just telling me about her first husband, weren't you, Ma. Must say it came like a thunderbolt.'

'I can only imagine.' Alice lowered her eyes as if sensing the matter private. 'I was only a little girl, too young to remember much ... but I was led to believe that ...' She hesitated. 'Captain Dugdale happened to be staying with us at the time after returning from the diggings with my papa.'

Henrietta lost herself in the moment. Hands loose by her side, steam rising from the spout of her Doulton teapot. 'Junius with his new cutter

– keen to show it off to William, and William, being William, was green with envy.' Everything went misty. She could feel the pent-up prickle, the pain, knowing that any second she might break down and make a dashed fool of herself.

'So I take it Papa was the last person to see my cousin alive?'

She nodded painfully.

Alice put a hand on her elbow and gave it a squeeze. 'I remember Mama relating the incident much later in life. There were other sightings, apparently. One from Point Lonsdale. A man swore he saw the cutter going through the Heads, jib and mainsail set in full flight, fairly scooting along. But the search party didn't bother looking beyond the Heads. It was Captain Dugdale's word they took.'

It felt like a knife had been stuck in her back. 'What are you saying, Alice?'

'Oh, I may well be mistaken. Memory is a very slippery thing and one should never believe what one is told, second, third or fourth hand.'

Henrietta's face fell. Of course she was not the same person she was fifty years ago, and yet she knew that what she felt right now was encapsulated by what she felt back then as a helpless young widow stranded alone in a new colony. Nobody had ever asked about it before.

She looked past Alice as a hard, dry sob rose in her heart at the memory, followed by great gulping soundless ones that ripped uncontrollably into her muscles and belly, her bones, into the very depths of her body and soul. Her fingers went instinctively to her mouth. She bit down hard, trying to stem the paroxysm, and considered for a few brief moments what her life would have been like had things been different.

Chapter 31

~

W hat a paradox it was for birth and death to coincide in such a way. Whose design was that?

The turning of the second year of the new century was marked by the Proclamation of Federation at Centennial Park in Sydney and the swearing-in ceremony. A sense of anticipation prevailed as everyone eagerly waited for the new Prime Minister to release details of federal policy. Would Mr Barton and his colleagues come around to it? Would they ensure a uniform federal suffrage that involved granting suffrage to women?

Each day dragged on. January was unprecedentedly cool – too cool for beaches or picnics. Here they were, half the season gone, and only four or five days had been really hot. Heavy banks of clouds gathered as the bay grew blacker and blacker, a fair gale and a downpour that flooded the streets and lanes. With everything awash in the city, she and Freddie were forced to spend the last of his Christmas holidays at home.

Finally came the news they were waiting for. Mr Barton, in his inaugural speech, said that he accepted the principle of women's suffrage. *That the Franchise should be uniform is not only desirable*, he pointed out, *but it seems likely to become necessary for the avoidance of confusion.* Freddie scooped her up in his arms and waltzed her around the kitchen floor.

The temperature rose fittingly in the days that followed. Golden sunflowers grew tall against the brush fence, their big brown eyes glistening as they smiled throughout the day. But by the end of the week, when news hit Melbourne that the Queen had died, they were already wilting. Nobody quite knew what to do, there being no precedent. The follow-on of official proceedings for the newly formed federation was cut short for the mourning of the old Queen. Suddenly everything nailed down seemed to be coming loose. Each evening, Freddie arrived home with another armful of newspapers from across the nation.

THE QUEEN'S DEATH
HER LAST MOMENTS
DIES PEACEFULLY
SURROUNDED BY HER FAMILY

With weary expectancy and amid clinging silence crowds watched the lighted windows of the wing from twilight to darkness. At a quarter to 7 p.m. one of the Royal servants reverentially placed a board upon the gate with the following medical bulletin: 'The Queen breathed her last at half-past 6 o'clock, surrounded by her children and grandchildren.' The crowds, except for a wail of anguish, silently departed to hide their grief, the bells of Chippingham Church meanwhile tolling.

Henrietta pored over the papers cover to cover, each one competing with the others.

The Queen's death a sad climax to the Boer War, which has undoubtedly hastened her end.

Tributes gushed forth as the weeks turned.

Only the actions of the just
Smell sweet and blossom in the dust.

The words, for some reason, made her think of Bloomsbury and the firstborn sister she barely knew. She was picturing Maria – three and a half years older than the Queen – now aged eighty-eight, gazing out of the window at St George's Gardens, an invalided old woman, long deaf and forgotten, with senile dementia.

The Handel Street Asylum, where Maria now lived, was just around the corner from their parents' Bloomsbury home. There were far worse places one might wait to die than in the heart of one's youth, Henrietta supposed. It would be winter there, but in springtime a soft vaporous air would hang over the old burial grounds. It was like looking at an Oriental watercolour or a piece of porcelain, with the delicacy of shades and the fine row of almond trees reaching upwards, paying homage to the dead. Twigs and branches mere wisps fragmented by a profusion of pinky-white blossom reminding her of hieroglyphics from some exotic land.

⁓

In May, the celebrations for the opening of the first Parliament of the Commonwealth at Royal Exhibition Building were to last a whole week. Passing glimpses of the procession along Swanston Street had come her lucky way, and from the Carlton Gardens, looking up at the balcony through the black sea of top hats, Henrietta had spotted the Duke of Cornwall and York on the stage in the centre, in full military uniform, and, fancy, a pointed beard just like Freddie's. Melbourne was ablaze with flags and banners in a brilliance of colours. The trains were packed each day.

The following evening, as she and Freddie rolled slowly into the city by cab, they were greeted by rows of plane trees with silver branches bursting into the stars, and masses upon masses of people, all classes revelling in fireworks, street bands, or concerts and theatrical performances. Street after street of buildings and balustrades magnificently lit up by thousands of electric light bulbs and, pointing into the black sky, towers with copper cupolas green in the light of the moon.

Henrietta sat back, arranging her evening silks. Merrymaking was all very well, she thought, but in Victoria there was still work to be done.

The week of twenty-four-hour festivities seemed never to end. Perhaps it had all been too much for William Lynch. Poor fellow, no longer young but such a great advocate of federation, dropped dead at table – a stroke while lunching at the Australian Club – leaving Freddie shattered and the whole of the Melbourne legal fraternity in shock and turmoil.

'My friend of forty years.' Freddie dabbed a tear from his eye with the corner of his handkerchief. 'To think, I'd only been discussing something with him this morning. I can't believe it. Work's not going to be the same,' he said. 'How the dickens am I to keep going?'

Freddie's equanimity began to leave him. Fagged out and faced with a growing backlog of work, he felt under enormous pressure. Once home, he drew into himself with a saturnine cast to his face.

Weeks of winter rains didn't help. But one day Freddie couldn't sit still. He was fidgety; constantly doing something that didn't then need to be done. Pulling at his wristbands. Straightening pictures on the wall, winding the clock. Finally, he sat down beside her, clutching either arm of his chair.

'What's wrong? You look worried, dear. Are you worrying for worrying's sake, or is it work?'

Freddie closed his eyes. 'Worrying about work – worrying about you.'

'Me? Whatever for?

Everything had suddenly changed for Freddie. Mr Hector MacDonald, Junior, soon to be admitted to the Bar, would be taking his father's place as partner of Lynch and MacDonald. Time was catching up with Freddie. He was catching up with her. The old brigade making way for the new.

'Think of my old friend, Lynch,' he said despondently. 'Like me, darn near sixty. Here one day, gone the next. Now, who would look after you if something happened to me?

A bombshell came one blustery day in August. Feeling unprepared and pale as a statue, Henrietta stood, supporting herself against the wooden pillar of her front portico. A cable had just arrived from Emma to say that she and the girls would be coming by train to Telko within the hour to bid their farewell. Their property had been sold up, their trunks, tea chests, crates and furniture were ready, waiting to be loaded at the docks. The ship had put in and the family was all set to sail for Fremantle.

Up until now, the reality of their leave-taking had failed to register with Henrietta, saddled as she was with so many preoccupations. Then again, correspondence had been sporadic.

'Come in, come in.' Quickly she closed the door behind them. 'Here, give me your capes.'

The young ones, animated in navy-blue serge trumpet skirts over shirtwaists with front sailor collars, took off their boaters and patted their piled-up hair.

'Goodness, you make me feel cold.' She rubbed her hands, directing them towards the blazing fire, suddenly realising she was still in her 'at homes', free from the trammels of everyday dress.

Emma chatted to her as she rustled around, offering them fresh cups of tea and a plate of buttered muffins, trying to be bright and cordial.

'You girls'll be all the richer for the journey, the experience ahead. And just think, once you've registered on the electoral rolls as new West Australians, you'll be entitled to vote in both state and federal elections. As for Victoria,' she sniffed, 'by the time they break the deadlock, I might be dead.'

'Oh Aunty,' cried Emma, reaching out in a clasp of hands, 'don't say that!'

Louie wore what seemed like a superior look, her chest puffed out like a pouter pigeon as she paraded about the room in her new fashionable clothes.

Louie suddenly stopped and, gawking at her, put a hand to her mouth.

'Pray, what are you laughing at, Louie?'

'I can't help it, Aunty.'

'Why, am I such a curiosity?'

'Louie, don't be so rude,' said Emma, stepping in with a frown.

'Sorry, Aunty.'

Silly ninny obviously had not seen plus-fours and spats before. Sometimes the cup of ridicule was too hard to bear, never more so than in one's own house.

Her visitors did not stay long, eager to board the ship. Wrapped in her camel cashmere duster coat, and with fedora atop, Henrietta took Emma's arm, walking solemnly in silence as the girls trotted off ahead down the road towards the station. The dark red berries of autumn had gone. In their place, masses of black crossing stems, the stark leafless outlines of the hawthorn hedges converging into the bend.

After they said their goodbyes, amid lots of clasping and kissing, Henrietta had barely the strength to wave. 'The world is thine oyster,' she sang out as the train left the empty platform.

'I never thought they had any real intention of going,' she later grumbled to Freddie. 'And now they've all upped and left and I suspect I shall never see them again.'

It felt like a desertion, a judgement, almost a personal affront. They were off to seek their fortunes in the great Wild West, leaving her to what was left of her little life in a place of no account in the backblocks of Boroondara. The harder journey would be hers.

∽

Within months, Hattie's surprise letter arrived from Benalla, no doubt generated by Emma's final parting.

You'll be pleased to know, Aunty, the hotel has been closed for good.

Good riddance! Anyone could see that the Vineyard Hotel had brought Hattie nothing but trouble – only the curse of alcohol and the curse of death.

Hattie, in her shrewd-headed way, had always managed to shrug off adversity. Against all expectations, she had turned the business around so profitably, reducing the mortgage by over half. But disaster struck yet again. Lying in bed awake one night, the poor woman had seen flames rearing up the face of her window. Her prized Vineyard Hotel engulfed in fire. Seven out of her twenty-one rooms were completely destroyed. Everything, family possessions and wearing apparel, lost. It was a miracle that everyone, guests and family, were not burned alive.

If Hattie had had any sense, she would have taken the insurance payout and run. Not Hattie. By her thrifty ways and hard work, she raked the hotel out of the fire. Every year since Martin's death, she had fought to keep the licence, competition always being fierce in Benalla. When the Licensing Board ordered seven hotels to be closed, Hattie had no option but to close and apply for compensation. In granting it, the arbiter said she was the most honest witness in the hearings.

Being a publican was a sorry calling, in Henrietta's opinion. Resonating in the corridors of her mind were lines she'd once heard read at a meeting of temperance women, a poem about the effects of alcohol on family life.

That would create together here
A dungeon and a star
Two things that lie two worlds apart
the cradle and the bar.

But, as Freddie justly pointed out, look to the good side. Hotels provided useful and often very necessary services and venues to society. Whereas many a publican had succumbed, Hattie had had enough self-possession to claim mastery over her domain.

I took stock of what you said, Aunty. Never you mind. I was always
upright and ladylike, and made sure I kept dry.

Freddie was right. Hattie was to be commended. How oft she had condemned her niece instead of holding her up.

I'm sixty, now, Aunty. Seem to have spent most of my life in the courts, one way or another. But I managed and paid everything off. I've done pretty well, all things considered. Now I'll be able to live in peace and never be a burden on anyone.

From the other side of the country, Emma wrote to say that Perth was booming and the sun always shining. The family had settled in nicely, proud that young James would be going across to Adelaide next year as the Western Australian delegate for the second annual Australian conference of postal and telegraph officers.

The amalgamation of the postal and telegraph services should have come as a boon. Women in Victoria had long fought for equality in pay and status in this service. Since the men's union had refused women admission, they formed their own, with Louisa Dunkley as their leader and delegate.

Henrietta followed this new piece of intelligence with highest hopes. She had always found James a fine, agreeable young man. Yet he was openly hostile to Dunkley's motion that there should be the same title for men and women undertaking identical duties. And what was his excuse? *It was tantamount to saying that women were as capable as men.*

Oh, her poor heart! The *Commonwealth Public Service Act* was supposed to embody the principles of equal pay. Yet what it gave with one hand it took with the other. Married women were still to be seen as 'psychologically unfit' for work. Single women to remain temporary staff until they married. Clearly, women were to be excluded from most occupations and every form of advancement.

⁓

Freddie, rugged up in overcoat and bowler hat, continued to take the early train to the city each morning. Oh, how she longed for a breezy remark, his brave *pompity-poms*. Someone to jog her along. Yearning for his company, Henrietta counted the stops. Richmond, East Richmond, Burnley, Hawthorn, Camberwell. Blood sluggish, she sat, book in hand, looking out of the vestibule window at the twiggy outlines, waiting for the mist to lift. When and if the sun did shine through, there was never quite enough. Damp air from the gully stiffened her joints, the cold, mean winter ache gripped deep in her bones. Chores that used to take five minutes now took an hour. More than often, her body chose not to work.

Black nights and empty days, everything an effort. Her slightest needs – a cup of tea, a light meal, even fetching a clean handkerchief or a few pieces of firewood – left her exhausted. Fumbling with handles and doorknobs. Feet that stuck to the floor.

Outside it was just as inhospitable. The land was spongy; nothing wanted to grow. A sinister midnight storm had stripped the few remaining leaves off the old roses. Not a bud in sight, and everywhere muted shadows swallowing the light. There, keeping her company, a pair of doves shuffled around, their soft hues blending into the swathe of fallen leaves banked against the door. In the deepening dusk came the drift of burnt coaldust and the whistle of the train from across the dale. Good. Freddie would be home soon.

As she waited, she detected a kind of flickering movement, little bursts of black and white that went hither and thither, almost silently, imperceptibly, across the lawn. It was their pair of resident mudlarks foraging for worms.

Birds, she realised, had been as much inspiration for her as for many a writer or composer. Mozart and his Magic Flute; funny Papageno and his panpipes. And what about Beethoven, Daquin? The jerky sway motif of the cuckoo, pieces she'd played since childhood. Mostly, though, the smaller wind instruments, the flute or the piccolo, were used to replicate the sounds of birds. Major keys, too bright, too sweet, to be convincing. More often than not, there was a sense of sadness and despair expressed in birdcall – a wistfulness or melancholy that composers never quite seemed to capture.

Songbirds she had heard in many a port in Asia. Sometimes, after being released with a flute bound upon their backs, these quaint little creatures would return faithfully to their masters to be fed. Fixed in her mind, a songbird sunning itself in an intricately crafted bamboo cage. Beneath it, a sparrow pecking frenetically at discarded husks of rice. Suddenly it stopped, put its head to one side. Each bird eyeing off the other. Suspicion? Or was it mutual envy? To be a caged but secure songbird, petted and fed, or to be a free but homeless bird having to bear the icy winds of winter and forage for its food? Given the choice, which would you be?

'Choice is but an illusion,' Junius once said. 'We can only think we are free. We can never be free of the past.'

What was that old saying? *Love begins with a song and music and ends in a sea of tears.* What came out of her mouth these days sounded shredded, thin, and her throat squeezed back in rebellion. Since she could no longer sing, she sat, casting the net of her memory.

∾

She lifted her weary wrists, closed the lid of the piano and turned the lock for good.

'Wretched fingers refuse to obey.'

Freddie did not look up. He went on inspecting his bow. Rubbed some oil on the wood, held it up to the light. Then loosened the frog. Set out a new hank of horsehair on the table, humming under his breath.

Often she had toyed with the idea of writing to Louie on some pretext or other. She was keen to learn firsthand about what Edith Cowan was doing for Perth, for Louie, it turned out, had met the famous Mrs Cowan. What a tragic life this woman had had as a child, her father hanged for murdering her stepmother. And yet bad experiences were often the catalysts for change.

No, thought Henrietta, I don't give a fig for Louie. It was Emma she felt for, gentle soul. Those dark eyes, sad with the sadness of too much experience of hard ways; her careworn smile. It was over a year now they'd been gone, and unlikely she would ever see them again, but at last Emma was happy.

Nice new brick house in Subiaco; a park across the street with croquet and tennis courts and tall gumtrees. Backyard big enough to build a cottage behind as well. And a stone's throw from the railway station and the tram. My dear husband, Gentleman Jim, with his name in the directory. Everything I could possibly want, Aunty. James, our son and heir, back from the goldfields, now a member of the Perth Symphony and a chorister at St Mary's. Three girls still at home, none married, not for want of me trying. I don't miss Mornington anymore. Old scars die hard, Aunty. The bay still holds its sorrows.

Henrietta closed her eyes. Out of a dark plume of smoke rose the bold stripes and bunting of the bay ferry, everything bristling against the blue. Sunbeams skipping across the water and the bridal-train breaking up behind. Oh, how she yearned to feel the rise and fall, the throb, engines roaring full steam, paddles thrashing and the bell and the band music and the three loud burps of the horn. To look up and see cliffs of orange clay. Spread out beneath, wooden bathing boxes like rows of brightly painted toys – greens into blues, red, bright as a pillar box, breaking into yellows across the shore.

Mornington, a popular watering place; otherwise, as she remembered it, a town in mourning. How she yearned for the sting of salt and the tickle of a breeze to tease some colour back in her cheeks.

Chapter 32

W hen time came for Melbourne to celebrate the new Commonwealth law for uniform suffrage in June 1902, Henrietta found
herself bed-bound with a severe attack of influenza. Her moment
of triumph a damp squib. Propped up with pillows and her writing
compendium, she picked up her pen and in large, wobbly hand wrote
her apologies to the Mayor of Melbourne, with throat red raw:

*I grieve at not having sufficient strength to be with you tonight. It would
have been so fitting that my last public words should have been those
addressed to a Parliament conscientious enough to have passed this act of
justice to women.*

That done, she lay back, sniffing and gulping, thumbing her watering
eyes in a fog of frustration. It was not until the day after the big event
that she was able to take it all in from the morning newspaper as she
sipped hot lemon tea in the vestibule.

WOMEN'S SUFFRAGE

A CITY CELEBRATION

A meeting convened by the Mayor of Melbourne, on requisition, was held in the Town hall on the evening of the 16th inst., primarily to celebrate the passage of the Uniform Franchise Bill through the Federal Parliament, and incidentally to impress upon the Victorian Parliament the desirability of falling into line.

With the Mayor (Sir Samuel Gillott), who presided, there were on the platform:– Mrs Lowe and other leading members of the Victorian Women's Franchise League; Miss Spence, of Adelaide; the Acting Prime Minister (Mr Deakin); Senators Dawson and Ewing, Messrs Watson and Higgins, M.H.R.s Godfrey, M.L.C., Maloney, M.L.A. and J.S. Butters. Greetings from Miss Rose Scott, secretary of the New South Wales Women's Franchise League, and Mrs H. A. Dugdale, one of the pioneers of the movement in Victoria, were read. (Applause)

Mrs Dugdale's message reflected the tone of the proceedings. Only one motion was submitted, as follows:–

'That this meeting expresses its gratification that the Commonwealth Parliament has affirmed the principle of women's suffrage, by the passage of the Uniform Franchise Bill, and naturally concludes that the Legislative Council will now no longer withhold the State franchise from the women of Victoria.'

In moving it, Mrs Lowe, who was one of the band of women who began the movement in Victoria for the enfranchisement of women 18 years ago, rejoiced that at last women were within one of the important gates, almost within the charmed circle of politics; that one more pigtail of prejudice had been shorn, and that the mother sex had attained their political Commonwealth majority. (Cheers.) 'My last words to our women will be,' said Mrs Lowe, in conclusion, 'that with greater liberty come greater and nobler duties. Let us fit ourselves for this great and sacred trust, and prove ourselves worthy of it.' (Cheers.)

Mr Deakin seconded the motion. The foundations of the
Commonwealth were now well and truly laid. Men and women would
not be transformed in their relations by this very necessary advance,
that was, not to the eye of the superficial critic. That we looked to this
reform proving a radical and permanent reform in course of time was
true, because at the outset we were not only doubling the number of
electors, but were undeniably introducing into politics and public action
a new element, whose appreciation, however powerful before, had been
indirect, sinuous, and unobserved. Now, entering into the full heritage
of equal power and authority, came an equal number of voters to those
who had hitherto exercised the franchise, but they came with all the
differences inherited and acquired which distinguished the mental and
moral characteristics of sex and sex. The innate conservatism of woman
choked, as it always had been, was a dangerous element. Set it free, and
it would prove a reasonable conservatism, ready to advance step by step
with husband, father, and brother.

The paper, fallen from her hand, lay in loose leaves upon the floor.
Nose blocked, her breath quivering between a couple of upward
hiccup sobs, she pinched her eyes and let out a gargantuan groan.
It was a victory tinged with jumbling sensations. She put a hand
to her dewlap, feeling the hot, painful throb of emotion. She could
see them all packed into the town hall, their faces waxing jubilant,
and Miss Spence, the simple way she had put it, 'that every female
child now born in the Commonwealth of Australia is a free born
citizen of the Commonwealth.' The commotion, the clapping, the
cheers and roars.

Meanwhile, the State of Victoria was in gridlock. How she abhorred
the continual stalling, and the repeated voting down of the Bills by a
conservative opposition in favour of a God-given natural order was
nothing but filibuster. Are we ever to have representative government
in our state? Or despotism by a handful entrenched behind a

constitutional anachronism? That was the issue, as Mrs Goldstein put it, and the only issue. If only people would listen.

Henrietta sat up in her pale blue dressing-gown, straining her ear. Again and again, the relentless ring of an axeman – in his rhythm, the heavy, hollow sound of a good axe rending the air and the inevitable thump. Yet another subdivision. Camberwell, the vanguard of suburbia. Once it had been city men who wanted a comfortable estate of ten or twenty acres. Now housing was rapidly closing in.

She should drop her new neighbours a line and make herself known. But she felt she was too old to be making new friends and did not need more acquaintances, feeling as low as she was. The old aches and pains had returned. She could barely move; her joints red hot and tender, her tongue coated, and the dread of yet another likely attack of rheumatism.

She gave a shiver and pulled up the rug. When she awoke three hours later, it was to hear steps on the gravel driveway, the click of the front door. Goodness, Freddie home already? She keyed herself to the sound of every movement, his footfall coming down the hall, the pause as he pushed open the door with his hip.

'What, napping in the dark?' He came over quietly to the day bed, and, feeling her hand, gave it a squeeze. 'And cold as cold. Here, come along with me and I'll light the fires.'

⁓

Men in boats, they came and went, passing through her life. When Einnim came to pay her a visit the following year, she was in much higher feather.

Carl had been made a famous, if not a wealthy, man by the most remarkable quirk of fate – a photograph of a colossal dust storm taken at Narrandera in February. He had immediately copyrighted it, and in a matter of weeks prints of the extraordinary incident were being sent all around the world. Now they were even making postcards of it.

'Fancy! Carl, eh? Who would have thought?' Einnim, having made time to visit his brother, was generous in his praise. Carl, he said, did not dabble in catchpenny affairs. His studio – complete with cellars and mysterious underground corridors, and the latest in scientific equipment, no expense spared – was nothing short of world class. He should be aptly proud of himself. His business was a wonderful example of application, industry and enterprise. His work, a constant advertisement.

Austin, always one to capitalise, would put his brother to good account. The artful little devil was now trying to tempt Carl into going back to New Zealand. Some half-cocked proposal setting up a joint venture in refrigerated export. Heaven forbid! Austin, now chief engineer of the Waitara Freezing Works, was not content with fifteen hundred workers slaughtering forty bullocks a day and four hundred sheep and converting blood and bone into fertiliser.

But Carl, being Carl, was gracious. 'Well, Austin has the engineering know-how, and I do have the means, but no, I prefer to work by myself. I love what I do.'

Einnim, it seemed, was at a juncture in his life. The *Nora Bradford*, the coaster he had built and captained, had sadly been wrecked. Einnim knew very early in life that farming was not for him. He was more comfortably employed with wood and water than with plants or animals. Shipwright, boat builder, carpenter, coastal trader, he had successively made a living around his interests. Things tried and true. After four trips to England and ten years' sailing up the remotest waters of New Zealand, the wild streak had washed itself out.

Nowadays, he appeared pretty much the straight-backed citizen, serving the community on the Waitara Harbour Board and numerous school and sporting committees, as vestryman, as well as going through the chairs of the lodges. No wife to speak of, no offspring to carry him forward into the new century.

Perhaps it was the time of year – the leaves falling crisp and brown in dull, cold June – that brought with it a feeling of foreboding. God knows, she and Freddie, Mrs Lowe and probably Mrs Rennick were about the only ones left standing, the rest of their merry band gone. Who would be next? There was always that fear of dozing off and never coming back. And now that blessed church bell again – or was it a passing cloud, a thump or a knock that made her open her eyes?

Stiffly she rose from her reading chair and opened the vestibule door. High and low she looked, smelling the banksia blooms.

Horror of all horrors! A large black bird lay limp among the first of her crocuses. Body rigid, claws clenched tight against its breast. Ants crawling from the eye-sockets and little drops of blood congealed around the beak, which reminded her of a pair of open secateurs. And the sun catching the blue in its outstretched wing, its raven gloss rich as rich against the golden saffron stigma and the purple bloom.

The scourge of God. Wretched things could often be heard around lambing season, annoying the neighbours' ewes. Their mocking caw a resounding profanity over the churchyard hill. It was not just carrion they were after; these pests had acquired tastes. Once she had caught them pecking Freddie's grapes on the vine. Bold and brazen. Another time, sucking marrow out of a bone, lifting and turning it as it so suited in a horribly human way. Was it a harbinger or some nasty local trickster? Don't be ridiculous, she told herself. Edging past, she ferreted around in the grass for a fallen stick and began poking at the bird, fluffing its bearded crop.

How had it gone unnoticed? Henrietta looked around for Freddie. Ah, half-hidden behind the henhouse, a figure of deep concentration, his hulk of a frame, arms this way and that spraying his parsnips and peas to ward off the possums.

She turned abruptly, hand to her good ear. There, again – coming from the other end of the house – someone banging the door down, ringing hard on the bell.

'Sorry to disturb you, Ma'am. I knew you was home.' It was the telegram boy, standing in the open doorway, holding a message in his hand. Her poor old heart nearly stopped beating. The lad shuffled from side to side while she fumbled about, trying to open the sheet of pastel paper, take in the news and put on her spectacles all at the same time.

Reeling, she reached for a threepenny piece and, having thanked the boy politely in a wave of calm, remained rooted to the spot in disbelief as he rode off down the laneway on his red bicycle.

When she told Freddie that William Dugdale had died, she felt as if an enormous burden had been lifted from her soul. Freddie finished washing his hands, patted himself dry, meticulously, and folded the towel. With a faint drift of Condy's crystals, he enfolded her in his arms. 'Oh, my sweet little lady.' She could feel the familiar curvature of his lips against her ear, the tickling point of his beard. It was a short delivery, a slight buzz deep in his throat: 'Then we are free to marry,' he said, 'at last!'

The sweet days of *lovey-doveys*, all jujubes and jellies, had somewhat melted. She didn't want to hurt him, appreciating all he had sacrificed for her: his reputation, his family, his friends, his career and the better part of his youth. But now, with the warm pot of his belly pressing urgently against her, she looked up and fastened her eyes on his.

'Does it really matter, Fred, darling? Nearly forty years together. Says enough in itself, doesn't it?'

He drew her in by the waist and gave her one of his stern looks. 'Of course it matters.'

She remembered the shock of discovering that her own parents had lived a life of deceit. Her mother, sweet, dear upright soul, had borne ten children under the name of 'Mrs Worrell', while on paper still a 'spinster'. To learn that her father had all that time been a 'widower', a Registrar, no less, with his rubber-stamp of approval! It was brother Charles, his deputy, who, by accident, had come across their secret after Papa had died. She had felt angry and duped. Mama and Papa had slipped off to Brighton to marry in 1851, not telling a soul. What had prompted this lily-livered act? This hypocritical humbug – all those years making believing they were 'Mr and Mrs Worrell'. She and the rest of her siblings bastards, yet each baptised in the church.

'Well?' Freddie was looking down at her, his long forehead wrinkled with expectation.

She reached up and, cradling his lovely face, pecked him again and again. A face, she remembered, of such promise and possibilities. His soft, fast-whitening whiskers and what was left of his hair, his warmth, his hand on her shoulder – always there – whether a gesture of love or protection, she never quite knew.

Up until now, the choice to marry Frederick Johnson had never really been an option. The law of old had denied her the right to take William to court at a time when she had most needed to, and William was untouchable in exile. Now he was gone, the legal fiction of their marriage forever over, and against her ear, the *drum-drum-drumming* of Freddie's heart marking time.

'Yes. Yes, dearest,' she murmured. 'You are quite right, as you always are, my darling wise man. A point of principle it must be.' Cupping his beard in her palms, she fixed her eyes on his. 'Are you sure you want to marry an old lady, half-cripple that I am? As for vows …' She wagged a finger. 'I promise to love and cherish you, as I always have, but I cannot obey you.'

Obedience, he agreed, would be simply impossible from either of two dear companions whose interests were mutual and who had always returned love for love.

A week later, on the Saturday, they were married without any fuss. Somehow, with more than a little effort on her part, Freddie managed to get her to the Registry Office, and suitable notices were put in the papers. Mrs Dugdale-Johnson had rather a noble ring to it, she thought, added newfound dignity to her name.

Chapter 33

⌁

Henrietta waited for the sweet release she had long been craving. Come 16 December 1903, she and other Victorian women would be able to vote in their first federal election and have the right to stand for and sit in Federal Parliament. What an achievement. In a new burst of energy, she applied for membership of the newly formed Women's Federal Political Association, and expressed her ongoing interest in and support for Vida Goldstein's candidacy for the Senate.

With little ceremony, she and Freddie were registered as a married couple on the Commonwealth electoral roll. Her dear old mate, first to remind her of how unstinting she had been, that with body and soul she had given back whatever she had taken. When logic failed her critics, they had turned to slate her manner – 'her contemptuous curl to the lip', 'her imperious sweep of the hand', 'her overweening withering look' – all vain attempts to silence her and keep her in her place.

For more than thirty years, she had been paving the way in Victoria, cutting a track through a dense scrub of ignorance and prejudice, publicly and privately. She had never missed an opportunity to advocate for woman's moral right to the franchise, admission to university honours, practice of the professions, and power over her own property. And it had always been done against a hail of idiotic insults.

Physical attacks, at times, too. Those were hectic days. 'Do you remember when you had to protect me, Fred? That awful fellow came rushing up, wielding his umbrella, and you, brave man, stood between us.'

'Ah, yes,' he chuckled.

'But I never forgot Rousseau's words: *although men are bad, man is good.*' They always brought to mind her own words in her *Far-off Age*.

Dream, or what else it has been, I see always the beautiful light bright
with truth and hope. No one can extinguish it!

'Are you happy now, love?' Freddie was wanting to know.

She hesitated. The long fight was still not over for the women of Victoria. Still they must wait.

Yet how could she not be happy? She was happy simply because, apart from her ageing health, she had no reason now to be unhappy. All the background of distresses in her life somehow seemed to have evaporated.

'It's just that ... well ... is it too late to suggest a honeymoon, or should I say, "holiday"?' Freddie patted her on the shoulder. 'Soon as weather permits. Not too far, mind. Eh, what say you to that?'

Come gentle night,
come loving black
brow'd night,
Give me my Romeo, and when he shall die
take him and cut him out in little stars

She closed her eyes, slipping into the slide of memory. The moon was a broken shell drifting in and out of the clouds. It was that other lamp out there she was picturing – the pulse of its white beam every time like a pail of milk sent splashing across the black waters – that would come to her as comfort. Beyond, in the darkness, the waves singing in her ears, the dull roar of the breakers.

Her nostrils quivered, but she dare not look from the open carriage, the furious downhill race of trees, houses and other inanimate objects through the sea-spiced air.

It was Carl who'd suggested Point Lonsdale, having been there the previous summer.

'Remember the feeling, coming through the Heads for the first time?' Freddie had to shout against the wind.

In their own different ways, she and Freddie had come full circle, so to speak, back to the entrance of Port Phillip Bay, where they had arrived in the new colony barely a year apart.

Now here they were again, a short ride from Queenscliff, and the property where they had lived at Spring Hill. Freddie gave her a sideways grin. 'Hang on to your hat, love, otherwise you'll lose it!'

Oh, and such a pace, too. No sooner had they left Queenscliff and the narrows behind than they were winding their way through the scrub and up the Esplanade, past the tearooms and the general store towards the guesthouses of Point Lonsdale.

So much for holiday ether. The trip from Williamstown by steamer ferry had left her a little unsteady and queasy. Her sense of balance not being quite what it was, she feared she would slide on the deck. Such was her initial apprehension that she had to probe her memory for Junius' well-worn advice for seasickness: not to fix attention on any near object and to go regularly to the table and eat moderately of plain food. Harder by night, she recalled, with the waters shifting and pitching about, as one tried to seek out a beacon or lighthouse.

Carl had forewarned her. 'You won't recognise the place, Mama. The town's done itself proud.'

She spotted it immediately, the long white line of cross-bracing jutting out in the Rip. There'd been no jetty there when Carl was a boy. Last winter he'd seen waves crashing over the boathouse, covering the length in spray. Lifeboat at the ready, he had tested it, too, felt the decking shudder and list, experienced the vortex during the worst of a storm. By late evening, the only sign of life she could see out there was the gloaming. Long streaks of pink flushing in and out of the black piles, the reef-ridden shallows awash with the blood of a dying sun.

Surely here, of anywhere in the world, she could be happy, beyond the Heads riding the white horses, which champed and ramped and tossed in the spray. Or safe inside the lee of the cliff on the Bay Beach, picnic basket spread out, beakers of lemonade and a half-eaten cake. She smiled, recalling the blur of blue lips and shivering limbs, splashing about in the water, trying to fend off duckings. She, always wanting to strip down and swim with the men.

꙲

'Do you think you'll be able to make it to the top, love?'

Henrietta was adamant she would walk. Together the next morning, she and Freddie made their way slowly up the sandy track, she leaning on his arm, stopping every now and then on her walking stick for a breather.

Up past Buckley's Cave, near the end of the point, the towering white cone of a lighthouse.

'Pretty ordinary kind of day,' said Freddie. 'Not much happening out there.'

'Ah! All in the waiting, Freddie, love. *Light comes but; but oh, how dazzling!*' She squinted at the bay – a sheet of violet glass under the feckless summer sky.

'Yes,' he murmured. 'Light does wondrous things.'

She let go of Freddie's arm and raised her field glasses, searching the opalescent shallows and the shore. Below the dunes, three young women were out for a promenade. No bustles, no unnecessary frills or adornment – such simplicity of line – their bodies lithe and slim in trottoir skirts that cleared the shore by at least a good two inches. Across the water, the lie of Point Nepean, gunmetal; the cold, calm cauldron of the Rip and not a blessed ship in sight.

'How about you take a pew there, pet.' Freddie eased her into a bench seat next to the flagstaff and threw a nod upwards. 'I'll climb and take a look-see.'

'Be my guest.'

A reed in a gale. Pity the poor nightwatchman. Imagine stepping out on the lighthouse balcony to the deafening roar of the wind.

And yet today, as she looked seaward, the wind was so scant she could scarcely see a distant sail. Here, grounded at the point, it was unusually still. A hush had fallen over the bay. It was between tides, waiting the turn, the outgoing stream. Stretched out before her, the slack water, thick and lush, a heavenly blue gloss melding into the sky.

There she sat, serenely oblivious, absorbed in its calm. What was more than due would come to pass as surely as the incoming waters replaced the old. And as she waited, restless faces gathered in the clouds. Above the lighthouse-keeper's cottage, a hem of woollen indigo hung dark and loose. Falling shadows shrouded the bay. To follow would come the inevitable dimpling, that noble sheet of water ever changing with the whisperings of rain. She reached again for the words she had written twenty years ago in search of a happy age: *No loss – no death – simply change, which constitutes one perpetual motion.*

Flashes of pearl descended amid distant cries of confusion. Fleet-winged seagulls, like memories crowding her soul. Eddies flushed in and out of the rocks below. Yes, there were times she had lived at such a pitch of anxiety. For the moment, she was out in the stand of the tide.

AUTHOR'S NOTES

Any attempt to re-create the past requires a leap of imagination. *The past is*, as Michel de Certeau puts it, *the fiction of the present.*

My understanding of my great-great-grand-aunt Henrietta has been informed by many years of research, during which I have accessed public records, parish archives, censuses, local histories worldwide, thousands of newspaper articles and letters to the editor, endless nineteenth-century journals, books and publications, and my own private collection of family memorabilia. The private side of Henrietta's story has to a large extent been untold, thus allowing me enough space between the facts to let her breathe freely as a character.

In representing Henrietta, it was essential to use the names of real people, especially family members and those close to her. While founded on factual biographical evidence, their characterisations are the renderings of my imagination.

Overall, history has provided the backbone upon which to rest my story. Key events have been drawn directly from the record, while others are the result of speculation. Some have been prioritised or rearranged to suit the story.

Trove, the online repository of the National Library of Australia, has provided me with a wealth of material. All newspaper articles and letters to the editor are genuine copies, though some have been edited or abbreviated. While letters to newspapers under pseudonyms may be commonly attributed to Henrietta, their authorship, to date, remains unsubstantiated. Personal letters and parts thereof are real copies other than Henrietta's letter to Alice on page 303, and those written by the fictional hands of Mrs Lowe, and Henrietta's two older sons, Einnim and Carl, and her nieces, Hattie and Emma.

I have quoted variously from Henrietta's works and abundant letters, passim. In some instances, I have taken the liberty of paraphrasing, adapting and filtering passages from her writing into free indirect thought and discourse. The accuracy of Henrietta Dugdale's values and beliefs is demonstrated within her own literary work and correspondence. In borrowing her words, I have tried to capture the uniqueness of her voice, her wit and wonderful sense of humour, and, above all, her humanity.

My interpretation of the Dugdales' marital breakdown has been informed by close readings of Henrietta's letters and her short utopian novel, *A Few Hours in A Far-off Age*, in which autobiographical grievances are aired presumptively through the 'I' of the narrator. The details underlying the Dugdales' property altercations are scant. Records from the Borough of Queenscliffe Rate Book do not correspond entirely with legal records of land transactions, thus presenting veiled gaps in terms of exactly who owned what and who was living where and with whom at any specific time. One can only read between the lines. Henrietta once described William Dugdale as a 'monster' – a telling exposé consistent with the prejudiced narrative viewpoint in the story. William left no account of his behaviour. Putting the issue of child custody aside, the fact remains that he was a bigamist, and by these actions alone proved to be an unlawful and untrustworthy man.

Of the many texts sourced, a number were influential in the writing of this novel. Susan Priestley's biography *Henrietta Augusta Dugdale: An Activist 1827–1918* (Melbourne Books, 2011) provided a good general background on Henrietta and the women's movement, and was useful to have at hand. For local histories, I often referred to Barry Hill's *The Enduring Rip: A History of Queenscliffe* (Melbourne University Press, 2004) and *Early Memories of Queenscliff* by pioneer resident Charles Dodd (Queenscliffe Historical Museum, facsimile edn, 2004). The Mornington drowning tragedy of 1892 is well documented in Australian newspapers of the time, accessible through *Trove*. Paul Kennedy brings some of the personal threads of this tragedy vividly to life in his account *Fifteen Young Men* (ABC Books, 2016). A number of recently digitised nineteenth-century texts were essential. Henrietta's *A Few Hours in a Far-off Age* (1883) is available free online, as are Caroline Norton's *Caroline Norton's Defense: English Laws for Women in the 19th Century* (1854), and Barbara Leigh Smith Bodichon's *A Brief Summary in Plain Language of the Most Important Laws Concerning Women together with a Few Observations Thereon* (1857), which sets out the legal rights of married women of the time very clearly for the modern layperson.

The term 'dower trust' on page 82 was a trust granted under Common Law but traditionally by husband or family member to a wife for her support in the event she became widowed. It was generally settled on the bride at the time of the wedding, or as provided by law – her own untouchable, unredeemable asset while her husband was alive.

The women of Victoria were not granted the suffrage until late 1908, when the Adult Suffrage Bill was finally passed by the Victorian Parliament. Two weeks later, on 5 December, Henrietta gave a speech at a victory celebration held at the Masonic Hall in Melbourne – probably the last time she stepped up on a podium.

WORKS CITED

Books, journals

page 24, 'Man is will, woman sentiment ...': Ralph Waldo Emerson, Address to Women's Rights Convention, Boston (1855).

page 24, 'The slavery of women happened ...': Ralph Waldo Emerson, 'Woman', lecture (1855).

page 50, 'Whether for love or money, it was too rash ...': William Shakespeare, *Romeo and Juliet*, Act 2, Scene 1.

page 115, 'Who steals my purse ...': William Shakespeare, *Othello*, Act 3, Scene 3.

page 125, 'Some men love women as children love dolls ...': Mary Walker, *Hit* (1872).

page 162, 'I stand in the doorway ...': Henrietta Dugdale, *A Few Hours in a Far-Off Age* (1883), p. 5.

page 345, 'That would create together here ...': anon., *White Ribbon Signal*, official organ of the Victorian Woman's Christian Temperance Union, 1 June 1916.

page 359, 'Come gentle night ...': William Shakespeare, *Romeo and Juliet*, Act 3, Scene 2.

page 361, 'Light comes but ...': Henrietta Dugdale, *A Few Hours in a Far-Off Age* (1883), p. 85.

page 362, 'No loss – no death ...': Henrietta Dugdale, *A Few Hours in a Far-Off Age* (1883), p. 98.

Newspapers

page 29: 'Australia', *The Times*, London, 15 June 1863, p. 6.

page 33: Henrietta Dugdale, letter to the editor, 'The Lady Dairy Woman', *The Times*, London, 16 October 1863, p. 11.

page 38: Joseph Worrell, letter to the editor, 'The Schnapper Point Post', *The Age*, Melbourne, 10 May 1864, p. 5.

page 102: Ada [Henrietta Dugdale], letter to the editor, 'An appeal to Mr Higinbotham', *Argus*, 13 April 1869, p. 7.

page 167: Henrietta Dugdale, letter to the editor, 'Rational dress', *Australasian*, Melbourne, 17 June 1882, p. 7.

page 174: Henrietta Dugdale, letter to the editor, 'Stays versus comfort', *Australasian*, Melbourne, 26 August 1882, p. 7.

page 189: Henrietta Dugdale, letter to the editor, 'Mr Shiels's just divorce clause', *The Age*, Melbourne, 10 September 1883, p. 6.

page 194: Henrietta Dugdale, letter to the editor, 'Woman suffrage', *The Age*, Melbourne, 17 May 1884, p. 13.

page 200: Sarah Parker, 'Rosanna Plummer', *Herald*, Melbourne, 27 August 1884, p. 4.

page 201: Henrietta Dugdale, letter to the editor, 'Mrs Sarah Parker's attack on the V.W.S.S.', *Herald*, Melbourne, 28 August 1884, p. 4.

page 201: Fred Johnson, letter to the editor, *Herald*, Melbourne, 28 August 1884, p. 4.

page 203: E.H. Rennick, letter to the editor, 'Victorian Women's Suffrage Society, *Herald*, Melbourne, 15 October 1884, p. 4.

page 208: Henrietta Dugdale, letter to the editor, 'Mrs H.A. Dugdale in reply', *Melbourne Punch*, 12 June 1884, p. 10.

page 219: 'Woman items', *Bulletin*, Sydney, vol. 3, no. 109, 13 June 1885, p. 18.

page 225: Henrietta Dugdale, 'Now, Mrs Dugdale, step up', letter to the editor, *Melbourne Punch*, 11 March 1886, p. 1.

page 228: Fred Johnson, letter to the editor, *Liberator*, 1 August 1886, p. 3.

page 230: Carl T. Dugdale, letter to the editor, 'Woman's suffrage', *Herald*, Melbourne, 11 May 1887, p. 4.

page 244: Fred Johnson, letter to the editor, 'Railway freaks', *Herald*, Melbourne, 9 December 1889, p. 4.

page 250: Henrietta Dugdale, letter to the editor, 'A war against women', *New Zealand Observer*, 20 October 1890.

page 253: Henrietta Dugdale, 'Obedience to husbands', *Herald*, Melbourne, 7 July 1890, p. 4.

page 267: article, 'Middlesex Sessions, Friday 13 October 1848', *The Times*, London, 14 October 1848, p. 6.

page 277: article, 'Shocking disaster in the bay', *Argus*, Melbourne, 23 May 1892, p. 5.

page 315: article, 'Workers in conclave', *Tocsin*, Melbourne, 12 October 1899, p. 7.

page 317: article, 'Mrs Dugdale', *Table Talk*, Melbourne, 20 October 1899, p. 6.

page 320: Henrietta Dugdale, letter to the editor, 'Mrs Dugdale writes to us as follows', *Table Talk*, Melbourne, 27 October 1899, p. 11.

page 327: Henrietta Dugdale, letter to the editor, 'Ordinary wife-beatings', *Table Talk*, 22 February 1900, p. 7.

page 331: Henrietta Dugdale, letter to the editor, 'The Legislative Council versus brains', *The Age*, 30 October 1900, p. 9.

page 340: 'The Queen's death', *Evening News*, Sydney, 24 January 1901, p. 5.

page 340: editorial, *Fitzroy City Press*, 25 January 1901, p. 2.

page 341: 'Newport Baptists', *Herald*, Melbourne, 28 January 1901, p. 4.

page 351: article, 'Women's suffrage', *Argus*, Melbourne, 17 June 1902, p. 6.

ACKNOWLEDGEMENTS

I began this project in 2008, by coincidence the centenary year of the granting of women's suffrage in Victoria. Luckily for me, commemorative events throughout the State had generated growing interest in the life of Henrietta, especially in the town of Queenscliff where she had first settled as an early pioneer.

I want to acknowledge the debt I owe the Queenscliffe Historical Museum for their assistance in my early research. Through the willingness and diligence of past President, Jocelyn Grant, a valuable compilation of archival material was made available to me on disc, including groundwork investigations carried out by senior member, Doreen Turner. My sincere thanks go to those involved in assembling the material, and to Rosemary Brown, for arranging for me to look over the original Dugdale dwellings during one of my visits to Queenscliff.

I would also like to thank Susan Priestley, author of *Henrietta Augusta Dugdale*, for sharing copies of photos and personal correspondence, previously held in a private collection and kindly passed on to me with the permission of Virgil Gill, a descendant of the Harding family. My appreciation goes as well to Penny Mercer for offering me copies of old family photos of Henrietta's third husband, Frederick Johnson.

The writing part of the project involved six years of countless drafts and rewritings. At times, the task of completing it seemed insurmountable. How blessed I am to have close friends, fellow writers and family who contributed in so many different ways and kept me inspired. Among those, my heartfelt thanks go to my trusted readers: Robyn Mundy, who suggested early in the piece that I start the story in Queenscliff instead of London; my two daughters, Georgia Leonhardt and Lucy Leonhardt for their valuable insight and generosity of time; and Bernice Barry, who together with her partner, Mike Rumble, encouraged me to take the plunge into independent publishing. At different stages of writing I sought and benefited from professional advice. My appreciation goes to Belinda Castles and Glenda Downing, respectively, for providing independent structural edits. I am especially beholden to my dear friend and colleague, Amanda Curtin, who played the vital role of helping me fully develop and fine-tune the novel through to final copy. Thanks also to my designer, Sandy Cull, and proofreader, Wendy Bulgin.

Last, I thank my wonderful husband, Peter, for the part he has played in bringing this book to fruition. His patience and support throughout the entire project have been immeasurable.